BRIDGER:

DEADLY PERIL

by

L. Sanford Nance

PublishAmerica
Baltimore

ISBN: 1-4241-7898-3
PUBLISHED BY PUBLISHAMERICA, LLLP
www.publishamerica.com
Baltimore

Printed in the United States of America

Dedication

BRIDGER: DEADLY PERIL is dedicated
to the men and women of federal agencies
and state and local police departments,
who put themselves on the line daily
to preserve our way of life.

CHAPTER 1

WPO Radio Station
Portland, Oregon

A black mini-van—bearing stolen Oregon license plates—slowed and pulled into the parking area of Portland's WPO radio station. Two male occupants were dressed in dark coveralls, virtually concealing their bodies from ankles to chin. Their dress was intended to give the appearance of auto service personnel and would serve to allay suspicions of any casual observer.

"That's it…the green Mustang," indicated the older man to the driver. "Pull up in the space to the right."

The van stopped next to a meticulously restored 1965 Ford Mustang parked sideways in two spaces in an effort to protect the expensive paint. Both men pulled on thin leather gloves and tugged baseball type caps down low over their brows.

The driver got out, removed a telescoping pole from the van and walked casually toward a single security camera mounted on top of the building. He quickly extended the length of the fiberglass pole containing a cutting tool used by tree trimmers to prune high branches. Hooking the sharp blade over the wires powering the camera and pulling sharply on the long cord, the wires were cleanly severed.

Inside the station, snow appeared on the security television screen long ago tucked out of sight in a cabinet. The single security guard sitting at his station would not be alarmed to find the camera malfunctioning once again—when and if he got around to checking it. If anyone did view the tape, with the dim light and cap covering his face, it would be impossible to determine any facial characteristics of the subject, much less identify him.

The passenger waited until the camera was out of operation and got out of the van. Wearing a small tool belt around his waist, he walked to the door of the vintage vehicle and quickly got down on his back searching under the doorframe. It took only seconds for him to locate the wires for a car alarm; he pulled a cutter from his tool belt and clipped the ground wire.

Getting to his feet, he pushed a "slim jim" (a thin strip of metal commonly used by policemen and wrecker operators to enter locked vehicles) down between the glass and side of the door; after moving it up and down a couple of times, he located the door-lock mechanism. A quick jerk upward and the door unlocked.

The driver returned the pole to the van and carefully picked up a small bundle wrapped in tin foil. The innocent-looking package contained a quantity of C-4 military explosive and two sticks of dynamite being used for a "booster." After handing the package to the bomb maker sitting in the passenger seat of the Mustang, the driver took the "slim jim" and returned to the van.

The bomber pressed the release on the glove compartment and the door fell open.

Good deal. Saves some time and being unlocked probably means nothing of value is kept inside, which might cause it to be opened prematurely.

He pushed hard on a sharp "cork screw" type tool, embedding it into the soft bottom material of the compartment; it required only a few turns to complete a hole large enough for the wires from the bomb to pass through.

It would have been a simple matter to place the explosive outside the vehicle and use any one of a variety of remote devices for detonation. During the planning stage, it was determined the myriad of signals from various sources in the downtown area would most likely create a premature explosion. This process was much slower with an increased risk of discovery, but the risk was worth the reward. *We're removing a scourge from the earth and sending a message to the Feds at the same time. This is going to be a great show!*

The wires from the detonator were carefully threaded through the hole and stretched out of sight under the dash to an electrical cable running up the steering post. Holding a small pin light in his teeth, the bomber found the wire he was looking for and deftly removed some insulation. He attached the wires from the bomb and giving them a twist, reached to the sleeve of his coveralls, pulled off a strip of pre-cut electrician tape and wrapped it carefully around the connection.

Take time to be certain every connection is fail-proof, he thought taking a deep breath and wiping a small trickle of sweat from his brow. Intensive training emphasized the need to "be quick—but don't hurry." The risk is all wasted if the package fails to detonate. A last piece of tape was secured around the wires to hold them in place, and the bomber moved backward out of the vehicle, pausing long enough to relock the Mustang.

The two men drove slowly out of the parking lot and circled the block until locating a parking spot along the street providing a clear view of the Mustang. It would be 15 minutes before Spoonbill finished his program and exited the station.

Surveillance over the course of the past month revealed the target's habits on Tuesdays were consistent. After the long 4-hour show, he exited the station within 10 minutes and followed the same route for several blocks to a favorite food and watering hole.

At *Ronzoney's Seafood*, fresh salmon arrived every Tuesday morning. Spoonbill usually drank two vodka martinis to unwind before the headwaiter served him a specially prepared order of salmon. He ate the meal, accompanied by a glass of white wine, while listening to the live entertainment.

Tonight, *Ronzoney's* would have one extra "VIP order" of salmon available.

***

WPO, a 50,000-watt mega station, specialized in talk radio. The powerful signal emanating from downtown Portland could be picked up along the west coast and inland into Idaho, Montana and Nevada. Programming substance tended to be liberal, ranging from a relatively moderate dialogue of environmentalists, to more controversial viewpoints of alternative lifestyles and politics.

The station broadcast twenty-four/seven and required heavy advertising dollars to keep the privately owned corporation healthy. Advertising revenues were determined by popularity of show and time of day. Little could be done to manipulate time of day leaving popularity as the wild card.

Station management operated from the premise, "any caller is better than dead air," and encouraged program hosts to be "bold in generating controversy on both sides of an issue."

Some program hosts took the directive more literally than others. One such host was Anthony Spoonbill (a professional name shortened to "T-Spoon"), whose show generated enormous attention—both positive and negative.

The show's format called for a combination of live interviews, call-in by listeners and monologue by the host. Spoonbill became a master at controlling the emotions of listeners, creating a surreal atmosphere of obsequious callers agreeing with his viewpoint, followed by a growing number cursing and spewing foul epitaphs. The former were often cut short followed by spicy comments of "air head," "Nazi," or similar terms designed to keep listener blood pressure elevated for the entire four hours.

On more than a few occasions, Spoonbill's callers made unveiled physical threats, the complete nature of which were left to the imagination when WPO producers made use of the built-in "censure button." (All radio broadcasts are delayed several seconds before actual transmission, thus allowing obscene or unwanted comments to be omitted.)

Producers, however, could do nothing about the letters, phone calls and e-mails containing an increasingly sober theme—more than a few of which were deemed serious enough to warrant turning over to the local police.

Spoonbill was beginning to have concerns about his show in general and the growing number of threatening communications in particular. In the glass soundproof enclosure from which the show was broadcast, he sat drinking a cup of tea. It was the last break before ending another show—another show monotonously like the countless number before. His attention turned to the last caller.

I had that last asshole pissing down his leg. The ignorant Neanderthal was buying every last word of my mind-numbing dialog. I wonder what threat he was about to puke out before my half-asleep producer finally got around to hitting the "nut button" and cutting him off?

Maybe I've pushed the envelope too far, he surmised. *It's been a good ride. Time could be right to move on and take my act to the east coast. My agent says there are a couple of great offers from Boston and New York. Tomorrow...I'll meet with him tomorrow and see what's on the table.*

The break was over, and the producer was giving him a hand count: four, three, two, one.

"Welcome back all you sophisticated, gifted, free-thinking stalwarts of the community. And a reminder about tomorrow. T-Spoon has an interview you will not want to miss. Our special guest from San Francisco—Councilman J. D. Cushing—will visit with us on the great strides 'the city by the bay' has taken to bring equality to an oppressed minority. The topic will be Gay marriages...reminding us of an interesting question. Has the time arrived for Portland to follow her big brother to the south and give this maligned minority its constitutional rights?

"Oh yes, lest I forget. I have a grooming message for you Neanderthals out there like my last caller. Throw your beer can in the pile on the floor, sit your wife down at the kitchen table and shave her hairy back!"

***

The two terrorists sat with their radio volume turned low. They listened quietly to the closing moments of the radio show of a man they were about to literally blow into small pieces. Neither man felt any sense of remorse or emotion of any kind. It was simply another assignment to do what they were trained to do; besides, it would rid the world of one more enemy of their cause.

"This is Anthony Spoonbill saying goodnight to all you loyal patrician listeners out there…and you geeks and freaks as well. Tune in tomorrow for more debate and edification, presented brilliantly and accurately, one T-Spoon at a time."

Moments later WPO's back door swung open, and the soon-to-be victim walked to his car. Spoonbill moved around the vehicle slowly, carefully examining the Mustang for any signs of damage it might have received from a carelessly opened car door.

The two terrorists gave each other a knowing smile. "In a few minutes, he won't have to worry about the paint job ever again," the older man remarked, causing both to laugh softly.

Satisfied there was no damage, Spoonbill got into his Mustang and pulled out of the parking lot, moving swiftly into the traffic before turning right onto SW First Avenue.

So far so good, the bomber sensed. *C'mon pal, keep on trucking down to Clay Street.*

The Mustang accelerated rapidly and the van fell back. The last thing they needed was to get stopped for speeding in a vehicle with stolen license plates. Both men were heavily armed, but a shoot-out with local police was not likely to have a successful outcome.

Ahead the Mustang's brake lights suddenly flashed, and the agile sport car slowed quickly. A Volkswagen convertible full of teenagers swerved recklessly into his lane and with tires squealing turned immediately into a parking lot. Spoonbill's arms left the steering wheel in an irritated gesture.

Damn, that was close. Don't want him switching lanes and using the turn signal, the driver thought.

11

A short distance ahead the victim approached Clay Street and the brake lights came on. He was staying on course. It wouldn't be long now. A hundred feet from the corner the left turn signal actually flashed once—the circuit was completed and the C-4-dynamite-combination exploded!

A fireball erupted in the early evening sky, ripping off the roof and sending the Mustang several feet into the air. The glass, plastic and lighter metals of the dash acted like shrapnel and added to the already deadly concussion effects of the bomb. Anthony Spoonbill was torn into small pieces of shredded flesh and bone. There would be body parts spread over the entire block—precisely as planned.

It was unerringly what their strategy envisioned—detonation on the first left turn. The bomber glanced at his confederate and smiled a tight grin. The van turned down Clay Street, and they slowly worked their way through stopped cars, broken glass and wreckage—the two terrorists exchanged a high five.

Pieces of the Mustang were everywhere with what was left of the once shiny body smoldering up against a building. Several cars, damaged by the explosion, were on the sidewalk or turned sideways in the road from collisions with other vehicles.

The lower windows of 1500 SW First Avenue—address of the FBI Portland Field Office—were mostly blown out and strewn on the road and sidewalk. The offices themselves were damaged—not severely enough to affect work efficiency—but enough to send a message.

"Those FBI assholes can walk to work tomorrow!" the excited driver shouted.

"Yeah and they can use a *spoon* to scrape that queer bastard off what's left of their windows, " came the chilling reply.

Being careful to drive at the speed limit down SW Harbor Drive, they turned off onto I-5 north toward Seattle, taking them across a bridge over the Willamette River.

The passenger held a disposable cell phone in one hand, punched in a number and waited three rings before speaking. "P-1...mission completed and clear." He then broke the phone in half and tossed it out the window into the murky water below.

Both men laughed, growing confident of their successful escape from a mission handled with bold efficiency. The black van proceeded north on I-5, and they crossed over the Columbia River into Washington.

After several miles and seeing the turn-off he sought, the driver exited the freeway turning down a secluded road for a mile before pulling into a small wooded lane. In the approaching darkness, trees on both sides concealed the van from view.

The two men got out of their vehicle and removed lengths of black magnetic covering off the metal sides and top. It took only moments to strip it clean. They threw the deceptive color materials into the back of the van, and one man swiftly removed the stolen plates and buried them under a pile of brush while the second replaced the van's registered Idaho licenses.

The entire procedure took only minutes before the two were back on I-5 destined for Idaho in their **white** van—just two more tourists enjoying the Washington scenery.

***

CHAPTER 2

Offices—*New York World* Newspaper
Downtown Manhattan
New York City, New York

John Chambers was not at all certain why his editor had chosen him to do this story. It would be his first trip to the West, and he knew next to nothing about the culture and lifestyles of the region. That would have to change in the next few days.

Following graduation from NYU, *summa cum laude*, Chambers attended Columbia School of Journalism. After Columbia, he accepted an entry-level position with *The Big Apple,* a small magazine with limited circulation but a reputation for innovative writing.

Friends and family were proud and expected great things, but time passed and expectations weren't being met. Professional journalism is a tough, competitive business; and the streets of New York are awash with out-of-work novelists, playwrights, reporters and writers of every variety.

At first, Chambers felt pleased about having a job; meager salary or not, the experience was priceless. Those close to him weren't so sure. Now characterized by some members of the family as the underpaid "retread" living at home with his parents, they watched with concern when he turned down more lucrative positions in advertising and other professions. Even his fiancée Carla was getting impatient and suggesting he pursue other more lucrative career choices.

Collective feelings seemed to be summed up when his favorite Uncle Jerome made a remark over Thanksgiving dinner intending to console him. "John, sometimes we have to forget about who we dreamed we could be and accept who we really are. Life is much easier on us when we do."

He could still hear those words and see the gloomy defeated look on his uncle's face. He looked like a man who had died of paper cuts rather than knife stab wounds. If he had any doubts about the choices he had made, they were all resolved with a single benevolent statement spoken from the heart with such unintentional potential for causing great pain.

Over the next few months when thoughts turned to quitting and trying another profession, his uncle's words came ringing back to life. John Chambers was determined to "pursue his dreams" and let destiny take him where it might. Whatever happened, he resolved never to be Uncle Jerome's age knowing he had given up his dreams and would never have a chance to pursue them again.

Starting at the bottom, it took two years to be promoted to staff writer. The lack of financial resources, combined with long hours spent working, took its toll on his personal life. His lengthy engagement to Carla Matthews (presumed to be "the love of his life," since first meeting her at Columbia) came to an abrupt and one-sided end.

Carla dropped the news on him out of the blue. "Someone else has entered my life and I'm *sorry,*" she indicated. When she moved in with the new "someone else," the day after breaking off the engagement, it devastated him. Recuperation was taking a long time in coming. Fact is, he still wasn't doing so well.

When 911 happened, many lives changed forever. It affected Chambers in ways he could not imagine. Perhaps his personal life in disarray provided a special empathy for the losses of victims and their families. His writing took on a new dimension and began to reflect an innate sensitivity, which soon began to attract attention.

One female reader wrote, "John Chambers' interviews with policemen, firemen and victims' families are moving and emotional without being too invasive. His is an empathy professionally expressed, but with a personal human touch."

Talents, honed working at simple assignments for a small magazine, blossomed in a crisis and were being recognized at a critical time and place. The entire world was focused on New York and readers couldn't get enough information on the horrific tragedy. Chambers' poignant stories were reprinted around the world.

Offers began to come in, some from unusual and exotic locations, magazines and newspapers scarcely known to him. Each seemed to feed off the last, and the number and quality of opportunities continued to get better. It was difficult, but Chambers made a determined effort to be patient and wait for the right opportunity. Finally when *New Yorker Magazine* and *Time* expressed "an interest in speaking to your agent" (Chambers wondered if it might be a good time to get one), he knew the right moment to make a decision on his future was close at hand.

Soon after, the call for an interview came from his current boss, Michael Gates; and following the interview, Gates extended an offer to work at what many consider the number one newspaper of all—*The New York World*. It was a no brainer, so far as Chambers was concerned. This was *the* opportunity for a print journalist, and he wasted no time in accepting the offer.

The next several months raced by, with financial and other benefits thrusting him overnight into an entirely new lifestyle.

The "underpaid family retread" moved into a small studio apartment in Manhattan. Chambers felt good about his new opportunity and the prosperity it brought. Suddenly, there were tickets to Broadway shows, athletic events and rock concerts at Madison Square Garden. He could now afford an occasional meal at the better restaurants and shopped at more upscale clothing stores.

Life was good, at least from the professional standpoint. There had been a number of "routine" assignments, and Gates seemed more than satisfied with his work. A meaningful personal relationship? That was an entirely different story. A couple of brief encounters, which only seemed to deepen his obsessive feelings for Carla, were disasters; he had now gone a full year without female companionship of any kind. In reality, his personal life was in the toilet.

Last Wednesday when Gates called him into his office, Chambers knew very little about Ted Bridger, only vaguely remembering the name associated with the investigation of 911. This was going to be his first really big assignment, and he resolved to make the most of the opportunity. Chambers would soon discover Bridger was a complex man—and their approaching relationship was to change his destiny forever.

***

Michael Gates was in his late fifties, with fine white hair and the potbelly and ruddy face of a man who liked his scotch and cigars—together when possible. He depicted the image of the tough city editor, straight from Hollywood movies of the thirties and forties. After many years in the role, he had his act pretty well together. In reality Gates was highly professional and would go the extra mile for "his people." Chambers both liked and admired him.

Chambers tapped twice on the editor's glass door, not waiting for an invitation before opening the door and stepping inside. The room immediately gave off the choking smell of many hours of cigar smoke seemingly spewing from every direction at once.

Gates sat behind his worn desk littered with the week's copy, chewing what remained of a long dead stogie and staring at the computer screen in front of him. He peered over his reading glasses with tired eyes and in his best impersonation of a hard-nosed boss, paused for a moment before speaking.

"John—take a seat and listen up. I've got a great assignment to do a series of interviews with a very complex subject. Ever hear of Theodore Bridger?"

"Don't believe so, Michael; give me a hint."

"Assistant director of the FBI…intelligence expert…predicted the step-up in terrorist activity in the U.S…. got on the shit list in Washington with the political big boys and probably got fired or forced to resign? Ring any bells?"

"Okay, now I'm with you. Bridger warned about the first World Trade Center bombing and then caught the perpetrators. He left Washington. Right? Seem to recall reading about him going home to his ranch in Texas…or Arizona or someplace."

"Actually he is "rusticating" farther to the north. Bridger's "home on the range" is in Wyoming, and it might be a good idea to remember, since you'll be going there to interview him," Gates said pausing to let the full impact sink in.

"Ted Bridger, actually Theodore Alexander Bridger II, is no ordinary cowboy; in fact, for the last 35 years, he's been anything *but*. Born and raised on a ranch in Wyoming, Bridger entered the FBI shortly after graduate school. Handling the complex and diverse investigations of the federal agency apparently came easily—superiors used the word "instinctively." In the beginning he worked a full gamut of the 180 federal statues of which the Bureau was then responsible.

"During the airplane skyjacking days of the late sixties and seventies, he was assigned to a skyjack squad on call across the country; as a young agent, even worked a short period on the notorious D.B. Cooper skyjacking. I had the opportunity of meeting him during the investigation.

"That case is still not officially solved. The FBI believes Cooper died when he parachuted out the back stairwell of a Boeing 727 with the ransom money in a leather bag strapped to his wrist. Experts agree the force of wind currents hitting the bag probably severed the poor bastard's arm from his body. Bold but ignorant, Cooper never realized the money he gave an arm for was useless. Marked for identification purposes, some of it was found floating in a river near where he exited the plane. Actually, that was the only evidence ever found.

"I mention this little morsel of dated information, to add to your woefully lacking appreciation of the *great* reporters of the past. Yours truly was a hot rookie who worked the sensational story from the Rose City—i.e., Portland, Oregon. Best lay I ever had, with a sweet young thing on the banks of the Rogue River. Rockier than hell on those banks. However, that's not a proper subject for such young ears. Another time perhaps.

"More to the point; as mentioned earlier, I crossed paths with Bridger. Found him bright, dedicated, enthusiastic…*imposing*. Definitely headed for bigger and better things than searching the wilderness for what was left of a one-arm body falling from 10,000 feet.

"He received a transfer to San Francisco assigned to Soviet espionage, where FBI superiors soon recognized his potential. Their early judgment proved accurate, and Bridger's entry into the sophisticated world of spying and counter-spying led to rapid advancement.

"Bridger's earlier exploits—excluding women since he's a handsome widower—revolved around the KGB of the former Soviet Union and the cases he worked in the U.S. and abroad. During the cold war, he became an expert in the field of espionage and counter espionage. Freedom of Information records reveals Bridger suffered gunshot wounds twice in the line of duty and was involved in numerous shootings and physical scrapes. You're going to discover this bloody chap sounds like the fictitious hero Ian Fleming may have had in mind when he wrote James Bond.

"On foreign assignment, he worked out of U.S. Embassies with the title of Legal Attaché, which frequently led to the need for cooperation from the CIA Chief of Station. It was not always forthcoming—his mounting protests of the lack of synergy were never acted upon in Washington but did manage to piss off a lot of people. Slowly but surely, the fair-haired boy was on his way to becoming prematurely bald.

"Early on, the Bureau's counter-espionage and counter-terrorism efforts were closely linked. Bridger developed an exceptional aptitude for identifying potential terrorist activities and methods for combating what he early recognized to be an overwhelming threat to the world in general—and the United States in particular.

"Bridger's growing expertise in all fields of the intelligence game led to his appointment to organize and train an anti-terrorist squad. The Bureau expected terrorist activity in the U.S. would be only a matter of time, and the duties of the squad were to investigate suspected terrorists' clusters to assess their latent potential for violent activity in the United States. People trained by

Bridger have made their marks in Afghanistan and Iraq and garnered respect from the international intelligence community—including the Israelis, who are not easily impressed.

"As you already mentioned, my boy, Bridger warned of the first bombing of the World Trade Center and played a major role in the identification and capture of those very bad boys. Did the turf-protecting, political appointees at the Federal Bureau of *Ignorance* learn anything? Efforts to warn of pending future violence of an escalating nature were totally disregarded.

"A lot of Washington insiders believe Bridger retired in a state of "aggravated frustration" with the politics of his superiors in the intelligence community. Part of your assignment will be to answer this question: Why did an acknowledged authority on a subject now paramount on the minds of governments around the world, choose to suddenly leave his position?

"Are there any questions or has my briefing extraordinaire covered everything?"

"Let's see—when, where, why and how?" Chambers panned. "I've got the where and know how...now all I need is when?"

"John, my boy, take all the time you need, provided you are on a plane heading for Horse Creek, Wyoming, by Monday morning. Yes—you heard correctly. Monday morning...Horse Creek. Check with Cynthia for the details. The travel people are making arrangements while we speak—do your research before you leave—and, John, better go buy a hat and some spurs. I hear those cowgirls like both! Get out, please. I'm very busy."

Leaving Gates' office, Chambers stopped to see Cynthia Kite. A long-time administrative assistant to Gates, she performed all the duties required of a receptionist-secretary and more. Cynthia was talking on the phone and held up one finger to indicate she would be only a moment.

Her black hair peppered with gray was worn short and complemented fine features and dark brown eyes. In her mid-fifties, immaculately groomed and with a voice on the phone sounding 25, Cynthia was a widow, leaving her free to spend her salary anyway she desired; fashionable clothes were close to the top of her list. A "girlish" trim figure permitted the wearing of the very latest from fashionable designers, and she was a familiar topic at the water cooler with very complimentary remarks coming from the men. Women, on the other hand, were more likely to express what Inspector Clouseau of *Pink Panther* fame would call, "rits of fealous jage."

Cynthia ended the call and turning to John using the low sexy voice, which undoubtedly contributed to her employment years before, asked, "How may I help you, John?"

"Gates gave me the word on the Bridger assignment and said check with you on details. What do you have for me?"

Reaching into a rickety wooden file cabinet next to her desk, she removed a folder and handed it to him.

"I believe you'll find most of what you need in here, including your travel agenda. The travel department will have your airline tickets ready tomorrow, along with a rental car reservation. I asked them to reserve tickets to both Denver and Cheyenne, and you can check a map and decide into which place you prefer to fly. Oh…and John, here are a couple of web sites to help with your research on Bridger. He's a very sophisticated man with a varied and, I might add, exciting background. If you need anything else, let me know."

"Cynthia, will you marry me?"

Reaching down, he gave her a quick kiss on top of the head and turning quickly toward his cubicle heard her say, "Leave a number and wait for a call, John."

Back at his desk, Chambers read the printout on Bridger.

The New York World contacted Bridger shortly after his retirement to request an interview. His refusal appeared adamant. "My plans are to return to private life at the ranch and make up for lost time with friends and relatives. Attention from the media is something I prefer to do without and appreciate your respecting my privacy."

The World didn't become the newspaper it is without persistence and patience, John realized with pride.

After a third and finally a fourth contact, Bridger agreed to do an interview—provided it would be conducted at the ranch, without interfering with whatever day-to-day activities might be taking place. In addition, he wanted approval over the content and accuracy of the interview before it went to print.

The last stipulation was heatedly debated at *The World*. Eventually, language was worked out agreeable to both parties. In negotiations, Bridger agreed to "consider" doing several lengthy articles in the form of serials depicting his long career in the FBI.

Part of Chambers' assignment involved preliminary dialogue designed to determine the suitability/desirability of such future articles. Potentially, a series of on-going stories represented a triumph for the paper and raised a red flag—

why? Why did he first refuse an interview and subsequently agree to consider a much lengthier and time-consuming series? Did Bridger have an axe to grind with someone? Was he planning to use *The New York World* to make it happen?

***

UST Flight 5509
O'Hare Airport
Chicago, Illinois

Chambers left Kennedy Airport in New York on Monday for the first leg of his flight to Chicago O'Hare. After landing in Chicago, his flight schedule didn't require him to change planes, so he decided to stay on board.

A new flight crew boarded the plane, and the first-class flight attendant stopped at his seat.

"Good morning. I'm Jan. I'll be working first-class the rest of your flight. Care for a beverage?"

"Good morning. Coffee please, with cream."

Chambers was the only passenger left in first class; everyone else disembarked.

Jan was a very attractive woman, probably in her early forties, a bottle blond with her hair worn mid-length; the airline uniform was a little tight, indicating she probably had added some recent weight. The uniform did little to conceal her full figure. *This is one sexy lady heading into middle age. I wonder how she's handling it.*

"Would you like a pastry? I'm sorry I can't offer you something more. A lot of our past frills are gone. So many of the carriers are in trouble financially after 911—everyone is saving money anywhere they can," she said smiling.

"This is fine. Coffee's very good and I ate earlier. Been flying long?"

"I've been with this airline about 12 years; before that, a commuter line. I make the run between Boston and Seattle with a layover in Denver."

"How about you? Are you living in New York? I noticed on our manifest you came on board at Kennedy."

"Yes…I've lived there all my life," Chambers added really hearing himself say it for the first time.

Damn, he lamented, *for a 27-year-old single guy, I really haven't seen much of the world. Virtually all my travel has involved destinations on the east coast, with the one exception of a college graduation present to Bermuda. My parents surprised me with the trip and even more by including Carla. (Mom insisted on double rooms and Dad gave me a conspiratorial wink. "Humor your Mother," he explained—"the rooms adjoin.") A week on the beaches making out and enjoying the nightlife, once the highlight of our relationship, now only represented painful flashbacks.*

The small talk continued for a few moments until people began reboarding the plane. The passenger load from Chicago to Denver was unusually light. Monday usually meant heavy business travel, and the older model Boeing 727 airplane had a small first-class section. One more example of an airline trying to cut operation costs by utilizing the smaller plane, when passenger traffic didn't require the larger wide-body airplanes normally used on longer flights.

Jan was closing the hatch; there were only five first-class passengers.

"Looks like we will be traveling light," she said, going to the front of the plane carrying a yellow oxygen mask in her hand.

Jan made the traditional emergency announcements and returned to where Chambers sat reading an article from an on-board magazine. She leaned across to retrieve some cups left by earlier passengers in the seat back beside him, and her generous bosom briefly brushed his face.

"Excuse me, John. Let me get this garbage out of here. People seem to leave it everywhere."

Going into the galley and throwing the cups away, she spent a couple of minutes reviewing the take-off checklist before moving to the jump seat facing Chambers, sitting down and strapping herself in.

Jan sat with legs crossed, squirming in the seat seemingly pulling her skirt down—in reality causing it to rise even higher, displaying her shapely thighs.

Chambers was staring at her legs and suddenly looked up to discover Jan had caught him in the act. Blood rushed to his face and he felt some relief when she gave him a slight smile. Was it his imagination—or was it a knowing smile? Even one of consent?

After they were in the air, Jan continued to inadvertently give him tantalizing glimpses of her shapely breasts. Each time she leaned to pour more coffee or offer another magazine, it caused the top of her uniform to open ever wider revealing a black bra straining to hold its luscious cargo.

Chambers picked up a magazine from the seatback pocket and attempted to read. Anything to keep his mind off the delightful body seemingly on display everywhere he looked. It was to no avail. Unable to concentrate, he decided on sleep; and soon his restless nap became an erotic daydream featuring Jan promenading down the airplane isle in scanty black panties and bra.

At last, the plane began to bump, followed by the grinding sound of the hydraulics as the flaps were lowered. An announcement to buckle up and replace tray tables came over the intercom.

The plane banked slowly to the left on final approach; Jan stopped at Chambers' seat and reached down to check his seat belt. Hesitating…she provided one more look at her magnificent chest. At the same time, the setting sun came through the window bouncing off snow-covered Rocky Mountains. The parallel was irresistible.

"Wow!" Chambers remarked, "That's not a sight you see in Manhattan."

A big smile crossed Jan's face. She had not missed the double entendré.

"John, our crew will be staying at the Airport Hilton. Stop by and I'll buy you a drink?"

"That's an invitation I would love to accept, Jan." *I haven't been with anyone in a long while, and a little roll in the hay may be exactly what's needed to get my love life going again.*

He was surprised to hear himself saying, "I have a great deal of work to complete before tomorrow, and I'm afraid I'll have to take a rain check. Do you ever get to New York?"

Both of them knew desire and opportunity had come and gone, but continued to play the mating game anyway.

"Here's my card. Next time you're in the City, call and I'll buy *you* a drink."

***

Denver International Airport
Denver, Colorado

Denver International Airport was far larger than imagined, and Chambers appreciated seeing the moving walkway designed to transport passengers overloaded with two types of weight—their own out-of-shape bodies and stuffed carry-on luggage. He had checked two larger bags carrying what he hoped was needed in the way of clothing and supplies deciding to carry only his Gateway laptop and a small bag of personal toiletry items on board the plane.

Before leaving New York, he carefully packed a couple of sports coats with matching slacks and appropriate accessories. That part was easy but what to wear on the ranch was another matter.

After a careful search through his closet and drawers, he settled on several pair of dungarees, a couple of sweaters and a pair of hiking boots. He tossed in his favorite Yankee baseball cap and a leather bomber jacket and then decided to include well-worn running shoes and sweats. Exercise had long been a daily routine, and the wide-open spaces of Wyoming would offer ample opportunity to do some jogging.

Chambers found himself standing in line in the airport men's room, wondering if he packed the necessary clothing. He'd seen the movie with Billy Crystal...what was the name of it? Big hats, boots and other cowboy clothing made the dudes appear comical. He'd laughed with the movie audience while watching Crystal and his friends' exaggerated efforts attempting to dress western style turn into a visual fiasco. *Surely, it wouldn't be expected of him...would it?*

After finally getting to a urinal and relieving himself of Jan's multiple cups of coffee, Chambers stepped to the lavatories, taking time to run a comb through his hair and straighten his tie. He left the men's room and returned to the moving walkways to cover what seemed like a mile to the baggage claim area. Along the way, he became ever more aware of the people around him dressed in western clothing.

The order of the day seemed to be leather or broadcloth western-cut sport coats with denim shirts and pants. The traditional Stetson style hats and pointed-toe cowboy boots often accompanied them.

Beginning to wonder if he was headed in the right direction, the baggage claim area for his airline finally appeared, and he lined up to wait for the baggage carousel to deposit his bags onto the revolving stainless steel apparatus.

The cold looking steel monsters moved around in circles, seemingly daring onlookers to find their luggage. Travelers always crowded close, as if expecting only one chance to grab their luggage before it gets whisked away and disappears never to be seen again.

Cripes sake please let my luggage make it.

The anxious moment passed when he spotted his large brown leather suit-bag careening down the chute to the carousel; the smaller matching duffel followed closely behind.

"So far so good." He slipped a dollar into a machine, "renting" a small cart to roll his luggage outside and waited for the rental car shuttle.

A small commuter airline offered flights to Cheyenne, but after checking distances on the map—and considering the small plane—he elected to drive. The plan was to spend the night at the Marriott Hotel near the airport and drive to the ranch early Tuesday morning for his meeting with Ted Bridger. The family ranch (Bar Double T) was some 120 miles away in Wyoming.

***

Marriott Hotel
Denver International Airport

Chambers decided to have a nightcap after his dinner at the Marriott restaurant and went into the hotel bar searching for a comfortable seat. The room was a high-ceiling atrium style with typical stools at a long wooden bar and assorted couches and over-stuffed chairs with accompanying low tables scattered randomly about. He spotted a large comfortable-looking seat in a secluded part of the room.

There were only a handful of people talking and watching baseball on several televisions mounted high on the walls about the room. The bar waitress followed him to his seat.

"What can I get you?"

"Scotch and water, please."

She was back quickly with his drink and setting it on a napkin asked, "Would you like to run a tab?"

"Please. I'm staying here. Room 310. Bill it to my room," Chambers said, showing his key card and putting it back into his pocket.

The drink felt good going down; he started to relax taking a long pull draining the last of it before deciding to have one more.

What the hell, only be taking an elevator ride and the booze will help me sleep.

As the waitress left to get his drink, a familiar face appeared at the doorway and looked about the room. It was the flight attendant from the plane.

*What was her name? Jan…*that was it.

Jan saw him and he waved in recognition. She smiled and moved slowly toward his chair.

"We meet again. You look so lonely sitting there—want some company?"

Before he could answer, she moved toward one of the larger chairs designed for two and said, "Let's sit over here so we'll be more comfortable."

It was obvious she had been drinking; her eyes and face had an unmistakable alcohol flush.

Shifting over to the larger seat, Chambers smiled, "This is a nice surprise. May I buy you a drink?"

"Thank you—I'm drinking stingers."

Wow. Stingers are brandy and white crème de menthe—easy going down, but with a deceptive kick, Chambers recalled from his days working bar during college.

The waitress left to bring a fresh round of drinks. Jan hooked her arm inside John's and nestled close nearly pushing him out of the chair. With her nose not quite touching his, in a pouty voice she whispered, "I enjoyed our visit today and was really disappointed when you said you would be working tonight. But here you are sitting having a drink alone. What am I to think, John…do you not find me attractive?"

"In fact, I have been working and simply wanted to take a break. To answer your question—yes, you're very attractive."

"Thank you. *You* are very attractive too. Cheers," she said touching her glass to his and taking a big sip of the potent drink.

They sat talking mostly about their careers, education, where they grew up. *All of the things two sexually attracted strangers find to lie about in a hotel bar in Denver, protecting their real emotional state, while selfishly searching for a temporary sexual release,* Chambers mused surprised at his cynicism. *The only thing is, I'm not lying. And for some reason, I'm willing to bet Jan isn't either. I sense emotional vulnerability, very apparent despite attempts to disguise it with alcohol.*

Jan liked to talk and put her hands on people for emphasis, and the trait became ever more persistent while they continued their conversation.

She downed the last of her drink, reached to John's thigh and squeezing it for emphasis said, "I have to be at the airport in the morning at eight sharp. If we're going to do anything but talk—we should go to your room."

Jan appeared slightly embarrassed at her own bravado, her face a bit more flushed, but she was not drunk.

This woman knows what she's doing, whatever the motivation may be. Damned if I'm going to walk away again.

"Waitress…tab please."

Chambers signed the bill, left a tip and rising from the chair offered Jan his hand. They made the elevator ride to the third floor in total silence with her snuggling against him but saying nothing.

Chambers opened the door to his room and started to turn on the lights when she put her hand over his.

"Let's leave them off. I'll open the curtains."

Walking across to the window and pulling the drapes, light from the parking area came through casting shadows across the dimly lit room. Jan turned toward him and began to slowly remove clothing.

She tossed her jacket across the chair and carelessly discarded her skirt and blouse. John stood mesmerized while his earlier daydream approached him in scanty black underwear.

Jan's body was even better than his earlier vision; large full breasts spilled out of the half cut flimsy bra and bikini panties revealed lush thighs not quite too large—and so very promising.

She put her arms around his neck and pulling his head toward her, gave him a very wet and long kiss. Her hot mouth sucked his lower lip building his desire.

John wrestled furiously with his belt, unfastened the top of his pants and let them fall to his ankles, quickly kicking them aside.

Jan backed slowly toward the bed, and he stepped away discarding his remaining clothes, before moving to take her in his arms. Their lips met again— this time he held nothing back. His tongue met hers, and they both began to breathe heavily with excitement.

His eager hands dropped to the fasteners on her black bra and fumbling with nervous anticipation, finally managed to work it loose. The objects of his earlier titillation burst free, and seeing her fullness for the first time, John felt his pulse quicken.

She ran trembling hands down his chest across his firm belly, and demanded in a barely audible voice, "John, please take me—please, John, take me now!"

Excited by Jan's eagerness, John picked her up and moving to the bed, laid her down very gently. She stretched her arms open to invite him and he positioned himself between her lush thighs. He felt himself giving in to the sexual frustration of the past several months—no longer possessing the desire or self-control to say no.

***

John began to wind down, feeling a strange sense of guilt. His last session in bed had been with Carla, and he hadn't been sure what to expect in the encounter. Casual sex was not part of his normal behavior pattern, making this totally foreign to him; for some reason, despite her aggressiveness, he believed it might be for Jan too.

They lay still for several moments, alone with their intimate feelings still too private to express.

Drenched in sweat, he rose from the bed and walked to the bathroom returning with two large towels. Gently he began to dry the small puddle of perspiration from the hollow between Jan's heavy breasts. She turned her head away slightly and said, "You must think I'm a slut, or worse. John, I'm recovering from a very messy relationship and…"

Before she could finish, he reached down and placed a finger gently over her mouth.

"So am I…recovering from a relationship. Let's be good to one another, okay?"

With that, he threw the towel aside and turned his attention once more to her tantalizing breasts. He discovered they were now salty and his dancing tongue soon drew a deep moaning response.

***

CHAPTER 3

G ood morning. This is your 5 o'clock wake-up call," the recorded voice announced on the telephone.

For John, Tuesday morning came very early. It seemed like only moments ago he walked Jan to the door where after a kiss, she once more refused the idea of his escorting her to the Airport Hilton.

Reluctant to leave the comfort of the bed after his short rest, stretching lazily, thoughts turned to last night. They had continued lovemaking until they were both exhausted and then lay in each other's arms relating the details of their lost relationships.

At one point, looking up at him smiling she whispered, "Thank you, John. I really needed this." The humor of the statement left them both laughing before she continued in a more serious tone.

The past several days were an anomaly, she explained. Normally described by friends as very conservative, she was experiencing a brazen personality change she found "frightening."

It all began when her ex-husband, caught cheating for the third time, no longer even tried defending his adultery. He packed a bag and heading for the door in a fit of anger, devastated her with a painful epitaph, of " fat old woman."

It worked on her mind for months, sometimes causing her to wonder if she was responsible for his seeking other women. All the while, she watched her weight actually go up, in self-fulfilling prophesy to her now ex-husband's cruel insults.

One week before, on her 40th birthday, some friends made what they believed funny comments about "downhill life after forty." She managed to laugh with everyone else but when the party ended, cried for hours.

A need to feel confident she was still considered a desirable woman by the opposite sex was becoming an obsession. She fought the battle to stay trim and attractive, even as the passing years and changing hormones made success ever more difficult. Her wandering husband's hateful comment did more damage than he might have hoped.

But, this was the first time anything remotely resembling this had occurred. The emotional assertion was followed by a desperate question. Do you believe me? She was obviously looking for validation—something to make what happened between them okay—even if it had to come from a fellow reprobate.

He now realized the importance of the answer to her. It probably came too quickly to be convincing. His reply was sincere at the time—and yes—he did believe her.

Reluctantly, around 2 am, they agreed it was time for both to get some rest before facing a long day.

"Our crew often stays here. The shuttle runs all night and they won't mind taking me to the Hilton," Jan explained. "There is no reason for you to get dressed. And, you probably shouldn't go like you are," she said with a smile looking down at his nakedness.

Jan gave him a peck on the cheek and with a devious smile said, "I'll be watching for you on your return flight. You're already a member of the 'mile high club.' You should be a member of the 'sky-high club.' It will be my pleasure to initiate you."

Chambers glanced at the red illuminated numbers on the bedside clock radio and suddenly came back to reality; it was time to get going.

Following a quick shower and shave, he opened the larger suitcase to look for something to wear; pulling out dungarees, a long-sleeved cotton shirt and one of the heavier sweaters, he quickly dressed. Styles of dress observed in the airport yesterday were giving him serious concerns about his choice of clothing for the trip, but that would have to wait. He was anxious to be on the road and slipping on the hiking boots, was glad to hear the knock at the door signaling the bellboy's arrival.

Chambers grabbed his leather jacket, followed the young man to the elevator and after a generous tip, asked the bellboy to hold his luggage at the front door until the rental car could be pulled around.

"What time does the your gift shop open?"

"At 7 am, Sir."

"Do you know if the Hilton's gift shop is open this early? I need to pick up a small thank you present," he explained.

"I'm not sure about the Hilton. Would you like me to call and check for you?"

"Could you please?"

Chambers paid his bill at the front desk and took a moment to ask directions to I-25 North. He had already looked at the map provided by the rental car company, but it never hurt to be sure.

At the front door, the bellboy returned to say the gift shop at the Hilton was open.

It was late spring and the mountain air offered a wintry chill as he left the hotel. He was grateful for the warmth the leather jacket provided while driving the long block to the Hilton.

Chambers found the gift shop and entering immediately saw a small replica of the Statue of Liberty. He asked the clerk if it could be wrapped, paid for it and wrote a quick note on the card:

Jan, for me last night will be remembered to be a "liberating event" and the beginning of a healing process. Hope you feel the same. The company was outstanding and in case you were wondering—the sex was greaaaat!! Travel safe. Signed—JC.

Locating the bellhop station, he gave the boy a twenty and asked him to take the hastily wrapped package to Jan Wilkerson's room right away.

Chambers was driving away from the Hilton when he saw a small shop advertising "fresh pastry and hot coffee." Feeling his mouth water in anticipation, he pulled into the drive through and ordered a bagel with cream cheese and a large coffee.

After pulling the rental car over to the side, Chambers worked feverishly with a plastic knife to spread the cream cheese. The handle snapped with the task half completed, and he finished using only the blade.

He let out a sharp breath of annoyance and glanced at his watch. It was only six o'clock and that would allow plenty of time (nearly two and a half hours) for the drive to Horse Creek.

To his relief, Bridger suggested John meet someone from the ranch at Horse Creek, rather than try and locate the Bar Double T on his own. They were to meet at Fitzgerald's Feed and Tack Store at 9 am.

Horse Creek sounds like some sort of suburb; it's quite a distance from Cheyenne, nearly 20 miles away, but people are moving farther and farther out of the cities these days.

When Chambers asked for an address of Fitzgerald's store, Bridger paused on the phone before responding, "The store is right on the main road; you won't have any trouble spotting it." Chambers thought he heard a soft chuckle before the phone disconnected. He never liked having loose ends and wasn't entirely certain it would be such a simple matter to find Horse Creek or the store.

31

There was a sense of relief when the clerk's knowledge of the freeways proved accurate and he found I-25 without difficulty. Traffic was light moving out of Denver; after a short time on the Interstate, a sign appeared—Cheyenne 100 miles.

Chambers made a lane change to the right and felt his stomach roll nervously. The reality of the situation seemed to engulf him for the first time.

Did this assignment really have the potential Gates had indicated, he wondered. On the surface it didn't appear to. But Gates had a "nose" for a story coming from years of experience; besides, his sources were among the best in the business. He smells a story and he trusts me with this—giving me a chance to prove myself—a mission to solidify my career. After mundane tasks, this could be the opportunity to move to bigger and better things—or what?

I've observed people who can't quite cut it staying at the paper doing menial work or simply being phased out.

Wait a minute. This is the break I've been waiting for, Chambers realized taking a deep breath and relaxing *and I'm ready. Enough with the negative mojo.*

The day was bright and the mountains to the west were spectacular. Taking a large bite out of the freshly baked bagel and swallowing a gulp of hot coffee, he felt better. Commuter traffic had already slowed to a crawl, and he was glad to be moving the opposite direction. The Ford Taurus cruised easily at the speed limit.

Denver was a beautiful city at the very foot of the Rocky Mountains. It would be a great city to visit with time to explore.

Chambers noted Denver was hyped as the "Mile High City" with its *Mile High* football stadium. Interestingly enough, his research revealed Cheyenne's altitude actually higher at 6,098 compared to Denver at 5,280; and surprisingly—Denver's population of 550,000 was greater than the entire state of Wyoming at 493,000.

Warm sun coming through the glass of the car felt good. He rolled the window down, and the outside air felt much warmer.

The drive was going faster than expected. Perhaps there would be time to look around the stores in Horse Creek for suitable clothing.

Cheyenne came into view to the east of the Interstate. Bypassing the main part of the city and continuing on, he needed to be alert for Wyoming State Highway 211, eight miles ahead; glancing down at the odometer, he made a mental note of the mileage.

Flat terrain seemed to extend for miles, broken only by the enormous mountains to the west. Chambers recalled more of the myriad of information acquired in researching this project. The Rocky Mountains formed in the Mesozoic Era dating to 138 million years ago; it is often called the cretaceous period and is responsible for creating oil and chalk deposits. Wyoming is also blessed with huge amounts of coal, and the combination is a substantial source of income for the state.

His reflections were interrupted as the road sign indicated 211 ahead. He slowed to make the exit and leaving the Interstate to the right, crossed back over the four-lane highway and read the sign pointing northwest to Horse Creek.

The highway narrowed to two lanes but the surface remained good. Glancing at his watch, he discovered it was only 7:50 am—still more than an hour before he was due at the store.

The road began to wind gradually into hilly terrain. He recognized Cottonwoods (Wyoming's State tree), which seemed to thrive in the dry soil. Growing in abundance in the sandy desert-like dirt and a climate with only 15 inches of annual precipitation, it was not uncommon for temperatures in Cheyenne to reach minus 30 degrees in the winter and 100+ degrees in summer.

Several vehicles passed him pulling long trailers, some containing horses wearing saddles and others with cattle. Mostly pick-up trucks or large SUVs, this country called for rugged vehicles to navigate the snow and rough terrain often encountered in travel.

John realized he had never seen anything like the vastness of this country. Until now, his previous experience with "wide open spaces" would have to be the Catskills of New York where he spent summer vacation at camp.

***

Fitzgerald's Feed and Tack
Horse Creek, Wyoming

Chambers saw a road sign approaching; this could be it. In bold letters the sign proclaimed: *HORSE CREEK—Elev. 6570—*and under that—*Pop. 29.*

"Twenty-nine. Twenty-nine," he repeated aloud. *Someone's probably painted over...*but before he could complete the assumption, he saw a small brick building with four or five children playing on swings. The little sign on the front of the building proclaimed Clauson Elementary.

The building was only large enough for a handful of students. *Could it be a one-room schoolhouse,* he wondered. Schools with a single teacher for all ages and grades were once very common; many of the country's most successful people were products of one-room schools. *It never occurred to me they still existed. I need to remember to get a photo or two for the paper.*

Shortly after passing Horse Creek's public school, Chambers spotted a large wood-frame building with a covered balustrade porch extending around the sides. In bold letters across the front were emblazoned: **Fitzgerald's Feed and Tack**.

The building's high gabled roof was covered with a green metal, designed to encourage heavy winter snows to slide off the slick surface, hopefully preventing the need to shovel the snow off and keeping weight from caving in the roof. A trickle of smoke swirled idly out of the brick chimney. Chilly early-morning temperatures still required a source of heat; and the fire was probably now being allowed to burn itself out, replaced by the warmth of a late spring sun.

The structure mirrored its age and the history that undoubtedly went with it, while at the same time reflecting careful maintenance. Windows in front were large to allow for light (probably installed before electricity was available) and space to display assorted products. John could make out a saddle on a stand and beside it a mannequin dressed in western clothing.

This looks like it could be the only store for miles and probably out of necessity carries a wide-ranging inventory, Chambers surmised.

It was early, still plenty of time to look around. Parking the Ford in an area to the west side and careful to avoid blocking fuel pumps in front of the store, he decided to look for something more appropriate to wear in this unfamiliar new environment.

Purely from habit, Chambers locked the Taurus and walked over to the wooden steps. The stairs led up to a large front porch full of various items ranging from rocking chairs, to saddles, shovels and other small implements.

He opened the front door and froze in his tracks, startled when a small bell rang above his head announcing an arrival. Moments passed before a very pleasant female voice asked, "May I help you?"

The voice appeared to be coming from a stack of boxes.

A young woman walked out of the messy pile—a very attractive young woman.

"May I help you?" she repeated. As she asked the question, she tossed her head to one side, allowing shiny brunette hair to rustle softly before falling back into place on her shoulders. Lively brown eyes sparkled from a tan out-of-doors complexion.

The young woman in front of him was blessed with what his best friend Mo called kissable lips—a full shapely mouth so many women were trying unsuccessfully to emulate with painful injections of collagen. It was unlikely these lips had never felt the sting of a needle.

A form-fitting western shirt silhouetted her shapely breasts. She stepped sideways to get through the boxes bringing her entire body into view, and the blue jeans were tight enough to reveal a sexy butt and long legs. With the low-heeled boots, he guessed her height at about 5'9".

"Is there something I can do for you, Sir?"

John realized he was staring. "Yes, uh yes, I'm needing some clothes," he blurted. *Good grief, what's wrong with me? I've been surrounded by pretty women all my life in New York. Why am I babbling like an idiot in a feed store in Wyoming?*

As she stepped closer, a pleasant smell drifted toward him and he felt mesmerized. *That fragrance isn't perfume; it's simply a fresh smell—probably from her recent morning bath. Holy shit. Get a grip! You're going to embarrass yourself.*

"Anything in particular?" she asked.

"I'm not really sure…uh…that is, I'm here to visit a ranch and really may not have the clothes I'll need. I'm…uh…coming from New York and have never been in this area before."

She looked somewhat amused by this information. Her eyes were laughing but her mouth only curled slightly in the smallest of smiles. "What will you be doing on the ranch—breaking horses?" Seeing his confused look and quickly realizing the cruelty of the statement, she felt instantly ashamed.

"I'm sorry. Please forgive me. It's…you are so obviously from another world. I can't quite imagine what you will be doing on a Wyoming ranch. I mean…what I'm trying to say is…I've been rude. Can we start over?"

"I'm Melanie Fitzgerald. Welcome to Horse Creek," she added and without waiting for an answer, stepped forward to offer her hand.

He was surprised at the firmness of her handshake and feeling her warm hand in his, could manage only a somewhat muffled greeting.

"It's a pleasure to meet you, Ms. Fitzgerald. No apology is necessary, and you are more correct than you may fully comprehend when you indicate—how did you put it—I'm 'obviously from another world.'"

"My name is John Chambers. I'm meeting someone here from the Bridger ranch," he added, still holding her hand.

"It's Miss—and I'm Melanie," she said, smiling warmly. "In the west, Mr. & Mrs. are for our elders."

She relaxed her grip slightly and looking down at her hand still firmly being held, slowly extracted it from his seemingly reluctant-to-let-go grip.

"I'm…I'm sorry…."

Before he could finish, Melanie interrupted, with her tone indicating she was getting back to business. "What you said earlier about not having the proper clothes—let's see what we can do. What kind of activities will you be involved in at the Bar Double T?"

"I'll be breaking some horses," he quipped with a smile. "I have a reputation for being one of the best in my neighborhood in New York."

"Touché. I deserved that. Seriously. Give me some idea what you will be doing at the ranch."

"I'm a writer for *The New York World*," he said, not attempting to hide the pride in his voice. I'll be writing a story on Mr. Bridger." *Surely, even Horse Creek knew of the greatest newspaper in the world.* Immediately, he felt guilty for the contemptible thought; it wasn't in his nature to put people down, especially when he didn't even know them.

"Mr. Bridger is out—I believe he said 'on the range'—doing something with his cattle. I'm supposed to meet him there and stay until he returns to the ranch."

"Will you be riding a horse?" Melanie asked.

"I'm not sure, but I should probably be prepared. I've ridden in Central Park enough to feel somewhat comfortable around horses and would enjoy the opportunity."

Melanie turned on her heel, struggling to keep from laughing out loud. "You'll be riding in a really *big* park at the Bar Double T," she said over her shoulder. "Let's see if we can find some proper gear for you."

Chambers followed her to the back of the store, wondering what that last comment meant. Looking around, he realized for the first time, there was no one else in the store. At least, not visible. This beautiful young woman did not appear at all concerned about being here alone with a complete stranger. Was it because she's confident of her abilities to take care of herself, or because people here are not accustomed to the violence of major cities?

Opening a door to what appeared to be a small office, Melanie spoke to someone, "You may come out, Bismarck."

A large German shepherd ambled out.

"Sit...stay," she commanded. The large dog immediately responded.

"John, meet Bismarck. He's my roommate and constant companion. Are you...okay with dogs?"

"I haven't really been around dogs very much. Hello, big guy. Okay to pet him?"

"Absolutely. I'll release him and he'll come to you for a smell. Stand still for a moment and then feel free to pet him."

"It's okay, Bismarck—he wants to meet you."

The dog immediately came over, smelling John's feet and legs before beginning to wag his tail. Chambers reached down and stroked the shepherd's big head, and the wagging tail picked up speed.

"He appears to like you. It's not normal for him to show affection when he first meets someone. You've made your first friend in Horse Creek."

"I'm glad to hear Bismarck likes me, especially considering the alternative; but I was actually hoping he would be my second friend in Horse Creek."

Melanie's expression barely changed with his lame attempt at flirtation, but John saw a hint of a smile and a slight twinkle before she coolly asked, "What size shoe do you wear? I'm going to look for a pair of flat heels. They will be easier to walk in and still give you enough protection to ride. I'm assuming you will not be doing any roping and won't need the higher heels."

"I'm a size 12. Before we run up too large a bill, what credit cards do you take?"

"No credit cards—only cash. If you don't have enough on you, bring it by later; I know where to find you."

Bring it by later? Damn, is she kidding? But there it is again, John acknowledged. *Her basic instincts are to trust with an assumption of honesty. This will take some getting used to, but I have to admit, it feels a lot better than living with suspicion and anticipating the worst from everyone.*

Moments later, Melanie reappeared holding out a pair of shiny calf-length boots. "We only have these in brown. Try them on for fit. Here, put these socks on first; you will need something cooler than those wool walking socks."

The cotton socks were thick on the bottoms and felt good after he pulled them on and followed with the boots. Standing up, he was surprised how comfortable the boots felt; a bit tight like all new shoes but not what he expected.

"Walk around a bit and see how they fit," Melanie encouraged. After a moment or so, she asked, "How do they feel?"

"Very comfortable for new shoes. These will do fine."

"They were designed by Justin, an old company bought out several years ago, but the new people still make a good quality boot.

"I'm going to give you a can of spray to waterproof them. After the spray dries, use this neets foot oil; be sure to apply it lightly and rub it in thoroughly. It will soften and protect the boots. And keep them from looking quite so new," she added softly.

What do I care if they look new, she reasoned. *You don't even know this guy...so what if he takes a little ribbing about new shoes from the ranch hands. Still, he is a guest of the Bridgers. You have an obligation to do everything possible to help him avoid embarrassment—for their sakes.*

There was little time for conversation. Melanie asked for sizes, made a change here and there and then moved on, confident of exactly what he needed. She moved about the store, selecting trousers, shirts, a western belt with a nice buckle and finally a waist-length jean jacket.

The trousers and jacket were pre-faded denim and would not give the awkward appearance of being new. Cowhand crews could be relentless in their sometimes cruel hazing of new people on the scene—especially when they considered them "dudes." New clothes often invited some teasing, even among close friends.

"Two more items. One I have and one has to be ordered to fit. We do not have *chaps* or *chinks* since they are usually fitted to the individual, but we do have a good assortment of hats. You're going to need a hat—a western hat. We have some fine Stetsons, but there are other brands equally good. Take a look and try some on."

What the heck are chaps and chinks, Chambers wondered. *I'm not going to embarrass myself by asking—surely if they're essential to my survival, someone will tell me.*

"I'm not so sure about a hat. I'm going to look and feel…well sort of strange in one of these," proving the point by placing a wide brimmed "Gus" type hat on his head. It was a large high-crowned hat named after Gus McRae—the role Robert Duvall played in the made-for-TV Western series, *Lonesome Dove*.

Once again, Melanie turned away to avoid his seeing her amusement. He was correct: strange didn't adequately describe what he looked like with this huge hat, without a crease or any styling added, sitting on his head. Hats of western cowboys are highly personalized, and the region a cowboy comes from can often be determined by the crease and style of the hat.

"I look ridiculous." John said suddenly. "I can't wear one of these. My Yankee baseball cap will do fine."

"A Yankee baseball cap will do fine—in Yankee Stadium. You need something to keep the sun and rain off. Something to keep your head warm at night and cool during the day. The western hat's high crown and wide brim is designed to do precisely that.

"Hmm," she expressed out loud.

"Would you mind wearing a hat if it's been worn already? My brother is about your size; he left a hat here, which he will not need again for quite some time. Care to try it on?"

"If you feel that strongly about my needing a hat, sure, I'll try it."

Melanie disappeared to the back of the store for several minutes returning with what appeared to be a new hat.

"My brother sent it to Laramie to have it cleaned and blocked right before he left," she said removing a hat keeper from the inside brim.

"Try it on and take a look in the mirror."

Chambers took the hat from her hand as if he expected it to break, walked over to the mirror and set it rather gingerly on his head.

"Do you mind," Melanie asked stepping close and reaching toward the hat.

Her body gently brushed John's arm. She moved closer still, intent on the task at hand and tugged the Stetson slightly down on his head lower over his eyes, unaware of the stir she was creating in him.

"There. Not bad."

Melanie took a couple of steps back and examined him carefully for a moment.

"Looking good, Mr. Chambers," she said with a sly grin. "How does it feel?"

"Mr. Chambers is my dad; my name is John." They both laughed.

"It feels comfortable enough and seems to fit fine; question is, do I really need a hat like this?"

"You're going to have to trust me on this one…John. After a couple days out riding, you'll be thanking me; besides, my brother promised me a bonus if I could sell this awful hat to some unsuspecting dude. Only kidding!" she smiled.

I can't remember the last time the company of a woman was this enjoyable. Great sense of humor, intelligent and amazingly beautiful, this is one lady I would like to get to know better—much better.

"Melanie, thank you for all your help—you've been awesome."

She looked directly into his eyes, "John, you are very welcome. "If you wish, go into the back and change into one of the outfits you're buying. They'll probably be more comfortable to wear on the ranch."

Melanie watched John shuffling through boxes on his way toward the bathroom/changing room and began to mull over this unexpected and unlikely meeting.

Her last relationship (if it could be called that) might better be described a terrible blunder. A whirlwind liaison with her college marketing professor—that stopped only short of becoming an affair—began with a cup of coffee and intellectual discussions. Soon, the conversations took on a more intimate nature, not offensive at first, but progressively more suggestive.

Melanie recalled being flattered a sophisticated and worldly man like Professor Strisand could be expressing interest in her. A weekend trip to Denver was arranged before she really knew him. Fortunately, she discovered shortly before leaving with him for the weekend—he was married. It was a devastating experience creating a distrust of men still not completely resolved.

Recalling her early college years living in the dorm, roommates often came in late, describing their sexual encounters in excited tones and sometimes teasing her for not having stories to tell. Foolish and immature though it may sound—looking back—she now realized it played a role in her agreeing to take the trip to Denver.

Recent personal losses in her family were a factor as well. Her goal was to major in Business Management and locate to Seattle or San Francisco after graduation to pursue a career. In her senior year, first her father and not long after, her mother became seriously ill.

Both parents died within months of each other. Older brother Raymond took over operation of the family store and ranch, with Melanie doing what she could to help out when home from school.

Raymond was a member of the Wyoming National Guard. Shortly after her graduation, his unit was called up for active duty, almost immediately leaving for Iraq. He sold off the stock and leased the hay fields of the ranch before leaving.

She was now operating the store alone with the exception of one part-time employee, who came in three days each week to help with the heavier chores when supplies were delivered.

Melanie's reminiscing turned back to John Chambers. *He's a healthy, good-looking man and...not wearing a wedding ring. Geez Louise, what a feeble idea. Nevertheless, I'm strangely attracted to him, even though it would be difficult to imagine two people with less in common. Perhaps opposites do attract.*

He's tall, with an athletic-looking build—bet he works out regularly; his slender waist really sets off his shoulders. Very handsome with facial features masculine without being coarse, dark hair and large intelligent brown eyes. His eyes sometimes carried an inquisitive look but also gave the impression of someone with serious ambitions. John has the appearance of a man driven to succeed. How old, she wondered. *Probably late twenties. Hhmm...interesting—I'm twenty-six.*

Melanie's musing was interrupted by the jingle of the bell; turning toward the door, she recognized Shane O'Grady. Shane was the senior foreman of the Bar Double T and was probably here to meet John.

It must mean his visit is considered important to the Bridgers. Shane doesn't waste his valuable time escorting peons, Melanie realized.

"Hey, Mel. How's the best looking girl in Horse Creek these days?"

It was Shane's way of kidding her. Since the mines closed, there were only 29 people—more or less—officially living in Horse Creek.

"She's fine, Shane. How's the most over-rated cowboy in Wyoming doing?"

Shane gave her a wounded look. He knew she could give and take with the best, and they never missed the opportunity to exchange friendly fire. Their relationship was special and both knew it. Recent events with the death of Melanie's parents and her brother leaving for military duty served to bring them even closer. Without her knowing it, Shane kept a watchful eye on her and encouraged the other foremen at the ranch to do the same.

Shane reached down to Bismarck and began to rub both of his ears. The big dog responded by turning his head from side-to-side moaning gently.

"Damn, if I could only find a woman around here who liked to have her ears rubbed," Shane commented dryly.

"See anything of a dude from the big city lurking around here anywhere? You haven't locked him up in the store-room planning to take him home for a pet, have you?"

Melanie gave him a big smile. She both loved and respected Shane O'Grady. After college, Shane had been drafted. He returned from Viet Nam a wounded hero to become the senior foreman at the Bar Double T—a position paying well into six figures. To the Bridgers, he was like family.

Shane is equally at home behind the controls of the ranch helicopter or on top of a pitching bronc.

He was probably nearing sixty, but you couldn't tell by looking. Over 6 feet tall, he looked in good enough shape to go out for the local football team. The mustache, mostly gray, matched the curly gray hair and finely wrinkled tan complexion of a man who spent a lot of time outside. His blue-gray eyes were always expressive, usually suggesting confidence and toughness, but sometimes reflecting the pain life had dealt.

Shane stood holding hat in hand, having removed it out of respect for Melanie. He wore typical western gear with a vest over a blue work shirt and faded denim jeans. Melanie took note of the chinks over his jeans and his high-heeled boots with spurs. (The chinks were made of leather and designed to protect a cowboy from the brush while riding as well as from the kicking feet of calves during handling.)

There's obviously going to be some riding in the "big park" today. Hopefully, John will be up to it.

Chambers came walking out of the back room before she had time to reply to Shane's question. He didn't appear too much of a dude; in fact, he could almost pass for a local. It was apparent the conversation between Melanie and Shane had been overheard through the thin walls.

John walked up to Shane, sticking out his hand and with a friendly smile said, "Good morning. I'm John Chambers."

Shane hesitated a moment before extending his hand—looking John straight in the eye; Melanie knew he was sizing John up.

Finally, he extended his big brown hand grasping John's and replied, "Good to see you, John. I'm Shane O'Grady. How's the trip?"

"Good! In fact, it's been great so far."

Chambers' enthusiasm caused Melanie and Shane to exchange glances.

"Glad to hear it. I've got a question for you. We need to get you out to the cow camp to meet the Boss, and there are two ways to do it. I may be staying for a couple days, so horseback would be best, but you can also fly in by helicopter if you prefer."

Chambers stood for a moment considering his choices. *Undoubtedly, I'll live to regret this decision—but I have a feeling if I said helicopter, I'll lose a lot of respect. I could live with it from O'Grady but—*"Horseback will be fine and thanks for asking."

The small talk continued between the two men, and Melanie completed the packaging of the clothing John purchased. She put the clothes he laid on the counter into a bag and placed the rest of the gear in two large boxes. Ringing up the charges on the ancient Dayton cash register, the cash drawer sprang open with a loud clanking sound, and Melanie turned to see John waiting at the counter to pay the bill. Shane was out of hearing range, looking at a new saddle near the front door.

"The total comes to $475," she announced. "I'm not charging you for the hat. You can return it when you leave; or if you want to leave it at the Bar Double T, someone will return it for you. If you don't have the cash, you can bring it by later."

"Not a problem. Could you please give me a receipt? This is a business expense. My new tax man loves receipts."

While he waited for the receipt, John pulled five one-hundred-dollar bills from his leather money holder and laid them on the counter.

Melanie picked up the bills, made change from the register and handed it to him adding with a smile, "Thank you for the business."

"Thank *you*. It was my good fortune to meet you. I'm sure you have helped me avoid some embarrassment, not to mention physical discomfort. Perhaps we'll see each other again. I'll probably be here for a week or perhaps more." *It could be more*, he reasoned. *It's obvious this assignment is going to be complicated. I need to take time to do the best possible job.*

"John, I'm planning to attend the 60th wedding celebration for Ted and Rebecca Bridger at the ranch this weekend. Maybe we'll see each other there."

Shane came back to the area where they were standing. "Let me help you with those boxes. It looks like you bought out half the store."

"Replacements for a few things left behind in New York," John replied. He looked up and gave Melanie a conspiratorial smile.

"Appreciate the help."

The two men walked out to the car and pick-up parked side by side. Carrying a box, Shane reached John's car first and took hold of the door handle.

After pulling repeatedly attempting to open the door, he finally realized—it was locked.

Melanie saw the growing look of amusement on Shane's face. He set the box on top of the car, looked over to John and with a straight face said, "Good idea keeping your vehicle locked in these parts. We've had a rash of car thefts lately here in Horse Creek!"

John did not reply as he stood fishing for the key in his pocket. Unlocking the door, he placed the packages inside, jumped into his car and with a wave to Melanie, fell in behind Shane's pick-up and disappeared from view.

***

CHAPTER 4

O'Grady's pick-up spun gravel moving out onto Highway 211, quickly reaching 65 mph, before he looked into the mirror to see if the *dude* was following.

Not quite fair, he admitted. Chambers was making an effort to fit in with what must be a surreal environment to him, rather than expecting people to make allowances. This was evident from his taking time to buy range clothes. He wondered how much Melanie helped with the selection.

The Boss, as Ted Bridger II was now known by the hands on the ranch (Ted Bridger I was Mr. Bridger), gave him very general instructions on meeting Chambers and getting him to the sight of the branding. There had been a brief discussion about Shane flying him in by helicopter. The Boss first suggested giving him a ride out in the chopper, but then changed his mind. "He wants to see the realities of life on a ranch—let's give him a little realism 'from the seat up' so to speak. Unless he objects, put him on a good horse and let him ride to the camp; just don't endanger his well being more than necessary."

O'Grady interpreted it to mean, "Get him there with the least amount of trauma possible." The last part about endangering him was unnecessary. Safety was an important consideration in every activity. Life on a ranch was plenty dangerous enough without recklessly adding to it. More than a few ranch hands were fired for failing to recognize that reality and placing themselves or others in unnecessary danger.

No one quite knew what to expect of Chambers from the standpoint of physical capabilities or attitude. He appeared to be in good physical shape, and O'Grady liked the way he shook hands with a firm grip and looked right into your eyes. This dude was sizing him up.

In the west, a handshake and eye contact went a long way in first impressions. In O'Grady's mind, Chambers was off to an okay start.

The fact he bought the clothes necessary for the ride out to the branding sites would save a lot of time and meant they wouldn't be scrambling around looking for gear for him to wear. Sitting in the saddle in thin pants, or wearing improper footwear, could quickly leave abrasions on the butt and insides of the legs and ankles, turning an otherwise pleasant horseback ride into pure torture.

He reached for the handset for his mobile two-way radio and punched the button for the ranch arena. "Randy? Shane here. We're fifteen minutes out and may be able to make the noon break if we can get right off. Get the two Fox Trotters saddled and loaded. Put the Syd Hill Australian saddle on Traveler; it's probably the closest thing we have to an English saddle. Throw in an extra *soogan,* will you, Randy? (A soogan is a cowboy bedroll containing a heavy outer canvas and often an inflatable mattress used for sleeping in the elements.) And Randy…be sure to put my .45 in my saddlebag. Thanks."

No point in getting John excited over seeing the gun. It was a Les Baer .45 auto pistol given to him five years ago by the Boss. Once after shooting at some tin cans with the Colt .45 O'Grady brought home from Viet Nam and only managing to hit a couple, the Boss finally remarked, "At least it makes a lot of noise, maybe it will scare something to death." Issued by the government in mass numbers, the old gun carried a lot of sentimental value. Sentimental value or not, the facts were it was sadly lacking in accuracy.

Bridger returned to work in Washington; and a couple of weeks later, a package arrived for O'Grady. When he opened it, he discovered a custom-made new pistol complete with holster, belt, extra clips and a note reading simply: "Hope you never have to use this fine weapon on anything but tin cans—but if you do—you're both up to the challenge."

Les Baer is a nationally prominent gun builder. He "accurizes" and hand builds .45s on a Para-Ordnance frame for FBI-SWAT. They're fine weapons and O'Grady carried his everywhere he went on the range, believing it necessary to carry "a tool" capable of putting an animal in distress out of misery when nothing could be done to help. This especially was true in the event of an accident to the horses he rode.

O'Grady had been at the Bar Double T most of his life. When he was only fifteen, his father died in a mining accident; being the oldest boy at home, Shane suddenly faced adult responsibilities.

Ted Bridger II had been a star athlete and student at Cheyenne High and was the subject of O'Grady's hero worship. Looking up to him in everything from the way he walked to the way he wore his hair, O'Grady was excited when he learned Ted would be visiting his old school to talk to the team. Fresh from his first year at the University of Wyoming, Ted was living every Wyoming schoolboy's athletic dream.

As Bridger stood visiting with the football coach, O'Grady watched for an opportunity and finally when Bridger was walking away hurried to catch up. He still remembered the conversation well and Bridger's genuine concern when he learned O'Grady would not be playing sports because of his responsibilities at home. The next day he received a message at school to call the Bar Double T and speak with Brock Lee, the foreman. He was offered a job on weekends and anytime he had time to spare. And Lee was careful to inform him—it would not interfere with his opportunity to play sports.

The senior Mr. Bridger took a special interest in O'Grady, virtually adopting him. With son Ted away at the University of Wyoming playing football on Saturday afternoons, Mr. Bridger took time to watch his younger son Timothy play high school junior varsity Fridays nights and then often stayed to see O'Grady participate with the varsity.

The young O'Grady worked at the ranch at every opportunity—including after school, on weekends and holidays. Mr. Bridger insisted he take time to participate on all the athletic teams at school he desired. He decided to play basketball, but elected to stay out of track and baseball because they took place in the spring and would cut into opportunities to work on the ranch.

He worked hard, learned quickly, and it soon became apparent Shane possessed a special talent and desire for ranch life. Tasks gradually became more complex, and he never failed to do all that was expected and a little extra.

Young Timmy Bridger was soon feeling the same adulation for Shane O'Grady that Shane earlier felt for his brother Ted. Shane still struggled with the belief hero worship probably led Timmy to follow in his footsteps and join the Army straight out of college. Timmy lost his life in that ugly jungle war of Viet Nam—and to some degree—O'Grady would always feel a sense of responsibility.

O'Grady did well in school academically and excelled in athletics. In his senior year he was rewarded with athletic scholarship offers to several colleges in the area. When the big one came—the Wyoming Cowboys—he wanted desperately to accept but knew he couldn't.

There were two younger brothers at home, and his mother needed his support. In the three years since the death of his father, the money he earned working at the ranch provided necessary income to supplement his mother's meager salary. How could he go away to college?

In addition to raising three young boys, his mother worked at a store in Cheyenne for minimum wage and without benefits. He learned the meaning of "without benefits" the hard way and never failed to appreciate having benefits thereafter. On several occasions, there were medical bills to pay, which were beyond their tight budget. The bills mysteriously disappeared.

Once, he went to Mr. Bridger to protest and was told he could pay him back "in the future." O'Grady started to say, "We don't accept char…" and got no farther.

"Shane, it is often far more difficult for a man to accept help when he needs it, than to do without," Mr. Bridger explained.

"Remember, it isn't merely *you* we are talking about here, it's your *family* too. It would be a wholly selfish act for you to refuse help and place your entire family in jeopardy. We will consider this subject permanently closed."

Mr. Bridger didn't speak for several minutes and O'Grady remembered starting to walk toward the door.

"Shane, I'm pleased to learn you've been offered a scholarship to Wyoming. I'm sure you know Wyoming is my alma mater, and the ranch endows several scholarships; some come in the form of cash grants to cover expenses unrelated to tuition and school itself.

"Since the athletic department will cover your room, board and tuition, you will be eligible for a Bar Double T grant. The grant is in the amount of $8,000 per annum. Our attorneys have inquired about the legality of this grant with the National Collegiate Athletic Association, and we were informed it is permissible: 'if the grant has been given to other members of the ranch community without regard to athletic utility.'

"We want all of our top hands to have the opportunity for college if they qualify, and we would be very disappointed if you did not accept this offer to better yourself—and your family."

O'Grady remembered leaving the office and literally running to his ancient rusty Chevy pick-up to rush home and tell his mom the great news.

At Wyoming, O'Grady soon found his 6'3" frame wasn't cut out for basketball at the major college level. After his freshman year, he concentrated on football and academics, having success in both.

In four years, he graduated with academic honors and made the Western Athletic All-Conference team twice.

O'Grady majored in Ranch Management with a minor in Business; and following his graduation, Mr. Bridger offered him a very lucrative position at the Bar Double T.

He appeared to have a promising future. Unfortunately, someone else felt the same. It was 1968 and things were heating up in a little known Southeast Asian country—Viet Nam.

The draft had been reinstated. It came in the mail. The US Army wants YOU! It wasn't a request.

Within weeks of his graduation, O'Grady was in basic training. After completing basic in Missouri, he was told his recent college degree and athletic ability made him a perfect candidate for OCS. (He discovered it stood for Officer Candidate School.) Following completion of OCS, he received the single bronze bar of a brand-new second lieutenant.

With the role of the helicopter being greatly expanded in Viet Nam, the Army needed aggressive, athletic young physical specimens "short on brains and long on guts." Fort Rucker, Alabama, became his home for the next several months, where he was taught the still developing tactics of the Army Air Cavalry.

The Army was still looking out for him; and following flight school, they pinned wings on his chest and provided an all-expenses-paid trip to Southeast Asia. O'Grady subsequently served two tours in "Nam" and returned to Wyoming a decorated, wounded and confused veteran.

His commendation read in part: "With a complete disregard for his personal safety, First Lieutenant Shane M. O'Grady successfully rescued a downed U.S. Naval fighter pilot in hostile enemy territory. Lt. O'Grady's helicopter was knocked from the sky, during repeated attempts to land in a small clearing receiving intense enemy fire. The co-pilot and door gunner suffered substantial injuries in the crash. Ignoring his own significant wounds, Lt. O'Grady proceeded to drag each man to cover, before returning to the unconscious pilot and carrying him through heavy mortar and small arms fire to safety. Lt. O'Grady's actions reflect the highest...."

The "significant wounds" were sufficient to get him sent home, and he was subsequently honorably discharged—with thanks from Uncle Sam.

He didn't, however, come home to "thanks" from his country—at least, not from those who were getting all the news coverage. There were marches in the streets and elsewhere. Some turned violent. The students were spitting at—and on—returning veterans in the airports and bus stations.

O'Grady was glad to get home to the Bar Double T; and when Mr. Bridger made available the position first offered out of college, he wasted no time in accepting.

Likewise, he did not procrastinate in proposing to his high school sweetheart, Helen Jo Spears. She accepted and they started married life living in one of the small houses on the outer limits of the Bar Double T.

The happy couple raised their two boys on the ranch. One was currently managing a sheep station—in Hobart, Tasmania Australia, owned by the Bridgers—with the second a professor of veterinary medicine at Colorado State University in nearby Fort Collins, Colorado.

Helen Jo was the love of his life. Five years ago she became sick quite suddenly and within ten days died of what doctors called "a virus of unknown type and origin." At first he felt her death was going to destroy him; then he did everything he could to fulfill his self-prophecy.

O'Grady began to drink. Initially, he told himself it was to handle his sorrow, but soon he was in danger of losing the battle to the bottle. Once again, the Bridgers came to his rescue. They sent him to Australia—"to check on the sheep station."

In Australia he spent a good deal of time with some old Aussie friends; Ray Woods and wife Sharon helped him find his way back to the world of the living.

Time away with the Woods and at the sheep station with his son allowed the healing process to begin; and upon returning to Wyoming, he focused all his attention and interest on the ranch. This was his home; he would live and die here. Someday he would be buried next to Helen Jo in the Bar Double T cemetery.

***

Bar Double T Ranch
Horse Creek, Wyoming

The brake lights on O'Grady's pick-up suddenly flashed, and Chambers gaped at a wooden archway with **Bar Double T Ranch** burned into a sign hanging thirty feet high on a massive cross timber.

The entire structure, built of huge spruce logs four feet in diameter, was set in rock and concrete. Black metal gates were completely engulfed sitting under the colossal wood entry.

The high arching gates swung slowly open, and Chambers surmised they must operate from an electric eye or remote opener. O'Grady pulled through the gates and stopped to be sure Chambers passed before they closed behind him.

Turning onto a paved road, they began to wind slightly down hill; looking ahead, Chambers caught his first glimpse of the ranch headquarters. In the distance, two structures, which appeared to be residences (one much older in appearance), were nestled in the valley with a snow-patched mountain peak silhouetted behind. It was an incredible setting.

The road to the ranch headquarters was lined along both sides by a post-and-rail fence. Scattered across the valley were large cottonwoods; enormous sprays of water irrigated lush green grass, to the obvious pleasure of the horses grazing in small herds on both sides of the road.

The valley seemed to stretch for miles along the base of the mountain. To the left, he could make out the outline of a helicopter and a very long building with the wide, high doors of an airplane hangar.

A long asphalt runway extended out from the hangar running parallel to the mountain down the valley away from the main buildings. Chambers' knowledge of airplanes was limited, but the runway appeared long enough to facilitate jet aircraft.

The first buildings they passed were of log construction with single gable roofs covered in green metal. These bunkhouses, Chambers would later learn, were designed to house four people; and each contained four bedrooms with private shower and toilet. The bedrooms surrounded a common living area, complete with fireplace and small kitchen. Built for the single employees whose duties required them to live on the ranch, they could also be used for special emergency situations.

A large native rock and wood building with pipe corrals extending out from open doors along one side came into view. Chambers noticed several horses leisurely eating fresh hay in the corrals; a dual wheeled pick-up truck hitched to a trailer in front of the building held two horses with saddles already on them. Chambers followed O'Grady's truck and pulled in beside the trailer.

Getting out of his truck, O'Grady was approached by a younger man.

"Mornin, Shane. Truck's fueled and horses are saddled and ready to go. Put the soogan in back with yours and throwed in an extree tepee too, just in case."

"Good thinking," O'Grady replied. "We'll only be out one night; what's the weather supposed to be?"

"Ya know how them weather guys are—they tell it after they see it. Sposed to be warm with no rain for next kupla days."

"Sounds good. Randy...say hello to John Chambers. He'll be a guest of the Boss for a few days, and I'd appreciate it if you would help him any way you can."

John extended his hand, and Randy gave him a firm handshake saying, "Anything you need, Mr. Chambers, only need to ask."

"Thanks, Randy—please call me John."

Randy looked straight into Chambers' eyes and replied, "Yes, Sir—John."

O'Grady had a look of amusement when he turned to Chambers and asked, "You need to hit the can? It's in the arena down the hall to your left."

"Thanks; I'm OK but do need to make a quick phone call to my editor."

"No problem," O'Grady replied.

"I'll show you the arena office; it'll be more private."

He walked ahead of Chambers into the arena, turned right and opening a large ornate wooden door said, "Make yourself at home; use the desk if you prefer."

The office was beautifully paneled with an array of back-lighted shelves containing trophies with hundreds of colored show ribbons hanging about the room. Several saddles on wooden stands wore attached metal tags attesting to when and where they were won. The walls contained numerous color and (older) black and white photos of horses, some with riders and some without.

A large wooden desk with a brown leather chair sat at one end of the room, next to a huge rock fireplace. A small wet bar extended from the wall with several cut-glass decanters filled with a variety of liquor on a large silver tray.

On one side was a conference table with eight leather high-back chairs; several leisure chairs along with various small tables and lamps completed the business-like décor. This was obviously a working office, clearly furnished for a sophisticated and broad-based clientele.

Chambers hit the speed dial on his cell phone, hoping to get reception. In a few moments a low feminine voice said softly, "Mr. Gates' office, may I help you?"

"Cynthia…John. Is Michael in?"

"Can you please hold, John?" she breathed into the phone, "Let me see if he is available."

"Hello, John Boy. Where are you?" Gates asked.

"I'm at the ranch. We're about ready to leave—by horseback—to find Bridger."

"Horseback, huh? Sounds like an adventure. The paper doesn't give extra pay for hazardous duty, you know. Be careful, John—you can't have much sick leave built up."

Gates chuckled and John politely followed suit.

"Michael, I'm sure to be out of cell phone range, but I'll try to check in each day. Plans are to return to civilization sometime tomorrow."

"Understood, John Boy. Let me know if you need anything here." The phone went dead.

John Boy? Obviously a reference to TV's Walton family. Ignore it and this too will pass.

Outside, Chambers spotted O'Grady leaning on the fender of the pick-up, sipping a Dr. Pepper.

"Want something before we leave?" he inquired holding up the drink.

"No thanks, Shane. There's some bottled water in the car—I'll grab it and I'm good to go."

Leaving the front gate turning west, they traveled along several miles before O'Grady broke the silence.

"John, I've got a question. Understand, I'm not asking to embarrass you; have you ever been on a horse?"

"I've ridden some in Central Park, but the horses are all trail broken and accustomed to the park. I'm sure it would—indeed be embarrassing if you put me on a wild bronc.*"*

O'Grady let his breath out slowly; "Won't happen on this ranch. The best of horses can be dangerous animals, and we take good manners with our guests seriously."

This guy may be okay. He had an opportunity to exaggerate his abilities and opted for a candid answer; it shows some confidence, O'Grady acknowledged. *He's smart enough not to embellish his skills trying to impress someone and get himself into trouble.*

A few miles passed and they turned south onto a hard-packed dirt road, becoming progressively rougher, finally stopping at the base of a small mountain.

"We'll leave the truck here and take the horses the rest of the way; about twelve miles over the far ridge and down the other side."

Chambers noticed when Shane said *ridge*, he was looking at a *mountain*.

Shane dropped the gate on the trailer and unloaded the two horses.

"John, this horse with the Australian saddle will be yours for the trip. He's a Missouri Fox Trotter. Name's Traveler. Ever ride a gaited horse before?"

"I'm not sure. What does gaited mean?"

"Basically, it refers to their way of going—in this case, you'll find a very comfortable rocking motion—which is far easier on the rider than non-gaited types of horses. We use quarter horses for working cattle because of their agility and cow instincts, but they really beat you up on long rides across country.

"We keep the Trotters for fast smooth travel; our 'Sunday-go-to-meetin horses.' They are good in the mountains or on the flat. Ride him with two hands,

English style, and he'll also respond to leg pressure. He's a good one; you two will get along fine."

Chambers felt a little rush of adrenalin, but was surprisingly confident this man would not mislead him. Shane was nothing like what he expected a Wyoming cowboy to be, and it suddenly occurred to him—he felt an innate trust for this tough-looking cowboy.

Walking over to Traveler and reaching out to stroke him gently on the neck, the big horse turned his head blowing softly through his nose in a friendly greeting.

Chambers watched Shane tighten the cinch, untie his horse and lead him around in a small circle, then tighten the cinch a little more. Chambers carefully emulated what he observed and was soon walking Traveler.

Taking the lead rope and looping it through his belt, Shane threw the reins over the neck of his horse, grabbed a handful of the horse's mane, put a foot in the stirrup and swung lightly into the saddle.

Traveler stood perfectly still while Chambers mounted and searched briefly before finally locating the right stirrup with his foot. Squeezing Traveler lightly with his legs, the big horse moved out, following Shane toward the base of the "ridge."

The trail was well worn, clearly used often, and Traveler and Nason Ridge moved smoothly at a flat walking gait, covering ground at a deceptively rapid pace.

"Traveler is really comfortable to ride. Feels a lot different than the horses I've ridden in the past."

"These are Cadillacs," O'Grady replied. "You won't want to get back on those Chevrolets when this trip is over."

The horses began to bob their heads up and down walking up the steep terrain, stepping nimbly over small fallen tree trunks lying across the trail.

"I need to get a crew up here to clear this trail," O'Grady said reaching into his shirt pocket and pulling out a small pad. Crossing the reins across his lap, he began writing a note while guiding the big gelding along the trail with his legs.

Nothing more was said for several miles, until Chambers broke the silence asking for a description of the ranch. "I'd like to use it for background material in my article," he explained.

"Sure," O'Grady replied. "The Boss said to help you any way possible. What would you like to know?"

Chambers briefly outlined the type of information his readers might be interested in learning. Several minutes passed; Chambers was preparing to say something and, O'Grady began.

"The Double T runs about 16,000 calves, yearlings and bulls...with around...13,000 mother cows. The ranch shears about 2,000 head of sheep; I'm not directly involved with that operation.

"We irrigate and raise our own hay, mostly alfalfa and orchard grass mixed. After meeting our own needs, we use it for a cash crop.

"There is some coal and oil in various places on the property, which is handled by Mr. Bridger personally.

"We have six foremen; each has responsibility for a particular operation on the ranch. Some ranches would call my position Ranch Manager—I prefer senior foreman. My responsibility is to supervise the other foremen and coordinate the overall ranch operation.

"Bar Double T employs about 120 hands with various skills. Every employee has full benefits. There are two pilots in addition to myself. My ticket is for both fixed wing and helicopter.

"We have one full-time veterinarian—Dr. Robert Lyle and his wife Margie have moved onto the ranch; they actually grew up with Ted. Doc ran a big vet operation in Denver. Also have a couple of farriers and a vet assistant. Of course, there are stable boys and various employees inside The Lodge and The Homestead.

Chambers was stunned, trying to gather his response. "Holy cow! No pun intended...I had no idea. How much land is involved?"

O'Grady considered hard for a moment. It wasn't a question of knowing the answer—it was simply a matter people in this part of the country were reluctant to discuss and rarely asked. "About 620,000 deeded acres with around 120,000 lease acres from BLM."

Chambers rode along trying to absorb the intricacy of the information Shane had provided. Until now, he was unaware a ranch of this size and complexity existed. Everyone has heard of the King ranch in Texas, but it's not nearly this diverse. The augmentation and magnitude of the Bar Double T provided a new appreciation for the knowledge and skills of the man riding in front of him.

"I really didn't expect the ranch to be this vast...or so diversified. What you've described is remarkable."

"It didn't happen overnight and probably be impossible to achieve today. Most of the big spreads now are corporations. You should speak with Mrs. Bridger to get the full story; she's the historian in the family."

Chambers realized, *he must be referring to Ted's mother; his wife was killed in an accident.*

They rode mostly in silence for the next hour with O'Grady occasionally pointing out a dangerous spot in the switchback of the trail or a particular point of interest on the horizon.

The trail began to slowly wind down the west side of the ridge, and Chambers spotted a small stream of smoke in the distance. He began to make out the movement of horses and cattle. Suddenly, Traveler startled Chambers as he sucked in his sides and let go with a loud whinny, answered immediately by several horses in the valley below. The big horse had signaled their arrival at Cow Camp #8.

Riding the horses to a rope corral and dismounting, they removed the tack and used the blankets to rub the worst of the sweat off before hanging the blankets to dry.

The horses were turned loose in the corral and immediately began to roll on the ground, stretching muscles and enjoying the dusty bath. (The dust would help protect them from the already pesky flies.) Traveler got up, shook off the loose dust and began to look for something to eat.

Chambers followed O'Grady toward two covered wagons carrying supplies. "Hey, Cookie, what kind of slop's for dinner?" O'Grady asked.

"We're hav'in road kill, Shane—wha'd you bring us?" Both men grinned.

"Cookie, meet John Chambers."

Cookie eyed John cautiously before speaking, "Been expectin' ya, Sir; boss said you'd be along soon. Surprised Shane didn't getcha lost gettin' here. I'm Cookie," he announced, wiping his hands on his long apron and sticking out his hand.

"It's a pleasure to meet you, Cookie," Chambers said extending his hand. "Something smells delicious."

Cookies eyes flashed and he showed enough smile to reveal tobacco-stained teeth. "Hope we finally got a body in this camp who 'preciates fine cookin. Gonna be ready ta eat in ten minutes, Mr. Chambers."

"It's John."

"Right—John."

Behind them a deep, strong voice said, "Shane, glad to see you found us okay."

"No problem, Boss. Let me introduce John Chambers. John, this is my Boss, Ted Bridger," he said, with unmistakable pride in his voice.

"Welcome to the Bar Double T. I hope the ride in wasn't too unpleasant," Bridger said, extending his hand.

It was both a statement and query, Chambers suspected. "Quite the contrary," Chambers answered, extending his hand to meet Ted's; "the ride was very enjoyable."

Ted Bridger was an impressive looking man at 6'5" and 240 pounds. Range clothes and a well-worn, deeply creased Stetson did little to conceal his distinguished appearance. What was the term Gates had used to describe him—"imposing"—that was the word. A faded blue denim shirt with a sleeveless vest over the top, cinch blue jeans held up by a western belt with a silver buckle and worn cowboy boots looked very much at home on his big frame.

Looks like Shane had to scare up some duds for Chambers, Bridger surmised. *He actually looks pretty relaxed; it's going to be interesting hearing about the ride to get here.*

They were interrupted by a loud clanging sound. Cookie stood in front of the chuck wagon ringing an ancient triangle dinner bell. "Come 'n get it or I'll throw it out," he shouted loudly.

The ranch hands came in a few at a time, stopping at the water wagon long enough to wash up before getting into line for the food laid out in hefty stainless containers on a long table.

The workingman's "dinner" included fried chicken, baked beans, potato salad and hot bread, with plenty of coffee or spring-chilled can drinks for the hungry crew.

One bowl contained a crispy looking fried food about the size of popcorn, and only a few of the hands were piling it onto their heavy plates of food.

It looks like fried zucchini, and Cookie may be offended if I don't at least try a little, Chambers thought and spooned a small amount onto his plate.

Everyone ate heartily and most returned for seconds. Chambers decided he would like some more of the mysterious fried food to finish off the meal.

"Cookie, this is delicious," Chambers said pointing to the dish. It's not zucchini—what is it anyway?"

"Why, John, them's fresh *Rocky Mountain Oysters,*" Cookie replied.

Chambers noticed a quiet lull in the conversation around the camp but no further explanation was given. *How many cow camps furnish fresh oysters to their crews for lunch,* he mused.

Following the meal, some of the cowboys stretched out for a short nap, while others sat visiting.

Chambers listened while Bridger and O'Grady discussed the details of work needing to be completed over the next several days.

"John, we apologize for not including you in our conversation. We needed to get our work schedule confirmed, not suggesting Shane needs my help; he likes to make me feel necessary once in awhile."

"Not a problem. It's been interesting listening, and I'm looking forward to watching the activities this afternoon."

Shane and Ted looked at him and then at each other. *Sounds like he means it,* thought Shane.

***

Men on horseback gathered, sorted and weaned the calves simultaneously. Chambers felt like he was watching an athletic event. Every move looked carefully practiced, and there was little wasted motion as each member of the crew performed his function flawlessly.

Several adjacent portable corrals were in use at the same time, allowing the crews to work in practiced unison. A mechanical device called a Nordfork roped the calves; and after being restrained, they were castrated, given shots and branded in quick unison. During a break, O'Grady explained, "It keeps stress on the animals to a minimum."

By sundown the dusty, tired crew was ready to wash up and see what surprises Cookie had for supper. Work had gone from "some light, to no light"—simply another day in the life of a cowboy.

***

Bar Double T Ranch
Cow Camp # 8

Smoke drifted lazily into the cool evening air away from the small campfire. The Bar Double T Ranch lies mainly in southeastern Wyoming, where high meadows of lush green give way to arid plains with sagebrush and buffalo grass. The seemingly endless Rocky Mountains and the Continental Divide dominate the landscape to the west; to the east stretches the great prairies and farmlands of Nebraska, South Dakota and Iowa.

The sun was completing a graceful setting, the afterglow of red, gold and purple quietly fading. Like a small child not quite ready for sleep, the sun raised its head one more time, before slipping slowly into slumber for another night.

Dinner—or "supper" in this part of the country—was surprisingly delicious. Huge steaks were cooked on large iron grates over an open fire, while potatoes wrapped in foil and buried in the hot ashes came out to be stuffed with fresh butter, chives, bacon and chopped onions. Baked beans, covered lightly with brown sugar and a homemade barbecue sauce, were ladled onto tin plates in generous portions. Fresh beer bread, hot from Dutch ovens, topped off the main course; steaming hot coffee with apple pie, completed a meal fit for the best.

"Those steaks were tender enough to literally be cut with forks," Chambers commented to Cookie.

"Grain fed," explained Cookie.

"A meal like you served would cost me a small fortune in New York," Chambers gushed. "You're not a cook, you're a cowboy chef!"

Cookie lit up with pride. "Tell them ungrateful cow pushers, will ya," he replied, barely able to contain a big smile.

Turning on his heel and walking toward a group of lounging cowboys he added, "It's good to make conversation with a true *cona sewer*."

Several fires were burning in circles surrounded by large rocks designed to keep the hot coals under control. Each fire had three or four cowboys, sitting contentedly finishing their meals, talking quietly over the sound of a guitar strumming in the background.

John Chambers sat on a large log across a small fire from Bridger and O'Grady. All three were alone with their private reflections, sipping steaming cups of hot coffee.

Everything experienced today is totally new for me; should be far outside my comfort zone, Chambers admitted. *Yet, I'm feeling at ease— even comfortable—in this primitive environment.*

Journalists often listen and observe candid behavior to gain insight otherwise unavailable, and Chambers had used the opportunity offered by the afternoon's activities to carefully scrutinize his host; he realized he was still doing so as he looked across at the big man stirring the campfire.

Ted Bridger sat by the fire with his cup of coffee in one hand and a long stick in the other, poking at the hot coals from time to time encouraging the logs to burn at a controlled pace.

Earlier, when Bridger helped the men unload the supplies and unsaddle the horses, Chambers couldn't help noticing how casually he lifted the heavy sacks of grain and saddles with minimal effort.

Physically, Bridger was not a typical sixty-year-old man. His size alone set him apart from most, but there was something else very noticeable about his style of leadership having little to do with physical presence. He stood and listened to a conversation, waiting to talk until he was sure the speaker had finished. When he did speak, it was with the quiet authority of a man accustomed to making decisions, giving orders—and having them accepted and obeyed.

Observing him give directions for setting up the camp and then briefly describing tomorrow's agenda in practical conversational tones, it was obvious from the reaction of the men they felt enormous respect for Ted Bridger. What did O'Grady say on the way down here today? *"The Boss is a man to ride the river with."*

These are rough men, made so by their physical work and the extreme conditions under which it is performed. Independent to a fault and tending to resist authority they don't trust or respect, these cowboys go about their duties without grumbling or comments.

Laying down the stick, Bridger got up slowly to refill his coffee cup, and his movements appeared different somehow, light and flowing with the grace and balance of a dancer or perhaps something more practical for someone in his former line of work. He would have to remember to ask Bridger if FBI training included martial arts.

"John, you keep complimenting our cook, and we'll have to give him a couple more "Little Marys" (the name given by cowboy crews to a cook's helper) and a raise," Bridger said chuckling.

"How about some more coffee or apple pie?" he asked picking up the steaming pot with a gloved hand.

"No thank you, Mr. Bridger. I couldn't drink or eat another bite. The meal was great; in fact, the entire day has been. Thank you for allowing me to observe this side of ranch life."

"John, we should probably have an understanding from the get go. My name is Ted; Mr. Bridger is my father."

Chambers nodded his head in acknowledgement, but said nothing.

One of the hands stopped picking the guitar and walked over to the fire. "Boss...would you play something for us?"

"I'm a little rusty, but I'll give it a shot. What would you boys like to hear?"

"Some of that 'high brow' stuff," one of the men suggested. "We're a class outfit and we only listen to the best." There was muted laughter followed by loud jeers, when a jokester in the dark, gave his loud rendition of assorted flatulent sounds.

Bridger sat by the fire tuning the guitar until he was satisfied before beginning to play. It was a beautiful melody, *Andante Cantabile,* from Tschaikowsky's 5th Symphony.

O'Grady looked across the fire to Chambers sitting leaning back on a log. *What an improbable setting for him, O'Grady imagined. What must he be thinking observing a group of hard, tough men sitting around the campfire listening to classical music? He may not realize the roots of such behavior are bathed in the past. Cowboys in lonely camps often read anything they could get their hands on—the Bible, Shakespeare, the classics, poetry—anything to bring relaxation and fight the isolation. Those who couldn't read often played the guitar, fiddle, mouth organ, harmonica—anything easily carried.*

Bridger's talent for the guitar combined with the day's strenuous activities soon brought a lull to the camp. Privacy is difficult to come by in such close quarters. A constant banter and machismo posturing is always part of the culture anywhere young men spend long hours together—equally true on the battlefields of war, or the battlefields of the corporate office. Each man welcomed the opportunity for a few quiet moments and sat immersed in his own private world—a world dictated by individual experiences, ambitions and limitations.

After several familiar melodies, Bridger played Brahms' Lullaby and the men could be heard laughing and joking as they shuffled tired bodies off to their teepees.

"Good night, Gentlemen. Great day today. Let's get some rest; going to have another long day tomorrow."

Chambers walked over to the pit dug earlier in the day to serve for a latrine and after relieving himself walked to his tepee. The lifeless *soogan* was on the ground—waiting. He blew into the air mattress to inflate it—wishing he had done so earlier in the day—watching it inflate ever so slowly and finally, feeling lightheaded, sat down on the surprisingly soft mattress.

He located the container of neets foot oil in his saddlebag, and remembering Melanie's instructions, poured some on his hands and began to rub it onto his boots. The oil began to absorb into the soft leather, and his mind flashed back to another time and place; he was sitting on the front stoop at home rubbing this same smelly oil into his baseball glove.

Hey, that's it; this is the same stuff used on my little league glove to keep it from cracking. Strange, how smells often trigger memories of the past.

After some rubbing, the boots took on a darker look—no longer appearing new—but he didn't mind; the oil would protect them.

Lying down, he was pleasantly surprised how comfortable the bedroll felt.

***

Chambers awakened to the sound and smell of Cookie doing his thing. The clanking of heavy lids on Dutch ovens was immediately followed by the whiff of fresh biscuits baking and coffee brewing.

All these aromas mixed with wood smoke are totally unfamiliar but pleasant, he conceded—his mouth literally watering in anticipation.

His stomach suddenly growled in expectation as he maneuvered out of the soogan into the cold morning air. Chambers wasted little time slipping into his clothes. The past two days were long days, and it came as a pleasant surprise to realize how energetic he felt. The boots slipped on easily and reaching for his hat reminded him of Melanie.

She was an unexpected bonus to this assignment. He could not remember the last time—if ever—a woman caused this early a reaction in him. Unmistakably beautiful, but there was more…much more. It was a feeling he could not yet explain. Chambers wondered if it was only he—or could Melanie possibly be sharing some of the same feelings.

Last night passed far more comfortably than he imagined it would. A long day, combined with a hardy meal, and he could not have fallen asleep faster in the bed of a five-star hotel. He pulled the plug on his mattress and the air came out with a whoosh.

It's a hell of a lot easier coming out than going in. Still grumbling to himself, he carefully rolled the blankets and mattress, doing his best to get them tight, before tying the bundle with the rawhide strings to secure it. Satisfied with the finished look, he placed the soogan near the door of his tepee and stepped out.

"Good morning, Cookie; breakfast smells great."

"Mornin, John. Grab yurself a plate and get to it fore these mongrels eat it all up."

Chambers loaded his plate with bacon, scrambled eggs, hash brown potatoes and fresh biscuits and stood spooning some blackberry preserves onto his crowded plate when Bridger walked up.

"Looks like your appetite is improving," Bridger said smiling. "Another couple of days and you'll be returning to Fitzgerald's to ask Melanie to resize your clothes."

The comment caught Chambers by surprise. *Shane obviously talked with Bridger about me. Why? Curiosity...or something more? Could they be suspicious of my motives? You don't achieve Bridger's success in the world of intelligence and espionage being naïve. Suspicion and intrigue were ingrained in his personality.*

"The food is really excellent," replied Chambers. "I never knew 'roughing it' could be this pleasant. I'm not sure, Ted, but it would appear the image of the cowboy half starved, freezing cold and asleep on his horse, has been greatly exaggerated."

Ted laughed heartily. "Let's say you may be seeing the best of it; things are not always this pleasant. When you're ready, we can saddle up and ride out to my pick-up. My appointment in Laramie is for two this afternoon. There'll be plenty of time to wash the trail dust off and change clothes."

"Sounds great. Will we get to Laramie in time for me to check into the hotel? My reservations are at the Best Western."

"John, the accommodations in town are several miles from the ranch and means both of us would be doing some traveling when we could be working. How about you consider staying with us at the ranch? I can promise no tepees, and it would make the work easier on both of us."

"It's very gracious of you to ask, sir. If it wouldn't be too much bother...."

"No bother at all, John. I took the liberty of telling Shane to have your gear moved into *The Homestead*; that's what we call our guesthouse. There's plenty of room, and it will be convenient for us to work at our leisure."

So they have discussed me. Probably sized me up to determine whether they wanted me around any more than necessary. Uptight asshole— hotel. Okay guy—guesthouse.

The two men saddled their horses and without further conversation rode out of camp. The 15 miles to Bridger's pick-up went without incident, punctuated only by polite conversation.

The horses loaded easily into the stock trailer, and 25 minutes later they pulled into an area in front of the riding arena.

Randy was waiting at the door and came out to greet them. "Hey, Boss, John. How'd it go?"

"The trip went very well, and John's becoming a real horseman."

"I'll take care the horses, Boss. Parked the Rover over there. You'ns go head and take it, and I'll get it later at The Homestead."

"Thanks, Randy—you're a good man. Let's go, John. I'll get you to your room."

They walked to the "Rover," and Bridger motioned for John to get in. When Randy said Rover, Chambers envisioned Land Rover. The open-air vehicle sitting in front of him had never seen Great Britain.

The Rover, he discovered, is a four-wheel utility vehicle with a small wagon bed on the back, used for moving everything from bales of hay to reporters from New York.

After bumping along for several minutes Bridger said, "Here we are; this is where I lived growing up. It's a great old house, and Mom still prefers it to *The Lodge*. Guess I do too."

The large wooden frame house appeared immaculate. Three large, faded redbrick chimneys rose out of the roof. The "hip" style architecture (common in the late eighteenth and early nineteenth century) with its subtle angles blended with the dormer-type windows visible on three sides.

A large wooden floored "sitting porch" circled the house with one section screened to protect against insects during summer seasons. (He recalled an earlier remark made by Shane. "In this country, the mosquitoes and horseflies have heavy-duty landing gear.") Several varieties of rocking chairs and small tables gave evidence of frequent use.

"Let me tell you about your hosts before we go in," Bridger began. "Chen Liao is third generation on the ranch. His grandfather came to work here for my great grandfather, Ivan Bridger in 1870. Liao's ancestors worked for the Union Pacific when it passed through Cheyenne. To get away from the harsh treatment of the railroad, they hired on here at the ranch for $20 a month, plus room and board.

"The Chens were newlyweds and so were Ivan and Celestine—my great grandmother who happened to be full blood Sioux.

"Liao was raised here on the ranch by his second-generation parents and became like a brother to my father. Liao accepted the culture to a point, but wanted to marry within his own race. Since few Chinese lived in this area, it was decided he should visit relatives in his native homeland. After spending a year in China and going through enormous red tape from both China and the

U.S., he returned home to the ranch with his young bride, Bai Liu. We call her Lucy.

Unable to have children of their own, they considered my younger brother Timothy and me to be their own. When Timmy was killed in Viet Nam, they both went into a state of mourning—no less than my parents. They're part of the family."

Bridger's telling me this to let me know my hosts are not servants—and are not to be treated as such. I'm sorry he felt it to be necessary and hope it doesn't indicate I've done anything to suggest otherwise.

Walking across the porch, Bridger pressed the large brass door opener, and the heavy hand-carved wooden door swung open. Chambers stepped into an ornate entryway with floors of stone giving way to highly polished hard wood, interrupted in places by oriental area rugs.

A huge cut glass and brass chandelier hung high overhead from the vaulted ceiling, which was covered with lightly stained tongue and groove wood.

The fireplace made from native rock appeared more than capable of heating the entire room. Walls were light colored plaster, with several large western paintings hanging under muted lights.

Leather couches and chairs, wrinkled and creased from long use, and an assortment of antique lamps and tables were scattered about the room promising casual comfort.

"Welcome," came a soft voice from behind them.

Turning, Chambers saw a small slender Asian man standing very erect, looking at the two of them.

Liao bowed slowly and walked toward them.

"John, this is my dear friend, Chen Liao. Liao, this is John Chambers."

Looking up at Chambers and extending a small hand, Liao replied, "L.T. tells us you will be our guest for the next few days. Lucy and I are very pleased to have you with us. If you have any needs, please make them known to us."

Chambers extended his hand to meet Liao's and replied, " Thank you for your gracious welcome. I'm looking forward to my stay."

"Please allow me to escort you to your rooms."

Turning, Liao walked with great energy for someone of his age—which Chambers estimated to be in the late seventies—to the long wooden railed staircase, where with a bouncing step, he quickly ascended to the top.

"I'll leave you to get settled. Will an hour give you time?" Bridger inquired.

"Sounds fine. Meet you here?" Bridger nodded agreement and headed for the front door. Chambers sprinted up the stairs to catch up to Liao.

Opening a set of double doors, Liao turned to Chambers and said, "I hope this will be adequate for you, Mr. Chambers."

"This looks wonderful," Chambers said peering into the attractively furnished room, "Please call me John."

"Thank you…John. I will leave to allow you time to prepare for your trip with L.T."

There it was again. L.T. obviously referred to Ted. Need to remember to ask what it stands for. It's apparent from his mannerisms that Liao has maintained many of the formalities of his culture. If he's willing, perhaps there will be time for a short interview.

***

CHAPTER 5

C hambers entered the room and noticed his suitcases stacked neatly on a corner stand near a large four-poster bed. Through an archway to the left, a small sitting room held a large recliner with table and chairs; to the right, a door opened to the bathroom.

Several decanters of liquor were on a silver tray near the recliner in front of large dormer windows, and a small refrigerator was built into the shelf below. They seemed to be beckoning the houseguest to sit and enjoy a favorite drink while unwinding to a view of the mountains to the west.

Chambers went in the bathroom and quickly undressed, shaved and enjoyed a stinging hot shower. Large oversize towels were soft and felt soothing as he briskly dried the last of the water from his legs before slipping into an after shower robe hanging to one side. Glancing into the steamed-over mirror, he could barely make out the Bar Double T logo in bright gold emblazoned on the blue cloth.

Chambers was surprised to pick up his suitcase and discover it empty. Opening the nearby closet, he found everything neatly arranged with sport coats and slacks pressed and hanging on wooden hangers; shirts and sweaters were neatly folded and lay on shelves.

He opened a drawer finding his underwear and socks—then slipped on a pair of tan slacks with a light blue button-down shirt and dark blue sport coat. Uncertain about a tie, he put one into his jacket pocket; it could go on later if needed for the occasion.

Finally slipping into a pair of soft calfskin loafers, he took a last look in the full-length mirror and walked slowly down the stairs. On the front porch, seeing Bridger had not arrived, he found a comfortable-looking rocking chair and sat down.

"Ouch!" His butt was tender from the riding.

It was pleasant, not yet summer weather, with the temperature in the 70s; and looking out at the mountain, he began to reminisce over the past couple of days.

It somehow surprised him to realize how much he was enjoying himself. The time spent with Shane and at the horse camp was unlike anything ever experienced. *What about Melanie? Wonder what her story is? Is she seeing someone? engaged? what? She wasn't wearing any rings and she did say she hoped to see me again at the party.*

Pleasant reflections were interrupted when a vehicle approached from the direction of The Lodge; drawing closer, he recognized Bridger behind the wheel of a pick-up.

Chambers walked to the road, waited for the shiny new truck to stop and opening the door, slid onto plush leather seats. He recognized the strings of a classical guitar playing on the BOSE stereo system before Bridger reached forward and turned it off.

"Afternoon, John. Everything okay with your quarters?"

"Great! Wonderful views of the mountains and the rooms couldn't be better. Thanks again for the invitation."

Chambers noticed they were dressed in a similar manner—with the exception of Bridger's tie.

"You hungry yet? I'd planned to stop at a small restaurant in Laramie, but we could ask the cook to put something together for us before we go."

"Cookie's big breakfast is still digesting. Restaurant sounds about right for me."

Turning the pick-up west on Wyoming 211, Bridger accelerated to the speed limit for several miles before leaving the asphalt for a bumpy gravel road.

"Sorry about the road. Cuts about 15 miles off the trip. It'll smooth out ahead and...."

Bridger was rudely interrupted when a white pick-up came roaring past throwing a cavalcade of gravel and small rocks mixed with the dust.

"Bunch of fools, driving like that on this road. Must be 'city slickers'," he continued before realizing the potential insult. "No offense, John."

"None taken," Chambers replied, a bit shaken by the suddenness of the wild driving.

"This road is full of side roads with ranchers entering with slow-moving heavy machinery, most of which would bring those old boys' Chevy to a very sudden stop," Bridger added.

A couple of miles bumped by, and the white truck came into sight a short distance ahead moving very slowly. Bridger moved to the left and passed; Chambers noticed that the truck bore a Colorado license plate.

Bridger drove a short distance in silence peering intently into the outside mirror of his pick-up before quietly saying, "Here they come again."

Moments later a horn honked loudly; the white pick-up veered recklessly along side of them. The occupants appeared to be in their late twenties. One of the three males inside lowered the passenger window extending his hand—the middle finger prominently displayed upward.

It was not necessary to be a lip reader to make out the profane epitaph. "You fuc.n' son-of-a-bi.h!" he shouted before throwing a half-filled beer can onto the hood of Bridger's truck. They sped off swerving recklessly in the gravel and going into a shallow ditch, before popping back out onto the road and disappearing in a cloud of dust.

"Geez, what was that all about?" Chambers asked in a voice sounding calmer than he was feeling.

Before Bridger could answer, they saw the truck stopped a short distance ahead, parked crossways in an attempt to block the road. One of them was out of the vehicle—and he was huge; at least Bridger's size and probably 25 pounds heavier.

"What the hell are they doing?" Chambers yelled.

"This could get nasty," Bridger said in a low voice showing no sign of excitement. "Hang on, John; I'm going to try and get past."

Driving straight toward the stopped vehicle, Bridger's timing needed to be perfect; waiting until the last instant before jerking the wheel left, the pick-up fish tailed in the gravel, straightened out and dropped into the ditch with two wheels. Chambers could hear the engine racing hard with rocks and debris hammering the underside of the truck. They literally flew past the would-be assailants before Bridger deftly turned back onto the road.

"Those crazy bastards were looking for a fight—or worse!" Chambers exclaimed, feeling his heart pounding. "What the hell's their problem anyway?"

Bridger seemed to be thinking for a moment before replying. "They apparently believed we intentionally threw dust and gravel on them when we passed. If they're going to drive these roads, gravel and dust is part of the program. Being from Denver, they probably don't understand. A classic example of 'road rage.'"

Chambers' heart was still beating faster than normal when he asked, "How do you know they were from Denver?"

"The license plate was Denver County. If you don't mind, grab a piece of paper from the glove box. Better write the license number down."

Chambers observed the number in passing, but made no effort to remember it. " I forget the number," he admitted.

"Understandable. It was 028-STN," Bridger replied. "The vehicle was a late-model, white Chevrolet."

Chambers was impressed. *But, why did Bridger say "understandable"? We've gone through a ditch evading what—assault or worse. He's treating the situation like a drive in the park; even remembers the license number.*

Then Gate's description of Bridger's exploits came back to him, *Write it off to experience,* Chambers realized. *He's been here before. This probably seems like "a Sunday drive in the park" for someone with his exploits.*

They were slowing down. W*hat next,* Chambers wondered, before seeing the highway. Thankfully, it was only the Interstate.

Bridger turned right and headed down I-80 west in traffic heavy with early vacationers. The highway was busy with every type of vehicle imaginable—cars, SUVs, motor homes and eighteen-wheelers all competing for space.

Chambers was thankful to see the traffic; traffic meant they were back in civilization, which somehow gave him a sense of security. The experience of the past few minutes would make a good anecdote to relate to friends in New York, who were certainly no strangers to violence, albeit not in this type of setting.

Soon they were slowing again, and Chambers saw the sign—**University of Wyoming—Next Right.**

"This is our turn, John. It's only 11:45. We've got time for a good lunch, and after I'll take you on a quick tour of my alma mater before my talk begins."

They drove a couple blocks north on Cheyenne Avenue before pulling into a small parking lot, serving a combination gas station and restaurant. Bridger stopped the pick-up next to the air and water hoses and both men got out.

"Need to check the tires on this side. One of them feels low; the ditch may have done some damage." Noticing Chambers looking at the tattered restaurant front, he decided some words of assurance might be in order.

"It looks like a 'greasy spoon,' but you'll like their food. I've been coming here since—well a long time."

"Looks like some of the eating places in my neighborhood back home," Chambers said reaching down to pull a clump of grass from the wheel well of the truck. "I'm sure...." Before he could finish, a white pick-up came to a screeching halt beside him.

A large angry man jumped out, slamming the door and moving toward him in a rage. "You fu'...ass wipes are askin' for it."

Chambers put both hands out in front, palms forward, "Calm down man! We didn't...."

An enormous left hand hit Chambers in the stomach knocking the air from his lungs, followed swiftly by a right catching him squarely on the side of the head. Hitting the ground hard, his first thought was...*sucker punched!* No stranger to school and neighborhood fights, he learned at a young age the value of the first punch; it usually decided the winner.

He had landed on his knees and felt the rough asphalt tear through his trousers. Chambers never saw the kick narrowly missing his head, landing on his shoulder and knocking him flat on his back.

What's happening? He could hardly move. Rasping for air he knew this hulk standing over him was going to hurt him—and badly!

Suddenly a booming voice yelled, "STOP!" It was Bridger approaching from the other side—the yell was meant to divert the assailant and it worked.

"You sorry mother fu'...You want some of this, old man? C'mon, you old fart...I'll pinch your head off and crap down your neck."

The next few seconds seemed to take place in slow motion. Chambers watched the angry giant charge toward Bridger with massive hands balled into fists, swinging first with a right, followed by a left aimed at the head.

Bridger waited in a deceptively casual stance with his left foot about shoulder width in front of the right. His left arm made a small circling motion deflecting the right hand punch—stepping quickly forward with the right foot—he deflected the left punch with the same circling motion of the right hand.

Surprised by the older man's agility, the attacker made a grunting sound and a smirk crossed his face. Stepping in with amazing speed for his size, he wrapped both powerful hands around Bridger's throat in a deadly chokehold.

Bridger's next movements were quick and precise—obviously practiced to the point of being instinctive. With his assailant's arms outstretched, he rotated his own hands between and quickly upward, arms passing over the top of the bigger man's arms and encircling them before lifting up with all his strength.

The attacker's elbows cracked sharply in a painful attempt to bend in the wrong direction.

Moving with cat-like quickness, Bridger stepped in close and with savage force drove his forehead hard into the man's nose.

"Aaah," he screamed! Anger mixed with pain as the blood gushed from his broken nose.

But Bridger was not finished as he drove his right knee savagely into the man's exposed groin with such force it lifted him off the ground. A look of shock flashed across the big man's bloody face. Crumpling to the ground in a moaning heap, he pulled his knees to his chest.

One of the two remaining men came into Chambers' view—attempting to approach Bridger from behind. His outstretched hand carried a long, ugly-looking serrated knife intended for gutting fish.

"Behin.!" Chambers managed to choke out.

Bridger spun around, instantly reacting to the new threat and began to maneuver in a circle to the man's left. It forced the attacker to reach across his body to strike with the knife held in his right hand.

Bridger's hand suddenly reached to his throat, quickly loosening and removing his necktie. Wrapping it around both hands, he left a length outstretched between them.

The man sprung toward Bridger, taking a vicious swing toward his stomach—the knife narrowly missing the mark.

"You bastard—you shouldn't uv done that to Sasquatch!" "I'm gonna cut yer guts out and feed 'em to you," the unshaven assailant snarled.

As he spewed threats, the man almost stepped on Chambers before turning his back and continuing to advance toward Bridger. Spotting the air hose hanging from a stand overhead, Chambers managed to grab the handle—maneuvering the nozzle under the man's butt—and press the release. One hundred-fifty pounds of compressed air came out with a rush.

The man nearly fell, then jumped forward startled. "What-tha hell!"

Bridger saw the opportunity and stepped in swiftly. With a figure-eight motion of his hands, he wrapped the necktie around the wrist holding the knife. Jerking the necktie hard, the knife spun into the air and clattered to the pavement several feet away.

Realizing his weapon was out of reach, the attacker rushed toward Bridger. "I don't need no blade to kick yer ass. I'll kill ya with my hands!"

The man stepped forward locking his left knee, trying to put all his power behind his punch and throw a right hand roundhouse.

Bridger delivered a swift kick with the heel of his right foot to the man's locked kneecap. There was a sickening loud popping sound. The knee dislocated and the leg caved in with the foot turned at a sickening angle to the side.

Lying on the ground, the once confident attacker cried out in agony. "You bastard, ya busted my leg! Aaah!"

Chambers grimaced while the man rolled onto his side retching hot vomit onto the pavement.

Not about to be surprised again, Bridger located the third man standing beside the white truck and started toward him.

"Hey, Mister—I'm not in this—I tried to tell 'em! They wouldn't listen. Both of 'em been crazy since they got back from fightin' A-rabs."

Chambers heard screeching tires and several police cars pulled into the drive, coming so fast he wondered if they would stop before running over him.

Bridger was bending over him asking if he was okay.

"Soon as...I get...my wind."

"John, you need to sit still for a minute. This is over," Bridger replied before turning to a husky middle-aged man in uniform. "Hello, George, good to see you."

"Looks like I'm a little late for the fun. What's gone down here, Ted?"

George Janzekovich was a Captain in the Wyoming Highway Patrol. In charge of the district, he would not normally be responding to domestic disturbance calls but had been on the way to the restaurant for lunch. It was obvious from their conversation he and Bridger were old and close friends.

Bridger spent the next couple of minutes relating the last half hour to the Captain and a gathering array of local police and sheriff deputies.

A Cheyenne County Fire and Rescue truck pulled in behind the police cars. Three paramedics got out and started toward the area where the two men were still sitting on the asphalt being corralled by deputies.

Bridger directed one of the three in Chambers' direction. *I must look damn foolish sitting here. Gotta get up.* Trying to rise, nauseating vertigo hit forcing him to quickly sit back down.

The young female medic bent forward trying hard not to smile. "Where does it hurt the most?"

Great question. "My head. He caught me pretty good."

"Stay put, I'm going to get some ice for your face. Don't try to get up until we can check you for a concussion."

After delivering the encouraging diagnosis, she returned to the truck where two other paramedics worked on the downed attackers.

Bridger went from human to animal and back again in a matter of seconds. It was an amazing display of controlled fury focused instinctively. He meant to win—without regard to how much damage the opponent suffered—and losing was not an option. The attacker would be neutralized with whatever level of damage was necessary.

Chambers felt himself shudder slightly with his next realization: *If the situation called for it—that undoubtedly included killing!*

Returning and placing an "instant ice" pack on Chambers' battered face, the demeanor of his caretaker changed. "Here, hold this on your face; you're getting a lot of swelling," she said with concern. Turning Chambers' face slightly upward, she shined a small light into each eye watching carefully for a response and then asked him to open his mouth and work his jaw from side to side.

"I don't see any sign of a concussion, and your jaw doesn't appear to be broken. But you should come with us to the emergency room and let one of the doctors check you out."

"I'm feeling better; I'm sure everything is okay," Chambers answered with more confidence than he felt. He realized he was embarrassed to be sitting on the ground like some nerd who took another beating from the neighborhood bully.

Chambers looked toward the still growing throng of people and saw Bridger talking to the only foe still standing, listening intently while the man made numerous gestures to emphasize what he was saying in an apparent effort to convince his audience of something.

He must be the genius of the group, Chambers surmised. *Sure as hell made a wise decision in not taking on the man who kicked the living shit out of his two friends.*

Bridger walked over to Chambers and with concern inquired, "How're you doing?"

"I'm...fine." Trying to rise to his feet, he wobbled a little and felt Bridger try to help. Instinctively, he pulled away and immediately regretted it. "Thanks—I'm okay—really."

He took a couple of steps and leaned on the truck; Bridger watched him with a growing uneasiness.

"Chambers, it's likely these two *gentlemen* who attacked us are in need of psychiatric counseling...more than jail. It seems they returned from duty in

Iraq recently, and their personalities are not recognizable by friends and family."

Chambers could not believe what he was hearing. "What are you suggesting, Ted? They should go to jail for counseling. You saw it…the bastard tried to".… Chambers broke off in mid-sentence. *I'm whining. What's wrong with me anyway? This sure as hell's not the first time I've been knocked on my ass.*

Taking a deep breath and letting it out slowly, Chambers' voice trailed off slightly, "Whatever you think we should do…this is your turf. I'll go along with whatever you recommend."

"You're a good man, Chambers," Bridger offered and walked over to speak with the waiting law enforcement personnel.

Why did such a simple phrase—heard earlier used with Randy—feel so good, he wondered. *"You're a good man."*

Chambers heard the aggressive debate from the combination of law enforcement officers; most were expressing opinions akin to his own first instincts. The consensus seemed to be, "These assholes should be charged with everything from 'reckless driving to assault with a deadly weapon.'"

The Captain appeared to be agreeing with Bridger, and it eventually seemed to sway the younger officers from the Laramie Police and Cheyenne County Sheriff's office.

One injured assailant was hand cuffed, lifted onto a stretcher and shoved into the waiting emergency vehicles. The Sasquatch was hobbling, limping along like every step jarred something extremely tender.

As Chambers listened to their apologetic statements to the indifferent cops, it was difficult to believe these were the two hooligans who had moments before viciously attacked them.

"We shouldn't have done what we did, man. Hey, we know that—but we could lose our jobs…"

"I've never been in jail before," Sasquatch whined to a young deputy.

"You aren't going to be able to say that tomorrow," the young cop shot back. "Watch your head—get in—and shut up!"

Bridger closed the door of the Captain's highway patrol cruiser, and Chambers heard him say, "See you at the University."

Bridger then approached Chambers and with a serious look finally remarked, "You know, Chambers, you don't look half bad…for someone who survived a train wreck. But we're going to have to find you some pants, unless you want to cut those off with my pocket knife and wear them for Bermuda shorts."

Looking down, Chambers saw bloodstained holes at the knees of both pant legs. "Damn, these were brand-new slacks. My knees will grow more skin— these slacks cost 250 bucks!"

They stood looking at each other for a minute, and then both burst into laughter. It felt good to release the tension.

"Come on; let's go find you a new pair of slacks."

***

University of Wyoming
Laramie, Wyoming

An hour and a half later, Chambers sat in the back of a small auditorium at the University of Wyoming. Dean William Shockley introduced Theodore Bridger, former Assistant Director of the FBI—relentlessly going over his lengthy bio before Bridger was finally allowed to approach the podium.

After acknowledging the appropriate dignitaries, Bridger introduced Captain George Janzekovich, "a close associate and friend."

"It's also my pleasure to introduce a new friend with whom I have already shared some very interesting experiences…Mr. John Chambers of *The New York World*."

The title of the lecture—*Terrorists' Plans for America*—attracted a lot of attention and curiosity. The "word" obviously got around campus, and students from various majors and political persuasions filled the theater to overflowing.

Chambers listened intently, occasionally scribbling notes. *This is at once interesting and revealing,* he thought hearing Bridger say—"It is not a matter of whether they will strike America again. Our enemy's agenda is clear and— they are extremely well funded, well organized and well motivated. It is rather a question of how, where and with what."

Bridger continued by speaking of the precautions already taken by the various agencies. His comments were both complimentary and critical, pointing to the necessity for further measures and going into detail regarding the weaknesses in the various policies being adopted.

"It is essential that those responsible for homeland security take whatever actions necessary to guarantee interagency sharing of information. We have all become aware, although admittedly after the fact, how important even seemingly unimportant bits of intelligence can be. We must never allow those mistakes to be repeated."

Bridger concluded with a challenge to the students. "Our enemies are strong, motivated and determined. We must meet their challenge with even greater resolve if we are to prevail. Clearly, our basic lifestyle and very democracy is being confronted. If you value our way of life, you must, and I'm confident you will, be prepared to make whatever sacrifices necessary to protect it."

There was enthusiastic applause mixed with some shouted questions from the students. Dean Shockley quickly rose and moved to the podium. "Mr. Bridger has graciously agreed to take a few moments from his busy schedule for a Q&A session. Please, limit yourself to one question."

Most of the questions from the student audience were routine. How may we pursue a career in the FBI? What would a dirty bomb do if released in a major city? Would it be possible for terrorists to poison our water supply? How could the world's intelligence community make such a big mistake regarding WMDs in Iraq? Then, a different question was raised.

"Mr. Bridger, I have read you are a professing Christian. Still, you represented a government responsible for taking innocent human life every day. Jesus said in Romans 12:17-18 we are to 'repay no evil for evil, and we are to live in peace with all men.' As a Christian, how do you justify your past actions?"

There was scattered murmuring from the audience—followed by an apparently snide comment Chambers couldn't quite hear—and muffled laughter.

Bridger stood patiently waiting for the audience to grow silent before answering. His presence at the podium was commanding, and he shuffled his position and looked about the room with a gaze that soon gained total attention from his audience.

"I am indeed a Christian and not simply a 'professing' Christian. You are asking a question which has plagued men for centuries. Allow me to refer to verse 18 of Romans you quoted in part. It says—'If it is possible, as much as depends on you, live peaceable with all men.'

"Should we fight—if necessary kill—to protect what we hold near and dear? How important is my family, my country, my religion…freedom? People have long been asked to make this decision—from entire societies in the days of Christian Knights in the Holy Wars, to individuals like Sgt. York in World

War I. There are many ways to participate in the fight to protect freedom, without the taking of life. In Proverbs 16 we are told, 'The most important battles are fought in the mind.' Each individual ultimately must search his or her soul and make the decision accordingly."

Chambers was impressed and perhaps a little surprised with Bridger's candid reply. He appeared sincere in his convictions; if true, it would make him a rare breed and would certainly make it more understandable why he became ostracized on the Washington political landscape.

Following a couple more routine questions, Dean Shockley walked to the podium and announced, "We must now conclude today's symposium. Perhaps Mr. Bridger can be persuaded to return at a later date."

There was a loud ovation and Bridger waved a couple of times before jumping down from the stage, trying to catch one of the students. It was the student who asked the question on Christian ethics.

They stood talking for a few moments, and finally the student offered his hand.

Closing his notebook and putting the pen in his jacket pocket, Chambers rose to his feet to leave the auditorium. A sharp pain rose from his cheekbone and followed the delicate battered nerves up through his eye into his brain.

Damn...my head is killing me...the aspirin must be wearing off. Reaching into the pocket of his new pants, he found a small package of aspirin the medic gave him earlier and went into the hall searching for a water fountain.

***

Coccimiglio's Restaurant
Chicago, Illinois

Every detail of the mission was carefully planned and rehearsed. The target, Judge Levi Rothstein, under surveillance over a period of several weeks, unknowingly made the operation easier by revealing a common pattern of habitual behavior.

Rothstein ate at his favorite Italian restaurant every Friday. In his role of Federal Judge, he was provided a driver and luxury automobile for all "professionally related travel." The driver—who also provided security—dropped Rothstein at the curb in front of *Coccimiglio's* precisely at noon, before proceeding around the block to access the restaurant parking in the rear. At approximately 1:15 pm, a call from Rothstein's cell phone would signal for the driver's return to the front of the restaurant, and the Judge would return to the Federal Building for afternoon court dates.

Rothstein was a man who adhered to precise routines—he didn't like surprises. Control was paramount in his personality and left him feeling most uncomfortable when circumstances prevented exercise of his authority. Following the same routines day after day gave him a sense of security, brought organization to the chaos he dealt with in court and kept him in control.

But following the same schedules for long periods is a dangerous practice for anyone who might be a potential target for violence. Judge Rothstein's driver and security guard would soon learn this reality—too late.

Noonday heat in Chicago was uncomfortably warm, and the roof atop the eight-story building where two assassins lay was tar and composition material; the sticky black covering held the heat. One of the two men wiped a trickle of sweat off his brow, and the second man looked at him and winked—it wouldn't be long.

Sounds of traffic, with an occasional honking horn and screeching of brakes, reverberated through the tall canyon of buildings. A single gunshot would go virtually unnoticed.

After time and location were decided, mission planning followed a simple time-tested formula:

Determine a firing position offering the best opportunity for success.

Ascertain the accessibility of the staging area and potential for concealment during the necessary enactment time.

Determine the distance to the target and compute variables for a successful shot. (The trajectory of the downward flight of the projectile was calculated by simple geometry. Using the Pythagorean theorem and cosine of an angle, a small calculator performed the calculations necessary to make sighting adjustments. Wind velocity and direction along with temperature and humidity also entered into final firing solutions.)

Determine and plan multiple avenues of egress to selected Raps (rally points) and Erps (en-route rally points).

The location selected placed external light at the best possible angle for the target coming out of the restaurant. A laser previously measured the distance from the rooftop where the snipers waited to the front door of the restaurant at exactly 197.7 yards and distance from door to curb at 28.5 feet. This gave the shooter a maximum of 8 seconds to fire a lethal shot.

The two men dressed in gray slacks with Velcro closures at the bottom securing them around the ankles and wore long-sleeve pullover shirts without buttons, thin leather gloves, baseball-type caps and cross-trainer athletic shoes. All labels were removed from clothing; neither carried any identification.

Choosing the color of clothing to resemble building maintenance workers, anyone who might observe them would assume they were performing repairs on one of the climate control systems.

The shooter lay in a prone position looking out over a low brick wall forming a perimeter around the rooftop. Beside him on the right lay a Remington Model 700 bolt-action rifle chambered in .308 caliber with a Burris Black Diamond 2.5x10 power scope attached; it was a lethal sniper weapon.

Distance to the target was less than 200 yards; but elevation, combined with tricky winds blowing off the various size buildings, complicated the shot.

Focus and take your time; maintain the same fundamentals employed a thousand times in training, the shooter reminded himself.

To the left, the observer lay armed with a 9mm Beretta pistol. Already having provided the precise target information necessary to zero the rifle's scope, all that remained was to be certain they were not interrupted.

It was time; the sniper carefully laid his weapon onto the low ledge of the roofline. The butt of the weapon rested on an ordinary sock partially filled with sand, held next to his cheek with the non-firing hand. This simple but effective tool fit between rifle and shoulder, keeping the weapon away from his body and reducing the affects of pulse beat and breathing on the shooter's accuracy. Balling the hand into a fist and squeezing, the aiming point could be moved in minuscule degrees.

The shooter gently placed the index finger on the trigger—ensuring it did not touch the stock of his weapon disturbing the rifle when the trigger was squeezed—and positioned his cheek into a "stock weld." *Place the cheek in the same place every time,* he recalled from training. *A change in "stock weld" decreases accuracy.*

Calmly peering through the scope to ascertain his "natural point of aim" (the point at which the rifle naturally rests in relation to the aiming point), the sniper closed his eyes, took a couple of deep breaths and relaxed; opening his eyes, the scope cross hairs were centered perfectly.

The adrenalin surged in both men but neither was nervous. This was not an unfamiliar situation for either; they killed before. The rush made them sharp; when the moment arrived, their training would take over.

The four-door black Lincoln appeared, moving slowly around the corner of the restaurant, and the waiting assassins made eye contact but didn't speak.

Regaining his stock weld and looking intently through the powerful scope, the shooter relaxed his breathing, concentrating on using only his stomach.

Precisely 197.7 yards away, the door to *Coccimiglio*'s swung slowly open. Rothstein stepped out into the bright sunlight smoking a cigar and looked over his left shoulder as if to speak. It would be the last voluntary act his body would ever make. The cross hairs of the powerful scope came to rest on the center of his head.

The powerful Remington .308 exploded deafeningly. An instant later the 180-grain bullet entered a half-inch above the right eye and exited through the left side of Judge Rothstein's neck, embedding itself into the heavy doorframe.

The soft-jacketed design of the bullet functioned to perfection with the gaping wound completely obliterating the back of the head and neck. Rothstein died instantly, crumpling to the ground with one leg twisted grotesquely under him. Pools of dark crimson blood streamed from his motionless body onto the sidewalk.

Sound ricocheted off the surrounding buildings. It appeared to be coming from every direction at once and made determining the position from which the shot was fired impossible. Taking cover behind the vehicle—pistol in hand in a now useless gesture—the driver searched frantically but saw nothing. Blood splattered on-lookers exiting the building and stepping over the lifeless body, milled about in a daze, unable to fathom what was happening.

On the roof, the shooter calmly removed wax hearing protectors, putting them into his pocket. Rotating the rifle stock to the right, he worked the bolt action catching the empty shell casing before it hit the roof, carefully depositing it into another pocket.

The weapon was handed to the observer, who placed it into an innocent-looking cardboard container; both men stayed low to the roofline and duck walked to the exit. They moved quickly, but not hurriedly, down the long flight of concrete steps and pushed open the door to a back exit where a vehicle waited.

Emergency sirens could already be heard in the background. Still, no reason to rush, they were on the backside of the building, fully two blocks away from the assassinated judge.

The box containing the rifle was placed into a concealed compartment in the vehicle's trunk, hiding it from view in a potential search. Getting into the non-descript car, they drove at a leisurely pace away from the area.

The shooter removed a cell phone from the glove compartment of the vehicle and punching in a number, waited for two rings and stated, "C-1…mission completed and clear."

Braking to a stop at a fast food restaurant, the disposable cell phone was wiped clean of prints, broken in half and tossed into a garbage can.

***

CHAPTER 6

I-80 Highway
State of Wyoming

Bridger was taking a different route back to the Bar Double T, explaining he wanted to check out an area of the ranch, but John suspected it was to avoid the scene of earlier problems. Casual conversation turned to background material for the article.

"What might best describe the techniques you used in the...encounter...brawl, whatever I watched this morning sitting on my ass? Was it some kind of FBI self defense?"

Bridger chuckled a couple of times before responding. "John, you're being too hard on yourself. But to answer your question, you met Chen Liao earlier, and you'll recall my telling you of our long relationship. I arrived home from elementary school one day with a split lip and Liao asked what happened. I told him 'a big bully beat me up.' He took me into the kitchen, cared for my lip and then asked me if I preferred to continue getting whipped or learn how to defend myself.

"I'm really not sure how I responded, but he told me to follow him; and Liao took me into the back garden for my first lesson in T'ai Chi Chuan. I was six years old. When I'm at the ranch, we practice every morning in the same garden."

"T'ai Chi is a martial art?" John inquired.

"Actually a very ancient form of exercise of mind, body and spirit. Many believe it is the origin of all Chinese types of martial arts. Chen style that we practice came from a family name. Liao traces his ancestors to the originators of the art.

"Please remind me to thank Liao for saving my life, will you, Ted," Chambers suggested with a wry smile but only half kidding.

"Your reception at the University was impressive. Could you give me some background on the time you spent there as a student?"

Bridger spent a few moments enthusiastically talking about his Wyoming football team and some of their accomplishments before suddenly growing silent, causing John to look up from his notes.

"It was after a game," he began, " when Katherine came into my life. The team attended a party for faculty and fans after every home game. On this particular day, we won the game, and everyone was in a light-hearted mood.

"I first noticed her sitting in a corner of the room staring at me as I moved around talking with alums and boosters. After a time I looked back expecting her to be gone—she was still there—still watching me. I swaggered over to her and arrogantly asked, 'Have we met?'

"She looked right into my eyes and responded, 'If we had, you would definitely remember,' and she gave me my first look at her wonderful disarming smile."

"Everything about her captured my attention instantly. It was much more than physical attraction, although Katherine was certainly very beautiful."

Bridger became quiet once again. John sensed he was in deep thought and decided to wait for a response. It was obvious, even after all these years, reviving this subject was still difficult for the complex man sitting beside him.

It's still like yesterday—seeing her for the first time, her short light brown hair parted on the left, and those beautiful brown eyes displaying her inner soul in such a special way, Bridger reflected beginning to feel the familiar pains of melancholy. *A slightly too large nose gave her a look of elegance and combined with full sensuous lips and perfect white teeth to make her truly eye-catching. When she stood up to meet me, she was taller than expected; her great legs, small waist and full firm breasts were stunning. At the time, I felt she was the sexiest woman I had ever seen. After all these many years, I still think so.*

Bridger returned to the moment and continued with a voice sounding faraway. "She caught me completely off guard again when she said, 'Well, Mr. Jock, you've inspected the goods. Do you plan to keep me or send me back for a refund?'"

"Wow! What did you say?"

"Seem to recall stammering several times before blurting out, 'You look like a keeper to me...' and then hastily trying to apologize."

Once again disappearing to the past, Bridger recalled the first meeting with what was to become the only woman in his life.

"Didn't mean it the way it sounded. I mean...."

"What did you mean, Mr. Jock? Your command of the English language seems to have escaped you," she said with a slight glint in her eyes. *"Perhaps you exhausted your tiny vocabulary schmoozing with your admirers and there is none left for me. Let's start with something simple, shall we? I'm Katherine Hallsey—and you are?"*

I remember being hurt—at the same time impressed—she didn't know anything about my football reputation. It was apparent any interest she might have in me would have nothing to do with football.

"John, I recall finding my voice long enough to introduce myself, and eventually we left the party together and walked back to her dorm. Our relationship grew and before long we both knew it was special. Katherine was a sophomore, same as me, majoring in Business. We held many interests in common.

"Katherine came home with me on school vacation to meet my family and they adored her. It was mutual. She loved my family and the ranch and looked for any excuse to visit, even for a few hours.

"I spent one nervous weekend with her parents in Boise—weathered the typical father to potential son-in-law questions. Her parents were and are great people, and we share a wonderful relationship.

"In the summer before our senior year, we were married. Our parents encouraged us to wait until after graduation, but they were easily persuaded to change their minds. We were married at the ranch. It was Katherine's desire and everyone acceded to her wishes.

"We both returned to the University and graduated." Bridger hesitated for several minutes mulling over the bittersweet memories.

Katherine was reluctant to attend graduation ceremonies in her pregnant condition. I tried to tell her she was the most beautiful naked pregnant woman I ever saw. It didn't make her laugh. Then I convinced her, no one would be able to tell a thing with the graduation gown on. Finally, she wrinkled her nose a couple of times and said, "You think not?" We went through the ceremony the next day. Several hundred unsuspecting fellow graduates—and the three of us.

"In August our first child was born. We named him Kevin, after her father and my grandfather on Mother's side. A year later Stephanie was born.

"Kevin is a pilot with UPS. Steph's a film editor, living and working in New York. Both have made their own way and I'm very proud of them."

Sitting quietly for a moment, making up his mind about something, he began slowly. " I had recently entered the Bureau, and Seattle was my first office.

Katherine left our apartment and drove to the mall to do some shopping. On her return, a drunk driver lost control of his vehicle on the reversible lanes of the Mercer Island floating bridge—commonly called suicide lanes—crossed into her lane hitting her car head on. She…Katherine never had a chance. Her vehicle crashed through the side barrier of the bridge into Lake Washington. It took a full day for them to recover her car from the lake. We took some comfort in the coroner's finding—she died on impact.

"Kevin and Stephanie went home to the Bar Double T. Katherine's parents were still raising two teenage children and were agreeable to the arrangement. Kevin was five and Stephanie only four. My parents, along with Liao and Lucy, basically raised them. Both children made frequent visits to be with their grandparents in Boise.

"I spent time with them—all that could be squeezed out of my often global schedule. But for all intents and purposes, they grew up on the ranch. I'm confident Katherine would have wanted it that way. She loved everything about the ranch."

Putting words to his inner thoughts, he began to speak again in a faltering tone with a hint of self-reproach, "It was best for them. All my transfers would have required an endless succession of housekeepers and nannies. It was best."

It sounds like he's still trying to convince himself he made the right choices. The guilt is still very much alive, John concluded.

The pick-up slowed and John looked up from his notes to see the entrance to the Bar Double T. The gates swung open; looking ahead, there was busy activity in the area of the airplane hangar.

"Looks like they're preparing for Saturday," Bridger offered. Mom and Pop are having their 60th Wedding Anniversary, and we're having a little 'shindig' for them. You're certainly invited; and you never know, it may provide something for the article."

Stopping in front of The Homestead, Bridger said in an understatement, "It's been quite a day. Why don't we take a couple of hours to catch our breath? I'll have someone come for you. Mom and Pop want to meet you, and we can visit before supper."

"Sounds great. Oh by the way, do you dress…how should I dress for *supper*?"

"Casual, John. Something comfortable."

***

86

Chambers shut the door to the pick-up, and Bridger grimaced slightly at the swollen lump on the left side of the young reporter's face. *Shit all mighty,* he lamented, *of all the people to get assaulted on a visit, did it have to be a writer from the New York World? It will be very interesting to see how this one looks in print; could have been worse if the "Sasquatch"—as his buddies called him—had been given a couple more minutes. Man, that's not a pleasant thought.*

Bridger entered the long parking garage and pulled into one of several stalls. A mechanic immediately approached him.

"Boss, someone called here for you a couple of minutes ago. Woman said it was the FBI. I gave them the number for the truck phone and...." The phone ringing interrupted him. "Probably them now."

"Thanks, Jake," Bridger replied reaching for the phone. "Ted Bridger, may I help you?"

"Ted...Bill Johnson. Got a minute?" Without waiting for an answer he continued, "We're working two assassinations: one a sniper in Chicago and the other a bomb in Portland. I've got a really bad feeling I'm missing something and could really use your input."

Bill Johnson was SAC (Special Agent in Charge) of the Seattle Field Office of the FBI. He was the first African-American to be appointed to this crucial leadership position and had served in several field offices across the country. They'd been best friends since entering the FBI and training together at Quantico.

"Bill, I have to ask, is this an official call or personal?"

"Ted, it's strictly personal—you don't have to talk to me. I understand your position."

Does he...understand my position? What is "my position" he wondered.

"Give me what you can."

"First, a bomb kills a radio talk show host last Friday in Portland. Blew the windows out of the Portland field office—you probably heard about it. Today a sniper killed a Federal Judge in Chicago. I think they could be related."

"Bill, we're not on a secure line. Maybe we should continue from The Lodge. Give me ten minutes and call back; you have the number."

"I'll call in ten minutes. Thanks, Ted. Appreciate it."

Bridger often reflected on their first meeting and wondered what form of primordial instinct pushed people like the two of them to test one another's physical strength and courage. Did it involve resolving some form of pecking order once essential to the well being of the tribe?

The two men introduced themselves with a pushing match during a basketball game at the Quantico gym. Both were young, former athletes, with a more than ample supply of testosterone and competitive spirit. The Quantico gym—with a combination of high-spirited young marines in officer training and FBI trainees hoping to become special agents—was a perfect place to get rid of some tension and frustration created by the intensive physical and mental testing.

Following the basketball games, the two combatants found themselves sharing a pitcher of beer at the same table of the *Globe and Laurel.* (A legendary bar located outside the gate of the Quantico Marine Base.) After the initial macho posturing was over, shared interests and ambitions surfaced; and over the next few weeks, a strong bond of friendship began to develop.

At Christmas, Katherine came to Washington, DC, to visit during the break from training school. Johnson introduced her to his fiancée Gloria. The two became instant friends, and Katherine was eventually maid of honor in their wedding, with Ted serving as best man.

The two men held much in common, and their relationship grew over the years. Both men felt guilt over children they saw all too little of because of their work. Both lost their wives—Bill to divorce after years of loneliness created by his work and Ted to accidental death. Their friendship endured through countless highs and lows—personal and professional—and was built on a loyalty and trust hardened by years of testing.

Going over to the mechanic, Bridger said, "Jake, if you get a chance, check the undercarriage of my pick-up, will you please. I hit a ditch pretty hard on the way to Laramie and want to be sure nothing too important is missing."

"Sure thing, Boss. We'll get to it right away, and if I find anything, I'll let you know."

Why did Bill feel these incidents were linked, he wondered. *Was there more than the fact they were assassinations? It could be coincidental. Both were large enough cities to have their share of crazies. The victims appeared to have no common link. Did he say a radio talk show host? Still, two assassinations in five days may not be coincidence. Well, when he calls back maybe Bill can offer more input to support his suspicions.*

Entering The Lodge, the housekeeper saw him and asked, "L.T., did you get the phone call? The man seemed in a hurry to talk to you. Saw you coming down the drive and called Jake. He tell ya?"

"Thanks, Hannah; he did. I'm going into the library to wait for a call. Could you please bring me a cold glass of iced tea?"

"Just made some sun tea. Be right back."

Bridger sat down behind a red mahogany desk in an oversize leather chair and pulled a legal pad and pen from a drawer. He liked to doodle when he was thinking.

Moments later, Hannah arrived with the iced tea. The glass was frosted and she added lemon and some fresh mint leaves.

"Thanks Han; this looks great."

"Anything else, L.T.?" she asked pleasantly.

"No thank you—I'm good."

Hannah was leaving the room when the phone rang, and Bridger waited for her to close the door.

"Hello, Bill. Perhaps we should start by your telling me what it is you suspect."

"Can't put my finger on it exactly, but Mike Fliege called me from Portland. You remember Mike—he's a brand new SAC, only on the job a couple weeks. The victim in Portland was literally blown up in front of their offices. Embarrassed the hell out of Mike, all of us for that matter.

Someone is obviously sending a signal loud and clear, but who and why? Something about the timing makes me very nervous. Cripe sakes, Ted, you know we've expected this as a potential terrorist scenario since seeing the turmoil the DC sniper created. This may well be only the beginning."

"Any Intel to support your concerns? Before or after?" Bridger asked.

"Nothing before and too early to have much Intel since. We're hitting our sources hard," Bill replied.

"Has the Fly Team arrived yet?" Bridger asked.

(The Fly Team—a small highly trained cadre of first responders—includes agents and analysts. Designed to respond to terrorism, based at FBI-HQ on call 24-7, they also can be called in on any sensitive investigation where their expertise could be useful.)

"When we talked last, Mike still hadn't called them—you think he should?"

"I believe this qualifies as a sensitive investigation, but it's obviously his call. What does SOG say?" (SOG—Seat of Government)

"Ted, since you left they've struggled finding someone to handle the Counter Terrorism Division and the new EADI (Executive Assistant Director of Intelligence) is still trying to get off the ground with the new enterprise. We can't seem to find anyone who has the background to handle the job and deal with the politics at the same time. We miss you, Man—and I'm not blowing smoke. Ted, can you hold a second?"

Johnson came back onto the line a few seconds later and blurted, "Shit, Ted, listen to this ComSum (Communication Summary): Chicago and Portland field offices are reporting voice messages to local radio and newspaper stations with domestic Al Qaeda cells taking credit for both hits. They are claiming they were trained in Al Qaeda camps in Afghanistan and are taking orders directly from Bin Laden.

"What do you think, Ted? Any gut feeling on this?"

"Not off the top; I'm totally out of the loop. Let me think on it for a day or two."

"Would you be willing to talk to Fliege if he called. Shit, you can imagine the pressure he's feeling."

"Bill, it might not be the kosher thing to do under the circumstances. It would probably be best to communicate through you. If you want to converse again when you have more details, you know I'm always only too damn willing to give my opinion."

"I'll be taking you up on it, Buddy. Thanks for listening; talk at you soon." Johnson's last statement would prove to be more prophetic than either man realized.

Hanging up the phone, Bridger looked down at the pad half filled with his doodling.

Victim nexus?

Location significance

M.O.

Details of forensic exam at scenes?

Common motive/what motive?

Timing significance?

It was second nature for him to listen to the early details of an incident and think of the investigative procedures to follow. The old axioms of Who, What, Where, When, How and Why came back to him. Feeling the pangs of disappointment, he reminded himself—*you're not responsible for the solution to this problem. The job rests with someone else, not you. Not now or ever again. At best, you are a resource to friends still fighting the battle; at worst, you could become a huge liability to them.*

The realization suddenly gave way to melancholy. *Damn! I miss it so fricking much. Skills it took a lifetime to develop going to waste. Put on a shelf in the prime of my professional life.*

Shit, hold the phone, what a pathetic attitude. Help where you can. Resentment has never found a home in your mind and it's not going to find one now. Remember what Pop says? "The knowledge we gain is only useful when we give it away." I've got to help Bill Johnson in every way possible—Kosher or not.

***

The Lodge
Home of the Bridger Family

Randy pulled the Rover off the main road and onto the long circular drive leading to The Lodge. He stopped under the high canopy covering the width of the drive, and Chambers gazed up to see huge entry doors at the end of a long ascending covered walkway.

It did look like a "lodge" he agreed. *The canopy certainly serves a purpose in the Wyoming weather, but there is something ostentatious, more or less commercial looking, about the building. It lacks the comfortable feel of The Homestead.*

"Randy, how long has The Lodge been here?"

"Let me see," he pondered. "I'm thinkin it was ready ta move into in tha…in tha late fall of '85. Makes it bout 20 years old. It's somthin else, ain't it?"

"It sure is, *something else.* Thanks for the ride, Randy; appreciate your saving me the hike."

"No problem, John. Wasn't sure how much hiken you felt up to. Heard ya had a rough day. You take care now, ya hear." And the Rover sped off.

So the word was already getting around. Somehow it both surprised and angered him. *Bridger didn't appear to be the type who would…who would what? Tell people the dude got knocked on his big city New York butt and sat like a pussy on the pavement, while Bridger vanquished the bad guys. Have I misjudged him that badly? What a disappointing thought.*

He was standing in front of a very large log and stone building, divided into a center dwelling of two stories with matching single-story structures on each side. Chambers climbed granite steps past mammoth posts and onto the rock floored porch, finally arriving at high double doors containing lead glass etchings of various animals and trees.

He agreed with Bridger. The Lodge really lacked the warmth and understated elegance of The Homestead. Reaching for the enormous metal knocker, Chambers was startled when the door suddenly swung open.

A middle-aged woman stood in the doorway and announced, "Good evening, Sir. I'm Hannah. Randy called to say you was headed this way. Hope I didn't surprise ya."

"No, not at all."

Hannah wore a casual housedress; her graying hair pulled back in a tight bun and her ruddy complexion combined with bright blue eyes to give her a friendly, maternal look.

"I'm the housekeeper," she announced. Everyone's in the library." Turning to leave, she added over her shoulder, "They've all been expectin ya; follow me, Mr. Chambers."

Hannah walked across the spacious entryway, past a winding staircase leading up to a long balcony with wooden rails and passed under a huge chandelier hanging from the high ceiling.

The doors to the library were open, and Chambers followed Hannah hearing her informal announcement, "Here's Mr. Chambers."

Turning to leave the room, she asked, "Could I get you something before I go?"

"Thank you, Hannah," Ted said. "I'll take care of his drink. How long before supper?"

"Should be ready in about 45 minutes; want me to ask Jock to speed it up?"

"No, timing sounds perfect. We want a little time to visit," Ted replied.

Looking about the large room, Chambers observed two walls covered with books and a third containing assorted photos of various sizes. Some appeared to be the very old "tin type" from the early days of photography. A large, deeply polished red desk dominated one end of the room. Behind the desk, double French doors opened to the outside. An assortment of sofas, chairs and tables with heavy brass sculpted lamps sat in a large semi-circle around an enormous stone fireplace.

Something else caught his eye—an obviously very old rifle encased in glass hung above the fireplace. Chambers was not a great fan of firearms, but this one obviously held some special significance.

Ted crossed the room extending his hand, "Welcome to our home, John."

"I want you to meet my mother and father," Bridger said, turning toward a distinguished-looking man and woman sitting behind him. "Mom…Pop, this is the man we were speaking of earlier, John Chambers."

Chambers moved toward them to shake hands; he couldn't help wondering if they'd been talking about the day's earlier incident.

Mrs. Bridger extended her hand, looking straight into his eyes, giving him the same assessing look he seemed to be getting everywhere.

Rebecca Bridger was small and thin with gray hair worn very short and parted on one side. Her clear blue eyes shone brightly from a tan face revealing the fine wrinkles of time but still very clearly displaying the delicate features of a woman of beauty.

The spring dress with its high neck bore a look of quality, as did her Italian leather sandals. Long thin fingers with carefully manicured nails displayed two unpretentious rings: a gold wedding band on the left hand and a topaz surrounded with diamonds on the other.

Mr. Bridger rose to meet Chambers. The older man surprised him with a very firm handshake. And, there it was again: that same appraising gaze into his eyes. *It's really not offensive; more like a curiosity. What exactly do they learn from peering into a stranger's eyes?*

Mr. Bridger was surprisingly tall, not quite Ted's height, but unmistakably his father. Wearing a western-cut shirt with a leather string tie, tan slacks with a silver concho belt and western style pointed-toe boots, he looked every inch the Wyoming cowboy. His features were regular except for a small scar down the right side of his face; thinning hair still contained some brown mixed with the gray and matched his neatly trimmed mustache. There was no sign of the potbelly, which often seemed to accompany age. Mr. Bridger, John would discover, was still a very active man despite his 80+ years.

"John, what would you like to drink," Ted asked. "We're having a glass of red wine, but I can mix you a cocktail if you prefer."

"Wine would be nice, thank you."

"Mr. Chambers," Mrs. Bridger began in a voice expressing regret, "We want to apologize to you for the incident of earlier today. It was most unfortunate and from what I'm told, you could easily have sustained even more serious injuries than you did."

"Mrs. Bridger, please call me John. And speaking of the incident, it really isn't anything requiring an apology. In New York, something similar could easily happen to one of my guests; there it may well be an attack from muggers. But this sort of violence can occur anywhere."

The difference being, muggers jump Ted and surprise, surprise; he probably beats the shit out of all of them.

"Well, John—I must say—you're taking the whole matter in stride," she replied.

"Let's talk about a more pleasant subject," Mr. Bridger interjected. John, tell us about your position at *The New York World.* You are our first visitor from such a famous newspaper, and we are interested in how you develop a story. You must have all sorts of guidelines to assure accuracy and fairness, lest you soon lose all credibility in the world of journalism."

Smart, he wants to know what I'm doing here and what my motivation is. Still protecting his son. This is a subtle way of getting me to start talking and he finds some answers. He dresses and looks like a simple cowboy, but this old man has been around the block and would not be a man to cross—especially where family is concerned.

Chambers response was interrupted when Hannah appeared at the library door.

"Here's Shane and Mel."

Shane O'Grady moved aside inviting Melanie Fitzgerald to step through the door. She handed her shawl to Hannah's outstretched hand. Melanie wore a colorful sundress with thin straps and a bow neck opened to the top of her breasts; a thin gold necklace accented her very tan neck and shoulders.

The light dress rustled gently when she walked toward them, and simple sandals highlighted the taut muscles of her bronzed calves. Every fiber of her presence radiated an unpretentious, casual sensuality, for which many women strive—but few achieve.

What a stunning sight, Chambers thought trying unsuccessfully not to stare. He looked away quickly but not quickly enough; O'Grady saw him, and it left a knowing smile on his rugged face.

"I'm bringing more appetizers. You need anything else?" Hannah asked.

"How about some 'Rocky Mountain Oysters,' Hannah? John loves them and they're hard to come by in New York."

"Shane O'Grady, you haven't. Oh you have! I can see it in yer face. You should be ashamed of yerself. I'll bring some nice shrimp for John and something special fer you."

"Good evening to you both," Rebecca said pleasantly. "Melanie, do come sit by me," she invited, patting the seat of the sofa with her hand.

"I'm glad you could come on such short notice."

"Good evening. Thank you for the invitation," Melanie replied, sitting down and kissing Mrs. Bridger lightly on the cheek.

"Good evening, John, nice to see you again."

"Good evening Melanie," John replied stiffly.

He was beginning to feel like the proverbial wet blanket.

"Mel, you have a beautiful tan. What've you been doing?" Mrs. Bridger asked.

"I've been working in the vegetable garden. The store keeps me busy, but after work I try to get in some time outside."

O'Grady broke into the conversation and Chambers was surprised to hear him say, "L.T., we're all anxious to hear about your adventure earlier today. How about telling everybody how John can blow hot air."

Crap, John grumbled to himself, *they're actually making fun of me in front of everybody!* He felt his face flush in quick anger.

"Well," Ted began, "John saved my bacon. A guy big enough to whip an army—his friends called him Sasquatch—ambushed him."

"Sasquatch? You've got to be kidding!" Mr. Bridger chortled.

"Not kidding—and you should have seen the size of this guy, huh, John?" Ted continued. "He surprised John with a vicious attack; even hurting and lying on the ground in pain, John never 'lost his head.' No pun intended," he added with a chuckle.

O'Grady laughed heartily and John managed a weak smile.

"Shame on you two! I fail to see the humor," Mrs. Bridger said in a scolding tone.

"Sorry," O'Grady said quickly, "but the story gets better. Go on Ted; tell them."

"You would undoubtedly be visiting me in the hospital—or worse right this moment—if John hadn't intervened. In a very unique way I might add," Ted continued.

Chambers sat dumbfounded listening to Ted embellishing the story of being rescued from a knife attack and ended by saying, "I'm in his debt," followed by, "he's a man I'd 'ride the river with,' anytime."

"My," Melanie exclaimed in mock admiration. "I'm in the presence of not one, but two—genuine heroes."

After a short pause, everyone in the room laughed.

Chambers quickly realized this was O'Grady's way of bringing the ugly incident out into the open. He went out of his way to open the subject, knowing full well Bridger would impart a fanciful tale.

"I've got a question," O'Grady broke in again. "What does a cowboy have to do around this watering hole to get a drink?"

"Sorry, Shane. You too, Mel. What may I get you?" Ted asked.

"It's such a beautiful evening, shall we take our drinks to the patio and watch the sunset?" Mrs. Bridger suggested.

O'Grady offered his arm to Melanie, and Chambers watched her accept a glass of wine from Ted and gracefully glide through the open French doors to the patio.

***

The semi-formal dining room was spacious (containing a beautiful antique table and chairs for 20 or more people) with a huge native rock fireplace in the center of one wall, uniquely serving the dining room and the room on the other side. A large lighted Pre-Raphaelite painting by *Rossetti,* hung above the fireplace depicting horses grazing peacefully in a mountain pasture.

Supper was served "family style." Hannah kept a fresh supply of food in the plates on the table, and each serving was passed on request. Jock—the cook—was Hannah's husband and could far better be described a chef of surprising quality.

A light Zinfandel accompanied the first courses of soup and salad, while a dry California Cabernet Sauvignon accompanied the main course, consisting of rare prime rib with a hint of wood smoke and steamed vegetables.

Dessert included a rich chocolate soufflé and a superb Australian after dinner wine.

The dinner conversation was light and revolved around local news of cattle and oil prices. Mrs. Bridger was careful to include Chambers by asking questions about his work, college and life in New York City.

Following the meal, everyone adjourned to the "great room" for coffee. The name said it best. An enormous room (too large to be considered "warm") with the double fireplace from the dining room dominating one wall, a grand piano and eclectic furniture that appeared chosen for comfort rather than any particular style. All four walls were covered, with photos and paintings of various sizes and shapes. The ranch possessed a long history, and much of it appeared to be revealed on these walls.

Rebecca sat her coffee cup back into the saucer on a table and walked slowly to the piano, sitting down and getting comfortable on the bench. She began to play softly, and in a few moments, Melanie joined her. Rebecca smiled at her warmly, and after making room for her to sit, the two were soon playing a piano duet.

They must play together often, Chambers realized. *They're far too skilled for this to be spontaneous. This is a scene straight from Victorian days, with ladies of sophistication displaying their music and artistic skills for the entertainment of houseguests.*

After playing for several minutes, the music stopped and everyone applauded. The two women, who might easily pass for mother and daughter, stood and gave a small mock curtsy to their appreciative audience.

"L.T., play something for us, will you?" Mr. Bridger asked.

"Only if Mel will sing."

After a couple of protests, Melanie agreed; and Ted selected a guitar from several on stands near the piano and tuned the strings. The two conferred briefly before he began to play the lead-in to *My Favorite Things* from the Broadway musical, *Sound of Music.*

"Rain-drops on roses and whisk-ers on kit-tens, bright copper kettles and warm wool-in mit-tens, brown pap-er pack-ages tied up with strings, these are a few of my fav-or-ite things."

Chambers was surprised Melanie's singing voice was considerably lower than her speaking voice. She sang effortlessly and Ted's accompaniment on the guitar was impressive. The song ended and again everyone applauded.

"More," O'Grady encouraged. "How about *Summer Wind*?" he asked. Obviously a song he heard them do before.

How many times, Chambers wondered. *How many times have they been together in this informal family setting, enjoying a simple way of life handed down for several generations? They were sharing one of life's most precious commodities—time. Taking time away from busy schedules (which he discovered were no less demanding here than in New York) to slow down and take time for social civility.*

He suddenly realized something missing—television. There was no sign of a television in any of the main rooms here or The Homestead. There may be some in the bedroom suites but not in the areas where people congregate. Those areas are reserved for sharing good conversation, reading, music, or perhaps only quiet reflection.

Ted was flipping through a large songbook; stopping, he asked Melanie, "Key of E^b okay?"

Chambers felt his pulse quicken listening to the romantic lyrics.

"The sum-mer wind came blow-ing in a-cross the sea. It lin-gered there to touch your hair and walk with me. We sang a song and strolled the gold-en sand, two sweet-hearts and the sum-mer wind."

The song ended and Melanie returned to her seat beside Mrs. Bridger while Ted played a guitar solo of *Danny Boy*. Chambers barely heard, still reflecting on Melanie's deep, sexy voice and the visions the words painted in his imagination. He could visualize her hair blowing in the ocean air while she strolled along a sandy beach. Fantasy returned to reality when he heard O'Grady signal a close to this exceptional, unforgettable evening.

"Well, Folks, hate to sound like Cinderella, but some of us have to work tomorrow. Thank you for another great evening," he said to Mrs. Bridger bending down and giving her a peck on the cheek. Walking to Mr. Bridger, they shook hands; and the older man patted him affectionately on the shoulder.

With a wave to the others in the room, he headed for the door. Hannah handed him his hat on the way out.

"Good night, Shane."

"Night, Hannah. Tell Jock the food was great like always." The heavy door could be heard closing and he was gone.

John had a sudden inspiration when he realized Melanie was not with O'Grady like he surmised when they entered together. *It would be nice to have a few moments alone with her, but how,* he wondered.

Melanie stood and thanked the Bridgers, pausing in front of Rebecca to give her a warm hug and kiss on the cheek, before saying something too softly to be heard.

Rebecca whispered something back into her ear before saying aloud, "Good evening, Dear. See you soon."

"We aren't ready for Carnegie Hall yet, but it's fun," Melanie said and gave Ted a light kiss on the cheek.

"Maybe next year," he replied.

Already on his feet, John walked to the Bridgers and offered a sincere thank you.

"It was a fabulous meal and a really enjoyable evening. Thank you very much for asking me."

"It's been our pleasure having you. I look forward to finishing our visit tomorrow," Mr. Bridger replied.

He's still fishing, John realized. Hurrying to catch Melanie, he hoped his game plan wouldn't appear too obvious.

"John, can I give you a ride to The Homestead?" Ted inquired.

His voice carried an amused tone. *He knows,* John suspected.

Before he could answer, Melanie said, "I'll give him a lift. It's right on my way out."

"If you're sure it won't be too much trouble, Mel," Ted said.

The facetious remark earned him a malevolent stare from Mel, "No trouble at all."

Outside, John followed Melanie to a vintage 280Z two-seat sports car. The roofs were out of the T-shaped top virtually turning it into a convertible.

The engine came to life and Melanie drove slowly up the long drive.

"It's been a great evening. The food was excellent—and the company even better," John offered.

Choosing to ignore the compliment, Melanie responded, "Always great food when Jock cooks. He's a big-time chef and could be working anywhere, but the two of them have become too comfortable to consider leaving the ranch. Besides, I'm sure the Bridgers are taking very good care of them—financially and otherwise."

"You have a great singing voice. Have you trained formally?"

She laughed. "Good grief no. Thanks for the compliment, but I'm afraid my 'training' consists of high school glee club and the church choir."

Stopping in front of The Homestead and shutting off the engine, Melanie turned in the seat with a worried look, "John, are you okay? Shane told me Captain Janzekovich was out today. He indicated the paramedics suspected you may have a concussion and should see a doctor."

She has genuine concern in her voice. Why? Probably because I'm a guest and she's feeling a sense of embarrassment for what happened today.

"I'm fine. She—the paramedic—was only being cautious."

Light from the full moon glistened brightly through the open top, briefly highlighting Melanie's face. *Gorgeous. What luck to meet someone like her a million miles from home.*

John started to speak, but before he could get the words out, she leaned toward him and gently touched his swollen cheek. Withdrawing her hand Melanie kissed her fingertips and reached back to again touch him—very gently. Before he could react, she reached forward and started the engine.

"Good night, John."

"Good night, Mel." Getting out of the car, he closed the door carefully and ambled slowly toward The Homestead steps—still pondering her affectionate touch—and watched her speed off into the night.

***

Melanie accelerated quickly, smoothly shifting the gears of the sports car into fifth and felt the rpm return to cruise speed. She loved her 280Z (having bought it used from the original owner while she was still in college) and cared for it like an only child. Most of the time she drove the old Chevy pick-up, choosing the "Z" only in good weather and on special occasions.

Her hair blew freely, and the cool air from the open top exhilarated the bare skin of her face. She surprised herself with a spontaneous screech of joy.

It's been a great evening. Great food and conversation with such good friends. Food and conversation? Who am I trying to kid? It was special because of John.

Strange how his face colored when L.T. told the story of the assault. At the time, I felt confused by my sense of pride when John was described as "someone to ride the river with." It's high praise in the west—doesn't get much better. No one is quite sure whether Louis L'Amour invented the adage or picked it up in his travels, but he used it often in his books. Whatever the origin, it has been a compliment heard since childhood.

How forward did it appear inviting him to ride home? Too aggressive? Rebecca didn't think so. She whispered the idea while we were saying our goodbyes; actually seemed to be enjoying the little conspiracy between the two of us—until L.T. chimed in.

L.T. was amused and took pleasure trying to complicate the situation with his offer to take John home. I'll get my chance with that "turkey." Everything that goes around....

Ouch—whatever made me touch John's face—and how about the cornball finger kissing routine? He probably thinks I'm an overly dramatic country bumpkin.

The gate to the Fitzgerald ranch appeared in her headlights, and for a brief moment she considered going on past and driving a while longer. It was such a pleasant evening, she hated for it to end.

But, Bismarck would need letting out. He usually ran for several hours after work, and he would be ready for some exercise. The big German shepherd gave her a great sense of security. Intelligent and loyal beyond words, he seemed to sense her needs and was even more protective with Raymond gone to Iraq.

Pulling the "Z" into the garage, she got out and carefully covered it with a custom tarp. It may be several days before she drove it again; and she didn't want Rocky, her cat, climbing on the paint.

Bismarck stood anxiously waiting at the front door.

"Bismarck, hey big boy. You ready for a run? Come on good boy, let's go!"

***

The Homestead

Chambers sat contentedly in a comfortable leather recliner looking out at the mountains; soft moonlight shining through the open window provided the only source of light in the room.

Taking the washcloth full of ice off his face, he went to the lavatory in the bathroom, dropped what was left of the ice into the sink and examined the nasty purple lump on his face in the mirror. The swelling had gone down some. *At least I don't still have two heads.*

Fortunately, the blow missed the delicate connection between upper and lower jaw. He was lucky nothing was broken and thankful he wouldn't be spending the next six weeks eating through a straw.

He walked back to the recliner and sat down. Returning after the evening activities, he was pleasantly surprised to find a hot pot of tea and cookies waiting on a tray in the sitting room. It was some type of herbal mixture and quite good; swallowing a sip and setting the cup down, Chambers began munching a cookie and reflecting on the day.

Supper was an interesting combination of succulent food, complete with wines, soup and soufflé together with the more simple fare of prime rib and steamed vegetables. Everything about the meal accentuated an understated comfortable lifestyle with the capability of being casual or formal, as the situation might dictate. Undoubtedly—The Lodge could host far more prim affairs with equal ease and style.

Taking another sip of the tea and reaching for another cookie, his thoughts turned to Melanie. He was disappointed when the seating at the table put him across from, rather than beside her. However, it gave him the opportunity to observe her without appearing to stare.

She participated in the conversations on cattle and oil; and to his surprise, the men sometimes nodded agreement with points she made. They were in no way condescending, and she was sometimes asked to defend her position. Clearly, Melanie's viewpoint was of interest—even valued.

Somehow, the "Wild West" to him conjured the image of men riding on horseback with their women trudging behind carrying their babies and epitomized the very definition of chauvinism. In fact, he was finding his first trip into the culture to be quite the opposite.

A slight chill ran up his arms when his reminiscing shifted to Melanie singing the words of the love song. *She probably has men beating a path to her door and could never have any inclinations toward me. Then again, the concern she displayed in touching me seemed genuine and was certainly unexpected. It seemed like a good time to kiss her—but she settled my indecision by starting the engine.*

Chambers finished the last of the cookies and feeling very relaxed rose from the chair and headed toward the bed. *Better get some sleep. After today, who knows what tomorrow might bring.*

***

CHAPTER 7

Homestead Rose Garden

Bridger was trying hard to concentrate on following Liao's lead. They liked to do T'ai Chi in the early morning at first light or at evening twilight; the Chinese believed the flow of chi could best be encouraged at these times.

Bridger's mind kept wandering to his conversation with Bill Johnson. His old friend seemed convinced these assassinations were connected, but if they were, what's the common denominator, Bridger wondered.

Finishing a difficult form calling for balance and control ("White crane spreads its wings followed by a heel kick"), a movement in the window distracted him. *Someone's watching.* Turning he saw it was Mom and Chambers.

Liao led through the last of the 112 movements. They turned and bowed slowly to one another, after which speaking quietly to him, Liao remarked, "Beautiful and graceful movements today, L.T. Remember, mind leads chi; today your mind was somewhere else—no Chi Kung!"

It was Liao's way of telling Bridger "you've mostly wasted 45 minutes of your time"—about as close as he'd ever come to a disparaging remark.

Mrs. Bridger turned from the window toward Chambers, "They've been doing their morning exercises since L.T. was a very young boy. Liao never misses a morning—rain or shine, he's out there."

"Mrs. Bridger, I've heard Ted called L.T...."

"It stands for Little Ted. There was some confusion with his being a junior, until noticing the hands calling him L.T. and my husband B.T. (Big Ted). It seems they were amused to see him walking around behind my husband mimicking him, even to the point of giving instructions to the men. They've been L.T. and B.T. ever since.

"Come, let us have some breakfast. L.T. and Liao will do some work in the gym and we need not wait."

A petite Asian woman, taking very small delicate steps padded softly to their table. Chambers stood and Mrs. Bridger said, "John, allow me to introduce my dear friend and your hostess, Lucy Chen. Lucy, this is John Chambers."

"Welcome, Mr. Chambers. Was your rest peaceful?"

"Very much so, thank you. Please call me John. Thank you also for the delicious tea and cookies. It was very thoughtful of you."

"We are glad you enjoy tea. Cannot take credit—John—it was husband Liao who suggested. He want rest to be peaceful and choose herbal tea to assist."

"Lucy, the food looks delicious. Will you join us?" Mrs. Bridger asked.

"Please to thank you. Liao and I share meal after recover from exercise. Please enjoy." Lucy slowly bowed and left the room.

"Mrs. Bridger, I'm trying to gain background information on the ranch. It will really add depth to my articles and give our readers a better understanding of something they have never experienced. Could you give me something of the history of the Bar Double T?"

"History of the ranch is a favorite topic for me. What would you like to know?"

"Would my use of a recorder distract you?" Reaching into his pocket he produced a small portable.

"Not in the least, John. Please tell me when you're ready."

***

"Ivan Bridger was my husband's grandfather and first settled on a small ranch near Cheyenne in 1868. There is a remote possibility Ivan was related to the famous mountain man, Jim Bridger, although we have never found clear-cut evidence linking the two, other than both came from Missouri. Through the years Ivan was often asked about his famous 'relative,' and no negative or positive response was ever recorded.

"After the Civil War, Ivan was discharged with the rank of Major. His service in the Union Army did not set well with his neighbors in West Plains, Missouri—a decidedly Confederate community. He returned to Missouri, finding the family farm in ruins and discovered both his father and mother died while he was away in the war.

"It seems both parents became desperately sick, dourly needing aid, and the neighbors showed their resentment of Ivan by refusing to help. Knowing he could never be contented in the area again, the next year was spent bringing the farm back into sellable condition, and when the first reasonable offer came for cash money, he quickly accepted.

"With thousands of returning veterans from both armies, times were tough everywhere. He used the money from the farm and his mustering out pay from the Army to purchase a horse and small outfit and left for Kansas.

"Ivan arrived in Abilene and soon determined the fastest way to make money was to hunt buffalo. He purchased a .50 caliber Hawken Rifle for $25—a great deal of money at the time but the Hawken was the best rifle of the day. Most of the mountain men and many of the scouts carried the Hawken, handmade in St. Louis by the Hawken family. Renowned for its reliability— something you very much wanted in fighting Indians or grizzly bears—and simplicity of design, it was 1874 before the Sharps appeared and replaced the Hawken to become the weapon of choice for the great buffalo slaughter still to come.

"John, you may have noticed the rifle used by Ivan Bridger is in a glass case in the library at The Lodge. It remains a symbol of harsher times when it was the most important tool a settler could have; it is still loaded and symbolically ready for use to this day."

"I recall seeing it," Chambers replied. "Perhaps there will be an opportunity for a closer look while I'm here."

Mrs. Bridger continued, "Grandpa Ivan bought a large wagon, a pair of strong mules, along with black powder and lead for making bullets and was in the buffalo hunting business. The American Fur Company paid $3 for a bull hide; he would make some fast money. There were still plenty of buffalo with an estimated 40,000,000 on the plains in 1868. That was to change very quickly!

"Ivan spent the spring and winter of 1866-67 sitting around campfires with other hunters and the occasional trapper, hearing many stories about the country north and west of Kansas. One area kept repeating itself in the stories—Wyoming Territory. The grass was 'waist high, water abundant, and Indians were only troublesome at times.' The land was there for the settling, and 'even a fool' could get rich.

"Grandpa Bridger had never ranched, having only milk cows on the farm in Missouri, but he believed he could learn what was needed to run a small spread. The next few years severely tested his naïve assumption.

"He faced two problems immediately: Where to get the beginning of a small herd and how to get them to Wyoming?

"One problem was soon solved. Enterprising men returning home from war were rounding up cattle that had been left to multiply on the Texas plains for years during the Civil War. The East was hungry for beef and it was still in short supply. Abilene had the railroad needed to transport cattle to Kansas City and Chicago, but how do you get cattle from Texas to Abilene?

"John Chisum of Wichita, Kansas, believed cattle could be driven from Texas to the railroad. This farsighted entrepreneur scouted out a trail beginning in Paris, Texas, curving southwest to meet the Pecos River south of Carlsbad, then moving north across the desert of the Texas panhandle and through Wichita to Abilene.

"In the summer of 1867, the first herds began to arrive in Abilene. From 1867 to 1871, one and a half million cattle moved up the Chisum Trail to railheads in Kansas.

"Ivan Bridger saw his opportunity and spent another winter, 1867-68, hunting and saving his money, seizing every opportunity to engage those with knowledge of the Wyoming Territory in conversation. The area around Cheyenne appeared to have the most promise for raising cattle and offered the most potential for population growth. By early spring of 1868, he was ready to make his move.

"When the first cattle arrived in May, he purchased two longhorn bulls and several cows. Already owning a covered wagon, he added four mules and another wagon, filled the wagons with enough supplies to get him through the first winter, and hiring two out-of-work cowboys looking for adventure, set out driving his small herd to Wyoming."

Mrs. Bridger sat forward in her chair and reached for her coffee cup. "And that, John Chambers, is how we came to be sitting here this morning enjoying this fine day."

Wow! What an intelligent and interesting lady. Her knowledge and recall of names and dates is very impressive, and she sure knows how to tell a story.

"Good morning," Bridger said approaching the breakfast table. Bending down, he gently patted his Mother and kissed her on the cheek.

"I'm starved! Save anything for me?"

"Lucy asked the cook to prepare more eggs and bacon. Sit down and have some coffee and fresh fruit with John and me."

Ted took his first sip of coffee, and Lucy appeared at the door.

"I am sorry to disturb, L.T. You have telephone call. Man say—very important."

"Excuse me," Bridger said, leaving the room.

"Hello, this is Ted Bridger."

"Ted, it's Bill. We're on a secure line; can you talk?"

"What's up, Bill?"

"Ted, I'm picking up some scuttlebutt you should be aware of—but don't kill the messenger, okay? I've got a reliable source in Homeland Security. They've been requesting a lot of background security checks. The new Secretary is driving FBI HQ crazy with requests for expedites. A select few—actually very few—have priority CTS-1. (Confidential Top Secret-1 priority)"

"Seems normal enough to me, Bill; the new Secretary wants to be sure of his people," Ted interjected.

"I couldn't agree more and here's the point—one of the CTS requests is on you!"

Ted didn't respond for a moment. *Why would they do a background check on me? I know I've upset some people along the way but—surely no one could suspect me of...of what?*

"Any indication what this may be about, Bill?"

"Nothing concrete at this point, but my source is going to take a closer look and get back to me later this afternoon."

"I appreciate the heads up. Keep me informed if you can—but don't put yourself in the line of fire."

"No problem, Ted—you'd do the same for me. I'll get back to you."

Concerned and a little angry, Bridger tried to regain his focus before he returned to where his mother and Chambers were still chatting. *What's going on here? My integrity and loyalty are a source of personal pride. Surely even my worst enemy would not have questions about me in that regard. Is there some kind of vendetta, something I don't know about? Stop overreacting*—he tried with only moderate success to convince himself—*calm down and wait for Bill's call.*

"I'm sorry for the interruption; it was nothing that couldn't wait. What have you two been discussing behind by back?"

"Your mother has given me the very interesting history of the ranch; our readers will enjoy reading it as much as I enjoyed hearing it. Mrs. Bridger, you are an excellent storyteller."

"Thank you, John. That is indeed a compliment coming from a professional journalist. But I've taken quite enough of your time. Please excuse me; time to say my goodbyes to B.T. before he leaves for Denver."

The men rose from the table, standing until Mrs. Bridger left the room.

"What a remarkable lady! She is in reality a great storyteller," Chambers added in genuine admiration.

"Mom loves the ranch and enjoys talking about its history in particular and the state of Wyoming in general." After a brief pause, Bridger continued, "I'm ready to get started with our work if you are."

"Do you mind the tape recorder?"

"Not a problem—fire away."

***

Near an Inner-City High School
Seattle, Washington

Rain cascaded softly down the windshield of the parked rental car. It was a typical late spring day in Seattle. Chilly with temperatures in the 50s.

The two occupants of the car maintained a close watch on a van parked two blocks ahead. They sat barely off 23rd Avenue, a carefully selected position giving the best possible view of northbound traffic.

The innocent looking van contained several barrels of fuel oil, sacks of fertilizer and C-4 plastic explosive. It was a bomb—crude, but very effective. A much larger amount of the same explosive combination accounted for the horrifying devastation and loss of life at the U.S. Federal Building in Oklahoma City.

In a few moments a small cavalcade of vehicles would approach. One of the vehicles transported U.S. Congresswoman, Charonda Granberry. A scheduled luncheon downtown required her auto to move down the one-way street directly past the bomb before turning west toward Puget Sound and the city.

Representative Granberry was an African-American. She was spending the morning speaking to students at her former high school a few blocks away. In the early 70s, she attended high school and then the University of Washington, to the north on 23rd Avenue.

Following graduation from law school, she practiced in Seattle for several years acquiring a wealthy clientele and prospered accordingly. Despite her success, she was not happy. Increasingly, the need to enlist in her community—to contribute in some small way—haunted her.

Finally, the opportunity came; she was asked to run for Congress from her home district in Seattle. It was the answer she sought, and after an aggressive campaign she narrowly beat out the incumbent and was now completing her first term of office.

Congresswoman Granberry was giving back. The trip to her old high school today represented an important part of her desire to impact young people from backgrounds like her own.

Standing on the stage at the high school looking out over the small podium, Granberry was finishing her lecture to the assembled students. *They look young—eager and still very fragile. But entirely different from when we were in high school. All things considered, one could say it's both good and bad. Innocence lost early to a rapidly changing world of communication bringing about exposures we never experienced until much later in life. At the same time, today's youth have greater and more diversified opportunities to expand and become the best they can be.*

Being home brought a flood of memories. Entering the school, familiar smells flooded her senses—the past came rushing back from her subconscious. Earlier while waiting to speak, she found herself listening for the inevitable bell to ring signaling the end of class. Favorite teachers, dances and athletic contests—it all came rushing back.

"Remember my earlier story of President Abraham Lincoln and his desire for public office despite many early failures. Success did not come without great effort, pursuit of a dream and the motivation of an intelligent woman— Mary Todd Lincoln.

"Allow me to leave you with this humorous image. 'Consider the postage stamp: its usefulness consists in the ability to stick to one thing till it gets where it's going.' Every time you see a postage stamp, take a moment to reflect on what we visited about here today. Thank you for your attention, and may God bless you and America!"

Students scrambled to their feet and their applause soon grew into a crescendo of noise.

They've actually heard, she realized. *It's a great feeling to return and try to make a difference—this is a far different response than I expected.*

"I'm sorry, the Congresswoman is on a tight schedule," she heard one of her aides saying to a young student.

"Wait, Jackson. What does she want?"

"She's wanting you to answer a question for the school newspaper. Already explained you're due downtown at Rotary Club."

"Rotary will wait a few minutes, Jackson. What is your name and how may we help you?"

"My name is Sharon Dickerson, and I'm the editor of *The Bulldog Barks*, our school newspaper," she announced without attempting to hide her pride. Adjusting her glasses, she continued, "I'm preparing an editorial on your career, and this will only require a few minutes of your time."

This could be me twenty-five years ago. Same attempts to articulate and present herself in a professional manner, despite her obvious inexperience.

Sharon wore her coal black hair in tight cornrows, and dark brown intelligent eyes peered out from glasses slipping down her nose at the slightest opportunity, requiring constant adjustment. Wearing a Seahawk football jersey and faded blue jeans with "style holes" in the knees, she was very much today's typical high school student.

"How could I refuse the opportunity of an interview with your paper, especially since I also wrote for *The Bulldog Barks* during my senior year. All right, Sharon, I'm going to treat you precisely like a reporter from the *Seattle Post Intelligencer*. You have five minutes."

Ten minutes later, the impatient aide returned; and Granberry was escorted out of the auditorium to a waiting vehicle. Two security people moved quickly, one in front and the other close behind, holding an umbrella over the Congresswoman. Reluctant to accept security, recent threats in the mail and nasty calls to her re-election offices in Seattle resulted in her decision to contact the Secret Service. This was the last day she would receive temporary coverage until the validity of the threat could be determined.

Outside, several students yelled their goodbyes or "right-ons" as she hurried past and got into the car, literally collapsing into the seat. It was going to be a very busy week—filled with meetings and speeches. An election year meant there would be much more ahead. *I'm up to it,* she concluded. *What I'm feeling right now makes it all worthwhile.*

"Jackson, wait here a few minutes and give me time to look over my luncheon notes. You know how easily I get motion sickness."

***

Two assassins sat with the engine running, calmly awaiting their prey; the defroster already operating on full was struggling to keep the windows clear. The driver reached forward and turned on the wipers to clear the rain from the windshield.

Sitting in the passenger seat, the bomb maker reflected on the design of the IED (Improvised Explosive Device). It was simple, stable and dependable—and having used the detonator on bombs in the past—he was confident it would work. He waited patiently with no sign of emotion, cradling a cell phone in his hands.

Vehicles of the motorcade were starting down 23rd Avenue; in front, a black Ford SUV moved at a slow pace honoring the speed limit in a school zone. Following closely was a four-door sedan with Congresswoman Granberry sitting in the rear of the vehicle opposite the driver. Another Ford SUV trailed behind. Charonda Granberry would pass within a few feet of the proximity bomb.

Traffic moved busily down the four lanes of the tree-lined street. Students from the high school pushed and chased one another in playful enthusiasm. Happy to be out of confined classrooms and on their way to lunch, they were enjoying themselves, despite the rainy spring day, perhaps contemplating the approaching summer recess. Too young to realize how fragile and unpredictable life is, they could not know they were about to witness the gruesomeness of death for the first time.

"Sharon, I can't believe you actually talked to her," the young girl giggled. "What was she like?"

"She was great, Jolinda! She actually made a guy back off so I could do the interview. Here she comes…let's wave to her."

Long moments ticked slowly by; and finally the driver, peering through a pair of small binoculars, advised his accomplice: "Approaching."

It would be only seconds before the target reached the van.

The bomber shifted the phone into his left hand and using his thumb punched in a number. *Wait…wait…*then pushing the call activation button—the phone dialed a pager in the van and the circuit was completed.

The blast made a deafening sound shooting fire and smoke high into the air. Debris rained down for several blocks, some of the hot metal coming to rest on the wet hood of the bombers' rental car causing steam to rise. Windows in buildings were blown out, and trees were severed from their trunks and strewn about the sidewalks and street.

All three vehicles in the small convoy were destroyed. Congresswoman Granberry's car catapulted into the air, broken pieces scattered over the area. The enormous force of the bomb caused the heavy engine to land a full block from the blast.

Granberry never knew what killed her. Death came suddenly and violently without warning on a familiar street in the city she loved.

The force of the explosion combined with flying metal snuffed the life out of two innocent teenagers. Like the Congresswoman they'd been listening to only minutes before, their lives ended piteously and without warning.

Jolinda's body was burned beyond recognition and lay smoldering against a nearby building. A blood soaked Seahawk jersey covered the decimated, limp remains of Sharon Dickerson hanging from the broken limbs of a nearby tree.

***

A slightly damaged rental car carrying the two assassins attracted little attention moving west toward downtown Seattle. The driver turned onto Interstate # 5 South, with a destination of Sea-Tac International Airport. The passenger dialed a long distance number on his cell phone, waited for two rings and stated casually, " S-1…mission complete and clear."

Looking around him for traffic, he picked an area over a high viaduct, broke the disposable phone in half and tossed it over the side.

***

The Lodge
Bar Double T

The morning passed quickly. Chambers made the most of several pages of questions previously prepared, and answers usually led to new questions.

They worked without interruption except for a jet passing overhead and sounding very low, which in fact it was.

"Pop taking off in the Lear," Bridger explained. "He has a board meeting in Denver today."

"I wasn't aware the Bar Double T was a corporation," Chambers said in a conversational tone.

"No…no it isn't. Pop has several corporate undertakings. The one today is hotel properties in the United States. He also has some holdings in Australia and Europe under a different umbrella."

And the Bridger saga continues, Chambers realized. *They really manage to keep a low profile with a lot of their holdings not showing in my research. Could be a lot of dummy corporations—created for business reasons or simply part of fitting into the community—to downplay the extent of their wealth?*

They worked through to the noon hour, and Lucy came in to say "dinner" was prepared and would be served when they were ready to eat.

After a simple but tasty meal, they got in another two hours, before Bridger asked if he could be excused. "I'm sorry, John. Need to meet with my foremen to go over some ranch business. Can we continue tonight or tomorrow morning?"

"Sounds fine to me. I've enough information to sort through and get into my laptop to keep me busy for several hours."

Bridger left and Chambers decided to go to his room to work. It was also time to bring Michael Gates up to date before too late in the day.

Chambers got comfortable in the big recliner, punched the button on his cell and was surprised when Gates answered the phone himself.

"John, just about to call you; are you up to speed on the assassinations?"

"Only what I've seen in the local papers."

Chambers listened while Gates gave a quick rundown on the two attacks before adding, "and get this—we've received information of a bomb killing a Congresswoman in Seattle. Still too early for any details."

"The dots haven't been connected, but this could be another terrorist attack. My source in Chicago informed me the paper possibly received a call from someone claiming to be Al Qaeda, taking credit for the first two killings. He indicated the FBI is asking them to hold off reporting for obvious reasons until they can authenticate."

"See what kind of comment you can get from Bridger. If you get anything we can use, get back. I'll have someone update you when we get more. Gotta go, let me hear from you."

***

Riding Arena Office
Bar Double T Ranch

Ted barely began his meeting with the foremen when a knock came at the office door in the arena.

Randy opened the door and stood for a moment before finally saying, "Boss, know you said not to bother ya, but a man called The Lodge on yer private line. Hannah says it's urgent and ta tell ya."

"Thanks, Randy. Gentlemen, can you excuse me for a few minutes? This shouldn't take long."

The men filed out. Looking at a row of buttons on the phone sitting on his desk, he punched the red one for his private line.

"This is Bridger."

"Ted, it's Bill. Crap's hit the fan here! A couple of hours ago, a Congresswoman and her entourage of five people were blown up by an AMFO (Ammonium Nitrate & Fuel Oil) proximity bomb. She finished delivering a speech to a local high school, and damnit to hell," Johnson's voice trailed off before he added—"Ted, the blast also killed two students." He spent the next couple of minutes giving details.

"I didn't call you earlier because I've been too damn busy following the latest protocol by informing every agency in the known free world. Hell, Ted, there isn't time to investigate; we spend all our time covering our asses!" he shouted into the phone.

"The Fly Team coming?" Ted asked calmly.

"Should be here in an hour. My people are doing "neighborhoods" (interviews of potential witnesses in the vicinity of a crime or incident) and have secured the scene. You know how much damage those damn things can do. Damn, Ted, there is flesh and body parts all over the area—and most of the eyewitnesses are kids."

"Any indication of it being dirty?" (Referring to "dirty bomb," more accurately entitled a Radiological, Germ, or Chemical Dispersion Device, which could facilitate the release of radiation, germs or toxic materials into the atmosphere.)

"None thank God. Our HAZMAT (hazardous material) people have been all over it from the start. Nah, Ted, what we have is strictly a *Badger Special.* (*Badger* refers to the University of Wisconsin athletic mascot. In the late sixties an ammonium nitrate-fuel oil combination exploded outside an ROTC building on the Wisconsin campus. A nearby chemistry building was blown up killing a late-working professor. It was the first FBI investigation conducted involving this type of bomb.)

"Ted, we've got another caller claiming responsibility. Call came in at 12:07 pm to a Seattle newspaper claiming to represent an Al Qaeda sleeper cell. The caller spoke briefly of the sniper killing and the bombings. The voice intonation was definitely domestic; voice techs say possibly southern or Appalachian.

There was also a warning with a familiar ring: "This is only the beginning. Death to the infidels! Praise to Allah!"

"Bill, give me the timeline again on the bombing."

"It exploded at around 11:54 am. The school lunch bell rang moments before they heard the explosion."

"The callers definitely referred to both bombs?"

"They definitely referred to both bombs, Ted. What're you thinking?"

"It was too soon after the bombing for anyone to hear about it on the news. Sounds like the call was legitimate."

"So, you think it is Al Qaeda?"

"No, not saying that at all. But it appears to be someone with bona fide knowledge of your event in Seattle for sure. Do you have a transcript of the call?"

"Even better. The newspaper has a recording and we've sent a copy to QAL (Quantico Audio Laboratory) for analysis."

"Sounds like you're on top of things. Bill, you have a full plate, but you're a good man, and you're more than up to the challenge. Call me if you want an ear."

"Thanks for the input, Ted. Talk to you soon."

Ted hung up the phone and sat for several minutes allowing his mind to mull over the information. Finally he looked down at the doodles on the pad in front of him. Some habits are harder to break than others.

Target connection to Al Qaeda ???

Motivation

Shock effect

Risk/reward for deep-cover sleeper cells???

US newspapers vs. Al Jazeera??? Islamic web site???

Something doesn't add up—but what? Wait a minute. This still isn't your call, which brings up another point. Bill's taking a chance communicating information on an ongoing investigation. It probably warrants serious discussion when we talk again. He's my best friend, but it might not be in his best interest to seek my assistance in view of the ongoing background checks they are conducting on me. I'm obviously persona non grata in Washington, and there's plenty of room in this doghouse for two.

***

"Rebecca, I'm calling to thank you for a wonderful evening. I'm not getting out much these days and it was especially enjoyable."

"Melanie, dear, you are quite welcome. We love having you with us and wish you would come more often. By the way, I was about to call you to ask for a favor."

"What is it, Rebecca?"

"Well, dear, it seems all the men of the house are busy this afternoon. B.T. is in Denver and L.T. and Shane are going out to one of the cow camps. I'm concerned poor Mr. Chambers will be left alone in his room feeling ignored. I'm asking a lot, Mel, but do you suppose you could take him riding? You could wait until after four when you close the store."

"Sure, Rebecca…if it would help. It's a great day for a ride and he seems to be pleasant enough."

"Oh thank you, Mel. I confess it was a growing dilemma. Randy will have the horses ready at the arena, and you can leave from there. You're a sweetheart, Mel—I owe you one. See you soon."

Now, only need to contact John Chambers and inform him—he has a date for 4:30 at the arena. Somehow, I doubt seriously he will object.

***

CHAPTER 8

Library of the Lodge
Bar Double T Ranch

Ted was still sitting thinking about the conversation with Bill Johnson when his private line rang.

"Bridger."

"I'm calling for Mr. Theodore Bridger II. Is he available?"

He was taken back slightly by the official tone of the female voice. "Yes, this is Ted

Bridger."

"Mr. Bridger could you please hold for Secretary Roberto Ramirez?"

Moments later, a pleasant articulate voice came over the phone.

"Ted, thank you for taking my call. I'm not sure you will recall, but we have met before."

"I do indeed remember, Mr. Secretary. Allow me to offer my congratulations on your recent appointment; it is a well earned and deserving honor."

"Thank you, Ted. I find myself wondering if the old proverb about 'being careful what you wish for, you might get it' doesn't aptly apply in my new circumstances. I'm barely able to find my way to my new office, and I'm already faced with a new terrorist threat with these recent assassinations."

When Ted failed to reply, he continued, "As you may or may not be aware, Al Qaeda has made a public statement claiming responsibility." He again paused, waiting for a reaction and was mildly perplexed when it was not immediately forthcoming.

"Yes, Mr. Secretary. I'm aware. The local news media has been filled with reports *and* speculation."

"Ted, let me cut to the chase and save us both some time here. Since assuming my duties, I have been less than…how shall I say…pleased with the ability we have displayed to react in a timely fashion to a catastrophic event.

I'm not referring to emergency aid to victims but rather to our investigative response. While the current events are not in and of themselves catastrophic, taken collectively they have the potential to become so. We have only to recall the effects of the recent DC sniper attacks and the trepidation and fear created. It is my opinion our early investigative response is fragmented and lacks coordination; it certainly does not have the synchronized efficiency expected."

"I'm very sorry to hear of your disappointment, Mr. Secretary. If you feel I can be of help, I'm at your service.

"Those are precisely the words I hoped to hear, since I do indeed believe you can be of service. Our current situation seems to be crying out for your experience and expertise on the subject of terrorism. Ted, I must request complete confidentiality with regard to the subject I'm about to discuss with you."

"Understood, Mr. Secretary."

"I'm formulating plans for a new investigative unit and would appreciate your feedback."

So that's it, Bridger surmised. *I've got too much baggage to be considered for any kind of position in the intelligence world, but it doesn't prevent the powers-that-be from searching me out 'confidentially' for my 'expertise' on the subject. I'm not sure whether to be flattered or pissed!*

"The director of the anticipated unit will have complete—allow me to emphasize—*complete* control of selecting and directing a division we will create under the auspices of Homeland Security," Ramirez continued.

"My idea is to create a highly sophisticated team made up of TDY (temporary duty) personnel from CIA, FBI, USSS, DIA and NSA. They will be asked to serve a three-year term, after which they will return to their respective agencies. Any comments thus far?"

"By forming this new organization you would be attempting to insure a free exchange of Intel from each of these agencies and expedite analysis of information being acquired from a variety of resources?" Ted inquired.

"Exactly. I seem to recall you were an early and vocal advocate of precisely what I'm suggesting, particularly where the exchange of information is concerned. However, of equal importance, this unit will have responsibility for a first response team and will coordinate investigations of particular threat to homeland security—including pre-eminence at the scene. The President and

I will make all decisions where and when the unit will be deployed. There will be no influences or demands from outside agencies."

"Mr. Secretary, on the surface this seems like a very interesting and timely concept. However, I'm certain you are aware it will not be well received in some circles. May I ask a question?"

"Please do."

"How many TDY personnel do you envision staffing this new undertaking?"

"There has been no definitive decision on a number. To a large degree, the decision is being left to my discretion in collaboration with the new director." *He's interested; throw him a couple more bones and see if he'll come to Washington for further discussions. He has some detractors in high places and it's best to tread lightly until I'm sure.*

"Mr. Secretary, it would seem imperative the unit personnel numbers be contained to a minimum to achieve the desired results. The last thing needed in the intelligence community is another agency further complicating a complex system already tending to duplicate itself."

He *probably thinks I'm suggesting the Department of Homeland Security is creating problems,* Bridger thought. *Whatever—at this point, I'm simply a casual participant providing resource information and helping him validate a decision, which appears to have already been made.*

"Your point is well taken and let me assure you my desires are to resolve, not complicate, issues surrounding dispersal of available Intel to appropriate agencies. We must obtain, evaluate and act on Intel in a more judicious and expeditious manner. Has anything I've outlined peaked your interest?"

Peaked my interest? Seems like a strange question to ask of someone to whom he is only seeking informed input. Maybe it's time to wet a finger and stick it in the air to see which way this wind is blowing.

"Yes, Mr. Secretary, it has. There are a number of questions and potential obstacles, not the least of which will come from the intelligence hierarchy. But your ideas certainly have merit and could be effective in filling a lagging U.S. security void."

"Ted, that's all I wanted to hear. How soon can you come to Washington to discuss this in detail?"

Damn, he's really planning to milk me dry. Unless...unless he's interested in me for the position. What the hell. This call's on his nickel, may as well find out what this is about.

"At the risk of being presumptuous, Mr. Secretary, is your request an indication you have interest in my assuming the position of Director for this new unit?"

The question had to be forthcoming, even though I hoped to avoid it, Ramirez conceded. *But he's earned the right to expect an honest answer to a fair question, even though I'm not totally prepared to give it to him.*

"At this point, Ted, I'm still in the preliminary stages of looking at the merits of this project, but the short answer to your question is yes. I have interest in further discussions with you on the subject, with the possibility of your becoming the Director."

"Undoubtedly you are aware, bringing me back into the intelligence community would not be a popular decision in some circles. With that being understood, I'm available at your convenience, Sir. It will be my pleasure to help in any way possible with whatever expertise I may have. When would you like me to be there?"

I like this man more all the time. No bluster or posturing here—none offered or accepted. Probably has a lot to do with why he isn't popular in some circles in Washington.

"Let me check my calendar and I'll have someone get back to you with arrangements ASAP. I'm very pleased you are interested and look forward to talking with you further."

"Thank you, Mr. Secretary."

Ted let out a deep breath and putting the phone back into the cradle sat back in his chair. *So that's what the security checks on me were about.*

He felt a rush and realized he wanted very much to get back into the "game." The past few months were pleasant and very enjoyable—to a point. But he was beginning to feel himself growing more and more restless over the last few weeks. It was becoming painfully obvious; without question he loved the ranch, but he was not yet ready to retire. This could give him the chance to make use of hard-learned skills and not face some of the politics and restrictions of his old position at the FBI.

There are many considerations before making commitments. Experience teaches a lot of tough lessons. At the top of the list is "get everything you feel is essential up front." Promises of future considerations are unlikely to come to fruition. With this in mind, he began jotting down notes on the pad in front of him.

Absolute requisites to acceptance of the position.

Assets not essential to the ultimate success but which contribute to attitudes and morale of the unit.

Non-essentials/wish list. Not likely to be approved in its entirety but any compromise additions will be a bonus.

The first two items on the list, he decided, would serve to determine how committed Homeland Security and Secretary Ramirez are to the success of this new unit. *I won't get involved unless I'm convinced of his total commitment,* he resolved.

Standing in the doorway, Bridger looked down the arena at his foremen pitching horseshoes.

"Crap, Tommie, the horse those shoes came off threw them better than you are."

The sound of laughter and good-natured ribbing was heard over the clanging of heavy metal horseshoes hitting steel pegs. He watched for a couple of minutes and was impressed how well they all seemed to get along.

"Gentlemen, I'm sorry to break up the game, but I'm ready when you are."

***

The Homestead

Chambers was very pleasantly surprised when Mrs. Bridger called asking him to escort Melanie Fitzgerald on a late afternoon horseback ride. She carefully explained her concerns regarding Melanie seldom taking time for herself, with responsibilities at the store taking most of her energy.

When he quickly agreed to go on the ride, Mrs. Bridger made his acceptance sound like he was performing a great favor on her behalf. *If she only knew,* Chambers lauged to himself. Reflections of Melanie continually interrupted his concentration all afternoon.

He spent most of the day organizing his notes and writing the first article, until finally wanting to stretch his legs, decided to walk to the arena. It was a warm, pleasant day and the fresh air and endless vistas on all sides were invigorating.

Entering the cavernous indoor arena, he located the tack area and spotted Randy saddling a horse. Traveler was standing nearby, cross-tied and unsaddled.

"Good afternoon, Randy. Want some help?"

"Thank ya, John. Never said no ta help before. Give'em a few strokes with one of them brushes an I'll gitcher saddle."

"You're not saddling Nason Ridge are you, Randy?"

"Na, this is Laramie. He's a Rocky Mountain horse. Shane got'em fer Mel from some friends of mine down in Kentucky, and she's th'only one rides em. Bred fer smooth travelin—kind uf a smaller version uf a Tennessee Walkin Horse. H'cn walk with th best ufem. No problem fer him to keep up, is there boy," he offered, giving the horse a pat on the neck.

John finished saddling Traveler and looked up to see Melanie coming in the arena.

Melanie was wearing the same type of western outfit as the first time he saw her in the store, and her figure seemed even more alluring than before. A western style hat with a "cyclone string" hanging loosely under her chin, sat casually pushed back on her head.

"Hey, John. Good to see you. *Nice hat!* Great day for a ride."

"Good afternoon, Melanie." Reaching for the brim of her hat and giving a small tug, he mimicked her earlier adjustment to his hat in the store.

"There, much better. Nice hat."

With a smile reflecting a hint of embarrassment, Melanie replied, "Message received and thank you for the compliment."

Turning away she said, "Randy, I brought some food and drink for a late picnic. Could you throw on a couple of saddle bags?"

"Sure thing, Mel. Ya gonna need somethin to sit on? I'm thinkin' one of th soogan's might work."

"Great idea. Tie one on if you don't mind."

The unlikely duo mounted in front of the arena and rode slowly through an open gate across the pastures in the direction of the mountain.

The air was fresh and crisp filled with the fragrances of late spring. Knee-high green grass, decorated with multi-colored flowers, displayed their subtle nuances in hues no artist could duplicate. It was only 4:30 and with the long days would be after 9 before the sun set.

"How are the interviews going with L.T.?"

"Going well, my initial article only needs a bit more material to fill in some gaps." *He could only hope his editor would like the drafts he would be e-mailing tomorrow and order him to stay and do the serial articles. It would take days, maybe even weeks, to complete. Of course, his assignment may well depend on what happens with the assassinations.*

"Good. It sounds like you will be here for the party on Saturday." Melanie shuddered. *That sounded pathetic. But the truth is, I'm dying to know.*

"Absolutely. Ted tells me it's going to be, how did he put it, 'a shin buster,' and this will be my first one."

Melanie smiled to herself but chose not to correct him. *He's probably referring to "a shindig." No point in correcting him. Strange how sensitive men can get about such things.*

Melanie's horse began to pick up speed. Laramie was smaller than Traveler but their gaits were similar, and both went into a running walk smoothly covering the uneven ground.

The combination of fresh air, running horses and Melanie made Chambers want to shout with sheer joy. *Not a great idea; she would probably think I've completely lost it and Traveler would likely run away on me.*

They seemed to be heading for a grove of trees at the base of the mountains; approaching some obstructions, Mel slowed her horse to a flat walk. The nimble horses barely broke stride when they began to step over small fallen trees lying across the trail. *Shane's description was accurate. Traveler is a Cadillac.*

"This is the first time I've been up here this year. Need to come back with a chain saw and clear some trail."

She did say chain saw—as in whooom, whooom, cut, slash, rip.

The grove of cottonwoods thickened; and small cotton-like puffs drifted about, falling softly to earth and accumulating heavily enough to give the appearance of snow in some places. Chambers heard a loud roar somewhere in the distance. He couldn't identify the sound; but whatever it was, they were getting closer.

The horses stepped through a clearing in the trees into a small lush meadow, and they were at the foot of a tall mountain watching water from the heavy winter snows melting and rushing down the craggy side. The source of the loud roar became apparent—a beautiful waterfall cascading off an ancient rock ledge into a deep pool. Droplets of water glistened in the bright sunlight, crashing on the rocks below, flowing rapidly down a narrow stream and disappearing into the cottonwoods.

Melanie stopped at a rope tied six feet high between two trees spaced twenty feet apart.

"This is it. I come here often in the summer, and Randy rigged this high line for the horses."

"It's a great spot, easy to see why you like it," Chambers replied admiring the surroundings.

Melanie slipped the saddlebags off her horse and removed the saddle placing it upright on the ground to dry. Chambers followed suit until the horses were tied with halter ropes to the highline with enough slack to allow their muzzles to reach the ground to graze.

"They're going to love eating this lush green grass—probably a lot more than you'll enjoy my picnic basket. Only fair to warn you, cooking is not one of my strong suits."

"I'm starved," Chambers replied to her self-deprecation. "Tell me you brought some Rocky Mountain Oysters."

"So you really do like those things? Everyone assumed Shane was exaggerating. They're only available certain times of year and I've never really liked them. *Sorry.*"

John helped Melanie spread the blanket and place the various items from the packs on top of it before she picked up two bottles of wine; he followed her toward the water.

"Feel of this water! Ouch—it's cold as ice!" It won't take long to chill the wine."

Reaching down to put his hand into the water, Chambers was surprised how frigid it really felt. "Wow! It's nearly freezing. How can it be so cold?"

"It's coming off the top of the mountain and is mostly snow melt. It will flow like this all summer and is great for the trout population. This is one of the best fly fishing streams in Wyoming."

They stood quietly for several minutes taking in the natural beauty of their surroundings. Bees buzzed from one wild flower to the next, working impatiently to complete the day's work and return to the hive with their nectar. In the distance two high-flying hawks were testing the late afternoon up drafts and drifting lazily over the mountain peaks, which still displayed large patches of white snow.

"What a fantastic setting!" Chambers exclaimed. "This assignment has been great; sometimes feel like I'm stealing from the paper."

They decided the wine had chilled long enough. Pulling one of the bottles from the cold pool, they ambled back to the soogan and sat down across from each other.

Melanie looked comfortable with her legs crossed under her Indian style, while Chambers sat with his legs awkwardly outstretched trying desperately to avoid getting a cramp—without success.

"Ow. Oh…ow!" He yelped when the cramp attacked his hamstring."

"What's wrong? What is it?"

"Cramp…cramp in my leg!"

Relieved and moving quickly across the blanket, Melanie reached for his foot. "Here, pull your toes back," and she pushed his toes backward with surprising force.

A couple of minutes passed and Chambers stopped squirming before finally saying, "Oh yeah, better, much better. Thank you. It must be from riding combined with missing my morning stretching. Sorry to startle you."

"Gosh, I was afraid you were terminal for a minute. Glad it feels better.

"I brought some light hors d'oeuvres, and, *Sir*, if you will open the white wine, I'll put some food out for us. Be careful of my wine glasses and don't break them—family heirlooms," she smiled, handing them across the blanket.

Taking the "glasses" he discovered they looked genuine enough, but in fact were plastic. Chambers pulled hard on the wine opener and the cork on the Ste Michelle Chardonnay came free with a loud pop.

"I love Ste Michelle," he said pouring two glasses and taking a small sip.

"Oh come on now. You've heard of Ste Michelle wine in New York?"

"Not only heard of it, but I also try to keep some on hand in my apartment. It's a very good wine from the state of Washington. Trust me, I know this wine."

He really is familiar with the wine. Wonder who he shared the last bottle with? Was she a steady girl, or oh my, even worse—his wife? He wasn't wearing a ring—but a lot of men don't. It hasn't even occurred to me to ask. I've simply assumed, because of the way he acted he wasn't.

"Mel. Melanie, what is it? Are you okay? Did I say something? Your face is flushed."

Taking a couple of very slow and deep breaths, she summoned the courage to look at him and ask the question to which she dreaded hearing the answer.

"John, I'm not sure how to ask this—other than straight out—so here goes. Are you married?"

"Whoa—is that what's bothering you? He began to chuckle and then burst into a loud laugh," slowly realizing Melanie wasn't joining him.

"Don't even try to laugh this off. I have a right to know! Are you married? engaged? what?"

John crawled across the soogan getting very close and looked straight into Melanie's tear-filled eyes.

"I am not married, engaged, nor do I have a steady girl friend or—before you ask—boyfriend. Okay? Okay?"

Battling hard to hold back tears of frustration combined with relief, Melanie finally found her voice.

"John, I know…I know I have no right…."

"Of course you have every right," he said quietly. Leaning forward slowly, he kissed her very gently on the lips. He didn't linger. "Mel, I would never hurt you with such a selfish deception."

Scrambling to his feet, Chambers said, "I better check the second bottle of wine; it could freeze before we have a chance to try it."

***

The Lodge Dining Room

Ted sat unusually subdued at supper waiting for the right moment to broach the subject of the recent turn of events with his parents. They were really happy having him home; it grieved him to think of upsetting them by leaving again.

"L.T., you're awfully quiet this evening. Something on your mind we should hear about?" asked his father.

Count on Pop to sense something going on. Even after long years apart, he still seems to have a sixth sense about what I'm thinking or when something is troubling me.

"There is a development I've been waiting to discuss. Secretary Ramirez of Homeland Security called regarding the recent assassinations. It seems he has concerns about investigative response capability and particularly free flow of information among agencies. You both know of my frustration created by much the same dilemma. He asked for some feedback on potential solutions for handling the problem."

He paused and there was no response.

"The Secretary has an idea for a new unit comprised of TDY personnel from various federal agencies. The director will report only to him and will have a lot of flexibility to select people, organize procedures and set parameters. Understand, no offer of a position has been made at this point, and it's unlikely the directors of the intelligence community in Washington are planning any parades for me in the event Ramirez brings my name up for consideration."

"Son, I've told you before," his father interrupted with an agitated tone in his voice. "Unfair opposition can be dealt with quietly behind the scenes. I know you've been adamantly opposed to any such political maneuvering in the past, but it really upsets your mother and me to see you screwed around by an ungrateful government for which you have sacrificed much of your personal life."

Is Pop referring to not being here for the kids, or my personal life in general? I understand, even share his feelings in that regard, but this is the first time I've ever heard the slightest reference to the subject, Ted lamented.

"Pop, I appreciate your concern and your offer of help. But, political maneuvering isn't something I could live with. I've been such a critic of Washington politics interfering in areas demanding advancement based on performance, it would be tough to take a new position based on influence.

"This could well represent a challenging opportunity, but it would mean leaving the ranch—and to some extent working out of Washington—although I've already decided to recommend Denver as the headquarters for this new organization."

"Teddy, for several weeks you have stalked around this ranch looking for something to keep you busy," Rebecca Bridger began. "Liao tells me you can't even concentrate on your T'ai Chi, and we know how much you enjoy your workouts with him. B.T. and I have worried about your growing unhappiness, and if you're waiting for us to respond in some way, here it is.

"Like any Mother, there are fears about your working in the awful spy business. But, you could be killed here on the ranch or—God forbid—like our dear Katherine in a car accident. You should and must do what your conscience and intellect direct you to do. Our Lord has given you special gifts and you must use them. You have our blessings and our prayers; you should do whatever makes you happy."

I'm not sure what I expected. Mom and Pop have always been ready to accept and embrace whatever Timmy and I wanted to do without regard to their personal desires. It's got to be tougher now, though, with both realizing their time is running short. Whatever happens, I must make every effort to be with the both of them whenever possible.

"Your Mother and I are assuming, of course, you have or will look closely at the position and be certain it carries the necessary commitment to make it less frustrating than your last position."

Pop is always thinking outside the box. He quickly assesses an opportunity and often sees obstacles most people only find the hard way—and usually too damn late.

"Pop, I'm looking at the essentials and trying to put something on paper. The Secretary wants to meet in person on Monday in Washington.

"It's all premature at this point. There are quite a number of potential problems to be resolved. Let's see how it goes on Monday. In the meantime, we have a wedding anniversary to celebrate."

***

The Homestead

John woke early on Friday morning and remained in bed for a few moments reflecting on the picnic with Melanie.

They enjoyed the food Mel served and took their time sipping the excellent wines, captivated by the scenery and hypnotic sound of a waterfall cascading down the mountain. It would be difficult to imagine a more romantic scene.

Melanie explained her all-to-recent experience with a married professor, making it obvious why she was upset to suddenly realize she might be on a picnic with "another" married man.

In turn, he spoke of his broken engagement and the difficulty of accepting the very real possibility it occurred because of his work. He shared the details of the break-up with Carla. What was it about Melanie that allowed him to trust her with private emotions his personality usually protected so fiercely?

A startling awareness came to him quite unexpectedly; he could think of his broken engagement without anguish. It was over. The emotional frustration and sense of betrayal when Carla left him no longer mattered...and it felt fantastic!

Tossing the covers back and springing out of bed, he started for the shower; having a sudden inspiration, he tore off his pajamas deciding to take a run. He hadn't worked out for several days and was really missing it. Pulling on his workout gear and lacing up his worn running shoes, he bounced down the stairs and stopped on the front steps to stretch his Achilles and hamstring muscles. *Man, my hamstrings are still sore from yesterday's cramps. Better take a little extra time and be sure to stretch them out.*

After a few minutes stretching, he pushed the small button on his wristwatch setting the time for 35 minutes and started down the drive at a quick pace. The cool early morning mountain air felt exhilarating, and he turned down Highway 211 and soon was out of sight of the ranch gates.

***

Ted was in the garden with Liao sharing a T'ai Chi workout and concentrating much better this morning. He imagined he could feel the Chi flowing from his dan tien and stimulating his entire body. (The Chinese believe the dan tien stores Chi; located below the navel, it is a point of concentration during Chi Kung workouts.)

Finishing the last of the movements, Bridger saw Chambers at the breakfast room window looking down at them and signaled for him to come down. *It's best to get this over with. I'm sorry to cut our interviews short, but I'm even more sorry to have to mislead him regarding the reason. It obviously would not do to let a reporter know what's really going on with my trip to Washington.*

"Good morning. Looks like you've had a good run. I'm going to do a little more work before breakfast; want to lift some weights?"

"Sounds good. I've missed my daily workouts on this trip, and it really felt great to get in some running."

"John, can you give me some idea of a timeline with our interviews? There's been a rather unexpected situation develop, which requires me to leave the ranch for several days. I'm concerned whether we have time to conclude what you may still need."

"When will you be leaving?"

"Monday morning."

"There are some gaps to fill for the current article," Chambers said slowly. "If we could find a couple of hours, this piece could be completed, but I planned to do some preliminary work on the potential serial feature." *What's up? Does he really have to leave or has he decided to get away from any further commitment on the series?*

"I'm sorry, it won't be possible at this time. Perhaps we will have another chance later; but for the present, I would like to see the finished article when it's ready. I'll try not to cause any undue delays, but per our agreement, I do have final approval of content."

"No problem. If we can finish today, there could be a draft ready for you to look at by Sunday."

The two men finished their workout in silence, with Chambers trying to hide his disappointment. After breakfast, they decided to shower and meet in an hour to conclude the interviews.

The interview session went rapidly with Bridger responding with surprising candor to some questions and careful articulation to others. After a couple of hours, Chambers finally exhausted his questions and Bridger left.

Hours later, Chambers stretched his arms wide and worked his neck from side to side trying to relieve the stiff fatigue brought on by sitting in one position for a long period. He decided it was time to e-mail the material to the paper.

Punching the "send" button on his computer, he sent a rough draft of the completed article and turned off the laptop. He switched to his cell phone and hit the speed dial for Michael Gates.

They spoke briefly of the article and then speculated on the possible motives Bridger might have for cutting the interviews short and leaving the ranch. Finally it was agreed, Chambers should return to New York, and they would decide whether a future series would be of interest to the paper.

Chambers ended the call and immediately felt a surge of disappointment at the realization he would be leaving for New York on Monday. He was enjoying Wyoming and would really be sorry to leave Melanie Fitzgerald and their potential budding relationship. Never seeing her again was haunting his thoughts at every turn; but thus far, he had not found an answer to that inevitable reality.

***

Ted was on his way to check on preparations for the anniversary party and realized how disappointed he felt knowing his son and daughter could not be here. Kevin was on a flight to China and the Far East, and Stephanie was still in Paris finishing a film.

Neither had married—both were in relationships from time to time, but nothing seemed to last; and he often wondered if he was in some way responsible.

How many times have special family events been missed through the years? I pray they never suffer the regrets I do.

Ted finished supper and went to the library to write some notes on the events of the past few days. He wanted to get input from Pop, and they sat for over an hour discussing strategy. It was pleasant sitting in the library sipping an excellent Christian Brothers brandy. Ted listened to his father finish a concept and realized how much he missed him all those years when his work took him away from the ranch. In some ways, he regretted not making a life on the Bar Double T. *Would Katherine still be alive? Would they be enjoying life together? Stop it! You know better than to go there.*

It never ceased to amaze Ted how his father could grasp a situation and contribute, even in the rare areas where he might possess limited knowledge of the subject. Theodore Bridger II felt great respect and admiration for his Pop; and moving over to the chair where he sat, placed a hand on his bony shoulder. Neither man demonstrated their emotions easily, and his father looked up in visible surprise.

"Thanks, Pop—I really appreciate your input. I'm going to get some sleep; tomorrow is going to be a great day."

Reaching up and patting his son's hand, Theodore Bridger I replied, "You're welcome, Son." Then in a somber voice added, "I hope you know how proud your mother and I are of you. I'll finish my brandy before going up to bed. Night. See you in the morning."

***

CHAPTER 9

Bar Double T Ranch
Horse Creek, Wyoming

O'Grady was pleased to find Saturday morning dawning bright and sunny. There were still some final touches to put on the day's celebration, and he formed a last-minute crew to help move tables and do the heavier work.

The airplane hangar was decorated in a cave motif with massive sprayed-on foam reaching down from the ceiling and up from the floor, looking amazingly like real stalagmites and stalactites. *If the "mites" go up, the "tites" come down,* O'Grady smiled, remembering the difference in the two. Everything seemed to be going smoothly. It would be a great day at the Bar Double T.

"Josh, do you have enough help? Anything you need?" inquired O'Grady.

"Can't think of anything. Checked our list through several times, and we're actually a little ahead of schedule. We're going to have an outstanding evening!"

Large round tables with seating for eight were spread across the enormous hangar. A wooden dance floor, capable of accommodating 100 couples at a time, spread out in front of two stages where separate bands would perform. The first band would play easy listening and era music as people were entering and during dinner. Band number two would play country and western for the next hour, with trade offs throughout the evening to provide an assortment of music.

Barrett Catering from Denver was responsible for all food and drink with Josh and Hannah supervising to see they received necessary logistic help for the sizeable undertaking. Over 400 guests (including the ranch hands and their spouses) were expected.

Several of the Bridger's "old friends," who were still physically able, would be in attendance. There were no invitations to business or political acquaintances—no governors, senators, or members of boards. This was strictly pleasure, a very special occasion reserved for extended family.

Mrs. Bridger made one firm request: serve soft drinks only before the meal. Wine and beer can be served with the meal and for a short time after.

"It would be horrible for someone to leave our party and kill or be killed in a drunken accident," she said with a grimace.

No one was surprised at her request. Rebecca never really recovered from Katherine's death. Their relationship was special from the start; no mother ever loved her own daughter more.

O'Grady walked slowly around the outside, checking both ends of the building. The Add-a-Johns were in place. With the number of people anticipated, he ordered 20 portable toilets and made sure they were placed far enough away not to appear unseemly and still be accessible. The two long sides of the hangar would be open during the hours of daylight, and they would close them as the temperature dictated. A crew had already sprayed the area to control insects and would spray again shortly before the guests were scheduled to arrive.

Everything was in place here, and he decided to go to the arena and check final preparations with Randy. The Bridgers would arrive at the hangar in an antique carriage drawn by matching black Morgan horses. Randy and some of the stable boys spent most of yesterday polishing harness and shining the silver in final preparation. The Morgans were high steppers (Morgan trainers referred to them as "park horses"), and they would be spectacular when they pranced right up to the open doors.

Pulling a slip of paper from his shirt pocket, O'Grady marked off a couple more items on the list and headed for the arena.

***

John Chambers rose early to get in another morning run. An endorphin flow (the feeling of well being the brain releases with exercise) might help offset a growing sense of dread associated with leaving Melanie right when he sensed something really good about to happen.

First draft on the article was completed, and Bridger reviewed it requesting only minor changes. Chambers saw no problem with any of the alterations and after only a few minutes at his laptop, returned the article for Bridger's sign-off.

Chambers wasted no time in e-mailing the document to New York. He then took the next half-hour scheduling arrangements for his trip back to New York. *Who knows, perhaps he would run into Jan on a return leg from Denver to Chicago.* The contemplation gave him a sudden unexplained tinge of guilt.

Gates suggested earlier he get some photos of the ranch for any potential future serials. He took his digital camera and for over an hour attempted to photograph the overall layout carefully labeling each building.

Chambers sat in the comfortable recliner in his room, sipping his second drink and reviewing the pictures. He couldn't recall the last time he indulged in two drinks of hard liquor in the afternoon, but the scotch was helping him relax until his cell phone suddenly rang. *Oh crap, Gates is probably nit picking the article. Shit, he seemed satisfied enough with the early e-mails—even complimentary.* It rang a second time.

"Hello, this is John Chambers."

"John, it's Melanie. Melanie Fitzgerald. I hope you won't consider this too forward of me. I've been thinking about the Bridgers' party; perhaps you might be more comfortable if you…if we met…." There was a pause on the phone and then, "Oh hell, John. Do you want to go to the party with me?" She asked expelling an exasperated breath into the phone.

"Melanie Fitzgerald. Melanie Fitzgerald. Do I know a Melanie Fitzgerald? "Are you the same beautiful cowgirl that took me riding yesterday? Melanie, my mother didn't raise any fools. I'd love to go to the party with you. What time shall I pick you up?"

"John, it would probably be a lot easier for me to come by for you; it may be difficult for you to find our ranch."

"Actually, I would prefer coming for you," John interrupted. I have the rental car and a drive will be nice." *Besides, it will give me some control over when we leave the party—and perhaps, only perhaps, give us some time alone.*

"It starts at 6:30," Melanie replied. "I want to be sure and see them arrive in the carriage, so let's say pick me up at six? If you'll grab a pen, I'll give you directions to our ranch and you can keep your cell handy in case you get lost."

Writing down the last of the instructions, he said, "I'll see you at six, and Mel, thanks for the invitation."

Flowers…going to need flowers. Geez, where do I get them? What time is it…4 pm. May have time to dress and drive into Cheyenne. Throwing the last of the Scotch down, he leaped from his chair and started getting ready.

Completely unaware of appropriate dress for a "shin buster," he had asked Bridger earlier in the day and was told no ties other than western and no suits; anything else goes.

Chambers slipped on a pair of Cinch jeans with a western shirt open at the neck, sport coat and the roper boots and stood in front of the mirror trying to decide whether to wear the Stetson. It still felt more than a little awkward. *What the hell, everybody else will be wearing one and Melanie will be pleased.*

Hurrying to his rental car, he impatiently drove past bustling crews readying for the party and turned east out the gate onto Highway 211 heading for Cheyenne.

Chambers checked the speedometer—75 mph—too fast and with two drinks on his breath if he got stopped. The drive to Cheyenne took a bit longer than anticipated, and he spent almost 30 minutes finding a flower shop and selecting a bouquet and corsage.

It was getting late and he was still several miles away from Melanie's ranch. Topping a small hill, he recognized the name of the road from her directions; his watch read 5:55. He might make it—barely.

The little rental car skidded sideways narrowly missing the ditch when Chambers turned abruptly into the drive. He hit the brakes hard and came to a sliding stop in the gravel driveway, dearly hoping it was Melanie's house.

Chambers got out of the car and felt a surge of relief—quickly followed by apprehension—when Bismarck greeted him. Hair stood up on the big dog all the way to his tail.

"Hello Bismarck. Nice dog—you're a good dog—be a good boy, Bismarck."

The German shepherd seemed to recognize his name and immediately began wagging his tail. *He recognizes me. They say these dogs are incredibly smart—it may be more than breeder's hype.*

Melanie opened the front door and stepping out onto the porch gave him an approving smile. "Good evening, John. It appears my brothers' hat has found a new home. Looks better on you than it *ever* did on him."

"Thank you, Mel. A beautiful and talented saleswoman helped with the selection. You look stunning and these are for you," he said holding out the bouquet and corsage.

"Thank you, kind Sir; they're beautiful but you shouldn't have gone all the way into Cheyenne. Here," holding the corsage out to him, "will you pin this on, please?"

Chambers fidgeted with the pin, trying to hold the flower in place with one hand; it soon became clear, this was a task he would never complete.

"Let me go in and do it in front of a mirror. Bismarck, come—you have to stay home and take care of things. I'll get you some milk bones."

Melanie disappeared into the house, and Chambers stepped off the porch to look around. The house was typical of many in the area. It looked solidly built and was probably well over 50 years old, mostly wood with some brick trim. The large front porch took full advantage of a pleasant panorama toward the meadows at the front of the property. Several implement sheds and outbuildings stood to one side of the house along with what appeared to be a large barn, all still in good repair despite no longer being used.

Melanie came out of the house closing the door behind her and in an apologetic tone, "Forgive me for not inviting you in. We're running pretty close so I'll make it up to you next time."

Sadly, there may not be any next time, Chambers pined.

Arriving at the entrance to the Bar Double T, a large sign hanging from the high cross bar proclaimed: **Welcome to the Bridger 60th.** A young man in a white coat directed them to a parking area farther down the drive.

Chambers opened the door for Melanie, and she recognized someone parking nearby.

"Excuse me a moment; want to say a quick hello."

When she moved around the car Chambers realized, *every time I see her, she is more beautiful than the time before.* She wore a simple dress with a light pattern of flowers—a V-neck showed tasteful cleavage—small earrings with matching necklace and bracelet provided accents, and stylish low heels emphasized her beautiful long legs.

"Sorry for not introducing you. I didn't want to get into a long conversation since it's nearly time for the Bridgers to arrive." She slid her hand through the fold of his arm and looking up gave him a big smile and suggested, "Shall we?"

They entered the cavernous airplane hangar to friendly greetings and gift-wrapped party favors and a band playing a familiar melody. Chambers spotted a large punch bowl; "Would you care for something to drink?"

"Please, thank you."

The "cave" facade completely hid the interior of the building making it difficult to recognize a working airplane hangar. The tables were covered with white linen, set with silver and matching candelabras, colorful china and crystal. Cut flower arrangements adorned every table, and huge potted plants were placed in strategic positions to hide items unable to be removed from the hangar. An assortment of colored lanterns hung below and around the stalactites to provide muted lighting after dark.

White jacketed servers balanced heavy trays of hors d'oeuvres and drinks, while they weaved through the growing throng of people. Friends greeted one another and moved off together selecting places to sit. Only one table was reserved for the guests of honor, leaving everyone free to select their own companions for the evening.

Chambers smiled to himself thinking, *damn these cowboys do know how to throw a "shin buster."*

"Scuse me John, Melanie, want ya ta meet my wife."

It was Cookie, standing with a slightly overweight, middle-aged woman. She had a very pleasant, but slightly uneasy look on her face.

"Hon, this is John Chambers and uf course ya know Mel. This is ma wife, Georgia."

"I'm very pleased to meet you, Georgia. You have a very talented husband. I've seldom enjoyed food more than during my recent trip to the cow camp."

Cookie looked like he grew three inches before he made an attempt to reply to the compliment.

"Heck...jus do th best I can. Georgia taught me most of it herself. Nuthin fancy, jus plain southern cookin—we growed up with in Mississippi."

The significance of Cookie's introduction of his wife was not lost. *It's a compliment he's chosen to introduce her to me,* Chambers realized.

Their conversation was interrupted when L.T. stepped to the microphone and asked for attention. The Bridgers were at the arena and would be leaving shortly in the carriage for the hangar.

"Would you please move to the west doors and be ready to greet the guests of honor?"

There was a buzz of muted voices and everyone began to move toward the massive open door. Chambers reached for Melanie, and she accepted his hand willingly. Feeling her hand in his for the first time gave him a tiny rush.

The magnificent black Morgan horses moved in high-stepping unison, their sleek muscles glowing in the early evening sunlight. They seemed to sense the excitement of the moment, and approaching the admiring crowd intensified the height of their step and the arch of their necks.

Randy looked proud dressed in his black frock coat, white shirt, bow tie and tall formal hat, sitting upright in the driver's seat, holding the reins in his skilled hands.

The silver conchos on the black harness glistened brightly, matching the trim of the immaculate antique carriage. Theodore and Rebecca Bridger sat facing the driver with Liao and Lucy Chen seated across from them.

Faint applause broke out and began to grow in intensity. Strobe lights exploded brightly and the professional photographer began to earn his money. *More history for the walls in the "great room" of the Lodge,* Chambers mused.

Randy stopped at the door where Ted and Shane helped the couples down from the carriage. The four then walked arm in arm to their table, and the band began to play *Always and Forever.* The female vocalist softly sang the lyrics, "Al-ways and for-ev-er—each moment with you—is like a dream to me—that some-how came true. I'll—al-ways love you—I'll always love you."

As the singer finished and the warm applause ended, L.T stepped to the microphone and thanked the various "people who made the evening possible." After everyone was properly recognized, he asked his father to come to the microphone and say a few words.

"We wish to thank each of you for taking the time to celebrate with us. You are part of the Bar Double T family, and it's fitting we should celebrate together on this occasion. Rebecca and I are fortunate to have shared much of our lives with many of you here this evening. We are especially grateful for the Chens who are sitting here with us tonight; together we have shared the very best and worst of times, and they have been our lifelong friends.

"I have composed a short verse intended for Rebecca and Lucy, and I wish to share it with you: 'Vestiges of age can never place its limitations on true beauty. Powerful memories allow me to see my mate at 17, with all her feminine qualities that seemed so significant at the time still clearly visible. Eons of time may wear away some outward grandeur, but it has replaced it with something far more alluring and difficult to find. For when I look at her now— I am attracted by far more glamorous qualities—I am captivated by my soul mate.'

The gathering stood and applauded loudly until Mr. Bridger held up his hands calling for silence.

"Let's all remain standing and have an invocation to give thanks for the meal we are about to enjoy, and then let's have a great evening."

The food and *Ste Michelle* wine were excellent with five courses served while the band played quietly in the background, creating a relaxing informal ambience. Conversations varied immensely from table to table, punctuated by sometimes muted and occasionally more raucous laughter.

Finishing the last of his dessert and taking a sip of after dinner wine, Chambers realized how comfortable he was beginning to feel in this unpretentious atmosphere. *Despite narrowly avoiding death in a pick-up and having my head knocked off my shoulders, I'm enjoying this surreal setting. There's a candor to the social life here long ago lost with many of the pseudo-sophisticated metropolitan cultures.*

His musing was interrupted when the band began playing a contemporary song with a slow tempo.

"Mel, would you like to dance?"

"I would love to."

Taking her hand, Chambers led her to an uncrowded spot on the dance floor. They settled into a simple box step, and with every sway to the music he could feel her body molding closer. Melanie rested her head on his shoulder, and he soon felt the warmth of her breath on his neck. Gradually in the beginning, but growing in awareness, warm thighs and soft breasts combined to create a total overload of erotic impulses.

Oh geez. No. Not here! Remember the trick you learned swimming at summer camp? Think of something else. Anything...mother...apple pie...Yankee baseball.

The music stopped. *What's happening? The bands are changing and everyone's leaving the dance floor. I feel like I'm in a nightmare walking naked down Broadway.*

"John, would you mind if we got some air. It's a little stuffy in here."

"You bet," John replied gratefully.

He closely followed her—trying not to step on her heels—until they were outside. She turned to face him, and he grimaced at the knowing smile on her face.

"Mel, I'm sorry I've embarrassed...."

She put her finger to his lips and whispered, "Actually, I'm quite flattered." Then she took him by the hand and moved toward the back of the hangar. When they were clear of people, she turned toward Chambers and slowly putting her arms around his neck, drew him close kissing him tenderly. Her moist lips lingered and did little to resolve the problem requiring their retreat from the party only a short time before.

Melanie looked down at his bulging pants. "*My*, what are we going to *do* if he keeps misbehaving this way?" she asked with a giggle.

"Mel, there's something you should hear."

"What is it John?"

"I need to tell you…I want to tell you…you're the most beautiful woman here tonight."

Melanie stared intently as if trying to read his mind and finally replied, "Thank you, John. That's a wonderful compliment."

What was that all about, she wondered as they started back toward the party.

Over the next couple of hours, Chambers attempted the western two-step without much success but did better with a line dance. Melanie was a good sport and always appeared to be laughing with him while she encouraged his efforts.

Leaving the dance floor after one more courageous effort by John to learn the two-step, Melanie suggested it might be a good time to approach the Bridgers. She led the way to their table and gave Rebecca a hug and kiss. Chambers offered his hand to Mr. Bridger along with sincere congratulations.

As they returned to their seats, Mel looked up and quite unexpectedly suggested they leave. Chambers picked up their party gifts and his hat and without comment followed her through the bustling crowd toward the hangar doors.

"Is anything wrong, Mel—are you okay?"

"Nothing's wrong. I thought we might go back to my house and spend some time alone. Of course, if you would rather stay…."

"Time alone sounds good to me." *He wanted more than anything to be with her—but what—it meant telling her he was leaving. It was a Catch 22.*

As they drove, conversation revolved around the party. Melanie opened her party favor to discover a gold necklace with a pendant in the shape of the Bar Double T brand and a small diamond in the center sparkling in the faint light.

"This is awesome! Wonder what you have. May I open it? Please?"

"Sure, go ahead."

She tore the paper and opened the box. "Look! What a great belt buckle!" she exclaimed, holding up a silver western buckle with the ranch brand and also accented by a small diamond.

Chambers stopped the car in front of her house and wondered if now was the time to tell Mel about leaving. *Hey, wait a minute. You're probably assuming too much here. She only wants to visit and have some time together. What's wrong with waiting? You can tell her when the evening is over.*

"Come Bismarck, you can go out for a run," she said letting the big dog go through the door and watching him head for the pasture. "What can I get you to drink, John? There's wine, soft drinks, water."

"A glass of wine sounds good if you'll join me."

Melanie put on some music and they sat sipping their wine and making casual conversation until she suddenly set her glass down on the table and in a serious tone said, "I'm really glad we could be together at the party; it's been a great evening."

Chambers moved closer and Melanie met his lips with a tender kiss, parting after a few seconds. Their eyes met and their lips came together again with unexpected passion.

He felt her shudder slightly—her tongue entered his mouth flicking lightly—and he reached an anxious hand to touch her full breast.

Suddenly John sat up straight and removed his arm from around her shoulders.

"John, it's okay. I know you would never do anything to take advantage...especially after our conversation...."

"Mel, no; it isn't what you think. I have to tell you something."

"Can't it wait? I kind of like what we're doing," she said with a slight giggle.

"No, we need to talk!" Getting to his feet and scrambling across the room, he recognized the need to get away from her; she was going to be impossible to resist.

"Mel, I'm having to leave much sooner than anticipated. Ted has been called away from the ranch and our interviews have been cut short. My editor wants me back in New York, Monday morning."

It took a few seconds for the reality of what he said to sink in.

"But, you said...you said you would be here for several more days and perhaps even weeks. You are talking about this Monday, correct?"

"I'm afraid so. It came up suddenly and...."

"Why didn't you tell me earlier this evening?" she asked in an angry tone. You allowed me to believe...to...to make a fool of myself. I'm embarrassed to say the least; how could you do this to me?"

"Mel, I don't know what to say. I started to tell you outside the party but didn't want to spoil the evening—but you have nothing to be embarrassed about."

"Oh really. Quite easy for you to say! I'm afraid you have the wrong impression of me and it's *entirely* my fault."

Pacing about the room and muttering more to herself than to him, she finally stopped and in a cold tone that made him shudder, " Thank you for a pleasant evening and goodnight...and, goodbye."

"Mel, we can't end on this note—there are too many things left unsaid. Please, let's sit down and talk."

"I'm sorry, John, it's too late for talk."

Melanie stepped quickly to the door and called Bismarck into the house; holding the door open, but keeping her back turned to John.

"Please leave."

As he stopped at the door, he turned to see she was trying unsuccessfully to hold back tears. He was still trying to console her, "Mel, please don't cry. I'm terribly sorry to,".... And the door closed in his face.

**

At the stroke of midnight, Liao and Lucy joined B.T. and Rebecca in a slow dance. The dance floor cleared and everyone admire the four of them gliding gracefully to the waltz music, ending with an announcement from Rebecca: "We must leave before we turn into pumpkins in front of your very eyes. Please stay and enjoy the music, and thank you again for celebrating this wonderful evening with us."

The party came to a close at 2 am. L.T. asked the band to play *Auld Lang Syne;* and those still dancing gave a final round of applause to the band before going to their tables to pick up belongings and say a final goodnight to friends.

It's been a long day, but it's gone very well. Mom and Pop really enjoyed themselves, and our guests seemed to have a great time.

He headed for The Lodge thinking about the enigmatic week ahead, knowing morning would come all too soon. Mom already made it clear—she expected to see one and all at church.

Sunday afternoon would be spent making final notes on his upcoming meeting. There was no need to be concerned about entertaining John Chambers. He watched him leave with Melanie and suspected they would have plans for his last day. *Good. Melanie needs some men in her life, and Chambers seems like a straight shooter; besides, he will only be here one more day.*

**

CHAPTER 10

John Chambers' Room
The Homestead

For Chambers, sleep took a long time in coming. The evening with Melanie went from bliss to bust in a matter of seconds. It was a mistake to have waited to tell her of his change in plans, but her reaction completely surprised him; but it was now obvious she was far more fragile emotionally than he had realized.

After a restless night, the ringing phone woke him with a start. "John, did I wake you. May we talk?"

"Mel—It's good to hear your voice."

"Do you have plans for this morning? Are you working or do you have some time?" Melanie asked.

"Work is all finished, and I basically have the day to burn; what do you have in mind?"

"You mentioned you were Catholic, and I thought you might like to attend mass with me. It's a small church in Laramie I've attended since childhood."

"Sounds great, what time?"

"Let me pick you up around 10:15; that should give us plenty of time for the drive. See you soon."

It was nearly 9—barely enough time to get dressed and have a cup of coffee before she arrived. Jumping out of bed, Chambers felt a sense of relief. *My last day in Wyoming might not be so bad after all. One thing is for sure: if it follows the pattern up to now, it won't be boring.*

***

The drive to church was punctuated with pleasant conversation and no mention of last evening's harsh words. Church service followed a familiar Catholic ritual, and Chambers found himself relaxing a bit.

They came out of church to discover the weather sunny and warm. Mel was driving the "Z" sports car and suggested they take the roofs out to better enjoy the day. Fresh spring air rushing into the open car felt invigorating, and Chambers was a bit disappointed when Melanie drove into a restaurant parking lot and stopped.

He had intentionally avoided touching Melanie by offering his hand, or arm at church and chose not to again going into the restaurant. *She deserves time to sort this out. I'm not at all sure what she may be thinking, but I won't risk having her believe I'm trivializing last night in any way.*

It was a busy franchise-type restaurant with an overflow of people fresh from church; after a lengthy wait, they were finally seated.

Neither could manage more than small talk before and during lunch, sitting uneasily, picking at their meals and leaving most of the food. John tried mulling over in his mind what he wanted to say but kept running into dead ends. His convoluted thoughts were like first drafts of an article; they seemed to all need rewrites. It was difficult to know what to say when the person you are addressing doesn't respond candidly.

On the trip back to the ranch, the need for conversation was mercifully denied because of the noise from the car's open top. Pulling up in front of The Homestead, he was relieved when she shut off the engine.

"Mel, could we…."

"John, we need to…."

They looked at each other and both laughed nervously, allowing tension to subside a little; perhaps they were ready to discuss the situation in a less emotional manner.

"Let's go around to the garden; it's lovely this time of the year," she suggested reaching for his hand.

When there hands met, Chambers felt an urge to take her into his arms but quickly realized his reckless desire for the blunder it would be.

Starting down the winding brick walk, they discovered Rebecca sitting alone under an umbrella in a comfortable wicker recliner. She appeared serene, surrounded by the bright colors and fragrances of the late spring, her frosty glass of iced tea sitting on the table. They hesitated, trying to decide if they should intrude on the peaceful scene.

Rebecca looked up and smiled broadly, "Melanie, John, what a pleasant surprise. Come and join me—it's such a beautiful afternoon and the garden is delightfully relaxing."

"Good afternoon, Rebecca," Melanie said, bending to give her an affectionate kiss on the cheek. "If you're sure we aren't intruding."

"I would very much like to share the company of two young people on this gorgeous day. Would you like some iced tea? There is plenty there on the table with some of Lucy's cookies."

Melanie stepped to the table and without asking poured two glasses of tea while John reached for one of the familiar delicious cookies.

"Mrs. Bridger, last evening was wonderful. Thank you for inviting me; I know what a special event it was and feel very privileged to have attended."

"You are quite welcome, John, and I'm very glad you enjoyed the evening. We were concerned you would feel uncomfortable among strangers and pleased to see Mel taking such good care of you."

Finishing the last part of the statement, an unmistakable glint in her eyes portrayed humor—or perhaps it was mischief.

Rebecca talked about the celebration and how delightful it was to see old and dear friends enjoy themselves.

John expressed the uniqueness of the experience from the standpoint of his background and cultural differences and delighted Rebecca with his comments. He failed to notice Melanie's sudden reticence to participate in the conversation and her sullen look.

Finishing her tea and setting the glass back onto the table, Rebecca rose and announced with a chuckle, "It's time to return to the *Spruce Goose*. It's my name for The Lodge—to B.T.'s great annoyance, I might add."

Chambers started to rise from his chair and Rebecca put out her hands signaling for him to remain seated.

"John, thank you, but please stay seated. By the way, it's time you started to call me Rebecca; Mrs. Bridger sounds too formal between friends, and besides, it makes me feel *old*. You two stay and enjoy the garden."

As they watched her closing the gate, John remarked, "What a special lady she is. Her wit and intelligence are rare in anyone but especially so...."

"But especially in someone from the—*boondocks* like Wyoming?" Melanie's tone was angry and wounded at the same time.

"If you let me finish, I was about to say, 'a woman of her era.'"

"Perhaps it would be well for you to study our state before insulting its history! You are obviously not aware—Wyoming was the first state in the union to grant women the right to vote. We're proud our history also reflects the first all-woman city government in the entire country. We've been out of the 'keep-them-barefoot-and-pregnant-and-they-will-follow-you-anywhere' mode for a very long time."

"Whoa, wait a minute. What the hell brought this on?"

They both remained silent for several minutes.

What's this all about, are we having a PMS moment? I deserved last night, but this is different; actually borders on ridiculous. Right now, returning to New York looks pretty appealing—and the sooner the better!

Melanie had risen from the table and was moving nervously about spewing out her angry frustrations. *What am I saying? Where is this coming from? I'm driving him away—is that really what I want?*

And then, it hit her. *You have strong feelings for this man—and for some reason it's scaring you away. Good grief, it's only been, what, six days? Whatever, there it is and you're dealing with it like a childish fool.*

Stopping in front of him, she gently touched his arm and said, "John, may we sit down and talk?"

What the crap is this? Some kind of childish game she's playing? Get mad, make-up, get mad again. When do we start playing doctor and nurse? Moving very stiffly, Chambers hesitated for a moment, before grudgingly sitting down across the table.

"What do we have to talk about?" he asked beginning to wonder how he could have misjudged her this badly.

"Let me start by apologizing, first for last night and every shameful, disgusting thing I've uttered since. I'm going to take a dangerous plunge and try to tell you honestly where I'm coming from."

Melanie stopped talking for a moment, clearly attempting to form her apprehension and feelings into words. Very subdued and sounding noticeably like she was speaking to herself, she began.

"I'm well aware we've only known each other a few days, and even thinking of having feelings for someone after such a short time, feels hauntingly familiar. I was counting on several days—even weeks—to find out what might develop between us when suddenly, everything changed."

"Mel, let me...."

Holding both hands out Mel signaled him to stop, "Please, John, let me finish while I can. I'm concerned about sounding desperate, even needy, to the point of being pathetic.

Taking a couple of steps away she began again. "This will probably sound very trite to you, with your recent history in a long relationship, but believe with all my heart the right man for me may come into my life only one time," she said pausing and expelling her breath forcefully.

"Understand, I'm not suggesting you're that man; it's obviously too soon, but I'm frustrated because circumstances may not allow time to find out. There—I've said it. This must all sound very premature, and I don't blame you if you want to run for cover."

She was looking away avoiding his eyes while she spoke. He waited for her to look up and directly at him before beginning.

"I anticipated we would have more time too, originally the interviews were projected to last several days—even weeks. It took a lot of courage for you to speak honestly, and I'm going to try and do the same.

"At this point, it's impossible to really know what I'm feeling. It's great being with you, and I'm attracted to you in every way a man is attracted to a woman. You know the circumstances of my broken relationship, and on that subject, please know Carla is behind me and of that I'm certain. I'm equally sure of one more thing; I want very much to know you better. The question is, how do we go about making it happen?"

He does have feeling for me, she realized with relief. *Maybe I haven't made a complete fool of myself after all.*

"What options do we have?" Chambers continued. "It's a long weekend commute between Wyoming and New York. We both have responsibilities and how can we...how can we what? Explore our potential relationship?

"How about this for a suggestion? Would you—could you come to New York? You could stay with my parents," Chambers added, his voice accelerating with enthusiasm. "They would love having you, and it would give us some time to get better acquainted."

They both sat in silence for a long moment; Melanie wondering whether she could work out the details and John wondering if he made a suggestion she considered offensive. After all, going away for a weekend was precisely what her *rogue professor* used in his attempts to take advantage of her.

"Are you serious—you really would like for me to visit you in New York?"

"Absolutely. Mel, I'm not suggesting we shack up together, okay? I have my apartment in Manhattan, and my parents have plenty of room. I've already spoken to them about you on the phone, and they would be very pleased to have you as their house guest."

"How soon are you talking about? Someone would have to run the store while I'm gone and...how long are we talking about?"

"Timing is totally up to you. Whatever you can work out and are comfortable with would be great."

"It sounds like a possibility to me at the moment, John, but let's see how you feel after you're back in New York." *It's not so much a lack of trust, but it's only fair to give him an out.*

"If you want to wait until then to decide, fine. But you have an open invitation, and it's your decision to make." *She doesn't trust me and is suspicious of my motives. I understand—but it still bothers me.*

***

Three thousand feet above Highway 211, looking out the side window of the Bar T's helicopter, Bridger saw Chambers' car moving toward Interstate 25. It was unfortunate he couldn't invite him to fly to Denver, but it was too big a risk to take. If John's reporter instincts smelled Washington, DC, in this trip, it could get complicated; besides, Chambers would get there nearly as quickly in the rental car.

O'Grady would set the Bell Helicopter down at a hangar in the private aviation section of the airport in Denver. The ranch maintained ground transportation for use in the area, but with all the security, it would still be a pain getting to the commercial flight. He briefly considered using a Bar T plane for the flight to Washington, but decided with the government bureaucracy, it would probably be far more complicated to utilize private transportation than simply allowing the Department of Homeland Security to cover the expenses.

The meeting with Secretary Ramirez was set for Tuesday morning. There was still some work to do on the organizational table, but all the important details were pretty much worked out; there would be time on the flight to polish the fine points.

***

John Chambers heard the helicopter fly overhead and watched it disappear to the south. *Where was Bridger going*, he wondered.

The chopper appeared to be heading for Denver, but from there they could be going anywhere in the country, or out for that matter. Chambers earlier tried unsuccessfully to finesse some information from Bridger and even casually mentioned the trip to O'Grady with the same result. His reply was simple and to the point, "The boss hasn't said—he'll let me know before the flight."

O'Grady would require lead-time to determine fuel requirements and file flight plans. Something's up—I detected a change in Bridger's demeanor, beginning about when? Friday morning, right after he told me the interviews would have to be cut short. What happened on Thursday?

He decided to call Gates before boarding his flight in Denver. Maybe putting their heads together, they could come up with some answers.

His mind turned to Melanie. Sunday afternoon was spent sitting in the garden and going for a long walk. They had no further discussion about her coming to New York, and he decided to wait and call her with another invitation from the city.

It was staggering to recall the events of the past week. One reality became clear: attitudes and basic passions about life can change abruptly. *Whatever else may come from this trip, it's been a great source of renewal and expanding of my awareness. Man, this trip has been stranger than fiction.*

***

Denver International Airport

Chambers arrived at the Denver airport with time to spare before his flight was scheduled to leave. After returning his rental car, the shuttle dropped him at the door to his airline; and he struggled from the van, bumping an elderly couple with his luggage before managing to get to a skycap station and checking everything but his laptop through to New York.

United Airline's lounge was located on the second floor. He chose the stairs rather than the elevator and quickly climbed to the top and pressed the button at the door. A loud buzz followed by a solenoid popping indicated the door was open, and he pushed through to be greeted by a pleasant, middle-aged woman behind a desk.

"Good morning, Sir. May I see your membership card please?" After a casual look at the date on the card and seeing it was issued to the *New York World,* she flashed a professional smile and handed the card back.

"Thank you. Will you be flying with us today?"

"Yes. I'm returning to New York," he indicated handing her his ticket.

After a moment to look at the computer screen in front of her she asked, "Do you prefer a window or aisle seat?"

"Aisle, thank you."

"Here you are, Mr. Chambers. Would you like to be alerted when your flight is ready to board?"

"Yes, thank you."

Looking about the room for an isolated place to sit and make phone calls, he settled for a corner near the window, far enough away from the nearest occupants to avoid creating a disturbance or being overheard.

It was after 10 am in New York. Michael Gates should be in. There were two rings before Cynthia answered.

"Good morning. Mr. Gates' office; may I help you?" came the husky voice on the other end of the phone.

"Good morning, Cynthia. Miss me?"

"Indeed I do, John. There's no one to replace our heavy water cooler bottle and I'm drinking from the lavatory. Please tell me you'll be home soon. Do you want to speak with Mr. Gates?"

"Please, Cynthia—but let me pull the dagger from my heart first."

John could hear a triumphant giggle before she transferred the call.

"Morning, John. Where are you?"

"I'm in the airport in Denver. Wanted to see if any information has come in regarding Bridger."

"You seem quite sure something's up. With all the diversified financial holdings the family has, maybe he's off taking care of some business."

"I doubt it, Michael. His attitude took a sudden change. It was like…like an athlete getting ready for a big game or something. His tone and mannerisms became more assertive and even his physical posture took on a different, more intense appearance."

"Were you able to get any idea of his destination? How much luggage did he take? Where was he departing from? Anything to give us something to start with?" *This sounds like a wild goose chase to me, but what the hell, can't stifle instincts on his first major assignment. Who knows, maybe it will lead somewhere.*

"I tried to work the employees on the ranch, and they either didn't know anything or wouldn't talk. No idea on the luggage. The helicopter left from the hangar and I didn't see them load."

Damn, I should have considered the luggage and tried to watch him unload the Rover.

"My best guess is, he's probably leaving from Denver on a commercial flight."

He could be going somewhere by helicopter; I really don't even know if he has left the immediate area. No way! Something is up; I can feel it. There's a story here somewhere.

"John, let me see what we can turn up through our sources. Any ideas of what airline or approximately what time he's leaving?"

"None. Can I check back with you after landing in Chicago?"

"It may be enough time to do some checking on flights. Our sources are a lot more sensitive with all the security issues involved, but we should be able to run this down. Call me when you land."

Please let there be something to this. If Michael burns a source for nothing, combined with the interviews being cut short, it would not be the success story I was hoping for.

This is not a business where you go only with the facts. You have to listen to your gut, something learned from experiences surrounding 911 and not to be forgotten. Listen to your instincts and don't let logic dominate your reasoning processes. This was a time to listen to those feelings. He was sure of it—almost.

***

Air America Flight 7845
Washington, DC

"Sir, *Sir* I'm sorry to wake you. We are landing, please return your seat to the upright position."

Opening his eyes, Bridger saw the flight attendant standing over him. After finishing his work, he did what he always did on long flights—slept. It was something acquired during several million miles of air travel. He could listen to the droning of the engines and doze enough to arrive rested and ready for activity. It made travel far less demanding and he considered it a hard-learned talent.

"Would you like a warm cloth, Sir?"

"Yes, thank you." He wiped his face and then his hands lightly with the wet cloth.

They were passing over the Potomac River and he spotted the Capital Beltway. It was the highway he would take into DC and meant Dulles Airport wasn't far ahead.

He had been stuck on the Beltway too many times to count and was glad to see the traffic moving at a good pace. It was 1:30 pm, which should mean missing most of the commuter travel, provided there were no accidents.

Bridger barely cleared the mechanical walkway into the terminal when a clean-cut young man approached him and asked, "Mr. Theodore Bridger?"

"Yes, I'm Ted Bridger."

"Mr. Bridger, I'm Special Agent Aaron Cohn," he said presenting the familiar blue-shaded FBI credential with his photo. "I'll be one of your escorts during your stay at SOG (Seat of Government). May I take your shoulder bag, Sir?"

"No thank you. I've got it," Bridger replied, extending his hand and exchanging a very firm handshake.

"Sir, we took the liberty of getting copies of your baggage check numbers from Denver, and your luggage will be taken to the Mayflower Hotel where you will be staying. Do you have any other business to take care of here at the airport?"

"As a matter of fact I do, Agent Cohn, and it will not require your help." Bridger saw the confused look on the young agent's face and decided to let him stew for a few seconds.

"Can you direct me to the nearest head? Missed the opportunity to visit the one on board before landing, and my eyeballs are starting to float."

"Yes, Sir. Right this way."

A slight smile crossed the young agent's face. Bridger well remembered his own early days in the Bureau when his duties involved so-called dignitaries, and all too often they were entirely condescending in treatment of those they considered underlings. He vowed never to be guilty of such a sorry attitude.

Following Special Agent Cohn through the busy airport, Bridger felt transported in time back to his own days as a young agent. How often had he volunteered to "escort" visiting VIPs? He never understood why the more experienced agents could not see the potential benefit from meeting the people who held the keys to advancement and success. *It would be interesting to know if Cohn did volunteer or was assigned the duty. And why FBI and not DHS?*

"Excuse me, Cohn, I'm going to pick up some newspapers," Bridger said stopping at a newsstand.

"Sir, there are copies of the *Washington Post, New York Times and Baltimore Sun* waiting in your suite at the hotel. There's also a *Washington Post* in your car, in the event you care to read en route."

"Thank you. Very thoughtful." *Lots of gusto and obtaining luggage numbers was a nice touch. This young guy is out to please, maybe even borderline obsequious. How much does he know about why I'm here? Or is he simply making the most of the cards he's been dealt?*

The two men exited through the automatic doors at the front of the airport, and Cohn moved to the rear of a parked four-door vehicle, swung the door open and stepped back for Bridger to enter.

"I'll ride up front if you don't mind," Bridger said opening the front door. Cohn was still standing at the back door unsure what to do next.

"We're good to go when you are," Bridger said over his shoulder.

Offering his hand to the driver, Bridger introduced himself. "Good afternoon. I'm Ted Bridger."

"Good afternoon, Sir. My name is Ron Strait. I work in the transportation section for the Bureau. Do you wish to go straight to the Mayflower?"

"Please. I'm sure you're not anxious to get caught in the commute traffic."

How about them apples, Strait reflected with the rancor of a man seldom appreciated. *Not many of these fat cats care piddly about my driving in this damn traffic. And how about this guy riding in the front seat? Cohn looked like he would pee his pants standing there holding the fricking door open.*

Strait moved effortlessly through the airport traffic and swung onto the Baltimore-Washington Parkway quickly accelerating to the speed limit. Traffic was light and they made good time. Turning off onto Highway 50, they were soon in the city. Looking up from his newspaper, Bridger recognized 11th Street and knew they were approaching the Mayflower.

Strait stopped in front of the beautifully restored hotel and asked, "Will you require transportation tonight, Sir?"

"I don't anticipate needing anything tonight. My meeting tomorrow morning is for 8 am. Will you be transporting me?"

Before Strait could reply, Cohn spoke from the back seat, "I'll be driving for you tomorrow. It will take us about 15 minutes to get to the U.S. Naval Security Station. (The temporary headquarters for DHS until new quarters are built.) What time do you want to leave the hotel?"

"I'll meet you in the lobby at 7:30 am. Thanks to both of you for your assistance."

Bridger picked up his laptop from the seat and swung the front door open feeling it hit something with a bang; it was Agent Cohn's leg. Exiting from the back door, he tried to open the front door and succeeded in getting a bruised knee for his effort.

A tight smile crossed Bridger's face seeing the embarrassment register on Cohn. *This kid's trying too hard; he needs to relax a little before he gets hurt.*

Cohn approached the doorman. "Mr. Bridger is checked in, and his luggage will arrive in the next hour. The bell captain has been alerted and will see it's sent to his suite." He handed over a bill that quickly disappeared into the doorman's pocket.

They must be paying agents a lot more these days. Looked like a twenty-dollar bill to me. The Bureau frowns on trying to recover tips on government expense forms, so he must be taking this out of pocket.

Bridger stood the huge lobby of the historic Mayflower and took a moment to look around. *They've completely restored the old girl and she looks great. Mr. Hoover ate lunch here every day for over twenty years, sitting in the same window seat every day. President Truman lived here for several months while he waited on restoration work to be completed at the White House. This is indeed hallowed ground.*

"Here's your key, Sir," Cohn offered. "Your luggage will be brought to your room on arrival. Will you require anything else at this time?"

"I believe you've considered everything. Thank you for your efforts. I'll see you tomorrow at 7:30 am."

Bridger opened the door to his suite on the 8th floor and was surprised to see the size of the accommodations. DHS had gone all out. It certainly wasn't necessary, but admittedly it made him feel appreciated. In the living area of the suite, a huge fruit basket and assorted bottles were on a table. There was brandy, bourbon and scotch, all high quality labels, along with several mixers; underneath several bottles of wine were chilling.

Are we having a party? If so, it must be the entire Washington Redskins football team. There's enough here to last a month.

He poured two fingers of Makers Mark into a glass. On another table, several newspapers lay neatly arranged with a card on top containing Cohn's phone numbers and included his cell phone and home phone. The note said simply, "In the event you need anything."

Bridger was having a second drink and reading a story on the latest assassination when he heard a knock at the door. Two bellboys dressed in traditional uniforms had Bridger's baggage stacked on a dolly.

"We have your luggage, Sir. May we put it away for you?"

"Please do." Stepping past him to the bedroom closet in the next room and placing the suitcases on the bed, they began to unpack. After placing undergarments, socks and incidentals away in drawers, they separated out his suit coats, shirts and slacks, placed them on hangers and returned to where Bridger stood mixing a drink.

"We will have these pressed and back to you within the hour. Would you care to have the suit you are wearing pressed? We can wait for you to change."

"No thank you. Is this part of the normal service at the Mayflower?"

"Mr. Cohn left detailed instructions, Sir. He has taken care of everything."

"He certainly has," Bridger said, holding out a tip.

"Mr. Cohn has taken care of that too," one of the bellboys, said with a smile indicative of a generous gratuity.

Where's this kid getting all the loot, Bridger wondered. *Damn, maybe Homeland Security has provided him expense money. That would sure be one hell-of-a deviation from the FBI.*

***

CHAPTER 11

Chicago O'Hare Airport
Chicago, Illinois

G ood afternoon, Cynthia. John Chambers—remember me, the water boy—is Michael available?"

"Oh dear, John, are your feelings injured from my water cooler comment? I wonder if there might be something I can do to make it up to you."

"I'm not sure. I'm pretty hurt, but let me try and think of something."

"Oh please do! One moment, John—I'll transfer you to Mr. Gates."

"John—we were able to track Bridger's ticket from Denver. He has a round trip to Washington, DC. There is an intelligence committee hearing going in Congress, and more than likely, that's were he's headed."

"It could account for his change in demeanor, but why not tell me he's going to meet with the committee? It's a matter of public record, isn't it?"

"It is indeed. But you know these spook types; they make a mystery out of everything. Whatever—it's our best guess for what he might be doing in Washington. If you need anything else, give it to Mo Mustafa. Mo is up to speed on everything you've done thus far and can do whatever research you might need when you get back. He's at your disposal for the next few days. Let's stay on this for a while and see where it leads. I'm here if you need me."

It didn't add up. Bridger would realize appearing before a committee meant coverage by the mainstream news. Why try to pass it off as a business trip? It was totally unnecessary—and besides—his testimony wouldn't require being in Washington long enough to postpone their interviews completely. Something else must be in the works.

Mo Mustafa was of Lebanese descent (a second-generation U.S. citizen with an Ivy League education at Brown), who came to work at the *New York World* in his late twenties. Many people, hearing him called Mo, assumed it was short for Mohammed. In fact it stood for Mozarab, a term referring to

156

Spanish Christians who were allowed to practice their religion during the Moorish rule.

Well-liked and respected, Mustafa's knowledge of the Middle East culture, along with Arabic language skills, proved invaluable to the paper and meant he was on his way to bigger and better things. Consensus among colleagues at the paper was he would be working in the Middle East as a correspondent in the near future and would probably already be there except for his reluctance to leave the American life style. Chambers and Mustafa shared tickets for the Yankees and New York Knicks; Mo was also a season ticket holder to Giants football.

Punching in some numbers on his cell, Chambers waited for the phone to ring. After two rings, a pure New York accent said, *"New York World,* Mustafa."

"Hey, Mo. What's happenin?"

"JC, my man. Hey, the Yanks need us, man. They can't hit Molly Pud. I'm glad to hear you're on your way back. Where are you?"

"Chicago. By the way, Gates indicated you would be working with me on Bridger for a few days."

"Right, he gave me the word. What can I do before you get here?"

"See what you can find on an agenda or list of people testifying before the Intelligence Committee in Washington this week. I'm going to contact some of my Washington sources and see what they know. Let's plan to get together first thing in the morning."

"I'm on it, JC. Have a good flight and I'll see you in the morning."

Mo's a cool guy. Some people would be a little ticked being asked to assist someone close to their own professional experience level. In fact, Mo has been at the paper longer than I have, which alone could be enough to cause some indignation; but that's not a part of his personality, he'll do the job assigned to the best of his ability.

***

Mayflower Hotel Suite
Washington, DC

Bridger awakened to the ringing phone at his bedside; picking it up, he heard the dreaded monotone voice familiar to business travelers across America say, "Good morning. It's 6 am."

From habit he responded, "Thank you." *Terrific, I'm having conversations with a recording.*

Getting out of bed, he felt a few kinks in his body from the soft mattress and a day's travel. *It's only 4 am in Wyoming and this damn bed is awful and the pillows even worse*, he grumbled. *But damnit, I used to be able to sleep four hours on the ground, or sitting up in a car and wake up feeling ready to go. Soft, pal, you're really getting soft.*"

After a trip to the head, he splashed some water on his face and came back into the spacious living area. Moving a chair to one side and removing his pajama top, he performed his routine morning stretches followed by a quick session of T'ai Chi Chuan. It was enough to work up a mild sweat; and after a shave, the warm shower made him feel almost human.

Bridger selected a dark blue pin stripe suit with matching accessories and after dressing took time to read the morning paper while eating a light breakfast ordered the night before. Gulping down a last swallow of coffee he checked his watch: 7:20 am—Time to go.

As the elevator door swung slowly open, Cohn came into view across the lobby reading a newspaper.

The kid is punctual. I've always liked that; in my opinion, nothing is more disrespectful than being late for an appointment.

Looking up from the paper, Cohn quickly got to his feet.

Bridger noticed the young agent was "dressed for success." *Too few recognize the importance proper dress plays in first impressions and opening opportunities for advancement.* Cohn's dark business suit, button-down starched cotton shirt and silk tie were definitely not "off the rack."

Slightly above average height, probably about 6'2" and 175, built like an athlete—the Bureau favors an athletic physical appearance in special agents—and Cohn really fit the profile. Dark hair and eyes combined well with a medium complexion and good features; overall, a well set-up handsome young man.

"Good morning, Sir. I hope you had a pleasant night."

"Morning, Cohn. No complaints. Are we ready to go?"

"Yes, Sir. Traffic on Massachusetts Avenue is normal this morning. We'll have no problem keeping your time schedule."

When they arrived at the security gate of the U.S. Naval Security Station, Bridger was not surprised to see barricades of concrete and steel. Designed to stop a vehicle from crashing through, it gradually squeezed entering autos into a single narrow lane to a first guard shack where a heavy steel gate barred their way. A second structure in the background contained uniformed personnel armed with automatic weapons.

A Naval Petty Officer wearing a sidearm stepped out of the small building and approached through a narrow opening in the gate to the driver side window of the car.

Cohn presented his FBI credentials, waiting patiently for the security officer to examine it and compare his photo.

Satisfied the credential was legitimate, he asked, "Sir, what is your business on station today?"

"I'm escorting Mr. Theodore Bridger to an appointment with Secretary Ramirez."

The guard glanced briefly at his clipboard before moving to the passenger side of the car and requesting Bridger to " please step out of the vehicle."

"Are you armed, Sir?"

"No," came the reply.

"Sir, please hold your arms out to the side and spread your legs apart."

The scanning device in his right hand ran up and down Bridger's body. Once again, the petty officer searched his clipboard and asked, "Sir, would you give me your former FBI credential number, please?"

"Yes. It was 71432."

"Thank you very much, Sir. Sorry for the inconvenience. Do you require directions?"

"No thank you, petty officer. Agent Cohn is familiar with the station."

The road serpentined through the second check point, and they proceeded to a multi-story building surrounded by well-manicured grounds.

"Sir, the Secretary's office is on the 4th floor. You are cleared by name, photo and fingerprint. There is a waiting area on the first floor. I'll be there when you're ready to leave. Is there anything else you require?"

"You seem to have covered most everything. I'm sorry I can't be more specific on timing; could be an hour or all day."

Too bad keeping this young agent waiting. His training and hard work were not intended to produce a chauffeur, but who knows where this meeting may go? In an hour, I may need a ride to the airport to return home to the ranch. Probably wouldn't be all bad—would it?

Bridger shut the car door and headed for the entrance of the Department of Homeland Security.

***

Temporary Headquarters
Department Homeland Security
US Navy Security Station
Washington, DC

Upon entering the building, security checks included a thumbprint, after which he received a thick "Visitors Pass" hanging from a necklace. Escorted to a private elevator, stopping on the fourth floor, still more security authenticated his electronic pass with a hand-held scanner.

Finally Bridger found himself following an armed SP into an office where a female administrative assistant was sitting.

"Welcome to Washington; or more accurately—welcome back to Washington, Mr. Bridger. I'm Sarah White." A very attractive woman, probably in her middle fifties, came out from behind her desk. Her hair was coal black with gray highlights, parted on the left and worn short. Dressed in a dark pants suit, the tan silk blouse underneath revealed healthy cleavage. An easy smile radiated from a finely featured face with only enough make-up to highlight beautiful green eyes.

"How do you do, Ms. White. I'm Ted Bridger."

He took her offered hand in his feeling its soft warmth. Low heels caused her hips to move provocatively when she returned to her desk, and Bridger caught himself admiring what he saw.

Sarah White possessed the full body of a mature woman. Somehow, the skinny "little boy butts" popular in today's culture failed to arouse him. He appreciated seeing something shapely enough to identify the gender.

Testosterone, he conceded feeling a tight smile cross his face. *Actually feels good to have some interest. It's been too long since a woman turned me on. All this unexpected action surrounding a possible new position must have jump-started some glands; and if the way I'm feeling is any indication, they may be working overtime.*

"The Secretary will be about ten minutes. He wants to clear his calendar for the next few hours to accommodate your meeting. Would you care for coffee or tea, Mr. Bridger?"

"Thank you. Coffee would be great."

As Ms. White passed in front of him, he looked at her more carefully. She was not wearing a ring on her left hand. Long floating strides caused her full bosom to jiggle provocatively, before arriving at the coffee and leaning forward to pour the beverage. The allure of cleavage gave way to an unexpected view of large full breasts. When she raised her head to ask if he wanted cream, Bridger found himself caught in the act.

His face flushed with embarrassment but was somewhat relieved when with a knowing smile and still bent forward at the waist, Ms. White asked "Would you like cream—in your coffee?"

"Only a tad…thank you," Ted managed to reply.

A few minutes crept slowly by, and Bridger sipped his coffee trying unsuccessfully to blend with the surroundings. Finally to his great relief, a buzzer sounded on Ms. White's desk.

"Mr. Bridger, the Secretary will see you now. Please follow me."

A heavy paneled door opened, and Bridger stepped into the office of Secretary Ramirez. Bridger gazed about the room. It appeared to have been recently renovated to accommodate the newly created cabinet level officer and looked long on expenditure and short on function. *Here's another example of taxpayer money being spent on a short-term solution. Most of what I'm looking at will be ripped out and disposed of when the new headquarters are completed.*

"Good to see you again, Ted. Thanks for coming on such short notice," Ramirez said stepping in front of his enormous desk and offering his hand.

"It is certainly my pleasure to be here, Mr. Secretary. Please allow me to congratulate you in person on your appointment."

"Thank you. It's proving to be quite a challenge. Let's sit over here at the table where we can be comfortable. I see you have some paperwork for me, and I likewise have some for you. Some things never change, huh Ted?"

Ramirez stopped at the smaller of two tables in the room, motioned Bridger to a chair, and the next two hours were spent discussing the details of the Secretary's proposal. Ramirez listened attentively while Bridger went into the specifics of how the proposed unit might be organized.

***

Greene County Courthouse
Springfield, Missouri

Prosecuting Attorney, Timothy Waters, lay dead on the steps of the Greene County Courthouse in Springfield, Missouri. A single shot from a .308 Remington 700 rifle killed Waters before he could enter the building.

A growing pool of blackish colored blood streamed from the gaping wound in what remained of his head. Disbelieving on-lookers, whose morbid curiosity drew them to the scene, stared in anguish. Some turned away in shock struggling to fight down the nausea burning in their throats.

The assassin and his spotter drove a ten-year-old red Dodge pick-up with its enclosed camper east on Chestnut Expressway away from the scene of the murder, being careful not to exceed the speed limit. The deadly shot was fired from inside the camper, and afterward the shooter crawled through the small interior window back into the front seat of the truck.

"S-2—mission completed and clear," the shooter calmly declared into his cell phone.

Arriving at Highway 65, the driver signaled a lane change and moved carefully into the right lane turning south toward Branson. They were looking for a place to dispose of the cell phone and approaching a river running into a lake saw the perfect spot. When the pick-up reached the bridge, the driver slowed; the passenger broke the cell phone in half and tossed it out the window, watching it spin end-over-end before splashing into James River.

Missouri Highway Patrol Corporal Gerald Burroughs was sitting a short distance away on the shoulder, partially hidden by a small grove of trees, and saw something thrown from a pick-up into the river. *Holy crap! Ten minutes until my shift's over for the day, and some red neck has to litter right in front of me. Jamie's recital starts at ten, and I could probably make it. What the hell, duty calls; besides, this littering drives me nuts.*

As the truck passed his patrol car, he noticed it contained two male individuals. Burroughs hit the switch for his lights; and stepping on the accelerator hard, the high-powered pursuit engine whined powerfully, quickly catching the pick-up. He glanced at his radar equipment; they were not exceeding the speed limit. *Good, may not have to write them a speeding ticket. Let's see what attitude we have here and maybe let them go with a warning.*

Calling in the license number and make of vehicle, he got out of the patrol car putting on his hat and approached the driver side of the truck.

"Good afternoon, Gentlemen. May I see your…."

Burroughs felt something hit him hard in the stomach, but never heard the loud boom of the powerful pistol. It felt like a hard punch—and then he realized—*I've been shot!*

*No! No! Why me…I have so many good things going…*lying on the ground feeling the searing hot pain in his stomach, he drew his knees up into a fetal position. *I'm going to miss Jamie's recital.* It was his last thought before darkness began to enclose him.

"What the hell did you do that for!" the passenger shouted at the driver. "Now you've done it you dumb meth-head! Shit! Shit! Gimme that damn gun!" he screamed jerking it out of the startled man's hand."

The older man reached into the younger man's shirt pocket and removed a small package.

"What the...."

"Shut the f...up! Stay put right where you are or I'll blow your stupid head off!"

Getting out of the pick-up from the passenger side, he carried a handgun in his right hand and the small paper packet in his left. Moving quickly around to where Burroughs lay in a rapidly expanding puddle of blood and taking careful aim, he calmly fired one shot from the .357 magnum into the fallen patrolman's head.

Kicking the patrolman's hat under the car, the shooter grabbed the feet, dragged the limp body around to the ditch side of the patrol car, and carefully placed a small package containing crystal methamphetamine into the Burroughs' jacket pocket.

That dumb shit, Bob Henry's going to have to make it home without his little pick-me-up. It may buy us some time. The locals will probably assume this was a stop gone bad when the Smoky found meth.

"You've put our ass in a real sling here, Bob. You better start thinking how you're going to explain this to the Colonel, because this one is on you! Let's get the hell out of here before any more 'rubber necks' get on their damn cell phones."

Highway 65 is a busy four-lane highway running south from Springfield to Branson—a popular entertainment destination attracting several million visitors annually. Several vehicles slowed and occupants caught horror-struck glimpses of the murder. (Most of the accounts would later prove unreliable to investigators.)

"We need to locate our nearest ERP," (En-route Rally Point used in military type operations to cache weapons, vehicles, etc., to aid in escape.) the passenger said in an irritated voice. He studied a Missouri road map.

"Highway 14 is about ten minutes with ERP #3. Pulling another cell phone from the glove compartment, he punched in a number. "We have smoky problems with our truck. Meet us at #3 with an extinguisher."

Closing the cell phone, he flung the .357 pistol far out the window into a roadside culvert. *We can't be caught with the weapon in our possession. Probably eventually be found by department of transportation workers, or maybe even someone working some community-service hours off a sentence. It really doesn't matter. We were careful to wear gloves and there would be no problem with fingerprints.*

He pulled a towel from under the seat, wiping down all of the truck he could reach. They were vigilant about fingerprints from the beginning, but it never hurt to be careful. It would take time for the two killings to be linked—if ever. The Feds would be working the queer PA's shooting under terrorism and "hate crime" mandates, but killing a highway patrolman meant the state and local cops would really be putting on the heat.

The Highway 14 sign appeared and they slowed, turning into a "Park and Ride" facility for commuters; finding a spot far away from the entrance, they parked the truck.

Both men got out of the vehicle and checking to be sure they were not being observed, quickly removed the Mississippi license plates and replaced them with stolen Missouri plates.

Moments later, a light blue Chevy sedan pulled into the parking lot and came directly to them. The cardboard box containing the sniper rifle was placed into a false bottom of the trunk for concealment; in the unlikely event they were stopped again, it would not be found without a thorough search.

Exiting onto Highway 65, the three terrorists drove south toward Branson and beyond to the Arkansas border. With several million visitors each year and scores of vehicles, it would be easy to lose themselves in the Branson-bound traffic. In a couple of hours, they would be safe—back at the farm in Arkansas.

Six miles behind on Highway 65, several stopped vehicles heard Patrolman Burroughs' radio suddenly come to life.

"Troop "F" headquarters to all units. We have a 1099-J4—be alert for a red pick-up with two male occupants possibly traveling east from Springfield center. License unknown—identity of occupants unknown. Repeat—1099-J4—1099-J4. Approach any suspect vehicle with back-up using extreme caution. (The J-4 designation—following the 1099 felony fugitive call—indicated Armed and Dangerous.)

***

Office of Secretary DHS
Washington, DC

Bridger and Secretary Ramirez were interrupted from time to time during the course of the morning with an aide bringing in fresh coffee and condiments. The door buzzed and Bridger expected to see more coffee rolling in. Instead of the young aide, a distinguished looking man about Bridger's age entered the room.

"Ted, this is Assistant Secretary, James Haugen. Jim, meet Ted Bridger."

"I've been looking forward to the opportunity, Ted. The Secretary's told me a great deal about you."

"Mr. Haugen, my pleasure," Bridger said extending his hand.

"Ted, would you please excuse the Secretary and me for a couple of minutes?" Looking at Ramirez before continuing, "Miguel, I'm aware you didn't want any interruptions, but you will want to hear this ASAP."

Ted was ushered to a small waiting room off the main office, barely hitting the seat when Haugen reappeared at the door.

"The Secretary would like for you to hear our discussion. Please," he said gesturing with his hand to invite Bridger back into the office.

"Ted, bearing in mind our conversation this morning, I'm certain you understand the sensitivity connected with what you are about to hear. Regardless of where our association may or may not go from here, we would welcome your input. Please continue, Jim."

"We have another sniper incident: a fatal shooting of a prosecuting attorney in Greene County—Springfield, Missouri—occurred at 9:17 this morning. The victim was killed on the steps of the county court house by a sniper's bullet. Details are still coming in from the scene."

There was a buzz at the door and the younger aide briskly entered the room carrying a file; handing it to Haugen, he left the room.

Haugen tore the seal off the folder and opened it, read a few lines and passed it to the Secretary.

"A male voice claiming to represent Al Qaeda called the *St. Louis Globe*, taking credit for the assassination. The message was similar to earlier calls. 'We can kill anyone, any time. No citizen of your decadent country is safe anywhere. Our holy jihad is Allah's will, and we will continue to kill infidels at random. Praise be to Allah.'"

"Shit! Is that all we have—reports of what's happened and more Al Qaeda threats? What the hell are *we* doing?"

Ramirez paced to his desk and flung the file down in obvious frustration.

"I'm sorry, Gentlemen, but this is really getting to me. We are one step away from seeing panic in the streets, and what do we get? After-the-fact action reports.

The Secretary turned and looked out the window toward the distant capitol seemingly searching for answers.

Finally letting out a deep breath, he turned toward Bridger and said, "I'm really searching, Ted. Realizing you are not fully informed, what is your take on the course this investigation is moving."

Bridger hesitated a long moment. *Careful. You know more than they are aware, but you could put Johnson in the line of fire if you reveal too much by your analysis of this situation.*

"Mr. Secretary, you were correct in pointing out my lack of investigative details required to arrive at an educated conclusion. The convoluted information I do have—raises serious doubts Al Qaeda is responsible."

Haugen's head jerked up from the file he was reading clearly stunned. "But…but CIA and FBI both agree this is a scenario they have been envisaging since the DC sniper created such national havoc. They are totally resolute in their view it is Al Qaeda and have concentrated their investigation on the single premise. If Ted is correct, Mr. Secretary—we've been spinning our wheels."

"Tell us more, Ted. What makes you believe it's not Al Qaeda?" Ramirez inquired uneasily.

"I'm reluctant to defend a position without having all available information. At this point, my position would have to be characterized as educated instinct; however, it is not my intention to throw out a bombshell and let it rest. This does not fit the Al Qaeda paradigm, and it is dangerous to see an investigation evolve with a predetermined mindset on what it is to conclude."

Terrific—absolutely great, you dumb ass. You get to defend a hunch with only half the available Intel—plus what Johnson told you, which can't be divulged here without getting him into a predicament.

"Could you be more specific?" Ramirez pressed with a hint of annoyance.

Bridger hesitated for several moments before responding, the Secretary of Homeland Security and his assistant anxiously awaiting his reply.

"The following questions come immediately to mind:

Why is Al Qaeda suddenly using newspapers and radio media in the U.S. to claim credit for terrorist activity? They have used Al Jazeera TV and a

Muslim web site exclusively in the past. Why not contact Al Jazeera's liaison here in Washington?

What is the motive? These cannot be called random killings at this point in time. With the exception of the radio talk show host—for whom I have only limited knowledge—there may be a basis for nexus.

The voices of the callers have been identified as "southern or Appalachian" dialects. This is totally inconsistent with what we have profiled as potential recruits to the Al Qaeda movement. Even allowing for recruitment from the growing converts in our prisons, an infinitesimal number are coming from a southern geographical and cultural background.

Al Qaeda has never shown the inclination or capability of training and using snipers to the extent suggested by the two shootings. Each event suggests highly trained expert riflemen using first-class technology in weapons and planning.

Risk and reward. Why would Al Qaeda utilize deep sleeper cells—which the callers have identified themselves to be—for such a limited pattern of destruction? Bin Laden has vowed to make the next attack bigger and more catastrophic than the World Trade Centers. While these attacks may well create a certain level of panic—as you have already suggested, Mr. Secretary—they will not succeed in bringing about Bin Laden's ultimate goal of destroying our economy and with it our society."

Secretary Ramirez stood for a long time pondering Bridger's disquieting analysis. Finally he spoke.

"Jim, this is exactly why we need this man working with us. Whether his theories prove right or wrong, he is the first person who has even suggested a new approach—a new focus if you will—which we have to consider."

"I agree Bridger raises some beguiling questions, Mr. Secretary, but I'm not sure we could convince FBI and CIA to modify their assessment based on what we've discussed. Why not make all information we have on each of the assassinations available to Bridger and let him give us a more definitive evaluation?"

"Sounds like a plan to me. However, let's not get ahead of ourselves. Jim, we have some more details to go over here. If you would have the pertinent files readied, we will have them available for Ted in the event he decides to join our little crusade—and, Jim, before you react, let me assure you—crusade is a term I would only use in closed quarters."

The remainder of the morning was spent with Bridger presenting what he considered essential details for a successful new enterprise:

An unspecified number of agents (not to exceed 10) from each of five existing agencies: FBI, CIA, NSA, DIA and USSS. (Federal Bureau of Investigation, Central Intelligence Agency, National Security Agency, Defense Intelligence Agency and United States Secret Service.)

Two additional agents to remain at the headquarters of each agency as liaisons. They receive all leads and act to expedite information within their respective agencies. Appropriate personnel in communications will be utilized from each agency to acquire and disseminate information.

Forensic liaison personnel, including specialist in bio, chemical, nuclear and conventional crime scene investigation.

Appropriate transportation specialists, to include fixed wing and helicopter along with appropriate ground transportation vehicles.

Autonomy from all agencies outside Department of Homeland Security. The director in charge of the unit to be responsible directly (and only) to the Secretary of Homeland Security and the President.

Unit to be headquartered in Denver.

The unit will assume investigative jurisdiction in all domestic security investigations assigned to them by the Secretary of Homeland Security.

Personnel will be given GS grade increases in salary upon selection. In addition, each employee will receive merit increases based on work performance. Upon the successful completion of their three-year commitment, all personnel will receive another GS grade increase before returning to their original agency.

Personnel will be staggered to provide continuity of capability when three-year commitments are fulfilled and individuals return to original agencies.

Criteria will be established allowing for a limited number of permanent transfers to the new unit.

A buzz sounded at the door again and an aide stepped in. "Your car is ready when you are, Sir."

"Thank you, Blake. I'll be right down.

"Ted, I have a luncheon to attend at the Senate Office Building. I foresee no impediments to implementing anything we've discussed. We don't have enough space here in our temporary quarters, and your recommendation for locating the headquarters in Denver is acceptable. It will provide a more central location in any case. There is space available at Denver Federal Center with temporary communication, support staff and transportation.

"I've already had preliminary talks with President Roark, and he is totally supportive of the concept. We're scheduled to meet again at 1:45 today. It will provide the opportunity to update him and gain final support.

"If the President is agreeable to the enterprise in the format we've discussed, are you prepared to come aboard as director of the new unit?"

"Mr. Secretary, it would be my pleasure to work under your direction. If it is your desire for me to undertake this assignment, it would be my privilege to do so."

"I'm very pleased to hear it, Ted. Welcome back to the battle," Ramirez added extending his hand.

"Why don't we plan to meet again around 4:30 this afternoon? In the meantime, I'm going to arrange for the VCFs (Virtual Case Files) with whatever we have on the assassinations to be available to you. After lunch, see Ms. White; she will direct you to a secure room where you can have a look see."

The Secretary pushed a button on his desk signaling for Ms. White, and seconds later she stepped into the room.

"Ms. White, can you please escort Mr. Bridger to the elevator. He will be having lunch and returning after to look at some SCI (Sensitive Compartmentalized Information). Please direct him to an appropriate space to provide security and privacy. And will you take steps to see he does not have to jump through all the security hoops to get back into the office."

"Yes Sir. Anything else?"

"I'm leaving for my appointment and will return this afternoon. Keep my calendar clear for a meeting with Mr. Bridger at 4:30. Thank you, Ms. White; that will be all.

The Secretary went quickly to a side door and out of the office. Bridger followed Ms. White to the elevator; and when the elevator arrived, she looked at Bridger, "I look forward to seeing you after lunch." The pleasant smile interrupted by the closing door appeared genuine.

***

CHAPTER 12

DHS Headquarters
Washington, DC

Aaron Cohn was in the lobby of DHS headquarters. He felt a bit lethargic from a morning of idleness but jumped to his feet and greeted Bridger.

"Good afternoon, Sir."

"Afternoon, Cohn. Hungry?"

"Yes, Sir. Do you have any preferences?"

"Let's go somewhere we can get decent food and not have a long wait. I have a busy afternoon ahead."

"I think I know the place."

Aaron did indeed "know the place"—the small out-of-the-way restaurant in Georgetown required only a short drive.

The maître d' recognized the young agent, and they were promptly ushered to a table. While waiting for the food to arrive, Bridger encouraged Cohn to talk about himself.

Bridger's earlier speculation proved correct; the young agent had indeed been an athlete in college. In fact, he was a big time basketball player at the University of California-Berkeley with enough talent to sign a contract with a professional team. Cohn spoke of his abilities in a very self-effacing manner. His "career" was cut short—no pun intended—when the larger guards in the league began to post him up and take advantage of his two weaknesses: a relative lack of size and "white man's disease."

Bridger laughed, remembering his own days at Wyoming in relating to the casual reference of not being an accomplished jumper.

Informal conversation continued over lunch until a name came up catching Bridger totally by surprise.

"By the way, Mr. Bridger, Bill Johnson said to tell you hello."

"You know Bill?"

"I had the privilege of serving under him and consider him a mentor as well as a good friend."

"You were with Bill in Seattle?"

"No, Sir—Los Angeles before he transferred north."

Could this be Johnson's "source" in DHS, Bridger wondered. *What was Cohn's connection to DHS? He was obviously still assigned to FBI Headquarters. Why was he selected to usher me around? Was someone on a fishing trip to find out what I'm doing in Washington?*

Finishing the meal and driving back to DHS, both men remained quiet— Bridger still wondering about Cohn's motives and the young agent wondering what he said to abruptly end the conversation.

They were stopped briefly on arrival back at Naval Security and waved on through; the same occurred in the lobby of the building. Sarah White obviously followed Ramirez's instructions to the letter.

When the elevator stopped at fourth floor, Bridger stepped out and Ms. White stood waiting.

"I have a private room for you, Mr. Bridger. Please follow me."

Hiking down the length of a long hallway, Bridger once again admired her sexy behind. The spike heels created a very suggestive swaying motion, making him sorry to see her stop at a door, insert a magnetic key card and push it open.

"I hope this will suffice. The VCFs are on the table along with some fresh coffee—and cream on the side. Anything else?"

"Yes, several legal pads please? I want to take some notes."

"Certainly. I'll only be a moment."

The files were from several different federal agencies. Bridger began to separate them into stacks, first by agency and then by title: forensic reports, neighborhood investigations, crime scenes, audio profiles, informant results, interviews with co-workers and relatives of victims.

There was a knock at the door, and Ms. White entered with legal pads and pens. She leaned forward and set them on the table, showing very ample white breasts under her silk blouse. Was he imagining things, or did she hesitate longer than necessary after setting the pads down?

The next three hours went by quickly, and after using most of a legal pad taking notes—his opinion was no different than before. In fact, after careful analysis of the available information, he was virtually convinced the assassinations were not the work of Al Qaeda.

There was a knock at the door, and Sarah White came back into the room.

"You've really been at it," she said looking at the scattered piles of files. "The Secretary has returned and will be ready for you at 4:30 as scheduled. You have about 15 minutes to get squared away here. I'll send a security clerk for the files."

"Thank you. You have been very helpful and I appreciate it."

"You are quite welcome. I'll be leaving soon and may not see you again today. If you don't already have plans tonight, would you care to have dinner with me?"

The invitation caught Bridger completely by surprise, and he sat momentarily startled.

"I'm…I'm sorry…I shouldn't…" Sarah stammered

"No—no plans for this evening; dinner sounds very nice, and thank you for asking," Bridger responded.

"Shall we say 7 pm in the Mayflower lounge?" she asked somewhat nervously. "We can have a cocktail and go to dinner from there. I can make the reservations if you like. Any preferences?"

"I'm a steak and potato man, but I'm sure anything you choose will be fine with me. It will be nice not having to eat alone; look forward to seeing you tonight and thanks again for the invitation."

***

The Secretary of Homeland Security and his assistant listened attentively while Bridger outlined his conclusions. From time to time, Bridger was interrupted by a question to clarify a statement or explain a technical term. The discourse continued for all of an hour.

I'm impressed, Bridger realized with some relief, *neither man tries to pass himself off as a professional intelligence expert and readily asks for explanations most bureaucrats would be embarrassed to seek.*

"That pretty well summarizes my assessment of the situation, Gentlemen. Decisions to limit the scope of our investigations to Al Qaeda appear to be a case of antithetical parallelism: 'This doesn't fit the Al Qaeda paradigm, but we are going to continue to investigate Al Qaeda.' The investigations completed thus far seem to support my original assessment; this is probably not Al Qaeda. At the very least, we should be considering other possibilities."

"Damn, Miguel, this is going to be a tough one to sell to those two arrogant clones tomorrow morning—but I believe Ted may be right. This is not the work of Al Qaeda, and we've been looking behind the wrong rocks all along."

"Couldn't agree more with both of your conclusions, Jim. Tomorrow morning will be interesting, to say the least, but then we've both known it would be only a matter of time," Ramirez replied without further explanation of his meaning.

"There is another subject you should be aware of, Sir," Bridger began. "I recently allowed a member of the national print media to spend some time at our ranch for the purpose of doing an extensive interview. The interview is completed and I have approved it for publication. It's going...."

"Forgive me for interrupting you, Ted, but I'm aware of your interview. In fact, we have read the article about to be published. It seemed quite fair; however, I'm not certain the Directors of FBI and CIA will agree.

"Speaking of which, let's get you into the water with both feet. I would like for you to attend a meeting with me tomorrow and summarize what you've given me. It will be with some heavy-duty bureaucrats. I realize you're hardly back in the saddle, so to speak; you comfortable with returning to the fray this quickly?"

"Sir, I'm working for you and I'm ready to do my best in whatever arena you decide I'm useful."

"Good. It's refreshing to hear. Allow me to say again, I'm very pleased to have you with us. Tomorrow's meeting is set for 10 am. Be here by 9 and we'll have time to discuss our strategy. You will ride over with me."

How long have they been looking at me? They probably had someone at the University of Wyoming lecture. It wasn't a big deal they knew about the article, but knowing the content was something else. Surely NSA would not be intercepting New York World electronic messages. Or would they? But if not, how would Ramirez be aware of what was going to be in the article. Does it suggest they have a source at the New York World?

***

Cohn drove Bridger back to the Mayflower, agreeing on an 8:30 am pick up for the next day, Bridger thanked him, apologized for the long day of waiting and dismissed him for the evening.

More mentally tired than physical, Bridger wasted little time getting to the suite and mixing a bourbon and water. Getting out of his clothes down to his underwear, he slipped into a bathrobe and sat down in front of the television.

Bridger found the remote and tuned the big screen plasma TV to a news channel where they were talking about the latest shooting in Missouri.

"Authorities continue to be clueless regarding the whereabouts of the perpetrators of these random assassinations. Al Qaeda is blatantly claiming responsibility, and neither the FBI or CIA will comment on whether they are any closer to determining how the terrorists entered the country or whether they are "sleepers" who have been in the U.S. for an extended time.

"The public is growing more wary each day, and one is only left to wonder—has anything really changed since 911? The terrorists appear to be operating with impunity and have now struck the very heartland of America. Are the various agencies responsible for our protection still embattled in petty rivalries? We have a right to expect more from the billions of dollars being spent for homeland security—haven't we?

"This is Jack Snow, WLDC, from the J. Edgar Hoover Building. Back to you, Mary Ann."

Taking a big pull from the glass of bourbon, Bridger took a deep breath and let it out slowly. *Well, I'm back in the game; and they are giving me the ball—time to show what I got.*

Getting up from the chair, he went into the bathroom, removed the robe and underwear and stepped into a huge two-person shower. He turned the nozzles causing the water to hit him from all directions and began to relax in the warm spray.

Why did I agree to go to dinner with Sarah White? There's a lot on my mind and I'm not sure I'll be much company. She's looking for good conversation and a pleasant evening, something always difficult for people our age to find.

Pulling a suit from the closet, he couldn't help being reminded of how resourceful Cohn was in having his wardrobe pressed and properly hung. There were still three more fresh suits available for the remainder of the week.

Selecting a light blue oxford cloth, he carefully tucked the shirt in, tied a Windsor knot in a silk maroon tie and zipped up the dark blue pin stripe pants. The black leather belt required one tighter hole to feel secure.

Good, at least the waistline is still reasonable. He worked at keeping the extra pounds off and was only 15 pounds over his college playing weight. It wasn't easy with age, but it was a matter of pride and self-discipline. He looked into the full-length mirror, straightened his tie, slipped into his coat and headed for the door.

Taking the elevator to the lobby, Bridger meandered slowly across to the main lounge. It was still 15 minutes away from their agreed meeting time, and he decided to have another bourbon to lighten up his disposition a bit.

The waiter was returning with his Wild Turkey when Sarah White appeared at the door of the lounge. "You look very nice this evening, Ms. White."

"Thank you...Mr. Bridger. But, do you suppose we can drop the Ms. and Mr. for the evening. I'm Sarah."

"Hello, Sarah; I'm Ted."

Her hair was still worn the same, but her make-up reflected the changes women make for evening wear, and the light blue eye shadow brought out the green in her eyes. Wearing a summer-weight dress, the medium low neck displayed her large breasts in a tasteful manner. A small gold bracelet on her left ankle contrasted with high calf muscles emphasized by spike heels.

"Would you care for a drink?"

"Look's like you're drinking bourbon, and I'll have the same, thank you."

How about that, a bourbon drinker, he thought signaling the waiter to bring another.

"How long have you worked in the Secretary's office?"

"Nearly a year. Actually came over from the Justice Department. I've been in government for 30 years."

A veteran civil service employee who's seen it all, Bridger concluded. *No attempt to hide her age; but with her looks, why should she?* He continued to ask questions in hopes of keeping her talking. It would make the evening simpler if he didn't have to carry a lot of the conversation.

In the middle of explaining why she never remarried after the death of her husband, Sarah suddenly stopped talking.

"I keep rambling on here and you've hardly spoken. Please forgive me. I'm afraid the truth is, I'm not getting out socially very much these days, and I'm afraid it may be showing in my manners."

"Not at all. You undoubtedly know more about me than you probably care to—from the security check—and there really isn't any point in my boring you."

Sarah laughed but offered no comment and looking down at her watch suggested, "It's probably time for us to go to dinner. I took the liberty of getting a reservation here. I'm told the food is very good, and it will save us driving in the traffic."

The Mayflower dining room was very busy, and it was fortunate Sarah made reservations. They were ushered to their table and given menus and water. Ted looked at the wine list and decided on a New York Merlot; the waiter returned to the table with the five-year-old bottle of wine and Bridger felt the cork for softness, smelled the wines bouquet and carefully rolled the dry Merlot on his palate.

"This will do nicely, thank you."

The waiter poured wine for the both of them and asked if they were ready to order.

"The lady will have Boston mackerel, with angel hair pasta and the house salad. You may bring me a filet mignon, medium, with new potatoes and a Caesar salad. Could we also get a small loaf of French bread, please?"

They sipped the excellent red wine and fell into an easy dinner conversation centering on their common experiences in Washington. By the time the blueberry cake arrived, they were sharing a California Vignoles after-dinner wine, and Ted realized he was more relaxed than he had been in a very long time.

What a handsome man! Wonder if he thinks I've been too forward asking him to dinner. This wealthy widower must have a lot of younger women throwing themselves at him. Probably only accepted to be nice, or perhaps hoping to establish a contact in the Secretary's office.

"Sarah, there's a band playing in the lounge. I'm no Fred Astaire, but would you like to take a chance?"

"Only if you understand, I'm no Ginger Rogers."

As they moved onto the dance floor and he took her into his arms, she realized how tall he was.

"My you are tall! Good grief, did I really say that? It's only…you don't look that tall…because you are so well proportioned…you know what I mean. Damn, are you going to let me die here?"

"Sarah, I think you are also 'well proportioned.'" And squeezing her a little closer he felt her warmth press up against him, when she whispered, "Thank you."

They danced one more dance, then starting toward a booth to sit down, Bridger stopped short.

"DHS provided some excellent brandy for my room. Seems a shame to let it go to waste. Would you be offended if I ask you to have a nightcap with me?"

"Not in the least, Ted. It's very nice of you to ask."

In the elevator Sarah remained silent, and Bridger began to worry whether he had offended her by his invitation.

Entering the spacious suite, she laughed and said, "My, this is beautiful; it must be where my tax money's going. I'll bet you have a wonderful powder room." *It better have. I've been waiting planning to use the facility in the restaurant before going home.*

"It's through the door to the right. Sorry, you may have to wade through the towels on the floor."

Ted put on some music and was pouring a splash of brandy into a snifter, when Sarah returned.

"May I pour you a brandy?"

"Only a small one. I still have to get home tonight."

Sitting down on the sofa, Ted handed her the brandy, and she sat swirling it for several moments.

"Here's to a successful stint with DHS," she said and held out her glass.

Ted touched his glass to hers and the crystal made a soft clink.

"Thank you, Sarah."

They each took a sip of brandy and half turning their eyes met. Ted leaned slowly toward her and she met him half way. There lips met very softly and parted. He set his brandy down on a table and reaching for hers put it down beside his. Slipping his arm around her, he pulled her gently toward him, and she responded by pressing her body into his.

Their lips met again and moving closer Sarah let out a jagged breath; Ted felt her large breasts pressing against him. They lingered at each other's mouths for a long while, kissing, nibbling and exploring playfully with their tongues.

Finally their mouths parted, and she nuzzled in his arms enjoying the comfortable feeling of being with a man she knew mainly through personnel files. Still, it was obvious from the little time spent together, he was a man of quality.

He's a wonderful kisser—something I've missed. It feels good and is really stirring some physical urges too long left undisturbed.

Ted moved to reach the snifters of brandy, and when he handed Sarah hers, she felt disappointed, realizing the mood was lost.

Taking a small sip of brandy, Ted looked away and said, "Its been a long time since I've enjoyed an evening this much."

Something in his tone and the way he looked off into the distance made Sarah wonder if he could be visiting the past. *Understandable. We both have a history with people we dearly loved. His personnel file details the story of the tragic loss of his wife and how he replaced her with his work. My file would probably reveal much the same.*

"Thank you, Ted, for such a nice compliment. I've really enjoyed it too, and I'm glad you accepted my invitation. We both have busy days tomorrow, and I'd better say goodnight."

Getting to his feet, Ted offered his hand helping Sarah rise from the couch. They strolled hand in hand to the door.

"My car is in valet parking and they will bring it to the front door of the hotel. Please don't feel you need to go down."

"It's not a question of need, Sarah." Bending he quickly kissed her on the lips, opened the door and still holding her hand started toward the elevator.

***

New York World
Office cubicle of John Chambers

John Chambers spent most of Tuesday contacting sources in Washington. Bridger was spotted at the airport the day before, met by a young man dressed too well to be with an intelligence agency. He was probably an aide to some congressman. A lot of the younger aides were recent graduates of Ivy League colleges and were still on allowances from wealthy families. Mo hadn't been able to find Bridger on any agenda lists for testimony at the hearings. Perhaps there were meetings taking place outside the public realm—or less likely, the FBI powers-that-be came to their senses and were asking his advice in the latest Al Qaeda attacks. No way—too many bruised egos.

"Mo, why don't you put these photos into your computer file. I took them at the Bridger ranch, and they may be useful in any future stories."

Mustafa took the digital camera to his desk. It was the typical "bull pen" style office with glass-enclosed cubicles containing a desk, chair and some filing space, along with a telephone and computer. Chambers occupied a similar space nearby.

"What is your best guess about what he is up to, JC? You have a pretty good feel for him by now. Could he be on a business trip like he told you? The Bar Double T must be working with several different lobbyists in Washington—coal, oil, beef—a lot of irons in the fire. Maybe he's meeting with one of those groups."

"Possible, but not likely. Bridger would have a representative of the lobby coming to him. He's not a big fan of Washington and probably wouldn't make a special trip to speak with lobbyist.

"In all probability, we only have one more day on this. Gates really wants to devote more personnel to the assassinations and said for us to begin contacting our sources ASAP. Since we'll be working together, why don't you go ahead and take the rest of the day to get started, and I'll finish up what we have on Bridger."

"Sounds good to me," Mo replied. "I'll need to leave the office. I have a new potential resource I'm trying to help find work and can only contact him during the day. He's involved with a mosque which may have some radical ties."

"Mo, why don't we meet each morning to compare notes and work out a game plan for the day? I'll take some time this afternoon to pull up the latest on the shooting in Missouri and see how it fits the earlier scenarios."

As Mustafa headed toward the elevator, John glanced at the time. It was approaching 11 am, which meant 9 am in Wyoming. He hadn't talked to Melanie since returning and she should be at the store. Picking up his cell phone, he punched the speed dial.

"Good morning, this is Melanie, may I help you?

"Good morning, Mel; it's John…John Chambers."

"Hello, John. How are you?"

"Great! How are you?"

"Fine." *He called! I really wasn't sure he would.*

"So, when are you coming to New York?"

"Do you still…are you sure you would like for me to come?"

"Mel, I miss you like crazy already. Please, say you will."

"I'd like to if you're certain. I've talked to my part-time employee, and he can watch the store for a couple of weeks. Have you spoken to your parents about this?"

"Absolutely, and they are very anxious to have you. How soon can you make arrangements? Do you need help with the airline tickets and travel?"

"No. No help needed. I'll check and see what's available. How soon?"

"Yesterday, tomorrow, the sooner the better. Okay?"

He does miss me. Better not tell him I've already checked the airlines and can be there on the weekend. It may sound a trifle anxious.

"I'll check the Internet and make some calls. Will you be home this evening? I can call and tell you what I've found."

"Let me call you. I'm really working hard to catch up, and it may be late before I get back to the apartment. You have my cell if anything comes up in the meantime. I'll try to call about 8 pm your time. Okay?"

"I'll be waiting—and John—it's been great hearing your voice."

"It's been great hearing your voice too, Mel. It will be even greater seeing you."

***

CHAPTER 13

Bridger Suite
Mayflower Hotel

It was 8:30 am and time to meet Cohn. Taking one more look into a mirror, adjusting his tie and closing the door behind him, Bridger stepped into the elevator.

Pleasant reflections turned to last evening, *been a long time since I enjoyed female company more. Conversation was excellent and it's strange how much I enjoyed kissing her. Felt like a damn teenager sneaking a quick smooch in his date's living room with her parents asleep in the next room.*

Still, those nagging feelings of being unfaithful to Katherine linger. Never mind the fact she would not want me to feel this way; it's still very uncomfortable.

Agent Cohn was waiting in the lobby reading a morning paper.

"Morning, Sir. Hope you had a pleasant evening."

"As a matter of fact, Aaron, it was a fabulous evening, thank you very much."

Damn! He called me by my first name and what's with the big smile? You'd almost think he got laid last night. Naw, probably only stayed up late and watched an old spook movie on the big screen.

"I'm very glad to hear it, Sir. Are we ready to leave?"

"Let's do it." And Bridger briskly moved out with the young agent scurrying to keep up.

Cohn made good time in lighter-than-usual traffic, and shortly they arrived at Naval Security.

"Aaron, this should be finished by noon, and you have things to do. Why not give me your cell number, and I'll give you a call when I'm ready. There is absolutely no purpose served in your waiting here."

"Whatever you say, Sir. I really don't mind waiting if it's more convenient."

"I'll call you when I'm finished," Bridger repeated as he closed the door.

Sarah White stood waiting when the elevator swung open on the fourth floor.

"Good morning, *Mr. Bridger.* Did you have a pleasant evening," Sarah inquired feigning a professional greeting. "Good morning, *Ms. White.* Actually had a very pleasant evening, and I'm hopeful there will be another like it very soon."

"I should think it could be arranged, and if I can be of help, please, call on me."

Wearing a long skirt with a side vent, her spiked heels displayed nice legs, and the dress was tight enough to set off another of her best assets. Sarah's silk blouse drew his attention to her magnificent breasts.

She looks gorgeous this morning.

"Secretary Ramirez asked me to bring you right in. Want to follow me?"

"Anywhere," he replied.

"Good morning, Ted. Have a good evening?"

"Outstanding, thank you, Sir." Sarah White smiled broadly as she left the office.

Ramirez's expression change slightly as he, too, caught the uncharacteristic big smile. Pausing for a moment while considering possible reasons for his administrative assistant's cheerfulness, with a slight shrug he said, "Good. Let's get down to business, shall we?"

"This is a press release prepared for your review. It is perfunctory in every sense and essentially contains some background and the fact you will be working as a director for DHS."

"I'm sure it's fine, Sir. However, it reminds me of a rather unusual request. As we discussed yesterday, I was concluding an interview with a journalist from *The New York World* when our business here made it necessary for me to cancel rather suddenly. It became necessary to fabricate an explanation. John Chambers, a young reporter doing the story, was undoubtedly placed in an awkward position with his paper, and it seems reasonable he be given a heads up before any release."

Secretary Ramirez paused for only a moment..."I fail to see a problem with your doing so. We can let it be our first confidential mutual understanding. Anything else?"

"No, Sir," Bridger said handing the press release back to Ramirez.

"Ted, we will be meeting with DCI (Director of Central Intelligence), FBI Director Goode, and the National Security Advisor, along with several of their subordinates. It is possible the Pentagon will have someone there from DIA (Defense Intelligence Agency) as well. President Roark will attend part of our meeting and wants to hear more about your—what might we call it at this point—*divergent conclusion*? Still convinced Al Qaeda's not responsible? Anything change your thinking?"

"Nothing, Mr. Secretary. If anything, I'm more convinced than ever."

"Good. You'll be making your case before—how best put—a very skeptical audience. Needless to say, we are ruffling some feathers with our new unit. What the hell, maybe it's time some feathers were ruffled! You have my backing, for what its worth, and President Roark is ready to hear some fresh ideas—especially if they produce results.

"You will be pleased to know your new office space in Denver is a top priority."

"Use these temporary credentials for the remainder of today, and you are scheduled to pick up a full set tomorrow at Justice." Ramirez handed Bridger a leather fold-over type case with photo and DHS shield and papers.

Bridger wondered where they got an obviously recent shot of him with a fuzzy background. Looking more carefully at the photo, he could make out what appeared to be a large column.

Damn! It's the Mayflower Hotel lobby. Someone took a candid shot of me since I've been here; wonder what else they photographed? If they have cameras in the suite, Sarah and I could be up for an academy award. Welcome back to a world of intrigue.

"How soon can you have an initial list of personnel requests?"

Still caught up in his thoughts, Ted hesitated before responding. "Sir, I already have several names to submit and will be adding to it daily. Do we have a firm commitment for cooperation from various agencies in transferring requested staff?"

"All directors of appropriate agencies will have memorandums crossing their desks this morning from my office," Ramirez said in an unequivocal tone. "My memo will be followed shortly by an Executive Order, signed by the President. There should be unconditional cooperation from all five agencies; if there is not, I want to hear about it immediately.

"I would like for you to meet with one of my assistant directors this afternoon and give him all bare essentials you require to get operational. The sooner you can get started, the better—even if you are only partially staffed.

"Any ideas what to call our new unit?"

"Mr. Secretary, *FIST* might be appropriate—standing for *Federal Investigative and Strategic Team.* It's an acronym used by U.S. Marshals Service in the 1980s when they inaugurated a temporary Fugitive Investigative Strike Team, (FIST) to capture violent fugitives wanted by Federal and local law enforcement agencies. They attempted—on a much smaller scale than what we are planning—to combine resources of several agencies working together. There efforts were discontinued in the mid-eighties, but for those who might still remember the name, it offers nothing but positive recollections."

Pausing for a moment repeating FIST aloud, Ramirez replied, "Good solid ring. Perfect acronym for what we're attempting to create. A combined elite team working together to investigate and strategize appropriate tactics. Excellent, FIST it shall be."

"Speaking of strategy, time to discuss our meeting. We should leave in about ten minutes or so."

***

The White House
1600 Pennsylvania Avenue NW
Washington, DC

The ride to The White House took only a few minutes. Security checks began several hundred yards from the entrance and continued through three different levels. Entering from the west entrance, they were escorted to a small waiting area outside the Intelmet Room, (Intelligence Meeting Room) where after one last ID check, the Marine guard opened a soundproof door, allowing them to enter.

"Good morning, Miguel," said a pleasant looking middle-aged woman.

"Good morning, Margaret. Meet Ted Bridger. Ted say hello to Margaret Fleisher, the President's National Security Advisor."

"Ted and I already know each other. He came to Columbia to speak on a number of occasions while I was still teaching there. Good to see you, Ted; glad to hear you will be joining us again."

"It's very nice to see you again, Ms. Fleisher. I'm looking forward to getting back in the saddle, so to speak."

"Ted, in this room, we tend to be very informal—except with the President of course—and I'm Margaret."

Fleisher was new to the Washington political scene. She was an academic with impeccable credentials, no embarrassing baggage and—she was Jewish. (No doubt helping to send a signal on the administration's pledge of support to Israel.) Ted guessed her to be in her early fifties. Dressed in a tan skirt with dark blazer, still reflecting her Ivy League background, her dark hair was worn short and contained streaks of gray. She was showing early signs of middle age spread, but was far from obese. Her dark brown eyes were penetrating and offered little to suggest what she might be thinking. It was an excellent trait to have in Washington.

"The door swung open again and three men entered. Harmon Barkley, (Director of Central Intelligence) came in followed closely by Jerome Goode (Director of FBI) and Malcolm Winter (a three-star general and Director of Defense Intelligence Agency).

Bridger could not help thinking: *Wonder if they entered in pecking order. Goode is a politician first and a leader second. Technically, Barkley may be considered more powerful, from a standpoint of global operation and budget. It will be interesting to see what status Ramirez has with these two and how he elects to use it.*

Walking toward the Secretary, Goode put out his hand, "Good morning, Mr. Secretary—Margaret. Hello, Bridger, how are you?"

Without waiting for an answer, or offering his hand to Bridger, Goode began talking to Ramirez.

He's precisely what I expected, Bridger concluded with regret. Average height and build, middle fifties, dark hair with gray at the temples, impeccably dressed in a dark suit with white starched button-down shirt and dark shoes. Nothing to call attention to or detract from his appearance—even his tie was muted carefully avoiding red or a color perceived to create confrontation.

Leaving the Secretary, Goode stopped at the table where a white-jacketed waiter stood serving coffee and pastries; Margaret Fleisher followed closely behind.

Barkley and Winter came to greet Ramirez. Everyone's movement appeared amusingly choreographed.

Barkley spoke first, "Good morning, Mr. Secretary...Bridger."

"Morning, Gentlemen," Winter added.

Barkley's a career bureaucrat, Bridger mused. *He's been in Washington for thirty plus years and knows how to stay out of the line of fire. He was CIA Chief of Station in Saigon. Many, including myself, will never forget Barkley's role in a dishonor forced on all of us.*

In his haste to get out of country, Barkley refused to recommend to Langley (home of CIA headquarters) promised support for Montagnard Tribesmen (along the Cambodian border) who were instrumental in fighting Viet Cong. Our "commitment" was broken when the pullout began and their traditional enemies, the Communist Viet Cong, massacred many of them. Veteran operatives who survived their missions in the jungle in no small part due to Montagnards were incensed to a point of rebellion but ultimately were forced to pull out or be left behind.

Barkley was in his late sixties and beginning to show a bulge around the middle acquired by too much time sitting and too many cocktails over lunch; his white hair was noticeably thinning.

A master of a clinched-teeth smile associated with Washington, he flashed one now to Bridger and in a tone edged with sarcasm, "We're looking forward to hearing from you this morning. We understand you have some very anomalous theories for us. Frankly, that seems somewhat curious for someone who has been—how shall I say—out of the loop with this investigation."

His tone was barely short of condescending and obviously meant to put Bridger on notice. *To hell with this Washington rhetoric! I'm not here to take crap from this political hack. If an assistant director, a professional intelligence officer, wants to criticize my assumptions—so be it. They have paid their dues and their comments would come from an informed opinion based on careful analysis. The DCI position is often little more than a political reward for past favors.*

"I certainly trust you will find my theories *entertaining*, if not *informative*," Bridger replied in a chilly tone.

"I don't think we've had the pleasure," General Winter interrupted an about-to-become tense conversation, extending a large, very black hand toward Bridger. He appeared to be in his early sixties and gray had mostly replaced black in his hair; he lacked Ted's height but probably outweighed him by twenty pounds, and it looked to be all muscle.

His uniform contained a chest full of ribbons and included a combat infantry badge with stars, two purple hearts, a silver star, two bronze stars and a blue and white ribbon signifying The Medal of Honor. Ted realized he was in the presence of a warrior.

The two men exchanged a firm handshake. Bridger caught a slight sparkle in Winter's eyes, possibly suggesting mirth at uncomfortable circumstances in which they both found themselves.

This is a business for which the General has little stomach; I suspect he's a guy you would like to have a drink with or take for a weekend to your favorite hunting lodge. This is probably his last assignment—accepted with a promise of a fourth star before retirement.

"It's my pleasure, General. I'm Ted Bridger."

Barkley turned away without further comment strolling over to a refreshment table to join Goode.

A door swung open and a young man stepped through, closely followed by Anthony G. Roark, President of the United States. There was an immediate hush and white-jacketed servers exited with an aide closing the door behind them.

"Good morning, Gentlemen...Margaret; please continue to get something to eat and drink." President Roark approached Ramirez and Bridger offering his hand to each in turn.

"Ted, it's good to finally meet you. Allow me to officially welcome you back to Washington I've met your father on several occasions. How is he doing?"

"It's a great privilege, Mr. President. Pop is doing well and still going full speed ahead."

"Please give him my best when you talk with him."

Moving to the front of a long conference table, President Roark took a seat.

Margaret Fleisher's voice broke into the quiet assembly, "Gentlemen, if you could take your seats, we are ready to proceed.

"In deference to the busy schedule for the President and Secretary Ramirez, Intel briefings on the domestic assassinations have been moved to number one on the agenda. We will hear from the DCI first followed by FBI. Mr. Barkley, you have the floor."

The next fifteen minutes were spent recapping Intel, which supported Al Qaeda being the perpetrator of the latest terrorist activities.

Barkley concluded by saying, "There is no creditable source indicating our conclusion Al Qaeda is responsible for the most recent terrorist incidents is, or might be, invalid. We will continue to pursue sources at Guantanamo Bay and around the world. I will let my counterpart, Director Goode, update us on where their domestic investigation stands."

"What you appear to be saying is: You really have no more information or leads regarding the identity of or the location from where these terrorists are operating? Am I correct?" It was the President asking the question.

"No...no, Sir. At this point, the forensic information and investigation at the various sites have provided numerous leads. I'm confident it is just a matter of time. Perhaps Jerome can provide us an update on what FBI has learned."

"Director Goode, we would like to hear the latest from the Bureau. Please tell me your investigation is taking us somewhere—anywhere would be good at this point," President Roark said in an annoyed tone.

Goode, feeling his seat get several degrees warmer, opened the file in front of him and began his version of the Washington two-step.

"We have some very good forensic evidence being evaluated from the scene in Chicago. It appears the Missouri shooting has the same modus operandi presented in the other shootings and in our opinion is the work of highly trained snipers, possibly trained at Bin Laden's camps in Afghanistan before we drove him to ground. This appears to be part of a relative large sleeper cell, which has very likely been in the country for some time—probably before 911. It's reasonable to believe some of the leaders may have entered under a foreign exchange program—or on student visas.

"We believe the perpetrators have likely been recruited in our penal system from the growing number of conversions to the perverted radical Islam faith. As you are well aware, Mr. President, more than 80 percent of all prison conversions are to Islam and generally in its most radical form. We are pursuing all leads in both of these areas and agree with Director Goode: 'It's only a matter of time.'"

"I'm always concerned when that particular idiom is used in such a critical and sensitive situation as this. Precisely how would you recommend I convey the message 'only a matter of time,' to the latest victim's family in Missouri? During my press conference today, are you suggesting the media be told, it's 'only a matter of time?' Is this the best we have to offer a nation nearing a state of alarm?"

The President's voice rose very little but was dripping with sarcasm and left little doubt of his frustration with the progress—or lack thereof—of the investigation.

The room suddenly grew very quiet. FBI and CIA were being reprimanded in no uncertain terms. The message was clear; President Roark was running low on patience.

"*Director* Bridger, we understand you have looked through various investigative files and have reached some interesting conclusions regarding the perpetrators of these crimes, which may not agree with what we've heard. We are really putting you on the spot in your first meeting here, but we are quite anxious to hear your analysis of the situation."

Bridger took a small drink from the water glass in front of him. *Well, here we go again. Been in Washington less than 48 hours, and I'm already about to piss off a bunch of people. What the hell, this is a boil that badly needs lancing.*

In a confident voice, he began to detail his analysis of the investigation and the controversial conclusion it supported.

"Mr. President, there are several profile deviations which lead me to question whether this is the work of Al Qaeda."

There was a sudden burst of murmuring about the table ending when President Roark injected, "Please continue, Director Bridger. I'm most anxious to hear what you have to say."

Bridger took ten minutes to go through each point and ended by saying, "and finally, it is a question of risk and reward. Would Al Qaeda be likely to use deep sleepers—who have been in this country for several years—for this type of reward? Bin Laden has made it clear, his goal is to bring down the financial institutions of the West and has repeatedly stated his next attack will be even more devastating than 911. Bridger paused and the frontal attack began.

"Are you suggesting, based on the minuscule information you have presented, our investigation should change course and move in an entirely different direction? If yes—precisely what direction are you suggesting, Mr. Bridger?" It was Barkley and his tone was barely civil. There was blood in the water and the sharks could smell it.

"Sir, I'm suggesting a change in the investigation only in the sense we should let it lead us—rather than leading the investigation. The investigation thus far supports...."

Goode interrupted him before he could finish speaking. *It's turning into a tag team match here,* Bridger realized with cynical amusement.

"Mr. Bridger, it is entirely premature to consider altering the course of our investigation. The impact on the public confidence in and of itself is enough to make such a move precarious. I'm sure you realize the importance of the Bureau retaining public confidence and the vital role it plays in the fulfillment of our mandate to protect the public."

Another tag and here comes Barkley again. These two only listen because they think it is their turn to talk next.

"I'm confident when Mr. Bridger has the opportunity to view our latest assessments from our sources in Afghanistan and Pakistan, he will realize these acts have been carefully orchestrated by Al Qaeda to create panic in the public *and* indecision in the ranks of our intelligence community."

"I have a suggestion to make." It was General Malcolm Winter speaking and the room became quiet for a moment.

"I would like to propose giving Mr. Bridger more time to evaluate all the information we have available. In the meantime, *Ted*, our resources at DIA are available to assist in any way possible."

Goode and Barkley stared in surprised disbelief at Winter's apparent support of Bridger.

Winter returned the stare, waiting for both men to look away before he diverted his eyes.

Then it was Secretary Ramirez's turn.

"We are hearing a very good example of why I have suggested the organization of a new investigative team. Combining personnel from the five agencies may be both timely and necessary to create a spirit of cooperation. Allow me to commend you General Barkley—you are one example here today of what is desperately needed in these trying times."

"Please, Mr. Secretary…" Barkley tried to break in.

"Allow me to finish!" Ramirez paused for a moment before continuing.

"It is imperative everyone in this room, and all those we are responsible for directing, understand one thing *emphatically*! Our commitment is to winning this war against *terrorism*—and we will not *tolerate* an attitude of competition among agencies blocking the free flow of information or in any other way impeding our ability to be successful. Are we *clear* on the subject?"

"For the record, Ladies and Gentlemen," President Roark injected, "I want to second what my Secretary of Homeland Security has so succinctly stated. My tolerance is great, but my patience in this matter is being woefully tested.

"Ted, allow me to say again, welcome back to Washington. Please know, my office is behind your efforts with the new unit and we wish you good luck and Godspeed.

"Ladies and Gentlemen, please carry on without me."

The President rose quickly from his chair, and there were sounds of chairs pushing back as everyone scrambled to their feet. He moved briskly to Bridger extending his hand, "Ted, thanks again for coming here today. Gentlemen, Margaret, thank you for your input."

Secretary Ramirez and Bridger waited until the President exited the room before leaving through the same door they used to enter.

"Nice job, Ted. The President was impressed and you may have won us a new ally in General Winter. Margaret is tougher to read, but we'll see. We've plowed some rocky ground—but there's an abundance of "bullshit" available around Washington—now we plant and hope for good weather."

Laughter from both men echoed down the narrow hallway in the West Wing of the White House.

***

John Chambers' Cubicle
New York World
New York City, New York

"Thanks, Ted. I appreciate your consideration in giving me the word."

Hanging up the phone from Bridger's call, Chambers wasn't sure whether to be angry or pleased. No question, Bridger deceived him, but he certainly didn't have to make the call leaking the news of his new appointment.

It may save me some embarrassment with Gates, and it showed a mutual respect; probably should feel good about this. Homeland security...and what did he say? FIST, wasn't it? Right, FIST was the name of the new group. Did it mean he would be working on the Al Qaeda linked assassinations? Do I dare think of Bridger as a potential source of informed leaks? Probably not; his integrity would be an obstacle unless—unless it was mutually beneficial. On occasion, the intelligence community wants certain information "leaked" to the public to serve strategic purposes.

Chambers went directly to Gates' office to clue him on the latest development. He would probably want a follow-up story.

It had turned into a busy week. Gates explained Mustafa's new source had dropped a bomb—no quip intended—in only their second meeting. The new informant indicated Al Qaeda was gearing up for the detonation of a "dirty bomb" (radiological dispersion device) in a major city but was uncertain whether it would be in this country or elsewhere. No details were available and the validity of the information was highly uncertain at best, since no substantiated information had been received from Mustafa's source prior.

The conundrum for the paper was complex. The obligation to protect confidential informants was at the very core of a journalist's ability to obtain copy from sensitive areas. What were the implications of providing the facts to the authorities, who would certainly want to interrogate the informant? Reporters and editors previously went to jail on contempt of court charges rather than reveal their sources in high profile cases.

Then again, what were the implications if the paper failed to provide the information and it proved accurate with an ensuing disaster? It was a decision for the paper's policy review board and would be going before them this afternoon.

Chambers headed for Mustafa's cubicle. Gates assigned him the follow-up on Bridger as expected, which meant Mo would have to continue another day working the assassinations on his own.

"Hey, John. I've been looking for you; someone here for you to meet."

"John Chambers, this is Shaquille Abumotte. He is going to be working the night shift in our area as a custodial engineer. Shaq is a visiting student from Kuwait and attends NYU."

Standing in the glass enclosure of Mo's workspace, the young man looked very uncomfortable. Dark brown eyes and hair complemented the young Kuwaiti's coffee complexion; with his medium build and in his collarless shirt, tan wrinkled cotton pants and running shoes, he appeared every inch the typical college student.

"Hello, Shaq. Welcome. If there is anything I can do to make your time here more comfortable, let me know."

"Thank you, Mr. Chambers. Everyone has been most nice to me already, and Mr. Mustafa has helped very much. It is Shaquille's pleasure to meet you and now I must go. There is much to prepare before return for work tonight."

As he walked away, John wondered. *Could this be Mo's new source? If so, he wasted little time getting him employment. It's possible management wanted him here where they could evaluate and control him better in the event his information was legitimate.*

Chambers told Mo of the new assignment with Bridger.

"It should only take a day. I have plenty of background and only need to do some editing and get it to Gates. Can you hold the fort in the meantime?"

"No problem, my man—piece of cake. What do you think Bridger is going to be doing with Homeland Security? Are they trying to shut him up with a token position or is this legit?"

"Bridger would be a hard man to silence if he had something to say, and he certainly doesn't need a token position. I'm thinking this is something to do with Al Qaeda and terrorism. I'll keep you posted."

Chambers decided it might be a good time to reach Melanie. It was already Wednesday and she would be arriving on Friday if everything went according to plan. He sat down and reached for his cell, punched the speed dial and listened to it ring twice.

"Good morning, this is Melanie, may I help you?"

"You certainly may. Tell me everything has worked out, and I'll be seeing you on Friday in New York."

"Everything has worked out—mostly anyway. There is one thing; would you be angry...or hurt...if I didn't stay with your parents?" And she quickly went on before John could respond.

"When I spoke with Rebecca about my trip, she offered me the use of their suite at the Cottonwood Plaza Hotel in Manhattan. The Bridgers own the hotel and keep the top floor for personal use; Rebecca pointed out it would be more convenient for us to meet and also allow me easy access to the city during the day while you're working. John, if you think for one moment this might insult your parents...."

"Mel, my parents would love having you, but Rebecca is right; it would be far more convenient for both of us if you stayed at the hotel. We can plan to have dinner with my family and perhaps see them in the city."

"Are you sure, John? Are you absolutely okay with this," she asked and he heard the relief in her voice.

"Absolutely okay, Mel. What about airline information? Are you ready to give it to me?"

Scribbling the information on a note card, he felt the hair on his arms tingle. *My life is due for a pleasant change beginning at 4:50 pm Friday— when Miss Melanie Fitzgerald's flight touches down at La Guardia.*

***

CHAPTER 14

DHS Headquarters
Washington, DC

The ride back to Naval Security Station was not wasted. The Secretary clarified again how anxious he was for Bridger to get FIST operational. "Plan to meet this afternoon with Assistant Director, Terrance Rainwater. His instructions are to expedite all requests and to facilitate a speedy walk through the bureaucratic maize. Rainwater is with Information Analysis and Infrastructure Protection. FIST will serve under IAIP's umbrella and receive funding through his division.

"Anything else come to mind needing the authority of my office at this juncture?"

"I don't believe so, Mr. Secretary. Following a brief stopover in Springfield, my plans are to be in Denver with a skeleton staff on Monday. Will it be possible to have the necessary rudimentary communication equipment in place by then?"

"We are in crap up to our knees and we've called the plumber. You know all too well how Washington operates; throw enough money at a problem and it usually goes away. Ask for what you need and for now, we will take care of the details."

It was nearly 11 am when they arrived back at DHS headquarters, and Ted decided to spend some time on the phone before he got too busy with the assistant director in the afternoon.

Getting off the elevator on the fourth floor, Ted was met by Sarah White.

"Sarah, two requests to make if I may. Would it be possible to make a number of secure phone calls from somewhere private?"

"Absolutely. Follow me please."

Stopping at a room a short distance away, she inserted a key card; the door swung open revealing an area with walls covered in a sound proof material. There was a series of small cubicles with sound proof "bubbles" and various types of communication devices, ranging from computers to satellite phones. The bubbles could be lowered over the individual workstation completely securing all conversations from any outside listening devices.

Sarah escorted him to a table with conventional looking phones and provided him with code numbers to facilitate use. "I believe you indicated you have two requests—what would the second be?"

"The second would be for you to have dinner with me again this evening. We could make it earlier than last night; and if you are agreeable, perhaps have something brought to my suite. Food at the hotel was quite good last night, and we could relax and enjoy a quiet evening. What do you think?"

"Sounds very nice to me. How early are we talking about?"

"What if you came straight from work? It would save you having to go home in the traffic, and we would have longer to enjoy our meal."

"Sounds good, except I won't be able to freshen up after a long day."

"Perhaps we can think of something," Ted suggested with a smile.

She wasn't exactly sure what he meant, but his smile hinted of something beguiling.

"I'll plan to see you about 5:30."

Bridger sat down at the phone, pulled his Franklin Day Planner from his briefcase and looked up Bill Johnson's private number in Seattle. He'd used the Planner for years and was reluctant to change over to the modern electronic type. All things new are not necessarily better—and to him, this was a perfect example.

The phone rang twice, "FBI, Bill Johnson."

"Good morning, Bill; how's the weather in Seattle?"

"Probably a hell of a lot better than Washington. Word is, you brought some storm clouds with you."

Damn him, Bridger fumed, *he has one hell of a source working somewhere in DHS.*

Deciding to ignore the comment, Ted went ahead with the purpose of the call.

"I'm going to get straight to the point, Bill. How much do you know about what I'm up to? Are you aware of the new team?"

"I've heard some rumors but can't say I know precisely what you have going."

Bridger took the next several minutes outlining plans for FIST and what the function would be. Johnson interrupted only once, asking the extent of cooperation he anticipated.

"I believe I'll have support from the top, meaning from the Secretary of Homeland Security and the President. Have to admit, the various agencies may be another story; there could be some ambiguity on that front."

"Sounds like an idea with merit on the surface; and if anyone can pull it off, they've damn sure picked the right man. How can I help?"

"You may be sorry you asked. You can help by becoming my assistant director, Bill. Really can't offer much except a grade increase in pay to start with, a lot of hard work and the unlikelihood you would ever be welcome back to the FBI. Take some time to think it over and let me know when you've decided."

"Ted, since Gloria left (referring to his wife of thirty years who divorced him two years before), I've pretty much spent my time at the office. We're spinning our wheels more than ever, and what you're trying to do is part of what motivated both of us to join the FBI. I'm the same age you are, been thinking about retiring, and this could be my last opportunity to do something really worthwhile. Hell, they shoot old horses don't they? If you can use me, count me in."

"Terrific, Bill. Frankly, I wasn't looking forward to trying to pull this off without your help. I'll get the ball rolling this afternoon. How soon can you be in Denver? Oh by the way; Denver's our new headquarters."

"Denver sounds great. Need to break this to my ASAC—he's been a good one—then give the cat away and I'm good to go."

"I'm going to try and be in Denver next week but first plan to stop in Missouri and check this latest shooting on route. Any chance you can be in Denver next week?"

"Should be no problem. What can I do here in the meantime?"

"I'm going to have to get back to you on that one. On another subject, what can you tell me about Aaron Cohn?"

If Cohn is his source, maybe he'll give it away or tell me.

"Ted, he's an echo of how we were out of the academy. Optimistic and ready to save the world from itself—full speed ahead and damn the torpedoes. Bright, hard working, loyal, tough, all the standard clichés, but true in his case; he worked some complex cases for me and never let me down once.

"Speaking of bright, get this: His parents gave him $10,000 at his bar mitzvah, and he promptly invested it in the commodities market, buying and selling short, or some such thing. Involved a complex system where he bought convertible securities in selected companies as a hedge against losing money in the commodities. He once told me his parents were sure he was going to piss his money away and were not happy to say the least. They were wrong. He made over a million and a half before he left high school—and, Ted, he's made a lot more since."

Explains his wardrobe and the generous gratuities, Ted realized.

"Would you recommend him to be one of the ten agents we bring in from the Bureau?"

"Without reservation, Ted."

Damn high praise coming from, Johnson.

"Good to have you aboard, Bill. Let's keep this discussion between us Indians for now; and Bill, if you have anyone in the other four agencies to recommend, let me know. Talk to you soon."

Johnson would be indispensable in getting this entity off the ground. He was first and foremost a leader capable of quickly generating a spirit of cooperation and rewarding effort in subtle ways that usually brought about even greater accomplishments. It was a mystery to Ted why the Bureau did not recognize Bill's unique talents and advance him beyond his position of SAC. It was true he could be coarse at times (even vulgar in his frustrations with anything interfering with successful performance), but his initiative and accomplishments far outweighed any perceived shortcomings in his personality.

It occurred to him a discussion on the merits of bringing Shawn Harmison on board might have been good to discuss with Bill. But it could wait; *besides, he feels the same as I do about Shawn's skills. First, let's see what's going on with Shawn's "little medical problem,"* the illusive terminology offered during their last conversation to describe his growing alcohol dependence.

Harmison was serving the FBI in one of several field offices sometimes used for disciplinary transfers—Butte, Montana. Agents in serious disfavor (but not serious enough to warrant dismissal) were transferred to an area to keep them out of the "line of fire" until a decision could be reached on their future. These agents usually fell into two categories: Those who grossly violated procedure—and those with dependency problems.

Young agents on their way up the food chain were being given a graphic illustration: "This is what happens when you fail to follow strict Bureau procedures and policies—resulting in 'unsatisfactory performance.'"

In Bridger's mind the valid inference was "Hey, look at those poor bastards; it's what happens when you take some initiative and screw up." It never failed to amaze him: An agency recruits the "best of the best" in terms of intelligence, loyalty, desire and work ethic and then promptly sets out to make R.U.R.s of them. (Rossum's Universal Robots from Karel Capek's play: The robots were built to do routine manual work for more intelligent beings.) Through the years, he watched too many of the best and brightest leave intelligence agencies in frustration.

The second type being disciplined (those with dependency problems—usually alcohol, but increasingly prescription drugs) were being given time to get their acts together.

Harmison was on very thin ice and really provoked some people at the highest level. Probably the only thing saving him was his connection with a certain powerful U.S. Senator.

Senator Adam Newell was Chairman of the Intelligence Oversight Committee, which in addition to reporting to Congress on the various branches of intelligence agencies, also made recommendations on personnel to fill key positions within that community. Senator Newell happened to be Harmison's uncle on his mother's side and thus far had succeeded in keeping the Bureau from cutting off Shawn's head and claiming the Grizzlies in nearby Yellowstone Park had done it.

Bridger had never known anyone with Shawn's ability to create a paradigm to facilitate the identification of suspected criminal or terrorist groups. It proved to be both his *kismet* and his *nemesis*.

Shawn went out on a limb with Bridger in describing the potential for terrorist attacks in the U.S., even predicting probable targets would include financial institutions. Ignoring repeated warnings from higher-ups, expressing concerns about creating panic and needless alarm among the population, they spoke out in closed congressional committee hearings on the dangers Bin Laden and Al Qaeda represented. Much of their "secret testimony," was promptly leaked to the press and the proverbial "snowball started rolling. "

Bridger received a demeaning letter of reprimand and was summarily ordered to "cease and desist from making statements of an imprudent and reckless nature." It really frosted him; looking back, it probably affected him subconsciously more than he realized at the time and may have been the final straw with his ultimately deciding to retire.

On the other hand, Harmison took a different approach to his letter of censure.

He committed sin "numero uno"—he went public. His comments were seen all over the world; Bin Laden probably has copies in his scrapbook in some cave in Pakistan. It took Uncle Adam's power of persuasion and clout to keep his brilliant but inflammatory nephew from being fired. Why Shawn decided to remain and take the vindictiveness of being exiled is another question. Nevertheless, it was his exceptional talent Bridger hoped to harness for FIST.

Graduating from MIT with honors (doesn't everyone who graduates from MIT) in math and computer engineering and responsible for much of the FBI's early efforts in the area of computers—including their use by the Bureau in investigation of computer related crimes—his early career was on the fast track for success.

We need to see what can be done to get him back on that track. Punching in the numbers for the FBI in Butte, Bridger went through the receptionist to get Harmison on the phone.

"Shawn, is that you? Calling to be sure you hadn't fallen into the mine pit and got covered up." (Butte is the site of one of the largest open-air copper mining pits in the world.)

"Ted? Ted, where are you…in town somewhere?"

"Well, sorta in town. I'm in Washington."

"Washington? Seattle?"

"No…the other one farther east. You remember, the one where we made all those friends."

There was a short silence, while Shawn tried to decide whether or not Bridger was putting him on.

"Shawn, how is 'the small medical problem' coming? Do the doctors think you can beat it, or has it become unmanageable?"

Need some careful wording here, both because I want to hear how he responds and because we may not be the only people participating in this conversation. It's secure on this end, but there are no guarantees on his end.

"I'm glad to say the medical problem is history and the '*doctors*' have found a much less invasive way to handle my minor disorder."

"Great to hear it, Shawn. Is there any chance you would consider leaving your assignment in Butte? The last time we talked, I remember your telling me how much you enjoyed the working conditions and case loads."

Not waiting for an answer to his facetious question, Bridger briefly detailed the FIST configuration and its primary function.

"What do you think, Shawn; interested in joining us?"

"Are you offering me a position? Can you make it happen? I mean—do you have the juice to really get me the crap out of here?"

"I've been assured by the Homeland Secretary, who is assured by the President, we can pull anyone from the five agencies for a three-year period. This is to be a totally synergistic project."

If we're under audio surveillance, it will be good for everyone to hear the last bit about the President. It may save the approaching pissing match from getting us wet before we can put on our raincoats.

"How soon are you arranging transfer orders?"

"Secretary Ramirez wants a skeleton operation going ASAP. I'm planning to be in Denver next week. Suppose your case load is too delicate and complex for me to expect you any time soon."

"If you're serious, I can be ready to leave Butte in 24 hours."

"How about taking 48 hours and be in Denver on Monday? I'll have the necessary paper sent on the next stagecoach and get you on our roster by this time tomorrow. Shawn, you may be asked to start on a profile shortly after I arrive in Missouri and can get some information to you."

"Sounds great, Ted…thanks! I'm really looking forward to working with you again."

"You're welcome, Shawn, and be assured, that old saw cuts both ways."

The clock on the back wall showed noon. The calls had taken a full hour, but produced two very key people in making FIST capable of succeeding straight away. There was a sense of relief having them aboard.

Suddenly he felt a rolling sensation in his stomach and realized he was hungry. Cohn answered his phone on the first ring.

"Aaron, how soon before you can pick me up for lunch? Got a meeting scheduled for 1:30 and it doesn't leave much time."

"No problem, Mr. Bridger—I'm in the waiting room downstairs. Figured you might be hungry after a busy morning and decided to come back, just in case."

"Be right down."

Damn, this kid is special. Maybe it is time to offer him a position. Johnson is really high on him, and I've seen him in action for the past several days. He's really what we want in a young agent—energy, intelligence and ambition—still full of aspiration.

Lunch went quickly at the same small restaurant in Georgetown. Bridger spent a few minutes telling Cohn about FIST and the mandate from Homeland Security. It was an opportunity to feel him out and, at the same time, make a decision on whether to offer him one of the FBI slots.

The young agent listened attentively, asked a couple of questions, but made no further comments.

Hmm, is he interested, Bridger wondered. *Probably not and why assume he would be? Could it mean Cohn's on a fishing trip at Bureau expense?*

Director Goode was providing transportation services as a direct result of Ramirez's request. The Secretary felt it served two purposes: first, it was an opportunity for FBI to show cooperation; second, it would be more comfortable for Bridger to have someone from his old agency.

Still, could someone be trying to stay one jump ahead in knowing what his plans for FIST are and then...then what? Crap sakes, get a grip and don't let paranoia ruin an otherwise beautiful mind.

Paying the bill for both lunches and leaving the tip, Bridger felt some pangs of aggravation. *What the hell,* he concluded, *you can't really expect a smart young guy like this to take a career chance on something new and precarious like FIST. It was still annoying—and perhaps disappointing—for some reason he couldn't quite explain, he wanted Cohn with FIST.*

***

DHS Headquarters
Office—Assistant Director Terrance Rainwater

Assistant Director Terrance Rainwater was a well-paid and highly skilled paper pusher with no illusions about becoming anything more senior. After years of civil service, his skills in navigating the maze of paper generated by the bureaucracy (a rare ability considered priceless to department heads) had finally been recognized and he was awarded a title.

Rainwater looked slightly rumpled when he entered the office after lunch. Appearing to be in his mid-fifties, a full beard matched his peppered white hair, and his intense eyes shown from beneath shaggy eyebrows. Heavy jowls of soft pallid skin jiggled when he plopped down in a chair behind his desk; and adjusting a back cushion, he peered out over a small mountain of paper and asked, "Where do you want to start?"

A great question, thought Bridger.

"The Secretary is emphatic in his desire for us to develop a staff ASAP. Let's start with the first two individuals we would like to have in Denver by Monday and on our roster by the end of the day tomorrow."

"Tomorrow as in Friday and you are referring to this coming Monday—four days from now, I assume."

"Correct." Handing a personnel request form across Rainwater's desk, Bridger added, "I personally contacted both Johnson and Harmison, and they are receptive to their new assignments."

Rainwater grunted something under his breath while he fumbled with a pair of reading glasses hanging from a cord around his neck. Bridger could not be sure whether it was a derogatory epitaph partially choked off or Rainwater saying, *"This is going to be tough, but for you, I can do it."*

"Do you have any other personnel to expedite at this time?"

"Not at this time; probably have several more by tomorrow."

Rainwater must have pushed a call switch somewhere on his desk. A young aide appeared.

"Jason, please put a *Tsunami* Priority on this, and get it to personnel at FBI in the next hour. Advise the Bureau this is I-3AP, (Immediate Attention Appropriate Administrative Personnel). And, Jason, be sure to time stamp it."

The next three hours were spent painstakingly going over the infinite number of details essential to getting an operation of this type off the ground. Finally, Rainwater must have concluded they had resolved all he could handle for the time being and brought the meeting to an end.

"Mr. Bridger, let me meet with my junior staff on this for the rest of the day. There may be some unforeseen delays in implementing some of what we have discussed. However, I see no reason we can't have you at Denver Federal Center on Monday with at least some of your new staff."

Sometime during the course of the afternoon, Ted's opinion of Rainwater changed drastically. Stopping their conversation from time to time, he would summon an aide and issue direct orders in an efficient and professional manner designed to cut through red tape and expedite the process of getting the new entity operational.

Whatever his appearance may suggest, this man is highly competent and skilled at his vocation. When he said, "meet with my staff for the rest of the day," he meant until the job is finished—it's already 4:30 pm. What is it they say about a book and its cover?

***

The ride back to the Mayflower with Cohn was subdued. Neither man seemed anxious to talk, and they spent the fifteen-minute drive in silence.

Could I have misjudged this young man, wondered Bridger. *Haven't actually asked him to join the outfit and therefore can't be really sure what his answer might be. Maybe another call to Johnson—the two may have made contact since my visit with Bill earlier in the day.*

"Cohn, let's plan on 7:30 tomorrow morning. First, some business at Homeland Security and then over to Justice for credentials before going down to Quantico."

"Will you need me tonight, Sir?"

"No. I'm fine at the Mayflower for dinner and have some things to look at later tonight."

Turning onto Connecticut Avenue, Cohn worked his way into traffic and finally reaching US #1 (locally dubbed Jefferson Davis Highway*),* headed for Alexandria. *How strange is it having a road named after the Confederate President who seceded from the Union,* he mused expelling a deep breath. *It's been a frustrating week thus far, with little to show for my efforts other than a very sore butt from sitting around and waiting.*

Maybe I've come across incompetent, he speculated. *My attempts to impress Bridger with taking care of minutiae may have looked like the traits of a gopher, satisfied with driving someone around and taking care of his dry cleaning.*

Probably should talk to Bill Johnson. He always gives me good advice, and right now my morale could use a little kick-start. An besides, Johnson's responsible for getting me interested in FIST after he picked up on the scuttlebutt of a new enterprise being formed under his close friend. Damn, I only volunteered for chauffeur duty because my heart was set on working in this new department.

***

Bridger's Hotel Suite
Mayflower Hotel

Pouring some bourbon over ice, Ted turned on the television to hear the five o'clock news. Jack Snow, the same commentator he heard last night, was giving the same report with only a slightly different narrative: same song, second verse.

Using the remote to click through the multitude of channels and finding nothing on the assassinations, he finally stopped on a channel playing classical music. Sitting for a few moments enjoying the music and the excellent Wild Turkey Bourbon, his attention turned to FIST. Everything was moving rapidly, and it would be all too easy to forget something vital in his haste. Getting Harmison and Johnson on board would help, but he really needed an administrative assistant to organize the office and train people to deal with the volumes of information they were going to be generating and receiving.

What was going on with Connie Long? She was the best ever, and wasn't she getting ready to retire? Something in her annual Christmas card…?

Jotting a note in his day planner, a ring at the suite door interrupted him.

"Good evening, Sarah." He reached out with his hand to take her arm and drawing her gently inside, gave her a tender kiss.

"Uumh very nice, Ted. Bet you kiss all the women who ring your door bell," she said smiling.

"Right you are. Got a bedroom full of women waiting to be serviced by this old cowboy from Wyoming."

They both laughed. "Could I interest you in a bourbon with a splash of water."

Bridger moved to the small bar to pour the drink and returned, handing it to Sarah who was still standing. She took a long pull from the drink and surprised Ted a bit by saying, "I feel really grungy. Come on Ted, you're the man with ideas. What can we do to alleviate such a disgusting situation? Any especially devious…sensual ideas come to mind?"

"Just had an inspiration; follow me, the *rapscallion* said to the innocent *damsel.*"

Strolling into the large bathroom and pointing to the mammoth shower designed to accommodate the Dallas Cheerleaders, he continued. "Observe, my dear, this invention is guaranteed to clean all the grunge and at the same time restore energy and a sense of well being. Two white Mayflower robes hang in yonder closet; allow your humble servant to fetch one for your comfort."

Returning with the robes and fresh drinks, Ted was pleasantly surprised to see Sarah stepping into the shower. Her shapely naked behind appeared irresistibly visible inside the glass enclosure, while she paused to wrap a towel around her hair.

Bridger hesitated, unsure what his next move should be.

Looking over her shoulder with a beguiling smile she asked, "Are you coming?"

Quickly undressing and entering the shower, Ted came in close behind her. Hot water from multiple faucets stung his naked body on all sides. The inside of the shower, already filling with steam, distorted their vision and added to a fantasy like atmosphere.

Bending forward he kissed the back of her shoulder, and she moved slightly backward, arching her neck and pressing into his nakedness.

"This feels wonderful. I've been thinking about it all day…ummh. Would you mind soaping my back?"

Reaching for the large bar of soap, Ted began to rub it gently on her neck working his way down, taking a long time lathering her lower body.

Slowly he moved back to her neck and massaged soap over the front of her shoulders and slowly down, pausing at her magnificent breasts to prolong the pleasurable task of "removing the grunge."

He gently massaged with his soapy fingers, bringing a provocative moan from deep in her throat giving promise of things to come. Ted consciously allowed her anticipation to grow, and Sarah writhed with pleasure when he worked his hands across her trembling belly. Her desire became overwhelming, and she half turned toward him.

"Can we…do you want to make love now?

Ted hesitated trying to decide how best to convey his feelings.

"Sarah, it's been a while since I've been with a woman in *that* way; but they say it's like 'riding a bicycle,' don't they."

Drying each other with the large soft towels, he was aware of her gentle touch and felt her shiver of excitement when he lightly passed his hands over her full body.

Taking his hand, she led him into the bedroom where she lay on the bed, displaying her nakedness in a provocative pose, denying any pretense of shyness and inviting him to come to her.

Ted's arousal soon became complete, and they spent the evening "riding the bicycle,"—all around the world—happy to prove some old adages were indeed true!

***

CHAPTER 15

After the bike ride—
Bridger's Hotel Suite
Mayflower Hotel

B ridger had been sitting for over an hour at a desk in the Mayflower staring at the FIST table of organization. Trying to re-evaluate for the hundredth time the vast organizational table basic to getting the new unit into motion, he now sat barren of ideas. *Paralysis by analysis*: isn't that what they call it?

The ringing telephone interrupted his agitation. It was after midnight and his first concern was for something happening to Sarah on her way home. Earlier, he insisted on walking her downstairs and seeing her safely to her car; he realized some of his old dread emanating from Katherine's tragic accident was still very much alive in him.

But as he had requested, she already called and indicated her safe arrival at her apartment.

"Ted Bridger, what is it please?"

"Ted...that you? Have I interrupted something? You sound strange."

"Cripe sakes, Bill, it's after midnight. What couldn't wait until morning?"

"Were you asleep? Hell, Ted, it's only 9:30 here. Ranch life must have made you soft with all the 'early to bed' stuff. Want me to call back in the morning? Ten-thirty too early?"

"Very funny. You may recall there are a few time zones between us, but now I'm dying to hear what couldn't wait until morning."

"You talked to Cohn about FIST today...yesterday?" Bill asked.

"I gave him some of the particulars, but frankly, he seemed less than captivated. Bill, could this guy be working someone's agenda in the Bureau to gain insight into the project...perhaps with the intent of preventing it from getting off the ground?"

"No way man—this kid is straight. He really wants to work in the new unit. He called me earlier this evening and was down in the mouth you hadn't asked him. If you're concerned about his loyalty, I'll vouch for him in that regard— without qualification. Ted, he's exactly the kind of young self-starter we're going to need."

"Okay, okay, you've sold me. I'll bring the subject up again tomorrow morning. How about passing the word to your protégé to be a bit more enthusiastic this time, will you please? Anything else?

Oh, before you go…Bill, what would you think of Connie Long to run the office for us? I'm not sure she's available, but she did a great job for me; I know you've worked with her as well."

"Long runs a tight ship, knows communications inside out; she would be good if we can get her."

"Talk to you tomorrow, Bill."

"Right, Teddy. Turn on Mr. Hoover's night light and get some sleep, you hear."

"Good night—Billy."

Bill's right about needing some "self-starters," and Cohn has been impressive. In the morning, we'll see if he wants to jeopardize his career by joining FIST. *We may not be doing this kid any favors by bringing him onboard.*

***

Mayflower Hotel
The morning after

As the doors of the Mayflower elevator slowly slid open, Cohn approached Bridger carrying several newspapers under his arm.

"Good morning, Sir. You made the news this morning; assumed you might be interested in seeing what they have to say and picked up copies of the *New York World* and all the local papers."

So he knows about the New York World. Now I'm really curious about his source.

"Good morning. You can bring me up to date on the ride. By the way, you up for some firearms work today? Need to pick up my permanent credentials at Justice and then go down to Quantico for qualification. They have a new Sig Sauer 9mm waiting for me to try out."

"Yes, Sir. When are you scheduled to be at Quantico?"

"Anytime in the afternoon. The head instructor is an old friend, and he'll be there until late in the day. He's promised to keep me from shooting myself, and they're preparing to protect civilians in the area from stray bullets."

Damn, I've watched some of the older administrators around FBI-HQ insist on carrying a gun and continuing to attempt qualification long after their bodies are saying—no way. Why can't administrators be satisfied with letting those of us who can handle firearms do so, Cohn reasoned. Somehow it was surprising Bridger might fit the category; even the possibility was a little disappointing.

As Cohn briefed Bridger on the newspaper articles, it quickly became apparent they followed the official release from Homeland Security and were in the middle of the various papers with a few short paragraphs. The *New York World* was a bit more detailed, as might be expected, but didn't contain anything in the least controversial.

Bridger stopped reading and abruptly instructed Cohn to pull over, pointing a finger toward the renowned Washington Cathedral Church.

"The church parking lot will be fine."

Cohn pulled into a space in the nearly deserted parking area, and Bridger hesitated for a moment looking at the young agent hoping to discern something confirming his instincts. Long ago, he learned to trust his first impression about people, and throughout his long career, it usually served him well.

"Turn the engine off; we need to talk for a few minutes.

"Aaron, I'm searching for quality investigators who can work closely with people from other federal agencies as well as local authorities. They will be expected to conduct sensitive and complex investigations under close scrutiny by public and government officials. Bill Johnson tells me you fit the bill in every way. I've great confidence in his judgment and know his respect is not easily won.

"You should be aware, FIST will create some controversy and perhaps even animosity in certain circles. At the same time, if we are successful, there is a possibility serving on this unit can be a catapult toward career advancement. Want to hear more?"

"Please, Sir."

"We would like to offer you a position with FIST—which will begin almost immediately. It will mean a commitment for three years before returning to the Bureau. If you need time to consider before responding...."

"No, Sir, I've been hoping you would ask me, and I'm ready to give you my answer right now. I'm well aware of the potential controversy FIST brings to the table, but the concept has great merit and can fill an investigative breach. Thank you for your confidence, Sir; I'll give you my best effort."

I've liked everything about this young agent from the beginning and Bill's right; this kid's enthusiasm rubs off on everyone around him. It makes me wonder why I doubted him.

"Aaron, we look forward to having you with us. How soon can you be ready to leave Washington?"

"Sir, I understand you are trying to get FIST up and running as soon as possible. My roommate here will stay in our apartment, and I'll continue to pay my share of the rent until he finds a new roommate. I'm good to go as soon I get packed."

He's obviously been thinking about this and has everything worked out ahead of time.

"Good, I'm headed to Springfield, Missouri, en route to Denver and would like for you to accompany me. We'll be leaving Friday afternoon—as in tomorrow."

"No problem, Sir; I'll be ready."

"I'm going to make some VCFs (Virtual Case Files) on the investigation conducted thus far in Springfield available to you. Take some time this morning to look them over, and we can discuss what you find on the trip to Quantico."

I'm not going to influence him at all at this point. It will be interesting to hear his theory with regard to the alleged perpetrators.

***

Sarah White's Office
DHS Headquarters

Bridger was glad to see the two dozen long-stem red roses were on Sarah White's desk. *When was the last time I sent flowers to anyone other than to a relative—or perhaps a funeral? You know age is sneaking up on you when you realize you're attending more funerals than weddings.*

"The flowers are very nice, but the card's even better," Sarah said smiling They both chuckled at the private joke.

It required careful thought to write something she would understand and yet could be spoken over the phone to a florist and then pass through security to her office. After some reflection he wrote:

"Thanks for allowing me to view the entire body of your beautiful works. They were indeed a rare delight. I'm looking forward to a more thorough examination in the near future." Signed, L.T.

After parking the vehicle at Naval Security, Cohn caught up with Bridger on the fourth floor.

"Sarah, like for you to meet Special Agent Aaron Cohn. He's with the Bureau."

"Hello, Mr. Cohn. It's a pleasure to meet you."

"Aaron is coming with us in FIST, and I've asked him to spend the morning going over the Springfield assassination investigation. Would it be possible for you to find him a workspace?"

Hey, now it's Sarah and Ted. Wonder if that's why he's been acting so chipper every morning; maybe there is life after fifty. Ms. White's a pretty sexy looking woman for her age, a little too heavy for my taste, but a great looking chest.

"If you will wait here, Ted, I'll take Agent Cohn to a secure room."

A few moments later she returned and looking at Ted with a warm smile said, "Really enjoyed last evening. I was sorry to see it end, especially knowing there can't be many left."

"Are you free this evening? I'm going to be leaving Friday for Denver, and it will be our last evening for a while. We can have a nice dinner somewhere and take some time to talk."

"Sounds great, except for the part about you leaving. Let's say about 6:30. Meet you at the hotel?"

The next couple of hours Bridger spent on the phone contacting potential personnel. Connie Long proved surprisingly easy. She had retired, still lived in the District and was getting bored being home with nothing to do. The clincher came with Denver being headquarters; her only daughter lives in Colorado Springs, a short drive south on I-25 from Denver. Connie would be ready to start work in a week.

Laura Rice was not going to be so easy. Bridger wanted her to head forensics for FIST. An African-American in her early fifties, with a background in the New York Police Department, Bridger first met her during 911 and after observing her work firsthand, convinced her to become a part of the FBI forensic laboratory at Quantico. The new position meant a substantial increase in pay, but apparently did little for her already shaky marriage, suffering from two workaholics attempting to adjust to impossible schedules.

Laura had no children and was recently divorced, but another move with this new outfit would be something she would not likely embrace. For one thing, she was east coast—born on Long Island to lower upper-class parents and educated at NYU. Big city culture was part of her personality, and it was going to take a great sales effort to get her away.

After a few minutes on the phone explaining the new squad and what her responsibilities would entail, he was shocked to hear her interrupt his sales pitch and say, "Sounds like precisely what the doctor ordered: new faces, new scenery and new opportunities. How soon do you need me?"

***

Bridger spent the remainder of the morning endeavoring to assemble key personnel from the various agencies. He was surprised to discover how many people he contacted were aware of the new team. By lunch break, four more agents had agreed to three-year commitments with FIST.

Johnson called with recommendations for three individuals they had both previously conducted operations with: Candice Urick from CIA, Steve Woolcock at NSA and Pat Hawes with Secret Service.

Two hours later he called saying all three were "like sheep following a Judas goat to the slaughter." Laughing heartily at his own wit, Bridger sensed Johnson's nervous excitement over the new challenge they were facing. As far as he was concerned, there was no one in the world he would rather be facing it with than Bill Johnson.

After providing the names to Assistant Director Rainwater, Bridger went to check on Cohn and found him with several files marked "SCI" (Sensitive Compartmentalized Information) spread on the desktop, along with a legal pad that appeared to be full of notes.

"Anything significant jump out at you in any of those files?"

"Yes, Sir; actually there are several factors not appearing to fit our profile. Perhaps we need to look at the possibility, this isn't Al Qaeda."

"Really? The intelligence community seems certain Al Qaeda's responsible. How do you explain the phone calls?"

Cohn hesitated briefly, "Sir, I know the direction the investigation is going and hope you don't think I'm being impulsive, but there are several red flags raising questions."

"Such as?"

"Well, Sir, take the FBI Audio Lab reports from Chicago. The voice of the caller taking credit for the sniper killing is 'a male Caucasian voice with southern to mid-southern enunciation vocal characteristics indicating extensive time living in that general geographic area.'

"Thus far, the report analysis indicates the voice is 'most dependably conjectured as being a recruited supporter of the Al Qaeda movement, with an indefinite milieu in this country.'

"Sir, I'm not an expert on demographics, but when was the last time we identified a Caucasian domestic recruit to Al Qaeda with a southern background? For whatever reason, it's a geographic area that has not produced individuals who meet the profile. The area is mainly Christian conservatives who are unlikely to embrace the radical Muslim ideology, and anyone who did would be so unique as to attract attention."

"That all sounds interesting, but certainly not definitive enough to convince anyone to change their investigative emphasis."

"Probably not, Sir, but two other things are also very intriguing: The bullets used in the sniper attacks were Nosler 180 grain Spitzers that are used by re-loaders. Powder evidence from the wall in Chicago the shooter used to support his rifle provided an interesting signature. That powder residue was Aliant 15, also used for reloading and for our military sniper ammunition.

Going through newspaper accounts on all the assassinations prior to and including today, there is an interesting event corresponding with the sniper killing in Missouri that—and I may be reaching here, Sir—may be connected.

"Shall I continue?"

"Please do; you have my attention and curiosity fully aroused."

"Sir, there was a Missouri Highway Patrolman shot and killed the same day as the sniper incident. The patrolman made a routine stop for littering, with his radio call indicating it was approximately 18 minutes after the sniper shooting. The pick-up truck carrying the shooter bore a Mississippi license plate. There was a small package of methamphetamine found at the scene, and the locals are assuming the patrolman unknowingly stopped a couple of runners.

"After looking at the locations on a highway road atlas and determining the approximate distance from the sniper attack to the patrolman shooting, I took the liberty of calling NRO (National Reconnaissance Office) and getting a satellite printout showing precise distances. A vehicle taking the most direct route—maintaining the local speed limit from the sniper attack to the scene where the patrolman was killed—would arrive in 17-19 minutes."

Cohn sat silently waiting for Bridger to respond.

"I know it may be far out, Sir, but it may merit a closer look."

This kid may be everything Johnson said and more, Bridger realized. *He not only saw some of the same inconsistencies, but also added a couple I missed. He shows innate investigative instincts combined with a willingness to stick his neck out. It's understandable why Bill was willing to go so far in recommending him.*

"Your assessment of the situation agrees with mine in several aspects. Let me rush to add, I am in a very small minority with that view; possibly only two people have it—and both are in this room."

Cohn let out a deep breath. *Woo, I was beginning to wonder if I'd gone too far too fast. Johnson said the guy wants input, agreeing with his theories or not. But, experience has taught me some lessons on that subject. More often than not, "don't be afraid to express your opinion," really translates "so long as it agrees with mine."*

"The theory on the patrolman is something we will take a closer look at when we get to Springfield," Bridger added. "It may very well have merit in being related to the sniper incident, and if so raises even more questions about Al Qaeda involvement.

"Let's give the SSRA (Senior Supervisory Resident Agent) in the Springfield FBI office time to receive the official word launching FIST; we can contact him tomorrow morning by FIDS (FBI Intranet Dissemination Source) before we leave. They should be able to get everything we need to bring us up-to-date on the investigation with the patrolman.

"Nice work, Aaron. Only goes to show, 'even a blind hog finds an acorn once in awhile.'"

Ignoring Cohn's confused look and turning toward the door, Bridger added, "Come on; let's get something to eat and go down to Quantico to see if I can hit a paper target with one of those sissy 9mm autos."

***

Interstate Highway 395
State of Virginia

Following lunch and a trip to the Department of Justice to pick up new credentials, Cohn and Bridger drove south out of Washington on Interstate 395 through Arlington and Alexandria, picked up Interstate 95 and arrived at the gate to the legendary Quantico, Virginia Marine Base, earlier than anticipated.

The armed Marine guard looked briefly at Cohn's credentials (FBI credentials commonly presented to access the FBI Academy on base) and then took several moments examining Bridger's "squeaky new" DHS identification in its stiff new leather case.

September 11 changed everything, Bridger reflected. Time was, a sticker on the windshield would have allowed entry with a wave of the hand. *Will we ever see those days again—probably not in my lifetime.*

Quantico, long the training base for Marine officers, was also the sight of the massive FBI academy with modern new multi-story buildings replacing the quaint old two-story brick structure.

It also included an outdoor firing range and its famous Hogan's Alley, a simulated city street with storefronts containing windows and various targets popping unexpectedly into view. The trick was to avoid shooting the woman carrying groceries or the guy with a broomstick sweeping the walk and shoot the bad guy with the shotgun or the perp holding a gun to the head of a hostage.

The range contained various areas to train with the handgun, shotgun, automatic weapon including the MP-5 submachine gun, gas gun and long-range rifle such as the .308 caliber Remington.

Cohn maneuvered through heavy traffic of people and vehicles across the Marine base past the FBI Academy, finally coming to a stop in the parking area of the firing range. As the two made their way toward one of the covered patio-like areas used for demonstration and instruction, two instructors hailed Bridger.

"Hey, Ted, good to see you. Welcome back to the world," Mike Hunter said shaking hands.

"We've missed you. Mind saying hello to some of my newer people," Bob Vontoure asked taking Bridger's hand and giving it an enthusiastic pump.

"Hell, we've told so many lies about you down here, they think you're a figment of my imagination," he said laughing and motioning for several other instructors to come over to the area.

"Mike, Bob, this is Aaron Cohn. He's with the Bureau and is going to be serving with me in our new unit—FIST.

"Aaron, say hello to Mike Hunter and Bob Vontoure, the two best firearms instructors in the world."

"It's a pleasure, Gentlemen. I remember your lectures from the academy."

"Good to see you again, Aaron. Do you want to do some shooting along with the boss? We can set you up if you like, and you can count it qualification or not."

"Thanks. Qualified two weeks ago, so I'll observe and maybe mark targets today."

"With your boss shooting, that will be an easy chore," Hunter remarked casually.

Shit, I assumed we would probably be here all afternoon, and then "the old friend/instructor" would use a pencil to punch enough holes in the target to qualify him, Cohn, thought. *Now it looks like I'll probably he using that pencil before the day is over.*

If these guys have been telling stories about Bridger, he must be really bad. I'll never forget an ex-CIA guy in training school who couldn't even hit the target, and the Bureau wanted his expertise in a critical area unlikely to ever require use of a firearm. On the final day of qualifying, one of the instructors handed me a pencil and said, "You're going to be marking Flynn's target today. He needs to qualify and you will note this is a 9mm caliber pencil." Flynn was my roommate—he qualified.

Hunter turned to the growing assembly of firearms instructors and said, "Gentlemen, we're nearly finished for the day. But first, want you to meet Ted Bridger. You will recall, my mention of his unusual abilities with a firearm on occasion, and today you're going to have the opportunity to see it was no exaggeration. Bring the remaining class over and let them observe. They may be able to learn something."

Vontoure opened a small canvas bag and removed a P-26 Sig Sauer 9mm semi-automatic pistol, with a black adjustable swivel holster and two extra clips. (A German-made weapon used by both the FBI and several other government agencies including the Department of Homeland Security; it is the finest of the finest and carries a price tag to prove it.)

"Ted, we did some test firing and ended up doing a bit of fine tuning with the trigger pull and slide action. We think it is set up well for you, and we're anxious to see you give it a try."

Reaching for the new pistol, Bridger commented, "These things still look ugly to me compared to a nice Smith & Wesson Revolver; but I have to admit, this weapon has a good feel."

After working the slide to be sure it contained no live ammunition and hitting the release for the clip, he carefully examined the new firearm. Raising the weapon to a firing position, squeezing the double action trigger, the hammer made a clicking sound landing on the firing pin.

"Man, this action feels smooth, Bob. You guys have done a great job. Hell, I might be able to hit one of those paper targets today. Let's go give her a try."

The entourage had grown and now included a half dozen firearm instructors, followed closely by 50 new agents in training and a very confused Cohn, who was beginning to wonder what this was all about. The group continued down a narrow path covered with an artificial surface to within seven yards of the paper silhouette target shaped in the outline of a man's upper torso.

Bureau statistics determined long ago, the vast majority of gun battles involving handguns took place from a distance of seven yards or closer; hence a great emphasis was placed on drawing a weapon, identifying the target and firing quickly and accurately at that distance.

Bridger adjusted a set of hearing protectors over his ears, inserted a full fifteen-round clip into the firearm, worked the slide to put a round into the chamber, holstered the weapon and made sure everyone was ready.

This should be interesting, Cohn imagined, *but why would he allow everyone to watch him make a fool of himself? Unless....*

Drawing the weapon from the holster and firing the pistol from the hip in two-shot bursts, Bridger fired eight rounds into the target with each round all but hitting on top of the next. Every shot was in the center of the chest.

"Nice balance, Bob, and the trigger pull is right on the money," Bridger announced to the smiling instructors.

Bridger turned and moved back up the path to a wooden barrier used to simulate firing from behind cover. The distance to the target was now 25 yards.

He inserted a new clip, grasped the Sig Sauer in a conventional two-hand combat grip and moving to the right side of the barrier, fired four quick rounds in two-shot bursts at the target. Switching the weapon to the left hand, he moved swiftly to the left side and fired four more rounds in the same two-shot bursts. Carefully letting the hammer down, he holstered the weapon and started forward to check the target. A mumbling group, beginning to appreciate what they were seeing, followed him.

Eight shots were in the area of the heart and could all be covered by a silver dollar; eight were in the head and looked like two eyes and a nose, with another five forming a smile.

There was an assortment of comments ranging from "that's great shooting." To Aaron Cohn's *holy shit,* followed by nervous laughter that accompanies seeing someone perform a task you know you will never duplicate.

Vontoure and Hunter stood smiling like proud parents at a little league game. It was the look of "see, we told you so," and "that's our boy," all rolled into one.

"Ted, you care to do some clay target shooting today? The range is wide open."

"Sounds like fun to me; let's take a crack at some birds."

On the way to the shotgun range, one of the new instructors asked Mike if he wanted him to get a shotgun from the lockers.

"Not necessary, Rance; we have everything we need, except the bird launchers have left for the day. How about a couple of you guys handle that for us?"

Cohn heard Mike indicate they would not need shotguns. *You've got to be kidding me. No one shoots skeet with a pistol!*

Arriving at the area used for launching clay targets, for shotgun practice, Hunter announced, "We're ready when you are."

Bridger loaded a clip into the new handgun, took a moment to adjust his stance and letting out a deep breath called, "Pull." The first five-inch round disk came flying out across the Quantico sky and Bridger calmly raised the pistol and fired a shot breaking the clay target in mid-air.

A second and third call for "pull," produced the same results; and finally moving to the doubles section of the skeet range, he asked for two targets at the same time. Once again both targets were broken.

Turning to Hunter, Bridger holstered the weapon and offered his hand. "Mike, you guys did a great job with this weapon. It's a fine piece and I'm going to be proud to carry it. Thank you."

The assembly of expert marksmen and trainees, fully appreciating what they witnessed, broke out in a round of applause. Aaron Cohn closed his gaping mouth and followed the group back to the shade of the patio.

Awesome! Johnson told me this guy was something else, but I imagined he was referring to investigative expertise and administrative skills. He's the real deal.

Before leaving, Bridger invited the firearms instructors to be his guests at the *Globe and Laurel Bar* outside the front gate of Quantico. It served the coldest beer on tap in the area, a first-class sandwich—and had a long history as a hangout for FBI and Marine personnel.

"This place holds a lot of memories," Bridger remarked looking around the old bar. "A lot of good men have sat here having a beer and enjoying good comrades—and too many left here to be killed defending their country in some far away action." Holding up a mug of cold beer he continued, "Here's to fallen comrades; may they rest in peace."

"Here! Here!" came the instant reply.

Cohn enjoyed hearing the "war stories" being recanted from years of experience and couldn't help wondering: *What stories will I have to tell in 20 years?*

Everyone had a couple of rounds, with their sandwiches, except for Aaron who Bridger pointed out "still has to get us home. Secretary Ramirez probably wouldn't be very pleased with either of us if we used our one phone call to ask him to retrieve us from a Virginia County Jail."

***

Dulles International Airport
Friday afternoon
Aboard Air America Flight 7226

Exhausted and glad to finally be sitting in the first-class section of the American Airline Boeing 757, Bridger exhaled slowly and began recalling a day filled with last-minute details. Some had been essential to the task at hand; most were more mundane, such as getting packed and out of the Mayflower Hotel to the airport.

Aaron had once again risen to the occasion, as Bridger discovered when he returned to his hotel room expecting to spend the next half hour packing and found everything already in suitcases sitting at the door. (He would be surprised on arrival in Springfield to see everything had been laundered and freshly dry cleaned before being packed.)

In addition, Aaron checked him out of the hotel and arranged for Ron Strait from FBI transportation to take them to the airport.

Since both men were carrying firearms, airport security escorted them to their scheduled flight ahead of other passengers. Bridger quietly handed his credit card to a member of the flight crew and asked them to upgrade Cohn's seat to first class. Not that the young agent couldn't afford it on his own, but he probably would be reluctant to upgrade, being concerned how it would look to Bridger.

Bridger pushed a button to lean back in the oversize plush seat and stole a quick look at the young agent in the seat beside him. Aaron was going over the latest personnel added to FIST from the various agencies.

He'll know everyone by name, organization and specialty before this flight is over. It will make him more effective in being able to function in the new unit. Many (probably most young agents) would be relaxing, having a drink and enjoying the first-class accommodations.

Accepting a bourbon and water from the flight attendant, Bridger took a long pull and felt his body relaxing as thoughts turned to last evening.

It was late when they got back to the Mayflower from Quantico, leaving scarcely enough time to shower and prepare to meet Sarah White for dinner. Until last night, time spent with Sarah had been pretty much one dimensional— purely physical. He looked forward to getting to know her better. She was a bright articulate woman with a lot to offer, besides the sexual attraction they obviously shared for each other.

The evening began with an outstanding meal at Union Station, followed by drinks and dancing at a small club in Georgetown, recommended by a friend of Sarah's.

It culminated with a kiss at the door of Sarah's apartment after both agreed it was late and Friday was going to be a busy day. Was it really the busy day, or had the two nights of ardor fulfilled both their needs for the present, leaving both to assume this marked the end of a brief fling.

Wonder when I'll see her again? She has a lot to offer a man, and it might be nice getting to know her better.

Strange, any contemplation of intimacy with a woman still created feelings of guilt. Physical relations somehow did not give him the same undertones of disrespecting Katherine's memory and his love for her. Would he ever be able to love again? He had serious doubts.

"Aaron, did we receive any response from the SSRA in Springfield regarding transportation?"

"Yes, Sir. I spoke with the ASRA (Assistant Senior Resident Agent) by telephone. They will meet our flight and provide us a driver or vehicle, whichever we request; and we're booked into a downtown hotel the ASRA recommended."

"Good. With our change in flights at St. Louis, we'll arrive too late to be fooling with rental cars and hotels. Anything in the FIDS regarding the highway patrolman shooting?"

"Nothing. There might possibly be some reluctance on the part of the resident agency to look at the two as being connected."

"Reluctance? In what way reluctant? As in won't provide us information—or some evidence which leads them to that conclusion."

"I would say it's more an indication of their apathy in believing Al Qaeda would have any reason to kill a highway patrolman on a routine stop."

"Aaron, that is exactly the type of horseshit thinking that gets us into trouble with an investigation! It's imperative we look at all possible scenarios, regardless of how unlikely they may be."

"Please turn off all electronic devices including cell phones and lap top computers until further notice," came the announcement over the airplane's intercom, interrupting their conversation.

"Damn," Bridger retorted, "I need to make a quick call."

Reaching for the airline telephone in the seatback in front of him, Bridger asked Aaron for names and numbers for the RA in Springfield. He calculated the time as just after 5 pm in Missouri.

"You sent the FIDS asking for the reports on the patrolman shooting this morning—correct?"

"Yes, Sir."

Punching in the numbers, Bridger waited as the phone rang several times finally answered by a male voice.

"FBI, may I help you?"

"This is Ted Bridger with Homeland Security; is Sterling available?"

"One moment, Sir. I'll transfer you."

"Sterling, how may I help you Mr. Bridger?"

"We are currently leaving Washington International and our schedule puts us in Springfield at 9:07. Understand you will provide us with a driver and transportation while we're in your area; and since our expected stay will be limited, I would like for you to provide some updated information. I'm requesting anything and everything relevant to the local investigation of the highway patrolman shooting for our review this evening."

"Sir...I'm not sure we can access that information at this late hour. Our local liaison is probably gone for the day, but we can have it for you first thing tomorrow."

Aaron is correct, there is some resistance here; this is probably as good a time as any to grease the skids.

"Sterling, 'that dog won't hunt'! You received our request this morning on FIDS. Get on the damn phone; even better, go down in person and make whatever contact is necessary to acquire all pertinent information on this investigation. Supplement the results with any information you have on the event, and have it at the airport when we arrive.

"And Sterling, don't hesitate to contact your SAC in Kansas City if you feel it necessary to validate my authority in this matter. However, allow me to recommend you not waste too much time; you have less than four hours."

Bridger hung up without waiting for a response. *I'll be damned if I'll live with this stonewalling. It's a good time to send a message; in federal agencies the word tends to travel swiftly through the ranks.*

"Aaron, make a note to contact Steve Woolcock with NSA and ask him to check for suspicious traffic on cell phone auditory records from the time of the shooting of the patrolman. Give him a timeline as accurate as possible.

"Let's provide Laura Rice with whatever forensic information is available and see if there is anything at either crime scene she needs to review or examine in more detail. Provide the graphics of both crime scenes to her and let's see what feedback she can give us.

"Finally, as quickly as it can be compiled, provide Shawn Harmison a complete update of our findings here, to go along with the information from each of the other assassinations. Please do what you can to assemble this hodgepodge of information into something coherent for him."

"Sir, what format will we be using for reports and communications?"

"New personnel will continue the same formats used in the specific agency they are coming from. It will avoid confusion and help us avoid extra training time. As FIST develops, we may decide on some internal formats that work best for us; any feedback in that regard will be welcome.

"Disseminate information wherever necessary, and error on the side of too much rather than too little. A vast majority of information given SECRET or TOP SECRET status through the years has been information readily available to anyone knowing where to search for it and didn't contain materials sensitive enough to be considered worthy of protection. More often than not, it served as a barrier to those who had legitimate need of what was so carefully being kept from them and hindered investigations, or needlessly complicated them."

A soft bell sounded signifying it was okay to move around in the cabin; Aaron immediately got out of his seat and retrieved his laptop from the overhead bin and sitting down began to look at some notes before beginning to type rapidly into the laptop.

I hate putting the heavy paperwork on Aaron so soon, but it will give me the opportunity to determine if he writes as well as he investigates. All too often, the two do not go together; and the result of an outstanding investigation is wasted due to lack of reporting and dissemination. Few people outside the world of intelligence (and too many within) understand the importance of the fundamental skills of the work we're doing.

***

CHAPTER 16

Offices—*New York World*
New York City, New York

M
ustafa looked distressed as he flopped down in the single visitor's chair in Chambers' bullpen.

"What's up, Mo? You look like your hamster died. You okay?"

"You got a minute, JC? Gates gave me the decision of the paper's policy board regarding the details my informant provided. They've decided to wait until the source has afforded confirmed information—get this—on more than one occasion before considering him reliable. It means they've elected not to provide the alleged dirty bomb threat to the authorities."

"Does that surprise you? That's pretty much SOP before paying an informant. Probably follows they would make the same decision with regard to dissemination," Chambers replied.

"I understand the policy in the case of money...but this could be a catastrophe in the making. Man—we're talking serious consequences here. This may well be considered actionable intelligence. If my informant's info proves accurate, this could be another 911 or worse!"

"What does Gates want you to do?"

"Gates wants me to squeeze my source hard for more specifics, including the obvious—where and when this is to happen. He's also suggesting I get involved with the mosque where my source is getting information. Crapola, JC, I'm a Christian, what do I know about Islam?"

"What's your gut telling you? You believe your source—is he hitting you for cash—or is his motivation more related to proving himself to you and his new country? I don't have to tell you, a lot of Kuwaitis still feel a strong debt of gratitude for *Desert Storm*."

"I'm struggling with that question. He really hasn't asked for payola directly; his parents have plenty but still want him to make his own way to some extent. Perhaps I can use a potential payday as leverage to encourage him to get me some verifiable information on the bomb.

"I'm going see him again today. Maybe I'll work that angle. Anything new on the assassinations?"

"Nothing we haven't discussed. We have a stringer working in Springfield, Missouri, who is meeting later today with our people already on the scene. (Larger newspapers often employ beginning journalists dubbed stringers to feed them information from areas not normally covered by full-time employees.) Apparently, the stringer has inside contacts with local authorities and may provide some useful information. Anything comes out of the meeting, I'll let you know."

Mo shrugged, still looking down at the floor in deliberation and then suddenly exclaimed with a freshly found enthusiasm in his voice, "Boston's in town tomorrow, JC. You interested? Hell, we could both use some time away from these glass cages."

"Next time, Mo. I've got some company flying in tomorrow, and I'm going to be tied up for the week-end."

"Company? Hey Dude, waz happenin? Relative company? *Female* company? Not to be pushy or anything…school me, man. You got a girl coming? Tell ol' Mo you have. Crap, I've been worried you were going to start hitting on *me*."

"If you promise to act civilized, perhaps you may be allowed to meet this lovely creature coming to the 'Big Apple' for the first time.

"So, this *is* a person of the female persuasion. When do I get to see her?"

"Soon, Mo. You will have to provide me with evidence between now and then that you have honorable intentions, are pure of heart and clean of spirit. Now get out of here so I can get some work done. And, Mo…be careful with Gates' idea of getting involved in that radical mosque. I wouldn't want to lose my only source for Giants tickets."

As Mustafa chuckled and walked away, Chambers couldn't help thinking about his last statement made only partly in jest: *It could be more than a little dangerous for anyone to get close to a group with the grisly nature of some of the radical elements of any cult, and what else could you call the perverted forms of Islam?*

***

Aboard Air America Flight 7226
Somewhere over Missouri

We will be landing at Springfield-Branson Airport in a few minutes," came the familiar announcement from the flight attendant. "Please check to be certain your seat belts are securely fastened and return all tray tables to the fixed and upright position."

I believe most of what Mr. Bridger wants disseminated is ready for communication, Aaron reasoned. *The file numbers and agency of origin will be in my report and available on SCION, (Sensitive Compartmentalized Information Operational Network) with whatever we develop here in Springfield as an attachment.*

Johnson's description of Bridger is proving accurate in every sense. He really cuts to the chase, and you get the feeling he's going to ask for your best and doesn't want to hear excuses; at the same time, I'm already sensing his appreciation of a job well done. This is shaping up as the type of work I came into the Bureau to perform, and working under Johnson and Bridger is going to be awesome.

"Sir, I have maps of the area for 2,500 square miles from NRO (National Reconnaissance Office operates satellites capable of providing photos of a given area), and I have a GPS unit to get coordinates from any evidence we discover at the scene. It could be helpful in getting the *signet* (signal intelligence) from the NSA satellites and also to help Harmison with an accurate delineation of both crime scenes."

"Good idea. Harmison is the best I've ever known at depicting accurate profiles with minimal information; the more we can give him, the better.

"It's nearly 9 o'clock and when we land, I'm up for a light snack before hitting the sack. How about the two of us grabbing a bite and going over the information Sterling has so feverishly prepared for us? It will save us both time in analyzing what we find and determining tomorrow's agenda."

"Sounds good to me, Sir. I'm more than a little anxious to see what the investigation is producing."

What did Bill Johnson say about him? "He's an echo of how we used to be." Perhaps that's the real reason I'm enjoying this young guy...narcissism...maybe even a little déjà vu. Whatever, I like this kid.

Exiting the commuter plane and stepping onto the still warm tarmac, Bridger and Cohn walked through the entrance to the small but modern airport over which hung a large sign proclaiming—WELCOME TO SPRINGFIELD-BRANSON AIRPORT.

They were immediately met by a neatly dressed, trim-built man in his early forties.

"Welcome to Springfield—I'm Henry Sterling."

"Good evening, Sterling. I'm Ted Bridger…this is Special Agent Aaron Cohn."

"Evening Cohn. Gentlemen, our car is immediately in front of the baggage area. When you've claimed your luggage, we're good to go."

The next 20 minutes were spent waiting for luggage, and it was approaching 9:30 pm when they finally saw the round carrousel lunge into motion.

Interesting, the difference in thinking between Sterling and Cohn on the luggage, Bridger considered. *One seizes the opportunity to make a first impression; the other plows straight ahead, his only goal to keep the rows looking tidy with the least amount of effort.*

Two BuCars (Bureau cars) were waiting at the front of the airport; a young woman exited one of the vehicles and stepped around to open the trunk lid.

"Gentlemen, meet Special Agent Karen Blackwell. Karen, this is Mr. Bridger and Agent Cohn," Sterling said.

Karen appeared to be in her late twenties, with short black hair, dark intelligent eyes peering through minimal make-up and a very tan face; a quick smile showed even white teeth. She appeared very fit—probably an avid runner from the look of her trim body, which was accentuated by her slacks and matching blazer.

"Blackwell is in her second office here in Springfield and is assigned to act as liaison during your stay. As requested, she has the latest reports on the murder of the Missouri Highway Patrolman and will provide those to you.

"We have space in our office for you to utilize while you are here, and our communication network is available as required. Is there anything else this evening?"

"That will be sufficient for now, Sterling. Thank you for your assistance in expediting the information requested; we will plan to see you at some point tomorrow."

"Tomorrow…sure okay…tomorrow. Blackwell has my numbers."

Turning on his heel, Sterling walked briskly toward the second BuCar, got in and sped off around a sharp curve in the airport drive disappearing from view.

Sterling's reference to Karen being in her 'second office' indicated this was the second office she had been assigned after entering the Bureau. Typically, the first office lasts about one year (a year of probation), and so she was still relatively new in terms of experience and in Sterling's mind, not key to the success of his day-to-day operation.

We've got a "five and five" guy here (five days a week until five o'clock), Bridger surmised. *My planning to see him tomorrow means he probably has to cancel a Saturday golf date. He's been in a small "fiefdom" too long, and now his comfort zone is being challenged by the demands of an agency changing before his very eyes. A few more days like today, and those I envision ahead of him, and he'll shape up or exit the Bureau for a nice private security gig.*

"Gentlemen, it looks like I'm your chauffeur; where do you want to go first?"

"Agent Blackwell, you've had a long day, and I'm sure you're ready for some rest. If you could drop us at our hotel, Aaron and I want to get a bite to eat and look over the report."

So the good-looking guy is Aaron. That ass-hole Sterling thinks he stuck me with yet another menial task. This may not be half bad after all. I could be of help in this investigation if they'll give me a chance. The older guy is probably hardcore Bureau chauvinist 'as in women don't belong in this dangerous work,' but maybe Cohn will cut me some slack.

"Mr. Bridger, I'm familiar with the Patrolman Burroughs' case. The "hate crime" investigation of Prosecuting Attorney Waters has been priority number one, and I was assigned to follow the patrolman investigation." *Damn, he may assume that to mean in the RA I'm considered the proverbial "third tit," and write me off without a chance.*

"If it would help, it would be my pleasure to assist you in looking over the report. If you don't mind my being candid, there is quite a bit of *fluff;* perhaps I could assist in getting you to the substance," Blackwell offered.

"I never turn down an offer of help. Are you up for something to eat at this late hour? The food on the plane was sadly lacking and I'm ready for some breakfast. Sound good to anyone?"

"Sounds right to me," Aaron injected.

"I know a little place near your hotel that stays open all night," Blackwell suggested. "We can have some privacy and get the best breakfast in town at the same time. It's not very fancy, understand...."

"Fancy's not a prerequisite. Good food and privacy fits the bill—let's go for it, Agent Blackwell. By the way, do you mind if we call you Karen?"

"Not at all, Sir—Karen is fine."

"Good. This is Aaron and I'm, Mr. Bridger," he said with a chuckle.

The two young agents looked across at each other; Cohn's laugh came easily with Blackwell managing a tight smile.

Blackwell moved smoothly out of the Springfield-Branson Airport and a short distance later pulled onto I-44 East. After a few miles on the interstate, she turned south on Kansas Expressway heading downtown.

"I-44 borders the city on the north and National Highway 60 borders it on the south. State Highway 65—the road on which Patrolman Burroughs was killed—runs north and south crossing both major highways. The perps had easy ingress and egress in multiple directions."

Stopping in front of a small restaurant in an older section of town, an ancient neon sign blinked *Jennie's Café* and under it another smaller sign proclaimed, OPE....24 ho....rs.

Blackwell pulled into a parking space and looking over the seat at Bridger sitting in the back said, "Sir, told you it wasn't fancy. We can go somewhere else."

"Looks like they probably have some fresh road kill to me; let's go get it 'before they throw it out,'" Bridger said, halfway out the car.

Bridger led the way into the antiquated café and was met by an array of appetizing smells. Whatever was being served here was being made here. The aroma of fresh baked bread combined with an appealing scene of pies freshly out of the oven cooling on wooden shelves, preparing to meet eager appetites of a new day.

"My sense of smell says you did *good*, Karen. I like this place already," Bridger added approvingly, eliciting a pleased smile and slight softening of the penetrating look in her dark brown eyes.

They selected a table near the back offering a degree of privacy and sat down, pulling the plastic covered menus from between the napkin and sugar dispenser. A tired and very plump waitress approached the table with coffee and after filling three cups, took their food orders. Repeating each order once but not writing anything down, she walked toward the kitchen and left the agents wondering how she would keep the orders straight.

Bridger looked across the table at Blackwell, already opening the first of several files and suggested, "Karen, why not give us a quick overview of what you feel are key elements of this case thus far."

Agent Blackwell cleared her throat and began, "The sniper attack fits the profile for all the attacks across the country that have been accredited to Al Qaeda. Although, I understand…uh, from the grapevine, you may not agree they are responsible for the attacks.

There was a brief silence while she awaited a reply, and when none came she continued. "The consensus by locals is Burroughs probably made a stop believing he had a routine littering and surprised two meth runners. (Methamphetamine: Illegal drugs for which Missouri leads the nation in production. Highly lucrative, due to the inexpensive cost of producing, the drug is extremely addictive and has replaced opiates as the world's #1 drug problem.)

"Sir, may I ask a question?"

"Fire away."

"Does your interest in the Burroughs' homicide indicate you believe his killing is related to the sniper incident at the courthouse?"

The grapevine my ass, this is cyber travel, Bridger concluded. *DHS, FBI, or both? How far would someone go to prevent FIST from being successful?*

"Karen," Bridger began, carefully selecting his words, "we don't really know for certain, whether the two incidents are connected. Aaron has looked carefully at some elements of the incident that suggests it is a possibility. We are not here to prove a theory one way or the other; we are here to look at the evidence and let it lead our investigation in whatever direction it dictates.

"What can you tell us about the evidence collected at the scene; anything remarkable?"

"Sir, there was a good tire track in the gravel, but no other physical evidence has been recovered. There were more than a dozen different people passing in vehicles who witnessed various parts of the crime being committed. Highway 65 is a four-lane; the media has asked for any witnesses who have not done so to contact local law enforcement.

"As usual, descriptions of the shooters vary so widely as to be more or less useless. The only consensus is number, sex and race." (Witnesses at violent crime scenes are notoriously unreliable with descriptions of perpetrators often giving wide ranging accounts of weapons, hair color, age and particularly height and weight.)

Blackwell reached into her jacket pocket producing a notebook and began turning pages. "The composite description is of two WMs (white males) with further descriptions of the driver being too vague to be of value. The shooter is described as a WM, husky build, light or graying hair, mid-thirties to early fifties, wearing a long-sleeve shirt buttoned to the collar and matching gray slacks."

"What do we have on the vehicle?" Aaron asked.

"Witnesses agree on the vehicle being a pick-up truck. We have the patrolman's radio call, indicating his stop of a 'red Dodge three-quarter-ton, with Mississippi license BOL-132.' The license was reported stolen from Tupelo, Mississippi, the day before the shooting, but was not yet entered at NCIC on the day of the shooting. (National Crime Information Center is a nationwide computer center for reporting and tracking stolen merchandise.)

"The patrol cars usually have a video camera in use, but Burroughs' camera was being repaired. Evidence from the medical examiner and eyewitness reports indicate Burroughs approached the truck and was shot in the lower abdomen. A shooter then stood over the downed trooper and shot him once in the head—with a .357 Magnum."

The last bit of information caught Ted and Aaron by surprise causing both to look up quickly.

"That's cold. Damn cold. Son-of-a-bitch! We've got to catch those crazy bastards—and '*sooner* rather than *later.*'" No one spoke for several seconds after Bridger's intimidating outburst. Finally, he continued with an apology, "Excuse my language, people. It's been a long day and I'm starting to get a little frayed around the edges.

"One of my best friends in Wyoming is a Captain in the patrol. These highway patrolmen are salt of the earth and put their lives in jeopardy every time they walk up to a stopped vehicle. They're on the front line for us, and we have to give them all the support we can in finding Burroughs' killers.

"You're doing great, Karen—what else do you have?"

"I'm afraid that's about it. No vehicle recovery yet. There are APBs out in all the surrounding states; and as you can imagine, the Missouri Highway Patrol is working overtime to locate the pick-up. They could have dumped it anywhere—a lot of ground to cover with so many states adjoining Missouri."

The waitress returned with the breakfast orders, accurately placing each in front of the correct person before pouring everyone a fresh cup of coffee. Sitting the coffee pot down on the table she said, "I'll leave this with ya all *and* save a few steps. Get'cha anything else? tabasco? ketchup?"

"No thank you. This looks fine."

Aaron wasted little time attacking his meal of steak and eggs over easy, hash browns and something yellowish-white and looking like cottage cheese.

"That's *grits*," Karen explained. It's made from hominy, a favorite southern dish. Like Crocodile Dundee said, 'you can live on it, but it tastes like shit.'"

Bridger looked up from his plate of biscuits and gravy long enough to show his amusement with the comment and then after a moment of reflection began to speak. "I remember working the Patty Hearst case in San Francisco; there was great emphasis following the kidnapping on finding her car. Because of the high profile associated with being the daughter of the newspaper-publishing magnate, there was a lot of wheel spinning. The call went out in every direction; the search went north as far as Canada and south to Mexico.

"Realizing this happened in the early 70s—when the two of you were still a glass of wine and an *erotic experience* away from life—anyone care to guess where the car was eventually located?"

"No?…Not even a guess? How about: hiding in plain sight, in the Federal Building parking garage. Agents were driving past it every day coming to work. Embarrassed the hell out of everybody. Media had a field day…but, it taught all of us some valuable lessons as well."

"Point being, we should focus our search on an obvious drop sight?" Aaron inquired.

"It would seem likely the shooters realized they were observed by people driving by in addition to the patrolman's call-in." Bridger continued, "They would, therefore, get rid of the pick-up and, I might add, any other evidence as quickly as possible."

"Of course," Karen began. "The .357 is probably out there somewhere close by as well. The local forensic team searched the immediate area, but it's doubtful they looked far beyond the crime scene. They are assuming this was a murder related to methamphetamine, and drug dealers might take the firearm with them."

"Probably a reasonable deduction, Karen. Let's plan to get an early start tomorrow and visit both crime scenes. In the meantime, how about we finish this delicious breakfast and get some rest," Bridger offered.

Bridger may not be so bad after all. It was enjoyable watching him look—quite literally—down at Sterling and dismiss him for the evening. I might even get to do some investigating if I play my cards right, Karen predicted.

***

University Plaza Hotel
Springfield, Missouri

At 5 am, a buzzing radio alarm rudely awakened Cohn from a deep slumber. He got slowly out of bed, stumbled into the bathroom and looked into the mirror.

"Damn, I look like something the cat drug in. I've got to get some exercise.

After taking time to hit the can, he scrambled into workout clothes, stretched briefly and headed out for a 3-mile run. Twenty minutes later he returned to the hotel weight room to complete his workout. There was still an hour before the agreed-on time to meet Blackwell and Bridger for breakfast.

Aaron opened the glass door of the small workout room and was surprised to see Bridger standing in the middle of the room performing some kind of martial art in slow motion. Observing discreetly for a few moments, he was amazed how light Bridger appeared on his feet. He displayed great balance for such a big man, and Aaron appreciated the overall body strength it took to demonstrate this kind of controlled movement. Bridger was surprisingly athletic and still extremely fit.

"Good morning, Aaron. Looks like you've been doing some running."

"Yes, Sir. I've been watching you exercise; and if you don't mind my asking, what type of martial art are you practicing?"

"It's called Tai Chi; probably the oldest in the world, and it's great for relaxation and general health in addition to defensive tactics. If you're interested, I'll help you give it a try sometime."

"That's enough for me in here; I'm going for a short swim and will see you in the lobby at seven."

***

Swan Lake Apartments
Springfield, Missouri

Not far away from the hotel, a female FBI Agent was also finishing a morning workout. Karen Blackwell completed her 5-mile run and entered the tiny room the apartment complex referred to as a "Health and Exercise Spa." *Is any of this crap equipment working today? Maybe at least some sit-ups and shoulder work on the Universal Gym* she thought with more than a little agitation.

A middle-distance runner at USC, she never felt her best without running before the day's activities began. It had not been easy for her to give up competition, but she could no longer train properly and perform her duties as an agent.

She hooked her feet in a rope at the top of the ancient incline board used for doing sit-ups and with hands clasped behind her head began to exercise. Her concentration was broken with plans for the day.

I'm going to suggest we start at the courthouse where the sniper killed Timothy Waters, then drive to Highway 65 and give them a feel for that crime scene.

Is it possible the shooter was the same in both events? It doesn't seem probable the patrolman inadvertently stopped the vehicle of two fugitives who committed murder minutes before. What are the odds? The description of the shooter did not fit the Al Qaeda profile—too old and no indication he was Middle Eastern—so that would mean if the shooter was the same in both events, Bridger's theory of someone other than Al Qaeda could have merit. He sure created a furor with it in Washington. If it proves correct, FIST could be off and running—but what if he's wrong.

Blackwell completed 30 sit-ups and moved to the Universal Gym, only to discover the cable still broken. *Damnit, I reported this thing twice already and they were going to.... Whatever, time for a shower anyway.*

***

Blackwell was surprised to see Bridger and Cohn waiting in the hotel lobby when she stopped the BuCar at the front entrance. She double-checked the time, relieved to see the dash clock read 6:58; she wasn't late. She made a mental note to be earlier in the future.

Both men were carrying briefcases and laptops.

"Gentlemen, do you have a preference for breakfast? We have a lot of chain type restaurants and...."

"How about *Jennies Café*? The food last night was great and it's close enough to be convenient," Bridger suggested.

Breakfast at *Jennie's* was simple and delicious. The conversation centered on small talk until Karen and Aaron discovered they had attended rival schools in the Pacific-10 Athletic Conference—USC and California-Berkeley respectively.

"Sooo, you attended "Latex U? (The reference being to the USC school mascot being the Trojans—derived from the hollow *wooden horse*—and not *safe sex*.) Is that an accredited institution yet?" Cohn inquired.

"Yes, Aaron, it is for everybody except male athletes. By the way, have they dropped men's athletics yet at Berkeley? Rumor is they decided to stop wasting money."

After listening to their friendly banter through most of the breakfast, Bridger finally interceded, "Is there going to be an end to this, or will I have to listen to it all day? You both attended nice universities—not as nice as Wyoming—but you can't be blamed for lack of opportunity; one does the best one can with what one has."

Bridger rose majestically from the table, picked up the checks, walked to the ancient cash register and paid for the meals.

Karen looked across the table with a puzzled looked and asked, "Did he say *Wyoming*—as in *Cowboys*?"

"I believe that's what he said all right. Remind me to tell you tonight over dinner about Theodore Bridger II." And with that comment, Aaron left the table to join his boss.

Was that a dinner invitation? Naw, he probably meant we'll still be working and the big brave boys will tell the little girl some war stories. Whatever—this guy is so hot!

***

"I thought it would be logical to start at the courthouse and then proceed to the shooting on Highway 65," Blackwell suggested.

"That's exactly what we had in mind. Aaron wants to trace a route from the courthouse to the second scene to establish a timeline, and we need your input on what you believe the most reasonable direct route might be. We should be able to verify whether the timing would allow the two shootings to be linked."

"After our discussion last night, I checked a city map to determine the quickest and shortest trek from Greene County Courthouse to Highway 65. It appears to be a no brainer; Chestnut Expressway is only two blocks south of the scene and runs directly east to the highway."

Blackwell drove past University Plaza Hotel, down Hammons Parkway to Chestnut Expressway and turned east to Boonville Avenue. The Greene County Courthouse was only two blocks north.

"This is it," Karen said simply. "You can see, there's quite a lot of activity, even this early on Saturday morning."

Bridger seemed to be deep in concentration about something, and when he finally began to speak it was with a questioning tone, "Karen, did you participate in the neighborhood investigations of this area around the courthouse?"

"No, Sir. I was assigned to the Burroughs shooting."

"It seems odd no one interviewed heard a shot. A .308 rifle makes a lot of noise, even if they used a suppressor. What could explain it not being heard in an area surrounded with people, in and out of buildings, passing by in vehicles and so forth?"

"The other sniper attack came from a rooftop," Aaron reminded. It would be difficult to suppress the sound of a rifle to the extent it couldn't be heard in an area with this many people. Could this be a "copy cat" of the DC sniper, shooting from the closed trunk of a vehicle?"

"If your theory of a connection between the two shootings here is correct, the vehicle used in the slaying of Burroughs was a pick-up truck. They wouldn't have had time to trade vehicles and get to the second shooting. Perhaps we should be looking for a pick-up with a camper on the back. It could account for not hearing the shot," Bridger replied.

"Are we ready to time the route to Patrolman Burroughs' shooting?"

"Give me a second to get a position on the GPS unit," Aaron replied.

Moments later Cohn gave the okay and switching on the stopwatch mechanism of his wristwatch, gave the go sign.

Blackwell, careful to maintain the speed limit, turned onto Highway 65 and drove several miles to the scene of the patrolman shooting—parking on the shoulder and turning on the vehicle warning lights. The red lights and strobes of the BuCar would attract too much attention, and there was no point in drawing onlookers to the scene.

From the backseat, Cohn announced, "17½ minutes—the timeline is right. We may be on to something."

"Aaron, give Steve Woolcock at NSA a call right now with the GPS coordinates," Bridger suggested. "I'm going to take a quick look around the scene of the crime and try to get a better feel for what went down here."

Agent Blackwell moved about the area with Bridger and pointed out the various elements of the crime. Blood from two areas—where the patrolman fell and where his body was dragged—was still evident despite attempts by a cleanup crew to remove it. The dark spots were deeply absorbed into the porous blacktop and would take sun and rain to eventually bleach them out. Until then, it would provide a visible chilling reminder of a life taken without reason or remorse.

People in passing cars were still slowing, attracted by the ever-present and inexplicable fascination associated with violent death. Circumstances seemed to make little difference, whether it's bloody auto accidents or the tragic shooting death of a law enforcement officer; morbid curiosity seemed to get the best of people.

Bridger stood still for several moments looking carefully around the immediate area mentally visualizing what had transpired during the commission of the crime. Aaron finished his phone conversation to NSA and joined the other two.

Finally Bridger began to speak, "In taking the time to drag the body around the patrol car, the shooter had to realize they were being observed by passing traffic. Combine that with the common knowledge, on a stop a patrolman routinely calls in the license and make of vehicle, and there is little doubt they abandoned the pick-up as soon after the shooting as possible."

"There is no reason to believe they reversed directions after the shooting. Highway 65 runs south all the way to Natchez, Mississippi, with the opportunity to divert east or west onto Interstate highways along the way.

"Agent Blackwell, have there been any reports of stolen vehicles in the immediate area on Wednesday last—the day of the shooting?"

"No, Sir. The locals were alert for that to happen, and there were no vehicles reported stolen anywhere along 65 that could be potentially connected to the shooting. The investigation has focused on looking for the pick-up in surrounding states, assuming the unsubs may still be traveling in it."

"Going back to our conversation last evening," Cohn began, "do you think the truck could be close by?"

"That is precisely what I'm thinking," said Bridger. "It's a nice day for a drive. Why don't we take a short drive down Highway 65 and use our imaginations a bit. Where do you dump a hot vehicle after multiple killings? Especially when you have eyewitnesses observe at least one of the shootings."

It was indeed "a nice day," and the rolling hills of the Ozark Mountains were in full bloom with dogwoods and red buds as far as the eye could see. Like so many scenes before and so many yet to come, the natural beauty and uniqueness of their surroundings were lost to the intensity of the moment. No one in the BuCar seemed to notice or comment on the scenery. The grotesque nature of the crimes they were investigating focused all their attention on the task at hand.

Going down a long steep hill into the valley below, Agent Blackwell suddenly broke the silence. "I have an idea. Actually more a suggestion," she added almost apologetically. "I've been thinking of the Hearst vehicle found in the parking garage; maybe these unsubs left this one in plain sight too. There are several park-and-ride areas off the highway where people leave their vehicles and carpool into Springfield or Branson. It would be a perfect place to 'hide something in plain sight.' We're coming to one at the next exit; shall we take a look?"

"Let's have a look see," Bridger said.

A short distance off the main highway, the park-and-ride was a relatively small paved parking lot holding about 15 autos, including one pick-up truck. They approached the truck and quickly realized it was too new and the wrong color for the suspect vehicle.

Blackwell circled the parking lot and pulled back onto the highway. "Do you want to take a look at a couple more? There are two within the next 12 miles or so."

"I think it would be a perfect place to make a switch, particularly if they set up ERPs ahead of time," Agent Cohn suggested.

"I agree. How about we hit the next couple ourselves and then give the "locals" (referring to members of local law enforcement) Karen's idea if we don't find anything. Every park-and-ride should be searched, and then we go into Branson and start looking through the hundreds of parking lots around the theatres," Bridger said.

Are they patronizing me, or do they really think it's a good idea? Don't go there, girl. These people have been straight with you—you're being treated like a professional. Don't let your cynicism spoil it.

The next park-and-ride was 5 miles ahead; they were disappointed to see only a few autos and not a single pick-up.

Blackwell felt disillusionment well up and doubted if she should have even suggested this impromptu search. They were probably wasting time, and the truck would be found in one of the myriad of parking lots in Branson. After all, she was discovering the hard way, lowly second-office agents (particularly female second-office agents) were expected to remain in the background and attract as little attention to themselves as possible. It would be much safer to simply go along for the ride and speak when spoken to.

Blackwell glanced down at her map and trying to keep the disappointment out of her voice said, "There's one more about 4 miles ahead off Highway 14."

A few minutes later, she slowed and drove a short distance down the narrow road before entering the park-and-ride. It was much larger than the previous two and contained a number of vehicles. There were several pick-ups but none appeared to be red. Then—just as they circled to leave—something caught Blackwell's eye. "There...at the back...isn't that a red Dodge?

As they approached closer, it clearly was a red Dodge—with a camper on the back!

"Pull up behind—what license number are we looking for?" Bridger asked.

Aaron thumbed rapidly through his notes and replied, "Mississippi...Boy, Oliver, Larry, 1-3-2."

The three agents sat staring at the red Dodge in front of them—it contained a Missouri license plate.

"I thought we had it," Blackwell groaned.

"We still may," Bridger stated in a matter of fact tone. "It would be a good move on the part of our perps to change plates to keep the vehicle from being noticed and found quickly. They would be much safer in making their get away if the search focused on the wrong vehicle."

"Let's get a VIN and run it through NCIC. I'm betting we get a hit; it's too much of a coincidence to have found a red Dodge sitting here matching the description *and* having the camper."

Cohn copied the VIN from the windshield and walked to the BuCar radio contacting FBI-Kansas City to request an immediate NCIC check.

Ten minutes later he returned, and looking at Blackwell with a big smile offered, "Nice work, Karen. This pick-up was stolen from a shopping mall in Fayetteville, Arkansas, last Monday. The Mississippi plate must have been put on the truck to keep the Arkansas Highway Patrol from picking up on it.

"The license plate currently on the truck came from Branson and was reported stolen Tuesday. They probably planned to dump the truck in a parking lot in Branson, but after the shooting decided to get rid of it as quickly as possible. Guess the big question now is: How do we handle this so far as the locals are concerned?"

"Get this area secured quickly," Bridger commanded. "I want Laura Rice here pronto for forensics—before anybody else contaminates the truck.

"Karen, you've been working with the highway patrol on this case. You handle notification on the discovery of the vehicle and explain to them why we want the lab work done by our people. Their forensic staff is free to observe—but make it clear: we are taking over jurisdiction and have concerns about contamination. Also, it is a good bet the .357 was disposed of between the shooting scene and here. Let's ask them to organize a search along the west side of the highway in the ditches.

"We need to get the photos of the tire track from the crime scene and compare them visually. It should give us some idea whether we have what we think we have, and the lab can confirm later. Any problems develop…let me know pronto.

"Aaron, you stay here and wait for the troops to arrive. Secure this area and under no circumstances does anyone touch anything until Rice is on the scene. I'm going to ask FBI to fly her in today by private transport.

"Karen, we need to go back to the RA for communication purposes.

"Questions? Good. This may be our first break; let's get the ball rolling," Bridger exclaimed already halfway into the BuCar.

"Agent Blackwell, I'm going to need to EC (Electronically Communicate) with a number of people in different agencies. Does the RA have a communication clerk?" Bridger inquired.

"No, Sir. We go through the field office in Kansas City for SCION and primarily use FIDS and FAMS (FBI Automated Messaging System) to do our basic reporting. We have access to secure land lines as well."

Blackwell turned onto James River Expressway and drove at a steady pace west to the Chesterfield exit and the sight of the FBI's Springfield Resident Agency. A total of six agents were assigned out of the Kansas City Field Office to live and work in Springfield.

They entered the building and moved quickly down the narrow hall to a set of what looked like wooden doors but in reality were armored steel painted to resemble wood. She entered a code to disarm the alarm and open the heavy bolt locks and waited to hear the solenoid click before swinging the heavy door open.

Bridger was not surprised to see the office empty. It was Saturday and he apparently had Sterling pegged correctly.

"I believe this is the space Sterling intends for your use," Blackwell indicated opening the door to a small office.

"I took the liberty of preparing codes to facilitate use of the various communication devices as well as the secure phone system," she said handing Bridger a card with the pertinent information.

"Thank you, Karen. Contact the Missouri Highway Patrol and let them know we have a suspect vehicle—I repeat—*suspect vehicle.* Ask for their assistance in securing the area until Rice arrives later today.

"Be certain everyone understands—I want no comments to the media on this until we can get confirmation on what we have.

"I'm planning to remain here and would appreciate assistance in handling the communications which will be forthcoming. Please let *Senior Resident Agent* Sterling know of my request," Bridger said in a clearly condescending tone.

"Questions…let's get at it."

The next couple of hours passed quickly. Laura Rice was set to depart from Reagan International via FBI jet and would arrive at 1:30 pm local.

The highway patrol assigned troopers to meet Greene County Sheriff Deputies and provide security at the scene of the recovered truck and to search the area for the weapon. It was agreed—they would have their forensic teams at the scene with Rice.

Blackwell handled her end of the assignment with professionalism, impressing Bridger with the skills acquired in a relatively short time in the Bureau.

As Bridger finished a telephone call updating DHS, Sterling entered the office. It was obvious from his attire that he was coming from a casual outing and had not taken time to change.

"How may I assist, Mr. Bridger?" Sterling asked.

"I suggest you check with Agent Blackwell and get an update on what we suspect we've found and where the investigation is headed from here. She's on top of the situation; in fact, it's due to her initiative we located the vehicle.

"It would be helpful if you could contact any personnel not otherwise assigned, and get them out to the area searching for the murder weapon. With a little luck—if it's out there—we may locate it before our forensic expert arrives."

The next several hours were spent doing what special agents do with a majority of their time—creating reports and disseminating information. To Sterling's credit, he participated in the mundane work without apparent resentment, even showing a certain amount of enthusiasm.

"Sir, it's nearly 1 pm," Blackwell reported to Bridger. I believe you indicated Ms. Rice would be arriving at 1:30. Would you like for me to…."

Blackwell was interrupted by the RA radio with a message from Agent Tillo.

"710 to RA…710 to RA…you copy?"

Sterling picked up the RA handset, "Springfield RA, copy."

"The focus of our search has been located, and we are in transit to the RA with the evidence in question…over."

"Good work, Tillo. Has the scene been secured, over?"

"10-4…the area is secure."

"That's good news," Bridger said. "Agent Blackwell, would you please meet Ms. Rice at the airport and transport her to the park-and-ride. She'll have some equipment; you may want to take an SUV if available. I'll meet you there."

As Blackwell started for the door, Bridger surprised her by adding, "Agent Blackwell, your performance has been very impressive. Nice work!

"Sterling, please coordinate incoming communications. We want to keep a no comment posture with the media until we're sure what we have. Anything from SOG calling for my attention, contact me by cell phone. Let's avoid radio traffic—better assume we could have unauthorized listeners monitoring."

"Would your forensic expert be comfortable using the facilities at the local police department? I can contact the Chief of Police for access," Sterling suggested.

"I'm sure Rice will need a place to work, and we've invited the Missouri Highway Patrol forensic people to observe. See what you can do; it appears investigations are put on hold on the weekend in this RA. Perhaps the potential national magnitude of this situation will help to change some of the apathy in that regard."

Bridger looked straight at Sterling for several long seconds after finishing his pungent remarks. *He looks like someone ran over his dog. Too bad! Now is not the time to be working on your golf game. This may be providing the wake-up call he needs.*

***

CHAPTER 17

Midtown Manhattan
New York City, New York

C hambers impatiently glared out the dirty side window of the slow moving taxi. *Damn! Never even imagined traffic would be this kind of problem.* It was 4:20 pm with Melanie's flight scheduled to arrive at 4:50. The cab hadn't moved a hundred feet in the past half hour.

Dialing the airlines on his cell phone, after three rings a recorded voice offered a series of choices and finally when "arriving flights" was offered he punched in the numbers.

Would you believe it, he mumbled to himself. *On time, how many flights arrive on time at La Guardia?*

Chambers held a twenty-dollar bill over the front seat of the taxi for the driver. "There's another like it if you get me to La Guardia in the next half hour."

The Puerto Rican born driver grabbed the twenty and said, "Yo man, hang on we gonna get down to business."

The cab turned at the next exit and picked up speed swerving down a narrow street for several blocks, weaving in and out of traffic until finally entering Queens Midtown Tunnel. The taxi, already showing wounds from past indiscretions, rocked wildly from side to side as the driver braked hard before shooting past another vehicle gaining another hard won *17* feet.

Traffic grew lighter on Brooklyn Queens Expressway, Chambers realized; *if we don't get killed, we might make it on time.*

The taxi careened onto Grand Central Parkway and a few frightening moments later, turned onto 94th Street for the short distance to the airport entrance, tires squealing to a stop with time to spare.

A big smile full of white teeth reflected from the driver's mirror, and a long black hand, palm facing upward, appeared over the front seat.

Chambers paid the fare, adding an additional *twenty-five* dollars and ran into the airport searching for United Airlines. He moved as quickly as the crowded airport would allow, found a display screen, located the flight number and rushed to the designated arrival area.

Chambers caught sight of Melanie; she saw him at the same moment and waved over the heads of the crowded mass of travelers. Waving back, he resisted the urge to attempt getting through the moving mob of people and forced himself to wait patiently for her to reach him.

He flashed back to his first glimpse of her appearing out of a pile of boxes in Fitzgerald's Feed Store. It was a pleasant memory feeling like it dated from the distant past, but in reality could be numbered in days. He felt a sense of pure joy, watching this gorgeous woman making her way toward him.

Melanie walked up very close, set a small carry-on bag down and purred, "Hey, cowboy, looking for a good time."

She put her arms around his neck and gave him a tender kiss. "I really missed you," she whispered and kissed him once more.

John picked up Melanie's bag and waited as she took his arm before strolling slowly toward the baggage area.

It doesn't get better than this, John concluded, glancing at the beautiful woman on his arm. *A few days ago, I doubted these feelings would ever be possible again. Easy pal. Give it time to develop; it's way too early to be thinking that way.*

"How was the flight? Could you see the city coming in or was there too much overcast?" John asked.

"John, I don't think I'll ever forget my first look at this city. Actually it was quite clear, and it was an incredible sight with all the buildings and traffic. New York City is impossible to imagine, if you haven't seen it before. It's…it's so big and so exciting," she added giving his arm a little squeeze.

"It's a great city with an incredible diversity of cultures. We're going to have a great time," John promised.

"But, you've had a long day and I'm sure you're tired. We can go by your hotel, get you settled and have an early dinner…supper, then you can get some rest."

"Actually got sleep on the flight and feel great. I'm too wired to sleep and don't forget—with the time zone change, it's two hours earlier for me. Maybe we could take a walk after supper and see some of Manhattan?"

The cab ride to the hotel passed very quickly, with Melanie full of questions about the city and still giddy with excitement.

The Cottonwood Plaza (located in Midtown Manhattan dotted with similar small hotels) had recently been renovated; the lobby reflected a combination of elegance and grace. Bright colors and fabrics highlighted the older grandeur of rich wood trims, antique lights and chandeliers.

The lobby was filled with people rushing about (many wearing nametags attached to their pockets suggesting a convention crowd)—going in and out of the bar on one side and the restaurant across the lobby on the other.

John was somewhat surprised to see how poised and confident Melanie appeared, as she paused in front of a dark ornately carved front desk waiting patiently until the first clerk was free.

"Good evening. I'm Melanie Fitzgerald."

"Do you have a reservation Miss…" came the tired response.

"Yes…Melanie Fitzgerald."

"One moment please. Yes, Welcome, Ms. Fitzgerald. We hope you had a pleasant flight." The clerk's demeanor changed abruptly; it was difficult to say whether it was because he finally looked up to see a beautiful woman standing in front of him or finally noticed a red-flag entry on the reservation.

"My flight was excellent, thank you."

"Could you excuse me for one moment please," the clerk asked turning quickly without waiting for a response and disappearing into a room behind the desk.

Moments later a neatly dressed, middle-aged man wearing a pleasant smile approached the desk stopping in front of Melanie, "Good afternoon, Ms. Fitzgerald. I'm Samuel Nichols and have the privilege of managing the Cottonwood Plaza. If we can be of service to you in any way while you are here, please let me know personally.

"Your suite is ready. How many keys will you require?"

"Two keys please."

"Here you are Ms. Fitzgerald…two keys. Your luggage will be taken to the suite.

"You also have a package from Mrs. Bridger, with instructions to present it to you upon your arrival. If you could wait one moment, I'll retrieve it from our safe."

Nichols returned, handed Melanie a small package and asked for a signature on a hotel receipt.

Melanie and John were escorted to a private elevator by a middle-aged bell captain where he demonstrated how to use the key to operate the elevator to the Penthouse Suite. Moving smoothly to the tenth floor of the hotel, the elevator opened revealing large, dark wood-paneled doors with tall potted plants on either side, under an overhead skylight.

The bell captain unlocked the tall door, swinging it open allowing them to enter. "If you will please follow me, I will acquaint you with the suite.

"Here are the climate controls for the main area, and you have separate controls for the bedrooms and baths. The television is built into this wall." Pushing a button on the table, a fresco slid silently aside revealing a large plasma screen television.

"Your surround sound switches are located here as well."

He continued walking through the suite to demonstrate various modern conveniences from kitchen to bathroom, culminating—to John's amusement—with the controls of the select comfort king-size bed.

It was, in fact, a small apartment with kitchen, living area, separate bedrooms and baths, furnished with a mixture of expensive paintings, bronze sculptures and comfortable furniture providing a tasteful warm ambience.

"What a fantastic apartment!" Melanie exclaimed. "Oh, and look; it has a balcony," she said grabbing John's hand and dragging him through the doublewide doors to the outside. They stood admiring a spacious garden balcony, surrounded by a high privacy fence and containing a wide variety of plants and shrubs. One corner hid a large hot tub completely encircled by vegetation. An assortment of rattan furniture, including table and chairs, made it an ideal retreat for casual eating or drinks.

Rebecca's influence is written all over this, John realized. *It's easy to envision her sitting here in the garden for endless hours, meditating in the serene atmosphere, while B.T. was somewhere in a city boardroom taking care of the demands of their business conglomerates.*

"My name is Taylor. If you require anything, please let me know," the bellman offered with a smile as he moved toward the door. "Again, welcome to the Cottonwood Plaza. Enjoy your stay."

John extended his hand with a gratuity that was promptly waived off.

"We can't accept gratuities from Ms. Fitzgerald. The Bridgers have taken care of that…very generously I might add. Thank you."

When the bellman closed the doors behind him, Melanie could not contain herself any longer.

"This is so awesome!" she squealed, dancing around the suite. Racing from room to room, her unbridled delight could scarcely be contained until finally—with the growing recognition she was acting like a teenager—she stopped in front of John.

"Sorry. It simply…."

"Nothing to be sorry about—this place is great!"

He pulled her close, "Mel, you are so beautiful, and I'm really glad you're here."

Their lips met softly and as they parted, Melanie rested her head gently on his chest and sighed, "I'm very glad too, John."

I can hear his heart beating, and his arms around me feel so natural. I've got to slow down and not get ahead of myself with all this excitement. It's been an incredibly wonderful and stimulating day.

The small package given to her by the hotel manager suddenly peaked her curiosity.

"John, would you mind opening a bottle of the white wine we saw in the wine cooler. Let's sit out on the balcony and have a glass before going to supper."

Melanie picked up the small gift-wrapped box and wandered out to the balcony, sitting down in one of the comfortable wicker chairs.

Carefully tearing the wrapping paper away, she removed the jewelry box lid and was astonished to see its contents. She gazed in wonder at a beautiful black pearl necklace with matching earrings.

Through eyes growing misty from emotion, she read the note from Rebecca.

My Dearest Melanie,

Hope you enjoy this jewelry as much as I have. B.T. gave it to me on our first wedding anniversary. Since we do not have a daughter to pass this to, B.T. and I decided to give it to the young woman to whom we could not feel closer if she were our own.

Enjoy New York and we will see you soon.

Love,

Rebecca

P.S.

Please note the enclosed gift certificate has an expiration date and is non-refundable; so you see, dear, you must use it while in New York. The two of you will enjoy shopping at Faconnable. Nordstrom owns it, and they have wonderful designs from Nice, France.

John stepped onto the balcony carrying two glasses of wine and saw Melanie clutching a piece of paper, tears streaming down her cheeks.

"Mel, what is it? Has something happened at home?"

Too emotional to answer, she held the gift box and note out to him.

First he saw the beautiful jewelry and then the gift certificate from Nordstrom and Faconnable on Fifth Avenue; it was in the amount of $10,000. "Wow!" he exclaimed.

***

Highway 65
Springfield-Branson, Missouri

Bridger returned to the park-and-ride area with Agent Tillo and quickly saw what he had hoped to avoid—media. "Damnit! It's the same all over. There's always someone willing to leak information for a few bucks or to return a favor.

"We need to get them back from the scene and keep them out of hearing range of any conversations Rice or the forensic team may have."

Bridger strode to the front of a still congregating crowd, held up his hand and called for attention.

"My name is Ted Bridger. I'm the new Director of FIST, an investigative unit from the Department of Homeland Security. I'm going to provide you what information we have thus far, and at this point in time will not...let me repeat, will not answer any questions beyond my brief statement. I'm requesting your cooperation in assisting us by preventing the compromise of this investigation through premature speculation or the release of inaccurate information.

"FIST is assisting state law enforcement officials in the investigation of the murder of Patrolman Burroughs. Federal jurisdiction in this case is based on the assumption the perpetrators have crossed state lines.

"Investigative initiative of a Springfield FBI Resident Agent has resulted in locating a pick-up truck fitting the description of the vehicle used by the subjects in the murder.

"A forensic team is imminent and will make a determination from available evidence regarding the validity of our speculation.

"No further statement will be made at this time or until we have time to properly assess any evidence recovered. We are requesting your patience in this matter, and you will be advised through normal media outlets when further information becomes available.

"Please give us your cooperation in moving back from the scene and not contaminating the area further. Thank you."

As Bridger walked away, several questions were shouted from members of the growing collection of print and television media—to no avail.

Cohn stood talking with two Missouri Highway Patrolmen and when Bridger approached, was introduced simply as "my boss, Mr. Bridger."

Good to hear and no mistaking what it means, Bridger thought—*an unmistakable sign we're establishing mutual respect in our relationship.*

"Gentlemen, please accept my sympathy for your loss. I'm sure working together, we can bring the sorry bastards to justice—and sooner rather than later.

"Aaron, you need a break. Why don't we wait for Rice to arrive; and while she's processing the truck, we can catch a quick lunch and I'll bring you up to date.

"Agent Tillo, take over here and provide whatever assistance Ms. Rice may request. And for cripes sake, keep those damn *Ozark paparazzi* out of the way!"

A few moments later, Blackwell and Rice drove into the parking lot, stopping near the red pick-up.

Bridger went to the passenger side of the SUV and opened the door.

"Hello, Laura. Good to see you again. Sorry about all the gitty up bringing you here, but drastic circumstances require"….

"Drastic actions," Rice said finishing the sentence.

"Nice to see you, Ted. By the way, are we going to be traveling this well all the time? This old body could get accustomed to private jets and the pampering that went along with it."

"Laura, if that's all it takes to keep you happy, you got it."

Rice had stopped at the RA long enough to change into work clothes, meaning white coveralls and rubber shoes. As she pulled on a pair of latex gloves, Bridger could not help noticing how great she looked.

Coal black hair with traces of silver provided the only vestige of age. Rice's fine features, bronze complexion and dark eyes complimented a still very shapely figure even loose fitting work clothes could not hide.

After knowing Laura for years, it was difficult for Bridger to imagine the type of man who wouldn't fully appreciate her. Once, early in their professional relationship, Laura alluded to physical abuse. Perhaps the abuse, more than her job, was the real reason for divorce.

Bridger spent a few moments introducing Rice to local law enforcement personnel. It was obvious she still had sensitivity for "locals" from her background at NYPD. Being pushed out of the picture when feds arrived on the scene was not something she could soon forget. A forensic team from Missouri Highway Patrol was immediately invited to participate.

"May I please see a photo of the tire track from the shooting scene?" Rice asked.

She took the photo and walked to the rear wheels of the truck. "This tire on the passenger side rear is, without a doubt, identical to the tire presented in this photo."

"Yes!"

Bridger looked around, startled to see it was Blackwell making an impromptu remark. She was now trying very hard to find someone large enough to hide behind.

Only Rice caught Bridger's smile as he turned away. *It's a pleasure to see and hear unbridled exuberance once in awhile*, he reflected. *She's traveling down the yellow brick road and why not? She's had one hell of a good day.*

Rice looked at Bridger with an arched eyebrow and asked, "First office?"

"Second," Bridger responded returning a smile. "Anything you need here Laura, let Agent Tillo know."

"Should have everything in the field kits, unless something really out of the ordinary surfaces; probably going to be a couple of hours."

"Agent Tillo will be at your disposal. We have some communications to get out, and I'll get back here when I'm finished," Bridger added moving toward the car.

Bridger opened the car door and looked back toward Rice who was measuring distance the driver sat from pedals of the pick-up. *She's trying to get some idea of the perp's size. We're really fortunate to have her with us. "Best of the best" is what we want—and in Laura that's precisely what we've got.*

***

Rice performed an exhaustive forensic exam of the unsub vehicle and crime scene and spent several more hours in Springfield's Police forensic lab performing preliminary tests and protecting a chain of evidence.

At 8:30 that evening, Bridger escorted a very exhausted Laura Rice to a waiting FBI Lear Jet.

"I'll have some final results for you by mid-morning tomorrow," she said, looking at Ted through puffy red eyes.

"I appreciate your efforts, Laura," Ted replied. Try to get some rest on the flight. You did a great job here, and we're fortunate to have you with us in FIST."

"You know I could never refuse your charm, Ted. By the way, speaking of charm—ha! ha!—I've heard scuttlebutt Bill Johnson may be joining our party. Anything to it?"

"Yes. Glad to say, Bill will be our assistant director."

"That's good to hear. He's an outstanding administrator and leader."

Bridger stood and watched the plane taxi to a holding point. The agile Lear make a quick turn lining up on an active run way; powerful twin jet engines roared as the plane picked up speed, climbed quickly into the air and rapidly disappeared into clouds.

Interesting question Laura asked. Bill is everything Laura indicated, but it leads me to wonder...is that the only reason she asked about him?

Bridger let out a long sigh and finally turned to Blackwell and Cohn, "Time to get some rest. Tomorrow could be another long day."

***

FBI Resident Agency
Springfield, Missouri

Sunday would indeed be a long day. Arriving at the Springfield RA, a few minutes after 8 am, Bridger was encouraged by a growing mountain of incoming communications. He was surprised to see SSRA Sterling in the office, organizing an effort to bring about some degree of order.

"Good morning, Gentlemen—looks like we stirred up a communication hornet's nest. Sterling, could you bring everybody up to date on what we have received since yesterday?"

"Yes, Sir."

Sterling picked up a small notebook from his desk and turning to the small group of agents asked for attention. He stepped to an electronic "smart board" and systematically began to highlight information received over the past 24 hours.

Tire print recovered at scene of shooting of patrolman is a definite match to pick-up located at park-and-ride.

Gunpowder residue found in camper of pick-up is Alipant 15, commonly used by reloaders and by US M1-18 sniper rifles. It is a match for GPR (Gun Powder Residue) identified at scene of sniper shooting in Chicago.

Fibers found in camper originated from Teflon-coated garment containing two additional protectors, Solarguard and Supplex. This combination of synthetic garment treatment is found in high quality outdoor clothing sold in upscale sporting goods stores in large quantities. Most common manufacturers using this combination are North Face and Columbia.

Ballistic tests conducted Smith & Wesson .357 Magnum, Serial #2L85049, located near crime scene positively identified weapon firing bullet causing fatal injuries to Missouri Patrolman Burroughs. Elemental analysis of bullet reveals manufacturer Speer, factory lot RJP. A search of NIBI (National Integrated Ballistics Information Network) failed to reveal any record of past submissions from subject handgun.

A partial print located on bullet casing of the recovered .357 matched to: MICHAEL WAYNE MATTHEWS, WM, DOB 02-21-65, Little Rock, Arkansas. (See attached information re: subjects military record)

Second partial print lifted from gas cap of pick-up matched to: ROBERT HENRY JONES, WM, DOB 08-07-70, Fort Smith, Arkansas. (See attached information re: subjects military record)

Bird feather recovered from radiator screen identified as Green Heron (Butorides Virescens). This species prefers wooded marshes, avoids wide-open spaces and frequents North-Central Arkansas. Feather extracted from bird in last 7-10 days.

"That's a summary of a forensic report provided by Rice," Sterling commented. "She must have worked all night. The report was on FIDs when I first arrived at 6:30."

How about that—he recognizes effort and dedication from Laura. Maybe there's hope for this guy yet.

"Can you give us a summary what military records revealed on both suspects?" Bridger requested.

SUBJECT # 1
Military record MICHAEL WAYNE MATTHEWS, WM, DOB 02-21-65, RA 183364261.

Summarily dishonorably discharged United States Army, 05-01-2003. Subject found guilty of repeated racially related encounters with civilian and military population resulting in serious injury and threat of injury.

Subject served two tours of duty in Afghanistan and Desert Storm-Iraq; assigned to scout unit. *Military training specialty reported—scout/ sniper.*

SUBJECT # 2

Military record ROBERT HENRY JONES, WM, DOB 08-07-70, RA 1889076393.

Summarily dishonorably discharged United States Army, 06-13-2003. Subject investigated on charges of using and selling various narcotic substances. Subject found guilty of racially motivated assault on member of unit resulting in serious injury. Subsequently served 1-year incarceration Leavenworth Federal Correctional Facility released 6-20-2004.

Subject served two tours of duty in Afghanistan and Iraq. *Military specialty reported—spotter scout/sniper team.*

***

The room was silent for several moments after seeing the last bit of information flash on the screen. The entire investigation had taken a completely new—and for some in this room—unexpected turn.

Bridger was the first to speak.

"Congratulations! You've been handed one *sensational* break. Sterling, you take charge of dissemination to the appropriate Bureau entities.

"Aaron, get this to Harmison right away. We need a profile report ASAP.

"Listen up people! Let's not have mistakes of 911 repeat themselves. Error on too much dissemination rather than too little."

05-29-2007
VCF # 911-009342
OO: Washington
TO: SAC Little Rock
FROM: SAC Kansas City/FIST Denver
RE: BuCom dated 05-25-2007.

Subjects considered ARMED & DANGEROUS.

EXPEDITE LEADS.

Will conduct interview Jerome P. Mullaney, 1412 South Dakota Avenue, Fayetteville, Arkansas, registered owner 2001 Dodge Pick-up, VIN 8927650-EKG. Vehicle reported stolen and subsequently connected to scene of shooting death of Missouri Highway Patrolman.

Ascertain miles vehicle driven since oil change on window sticker dated 05-21-2007.

Partial print lifted from gas cap above pick-up identical to that of ROBERT HENRY JONES, WM, DOB, 08-07-70, Fort Smith, Arkansas. JONES believed to be unsub accompanying MICHAEL WAYNE MATTHEWS during slaying of Missouri Highway Patrolman.

Partial print taken from .357 revolver found near crime scene, identified as murder weapon of Missouri Highway Patrolman, matched to MICHAEL WAYNE MATTHEWS, WM, DOB 02-21-65, Little Rock, Arkansas.

Will conduct credit and criminal check above individual and known relatives your area, identified in attached military records. DO NOT CONTACT, INTERVIEW, OR CONDUCT ANY INVESTIGATION THAT COULD ALERT SUBJECTS.

Identify commercial sporting goods type stores your area selling Columbia or North Face clothing with UPF sun protection (trade name Solarguard and Supplex) woven into fabric.

Identify sources your area selling caliber .308 Nosler 180-grain Spitzer bullets and Alipant Reloader 15 gunpowder. Bullets bear factory-marking C.T.

Identify sources your area selling .357 Speer 180 FMJ Blazer ammunition from factory lot RJP.

Bird feather recovered radiator of pick-up identified Green Heron (Butorides) known to habitat limited area North-Central Arkansas, with preference wooded marshes avoiding open spaces. Attempt identification viable areas of potential interest for location of subjects.

05-29-2007
VCF # 911-0009642
OO: Washington
TO: SAC Seattle
FROM: SAC Kansas City/FIST Denver
RE: BuCom dated 5-19-2007

EXPEDITE LEADS.

Will conduct investigation SeaTac Airport and vicinity rental car agencies for vehicle returned with damage from potential explosion at scene on and around 5-19-2007.

Will contact local authorities in effort to determine any reports of stolen ammonium nitrate fertilizer meeting chemical properties identified in BuCom dated 5-19-2007.

Review records Fort Lewis, Washington, for Ranger trained (ordinance trained) individuals discharged less than honorably over period last five years.

EXPEDITE AND COPY SAC KANSAS CITY—FIST DENVER WITH RESULTS

***

CHAPTER 18

Bridger Penthouse
Cottonwood Plaza Hotel
Midtown Manhattan
New York City, New York

After opening Rebecca's gift, Melanie called to thank her. She found it difficult to express her feelings for such an incredible gesture; and after listening to her sincere but frustrated efforts for a few moments, Rebecca politely interrupted.

"My dear, Mel, you should realize B.T. and I consider you part of our family. The gifts were simply an expression of our love and joy in having you in our lives. When you have a moment, call and let me know what you are doing and especially about new sights you have seen. Enjoy your stay in New York, and please give our best to John and his family."

Mel hung up the phone fighting tears of emotion and feeling a sense of security and belonging not realized since the death of her parents. Having no clue what was happening, John put his arm around her and held her closely until she quieted.

"Rebecca has been like a second mother to me. At first, I felt it was out of loyalty toward my mother. They were very close friends and confidants for many years. But now, it's much more; I've become the daughter she never had. I love and respect her more than I can say, but every time I try to express it, I'm at a loss for words."

"She understands," John said softly. "When you're together, it's very obvious. It was apparent to me watching you play the piano together and in the garden behind The Homestead; she knows exactly how you feel and it is indeed mutual.

"I have a favorite little restaurant for your first meal in New York. Let's have supper and take that walk."

***

On Saturday John and Melanie spent several hours at Faconnable with John enjoying the fashionable men's section and Melanie trying on an endless stream of outfits. After returning to the hotel with their packages, they walked the busy sidewalks of Manhattan.

The endless streams of people and the energy they gave off with their hustle and bustle enthralled Melanie. Everyone seemed to be in such a hurry. What a contrast comparing life in New York to Cheyenne or Laramie.

"Oh John, it's so exciting! It's understandable why you love it so. There is so much to see and so many people. Who are they? Where are they going? And why are they in such a hurry?"

"I'm really glad you like it; to be honest, I was concerned about how you might feel."

"So…you were worried this "little country girl" might be overwhelmed by the *big bad city,* huh? I have to admit, it would be far different being here alone.

"John, you know what might be nice? Let's go back to Cottonwood Plaza, order some supper and eat out on the balcony. We can watch a sunset through all these tall buildings. It will be a perfect end for my first full day in New York City."

"Sounds great, Mel. I'm getting hungry and a good meal with a *country girl* may be exactly what I need to get rejuvenated. Since the Bridgers own the hotel, maybe they have some of those delicious Rocky Mountain Oysters on the menu."

Looking at John with a curious grin on her face, Melanie finally replied, "Somehow I have my doubts."

***

Sunday Morning
Cottonwood Plaza Hotel

Melanie awoke to a pleasant sound of falling rain outside her bedroom window. It took a second to realize she was in New York. A rush of adrenaline tickled her stomach; it was a familiar feeling discovered in childhood. She first felt this sensation sitting in a classroom anticipating recess and soon learned she could create the rippling of pleasure with her imagination. It remained her little secret, believing it to be a unique ability, until years later in psychology class she first studied biofeedback and its use in stimulating the mind to create controlled responses.

Here I am, my first Sunday morning in New York. What will today bring? I wonder what John's parents are like? We have so little in common; we may have zero to talk about, and I so much want them to like me.

Saturday evening had gone perfectly so far as she was concerned. Supper was delicious and afterward they remained on the patio sipping Rebecca's favorite liqueur. Whidbeys Liqueur was a rather sweet loganberry from Washington State, and Melanie recalled Rebecca saying she and B.T. had discovered it during a second honeymoon trip to Whidbey Island, north of Seattle in Puget Sound.

With the sun setting slowly over the tall buildings, John invited her to attend church with him and his parents, suggesting they might have brunch afterward at their home in Brooklyn Heights. She accepted the invitation, they had kissed several times and John left—but not before giving instructions to "lock the door behind and not venture out too far without him until she was more acclimated to the city."

Melanie actually enjoyed his concern for her safety and was surprised it didn't conjure negative fears of control. It really was no different than her attempts to help him be more comfortable in Wyoming.

Applying the final touches of her make-up, Melanie heard the melodic doorbell chime. She opened the door to be greeted with a bouquet of flowers and a good morning kiss from John.

"You look beautiful this morning, Mel. I'll be the envy of every lad at St. Mark's."

"Thank you, kind Sir, and I will be the envy of every lassie as well."

Mel turned to retrieve her small purse, and John let out a small sigh of appreciation.

The lightweight flowered dress with matching scarf (he had helped her select at Faconnable) flowed with her movements and drew attention to her long tan legs and strap sandals. The black pearl necklace and earrings drew attention to her natural beauty.

"What...what's wrong? Is something showing?"

Finally realizing he was staring at her, John blurted, "No, no, everything is where it should be...in place...fastened...Oh hell, we're good to go."

He held the door open and Melanie went past with a puzzled look. *Man, she must be thinking, what a dork. You got to get hold of yourself or you're going to blow this before it has a chance to happen.*

The taxi ride took them through Greenwich Village, Soho, Little Italy and China Town into the Financial District of lower Manhattan. John pointed out the various points of interest, and Melanie listened intently with only an occasional question or comment.

As they crossed East River on the Brooklyn Bridge, Melanie turned toward John. He could see the exuberance in her eyes as she asked, "How have so many people with such different cultures and backgrounds created such a wonderful city?"

"The city has experienced enormous growing pains along the way, Mel. Many of the early majority cultures—English, Dutch, Irish, Italian and African—have been slow to accept the newcomers: Asian, Indian, Hispanic and so on. Likewise, various religions have created antagonism and friction among ethnic groups.

"Disagreements have not always been settled peaceably. There is a history of clashes, which too often became violent. Eventually differences were worked out and people have learned to live together in some form of harmony. Ultimately, New York—perhaps more than any city in the world—has come to epitomize cultural diversity."

The taxi stopped in front of an older but well kept two-story house with a tiny front lawn separating it from a sidewalk of the nearby street. The rain had stopped and John folded his umbrella, paid the driver and held the door open for Melanie. She stood staring—amazed how closely houses were situated to one another.

I wonder if I could ever be comfortable being this near so many people. I've never known anything but wide-open spaces.

"Here we are. This is home for me. My family has lived here since before I was born, and Mom and Dad will probably die here."

Taking Melanie's hand, John led her up a short walk lined on both sides by carefully maintained flowers. Arrays of colors displayed by daisies, petunias and salvia gave way to fragrant smells of the geraniums and roses at the entrance to the house.

The front door opened and a tall, neatly dressed middle-aged man and slightly overweight woman stood smiling.

Jack Chambers looked very much the successful mid-level business executive. Average height with a hint of gray at the temples, his pale features were clearly indicative of little time spent out of doors. The tan suit, blue shirt and matching silk tie gave a stylish tailored look, without any suggestion of formality.

Grace Chambers' hair also showed a small amount of gray at the temples, sending a clear signal vanity was not a concern. The remainder of her hair was dark black and worn tucked back into a bun. Dark eyes with a hint of laugh wrinkles matched her pleasant smile, and her tan complexion left little doubt of who cared for the flower gardens. Grace's stylish spring dress was multicolored with matching silk scarf.

"Mom, Dad, this is Melanie."

"Welcome to our home," Mr. Chambers replied, stepping back inviting them to enter. I'm Jack and this is my wife Grace."

A small entryway opened to the main living area of the house, a large room tastefully furnished and featuring a baby grand piano with music open on the shelf suggesting frequent use. Vintage plaster walls were decorated with several paintings, and furnishings were mixed including a sprinkling of what appeared to be antiques. The fireplace was large enough to heat the room— and probably had at times, judging from the darkened brick around the edges.

"It's a great pleasure meeting you. You have a lovely home."

"Thank you, Melanie. We've lived here for over 30 years, and both our sons were raised here. It's home to us and our boys as well.

"Would you care for something to eat or drink? We have coffee, juice and fresh cinnamon rolls. We like to have a little something before leaving for church," Grace said moving to a serving table.

"Keeps your stomach from disturbing the people around you when they're praying," Jack offered reaching for a warm roll.

"Jack, that's crude," Mrs. Chambers replied sharply.

"I would like a cinnamon roll and coffee. They smell wonderful and my stomach has been known to rumble at the worst possible times."

Melanie's last comment brought a smile of acceptance from Jack. *I'm going to like this girl. No pretense and what you see is what you get; and what you see ain't bad.*

The amenities were out of the way quickly and Melanie soon found herself wiping her sticky fingers and accepting an invitation to join Mrs. Chambers at the piano for a duet. They giggled like schoolgirls at the simple mistakes they were making in adjusting to one another's style of play.

"I've been admiring your black pearls, Melanie. May I say, they are absolutely exquisite!"

Melanie gently touched her necklace. "Thank you. They were a gift from Ted and Rebecca Bridger. Rebecca had them delivered to the Cottonwood Plaza for my arrival. She said they were a gift from Ted on their first wedding anniversary."

"What a special gift! They must love you very much."

Jack Chambers watched the two women enjoying themselves and being careful not to be seen, caught John's attention and gave a thumbs-up sign.

It's not taking long, John realized. *They're as taken with her as I am. This is one very special lady.*

As the music ended, Mrs. Chambers looked toward a grandfather clock whose loud ticking seemed to be sending an urgent message.

"We have barely enough time to make morning mass. Mel, we are so pleased you have decided to join us in church; perhaps *you* can bring the wayward lamb back to the fold," she said casting a mock frown in John's direction.

"As a matter of fact, Mother, I even made a special effort to attend church in Wyoming. So you see, I'm not such a fallen Saint after all," John replied.

"Did you by chance attend Melanie's church, at Melanie's invitation, with Melanie?" Grace asked.

John did not reply but his expression left little doubt.

"I rest my case," his mother said with a wry smile.

***

FBI Resident Agency
Springfield, Missouri

Sunday passed swiftly in Springfield. A steady stream of reports coming and going taxed the capability of the small office to the max.

Bridger called Secretary Ramirez at home (as requested earlier) to update him on the progress of the investigation.

"My apology for calling you so late, Mr. Secretary; I wanted to wait and provide all the information possible."

"Not a problem, Ted. We are all on a short chain until this matter is resolved. What do you have for me?"

Bridger spent several minutes with details of the investigation; Ramirez interrupted to ask questions on several occasions.

Finally in an uneasy voice Ramirez asked, "What do you think we're dealing with here, Ted? Give me your best assessment?"

"Sir, I prefer not to speculate at this point. I've asked for Special Agent Shawn Harmison to give us a profile, and I'll update you as soon as his report is available."

"Harmison you say…Director Goode contacted me personally when your request for Harmison's transfer was received at the Bureau. He gave a…how shall I put this…less than glowing account of Harmison's career achievements.

"Believe his comment was 'a loser who is drowning his mistakes in the company of *Mr. Jack Daniels.'* I'm told he maintains employment in the Bureau due to his personal connections to a high-ranking Senator."

So Shawn really has pissed off the brass—all the way to the top. Well, this is where we find out if Ramirez is going to keep his word in giving me the personnel requested.

"Mr. Secretary, I have absolute confidence in Shawn Harmison's ability to perform the duties required. He is the best of the best in the area of profiling, and I'm convinced his bout with the bottle was an anomaly brought on by an array of professional disappointments.

"If you care to look at his Bureau career impartially, you will find a long list of successes punctuated by letters of commendation and in-grade pay raises. His trip from the 'penthouse to the outhouse' correlated closely with my own."

"Ted, you have authority to select the people you need. If Harmison is your choice, you have my total support." *If Goode's assessment proves accurate, at least I have Harmison's Uncle—Senator Adam Newell of the Intelligence Committee—to deflect any political fallout,* Ramirez caught himself thinking. *Damned if that doesn't sound a lot like something one of these power-protecting politicians might be thinking. Better not forget the old adage: "If you choose the middle of the road, you get hit from cars in both directions."*

"Thank you, Sir. Your confidence and support is appreciated." *Get it while you can. Like Pop always says, "People and their promises are like old jock straps—with time they fail to provide support."*

"Ted, allow me to compliment you on the progress you're making. We certainly did not expect to see results this fast. Let me know if you need anything; great start for FIST! Keep it going," Ramirez said ending the conversation."

It was 8:35 pm. Every agent in the office had been going non-stop the past 12 plus hours, with only quick breaks to stuff a sandwich and drink endless streams of black coffee. Looking about the room, he saw a lot of very exhausted people trying to perform tasks requiring an alert mind and body.

"May I have your attention, please?" Bridger requested.

"It's been a long and promising day, and it would be a shame for us to screw it up at this point. Tired people make mistakes; I'm looking out through tired eyes at tired people.

"Unfortunately, we will have to develop a plan for having a 24-hour presence here in the RA until further notice. Any information coming in requiring immediate response should be brought to SSRA Sterling and my attention. We can divide the night into three, four-hour shifts, and I'll take the first."

There was a look of surprise on the faces of everyone in the room. *Bridger* was going to take the first watch?

"I'll take the second shift," a female voice said from the back of the room.

Why doesn't that surprise me, Bridger mused. *This young woman is more impressive all the time.*

"I'll take the third shift," said SSRA Sterling. "That takes care of tonight and we'll make new assignments tomorrow. Everyone get some rest and be here early tomorrow for a fresh start," Sterling added.

And Sterling's comment brought another look of surprise—this time on the face of Bridger.

***

New York World Offices
New York City, New York

The elevator door swung slowly open and John held it in place until Melanie could step off into a room filled with working reporters of the *New York World*.

Melanie stood looking about her at the lively activity and listened attentively to John explaining responsibilities of people on this particular floor.

Mustafa saw the two of them and gave a friendly smile and wave in their direction.

"That's my best friend, Mo Mustafa," John said suddenly realizing his surprise in calling Mo, *his best friend. Mo probably is my best friend. Strange, hadn't ever really considered it before. Wonder if it's mutual.*

John could not resist a surge of pride as colleagues turned to have a second look at Melanie. Obviously, she was a stranger and that would create a certain amount of scrutiny; but the looks varied from stares of admiration by the males, to cool competitive glances from the females.

"Melanie, I would like for you to meet Mo Mustafa. Mo—Melanie Fitzgerald."

Taking Mel's outstretched hand, Mo's admiring smile grew wide as he spoke, "Happy to meet you, Melanie. At last, it's clear to me why John has been speaking so highly of the great state of Wyoming. Welcome to New York."

"Thank you. I'm really enjoying the city. John has spoken of you often and I've looked forward to meeting you."

"Hopefully you haven't believed all of his mercenary comments regarding my personality flaws. Actually, I'm not a bad guy once you get past the rough edges. May I offer you something to drink? Bottled water, soft drink...*champagne?*"

"How about giving her hand back to her, Mo; she may need it again before the visit is over," John said with a sarcastic tone.

Looking down at Melanie's hand, which he was still holding, Mo said, "I apologize for the rudeness of my friend in not understanding the centuries old custom of my Bedouin ancestors in welcoming a beautiful desert flower to our oasis."

Bending forward from the waist in an exaggerated bow, Mo brought Melanie's hand to his lips and gave it a mock kiss.

"Knock it off, Mo; since when do Bedouins kiss a woman's hand?"

"Thank you, kind Sir, for your gracious welcome," Melanie said with a curtsy. The trip across your parched land has left me thirsty indeed, and if you could draw some cool water from the well it would pleasure me greatly."

"Your wish is my command. John, would you be so kind as to *draw cool water* for our guest. You know where to find it and don't hurry back," Mo said turning quickly back to Mel.

"Please step into my sprawling office and have a seat on my designer metal folding chair while we await John's return."

Mo and Mel stood watching unable to make out John's soft muttering as he slowly crossed the large room toward the employees' lounge. As they turned to face each other, they broke into triumphant chuckles.

She's awesome! It's easy to see why John could be so enamored. Not only gorgeous to look at, but a quick sense of humor and intelligence to match. Damn, maybe she has a sister.

The two sat in the small cubicle and Mo listened with genuine interest as Mel described her big-city adventures. She was in the process of telling Mo of plans to see Billy Crystal's one-man show on Broadway when John returned with the water.

"John, it sounds like you have mid-week all planned. Only one thing missing."

"I'm afraid to ask what that might be," John retorted.

"Hey, I'm referring to the Bronx Bombers my friend. You may recall they are currently in town playing the boys from Bean Town. Since my intense work ethic and loyalty to my fellow peasants requires my presence here, it would be my pleasure to make Yankee tickets available to this beautiful fair maiden and her unworthy escort."

Seeing John's excited expression at the prospect of attending the game, Melanie quickly asked, "John, can we? Can we go see Boston playing in Yankee Stadium?"

The admiring looks from both men made the idea of spending long hours listening to belligerent beer-drinking fans shouting insults at the players (as well as each other) and watching grown men kick dirt onto the shoes of the sheriff (in this case called the umpire) almost tolerable.

***

FBI Resident Agency
Springfield, Missouri

Agent Karen Blackwell awakened suddenly as her chin hit her chest. She was sitting in the most comfortable chair in the office—an oversized leather chair retrieved from behind the desk of SSRA Sterling.

The incoming communications pretty much stopped at 2 am (12 midnight on the west coast). There had not been anything requiring alerting Bridger or Sterling; it was 4:15 am and she would be relieved before long.

She pushed Sterling's chair back into his office and began pondering the past few days. Not really aware of how unhappy she had been in her job until recent days spent working with Mr. Bridger and Aaron, it was now painfully obvious she would soon have to make a decision about her future.

After completing an MBA at the University of Southern California, Blackwell surprised most of her friends with her decision to join the FBI. It was a professional choice discussed only with her parents.

Training at the academy passed quickly and for the most part was what she expected. Instruction was first class, and virtually every member of her class was crème de la crème. Likewise, first office went very well with an assortment of assignments designed to give an overview of Bureau statutory responsibilities.

Beginning with her transfer to Springfield, everything changed. Assignments were so monotonous as to be demeaning in nature. And it didn't seem to matter how much enthusiasm or effort she put into the mundane tasks—she never seemed to be given a chance at the more interesting assignments.

Sometimes she felt like a hamster whose daily life was on a wheel—no opportunity to advance or alter the course of events. Opportunities outside the Bureau were looking more appealing, and expiration of her three-year commitment made upon entering the FBI was about to expire.

What had changed over the past few days? Obviously she enjoyed, as everyone does, being given credit for the success of an undertaking. Had Bridger done so only to be "politically correct"—throw a bone to the token female and avoid any potential for cries of discrimination? Somehow, that didn't ring true for this man. He was the type from whom you had to earn respect, regardless of gender.

The sound of the heavy bolts on the front door brought her attention back to the present. Adjusting Sterling's chair carefully into its original position, she walked slowly back toward her desk.

"Good morning, Karen. Anything new come in?"

"Morning, Henry. Nothing since around 2 am; placed some copies on your desk. Would you like for me to stay while you read through them?"

"No. That won't be necessary. Go home, get some rest and don't plan to be back until afternoon."

"I'm fine really. I'll be back…."

"*Afternoon*! Do not want to see you in this office until afternoon," Sterling repeated.

As Karen left the building and walked to her car, she pondered the difference in Sterling's tone. *There was a change in his attitude that was unmistakable. Was it due to his recognizing her contributions of the past few days or something else? Perhaps Bridger was having an affect on Sterling's attitude, and it was spilling over into his treatment of those working under him. Whatever, it'll probably go away when Bridger leaves,* she bemoaned, saddened by her growing cynicism.

Blackwell felt her body slump with fatigue, sinking deep into the leather seats of the Acura Coupe. She was more tired than she realized.

Leaving the RA and turning onto James River Expressway, the first signs of early morning light were beginning to show. This was her time of day—the time she chose for workouts in junior high school when competitive running became more than a hobby.

Red and pink colors stretched across the eastern horizon, marking the beginning of something new, something never seen before and never to be seen again. Only a handful of cars were out this early, with most people still in bed trying to catch a couple more hours of sleep before meeting the demands of another dull week.

I'm not very happy with my work assignments right now, but the past few days have been anything but boring.

She felt her stomach roll and heard the soft growl. *Think I'll hit Jennie's before going home. No sense in trying to get to sleep with hunger pains gnawing my insides.*

The parking lot at *Jennie's* held only two other vehicles, and she slid the Acura into a spot close to the door. *They're not busy; should be able to get an order quickly and eat before falling asleep in my plate.* Taking a closer look at one of the cars, she realized it was the BuCar assigned to Cohn.

As Karen went through the squeaking door of the vintage Café, she spotted a familiar smiling face.

"Good morning, Karen. Wow—you look like something the cat drug in. Busy night?"

"Good morning to you too, and thanks for noticing. What are you doing up so early? Let me guess; going home after getting lucky with some bimbo," Blackwell retorted, quickly wishing she hadn't made the sarcastic remark.

Aaron didn't respond but stood staring until she finally looked away. *Whoa, did my remark really sound that nasty or is she overreacting?*

"I felt it might be a good idea to get to the office early and wait for the profile to arrive. Mr. Bridger figures Harmison has probably been up all night putting it together and expects it first thing this morning. He's putting a lot of eggs in that basket.

"By the way, in case you're interested, Mr. Bridger has been very complimentary of your work. Let me see…how did he put it, 'you have the qualities of a potentially outstanding investigator.'"

Blackwell's head popped up in surprise.

"He said that? Bridger…Mr. Bridger said that?"

"Why is that so shocking?" Aaron asked.

"It's a little unexpected coming from someone with his background and experience. It also seems a bit premature."

"I've only been with Mr. Bridger a few days, but one thing comes through loud and clear. It doesn't take very long for him to form opinions regarding people's work ethic, loyalty and their instincts for investigating; and once he has—as evidenced by his loyalty to Harmison—it takes a lot for him to change his mind."

Blackwell shot Aaron a cynical smile and snapped, "And of course he recognized those qualities in you immediately." *Holy shit—shut up, bitch! He's trying to compliment you, and you seize another opportunity to attack him.*

Once again Cohn ignored her comment, looking at her with a somewhat puzzled expression before adding simply, "No…he recognizes them in you. You must be tired and probably want to eat and get some sleep. I'll get out of your way; see you later at the RA. Mr. Bridger wants to wrap everything up here before we leave for Denver."

"Leave? When…when are you leaving?"

Once again Aaron gave her a long quizzical look before responding.

"We'll be heading for Denver in the next day or so. As you know, that's to be the new headquarters for FIST."

"Sure…sure I knew you would be leaving soon; hadn't realized it would be this soon." *Why is this news so disturbing? You knew they would be leaving and that isn't surprising. What then? They've brought changes; the environment here will soon return to normal, and you'll be back to hating it.*

Cohn sat without saying anything. *Despite all the mixed signals she puts out, Karen is the most interesting female I've met in a very long time. Damn, it might be nice to get to know this woman, and at times she acts like it could be mutual. Whoa there, hotshot, don't get ahead of yourself; she was surprised at the news—nothing more, nothing less.*

Aaron tossed a couple of bills on the table for a tip. "See you this afternoon; and Karen, the 'cat can drag you into my life anytime.'"

Turning quickly on his heel, he was gone before she could reply.

***

Aaron had been in the office a couple of hours when Bridger arrived. He entered the Com Room, handed Bridger a cup of coffee and began to summarize the communications of the past few hours. They were interrupted when a bell rang indicating an incoming message. Harmison's profile was on the secure network.

05-30-2007
VCF # 911-0009342
OO: Washington
FROM: Fist Denver
TO: SAC Kansas City/ Director FIST
RE: BuCom dated 5-19-2007.

The following profile is being submitted after consideration of available investigative information received on or before 05-30-2007. Reference list of reports on which this profile is based follows as addendum # 1-01.

SUMMARY:

Examination of investigative results from the individual assassinations reveals credible evidence indicating high probability of nexus of perpetrators.

Evidence suggests incidents conducted with overtones of centralized organization as indicated by cell phone calls subsequent to each incident. GPR (Gun Powder Residue) from wall of building in Chicago and interior bed of pick-up in Springfield produced by same manufacturer. (Ref. NSA reports of cell phone conversations on related dates and Chicago forensic report.)

Explosive C-4 used in Portland and Seattle contained chemical signatures indicating same source for each.

Details of individual incidents suggest perpetrators acted in pairs and functioned in a military style format.

An extremely high degree probability exists perpetrators have military background with sniper and IED (Improvised Explosive Device) training. These individuals projected to have record of unsatisfactory performances— possibly unrelated to military duties—linked to social adjustment. [Ref. TEDAC (Terrorist Explosive Device Analytical Center) and CIRG (Critical Incidence Response Group) reports.]

Victims appear to have been selected in support of a premeditated violent agenda against specific profiled individuals. A comparison of backgrounds of victims relating to motive reveals common nexus of one or more of the following: (a) race, (b) religion, (c) sexual lifestyle, and (d) public support of similar social, cultural and ethnic individuals.

Auditory comparisons of cell phone recordings by NSA disclose identical subject involved in Chicago and Springfield sniper incidents. Similarly, comparisons of Seattle and Portland voice interceptions indicate identical subject to be involved in both bombing venues.

The results of the investigations conducted to date appear to support the following conclusion with regard to perpetrators:

The motive for commission of the series of events accurately fits the profile of a variety of racial supremacy organizations.

A profile search of the DTSC (Domestic Terrorist Screening Center) reveals several potential organizations with the national affiliation required.

Several organizations fit the basic profile outlined. However, when all factors are given integral weight including known personnel, locality, avowed goals of various groups and potential for violence, orchestrated on a national scale, we can reach a conclusion with a high degree of probability.

The Brotherhood of Aryan Warriors has the synergy and financial resources. (Ref. Addendum # 17 regarding personnel and known locations for various domestic cells.)

Bridger took a sip of strong coffee as he read through the communiqué from Harmison one more time. He felt a slight chill come over his body as he noted Idaho and Arkansas were both on the list of known locations for—The Brotherhood of Aryan Warriors.

Could we be this lucky? Has Shawn hit a homerun on his first at bat with his new team?

Cohn came in and handed him a VCF communication from Seattle.

"Knew you would want to see this right away, Boss."

05-30-2007
VCF # 911-0009342
OO: Washington
TO: SAC Kansas City/Director FIST
FROM: SAC Seattle
RE: FIST Com. Dated 05-28-2007.

Result investigation SeaTac Airport Rental Car follows:

Rental car employee Richard T. Jackson, DOB 05-19-66, resident address 9410 152nd Avenue S.E., Seattle, Washington, advises two men returned vehicle 05-19-2007 with "pock marks on hood, roof and trunk which appeared to be burns." Jackson remembers date being his birthday, and he subsequently argued with two individuals regarding condition of the vehicle. Jackson could recall little detail apart from fact they were Caucasians and "appeared to be quite anxious to leave the airport." Jackson indicated he might possibly identify individuals if observed again.

SeaTac Rental Car records reveal 2007 Pontiac Gran Prix, VIN 777D0984190, reported to insurance company damaged and subsequently transferred to Hood's Body and Paint, 2000 Aurora Avenue South, for repair. Records further indicate vehicle rented 05-18-2007 to ARTHUR ALLEN SHIPMAN, Idaho Drivers License # 480-23-6756, residence listed as RR 4, Rocky Creek, Idaho. Rental paid by MasterCard # 4780-7766-0987-0874, expiration date 08-2009.

Cross check of records Fort Lewis Washington, indicate ARTHUR ALLEN SHIPMAN, DOB 11-22-69, army serial number, RA 173471189, Dishonorably Discharged United States Army, 06-24-2003, following summary court martial for repeated physical confrontations with racial minority members of his unit. Subject served Ranger unit with designated expertise in assembly and detonation of explosive devices. Psychological profile indicates "high degree of potential for violence, particularly toward minority ethnic and religious groups or individuals."

On 05-30-2007 Sgt. Ronald Colquist, Spokane Police Department, advised a large quantity of fertilizer matching chemical properties provided BuCom dated 4-19-2007 reported stolen on 05-06-2007, Hidden Valley Golf Course, Spokane, Washington.

Seattle Field Office will conduct following investigation:

Will conduct appropriate investigation Hood's Body and Paint including forensic examination of the SeaTac Rental Car vehicle.

Spokane will follow leads at Hidden Acres Golf Course in effort to determine perpetrators of theft of stolen fertilizer.

Reading the report from Seattle, Bridger could not help a feeling of vindication for Harmison, whose earlier loyalty had proven costly.

The profile appeared to be unerringly on the mark. The evidence was really starting to corroborate all the conclusions, including the likelihood the perps would be—"white supremacy types, with a history of overt action and potential for violence against ethnic and minority individuals or groups."

As Bridger finished reading the latest report, he looked through the glass wall; Cohn was talking with Karen Blackwell, and he motioned for them to come into the Com Room.

After entering the Com Room, Aaron was first to speak.

"You want to see us, Sir?"

"Have a seat. Need to give you a quick outline of the various communications that require immediate attention. Put your heads together, go through the list and get back to me with what I've missed.

"I'll be responsible for all communications to DHS. The two of you will handle dissemination of information to all other pertinent agencies. If you have questions, don't hesitate to direct them to me.

"All communications that may alert the potential perps we are on their trail are to be protected—that means using SCION (Sensitive Compartmentalized Information Network)—and information provided on a 'need to know' basis to all local agencies.

"Karen, you will be responsible for handling communications with the Bureau and maintaining liaison with the locals. Be circumspect—to the point of caution—in any area you suspect may result in leaks to media outlets. We do not want "premature articulation" making a mess of this before we can act."

Bridger spent the next several minutes designating the various agencies and specifying the type of communication appropriate for each.

This is a lot of responsibility to place in the hands of two young agents, but I'm confident they can handle it. Next, Bridger dialed Ramirez.

"Good afternoon, Ted. Do you have news on the investigation?"

"Good afternoon, Mr. Secretary. Yes, Sir. We have several developments."

Bridger described the latest investigative results, concluding by identifying the Brotherhood of Aryan Warriors as the suspected perpetrators.

"Ted, I'm extremely pleased with the progress you're making, but have to ask—what kind of DEAF (Definitive Expected Accuracy Factor) can you give me?"

"Mr. Secretary, we are sending out appropriate leads to corroborate what we have learned thus far and to fill in some gaps. If I had to assign a percentile factor at this point in the investigation, it would be 90+ percent. We should be able to give you a definite answer in the next 24 hours."

"Terrific, Ted! I meet with security agency heads and the President day after tomorrow for a PIA briefing. (Presidential Intelligence Assessment) No need to tell you how important some good news could be. Anything we can do here?"

"I'm sending a synopsis of our investigation directly to you within the hour. FBI and CIA are being updated along with appropriate other agencies. Our leads will determine potential locations and identify suspects in the areas mentioned to you. Sir, I would like to call your attention to the outstanding effort of Shawn Harmison. We pressed him hard for a quick response, and I'm not aware of anyone else who could have looked at the volumes of material and produced a profile with such unerring accuracy."

"Once again, Ted, the new unit has been impressive. If this goes in the direction we're projecting, you can be sure I'll not miss the opportunity of pointing out Harmison's contribution to interested parties. Keep me posted."

"Yes, Mr. Secretary."

***

CHAPTER 19

New York World **Offices**
New York City, New York

Mustafa had decided to complete some work on the Bridger file updating information coming in from the *stringer* in Springfield, Missouri. It was the bottom of the 2nd and the Yankees and Sox were tied 2-2.

Mo sat listening to the game through an earpiece plugged into his ancient Sony portable to avoid disturbing the half dozen or so people working on the other side of the room. They probably wouldn't have been able to hear the radio playing through the speaker, but it was a matter of courtesy.

He had opened a file on the computer and started to read when he noticed someone at Chambers' cubicle.

What would JC be doing here at this hour? He's supposed to be at the game with Mel using my tickets. Maybe it's Gates looking for some information on the Bridger story.

It was difficult to see clearly because of the reduced lighting, a "politically correct" conservation effort mandated by management for the evening hours. Mo could see someone bent over the keyboard—and it definitely was not Gates or Chambers. Reaching the enclosure, he failed to hear the muffled footsteps of someone approaching from behind.

"Excuse me! What are you...aaah"

Mustafa felt intense pain, lights flashing in front of his eyes—followed quickly by the deep silent blackness of severe head trauma associated with death.

The hard strike to the head came from a short length of taped pipe meant to knock the victim unconscious with one blow—if it killed, so much the better. The second assailant turned from the computer, hovering over Mo's prostrate body; mercifully, Mo never felt him drive a serrated tactical knife into his lower chest; it was a killing thrust, intended to enter below his sternum, missing the rib cage, moving straight upward into the heart.

Mustafa's limp body lay on the floor with a growing pool of dark blood leaking out from the head and chest. There was no sign of life, and neither attacker bothered to check the body for vital signs. Experience had taught them, if he victim weren't dead, he would bleed out in a matter of minutes.

Taking the disk they copied from Chambers' computer and carefully wiping the keyboard clean of potential fingerprints, the two men stepped over the lifeless body and walked slowly toward the elevators.

It was unlikely anyone would stop them, but if they did, they were dressed in work clothes with appropriate identification badges hanging from their necks. The badges had been good enough to get them past entrance security, and now if stopped, they were simply taking a short break. If there was any argument…well, they could handle that scenario too.

***

Yankee Stadium
The Bronx

Yankee infielder, Alex Rodriguez, hit a home run driving in two runs and putting his team ahead of the hated Boston Red Sox. Melanie could feel vibrations from the noise the crowd was making. John earlier explained the feud dated back to 1920 with the sale of Babe Ruth to the Yankees by the Boston owner in order to keep his team from going bankrupt. The sale was for $100,000—a lot of money in the 1920s. Boston fans believe the Babe's sale began a curse, which prevented them from having success against the Yankees until recent years when the American League Pennant and World Series victories broke the spell.

Rodriguez, the Yankee player who hit the home run, was paid millions of dollars a year. Melanie could not believe she was hearing correctly—when John told her before the game in his excited dialogue on each of the Yankee starters—Rodriguez was under contract for $200,000,000 over the next ten years.

"Isn't he the greatest! Have you ever seen anything like this guy?" John yelled looking down at Mel.

"Does he do this often?" Mel asked.

"Absolutely! He's positively awesome." John replied.

"For $20,000,000 a year, I would expect him to do it every time he batted," Melanie, said more to herself than to John.

"I'm sorry…missed that. What did you say?"

Leaning over and shouting into John's ear, "You expect him to do it every time he bats."

The field lights came on, and the crowd let out another loud roar. It wasn't really dark enough to require lights yet, but John explained the transition from daylight to darkness was difficult for hitters and fielders alike; and thus lights hanging on huge towers were turned on before the first shadows could hit the field.

It would be easy to compare the game she was watching to the stage play they attended last night on Broadway. It had been an experience she would never forget, and John must be enjoying this experience in much the same way.

The beautiful green field with the carefully mowed grass provided the stage for the actors to perform amazingly graceful acts. They ran and jumped in such an effortless way as to suggest what they were doing was easy. The smells of peanuts, popcorn, smoke and spilled beer were all part of the scene playing out around them.

Suddenly and without understanding why, she reached over and hooking her arm in John's arm pulled him toward her kissing him softly on the cheek.

"Thank you for bringing me to the game, John."

The expression brought to his eyes by her comment, sent chills through Melanie's entire body. He was about to speak, when she heard the sound of a cell phone ringing. It rang once, twice, three times and John seemed unwilling to answer.

"Hey, lover boy. Stop gazing into her baby blues and answer the damn phone already!" a hoarse voice behind demanded. The indignant suggestion was followed by laughter from fans sitting nearby.

Reaching into the pocket of his Yankee jacket, John reluctantly pulled the phone out flipped it open with one hand and put it to his ear.

"Hello, this is John."

"John! John! It's Gates. I'm at the office. I got a call a little while ago and came down to find a gruesome scene. Mo's been beaten and stabbed! He may be dead. Cripes sakes—it happened right here in the office at your desk!"

"Michael, I'm at the Yankee's game. I'll grab a cab and be there as soon as I can. Anyone else hurt or injured?"

"No...no—only Mo. What the hell is going on when you aren't even safe in your office working? This is unbelievable...."

"Where have they taken Mo?"

"To Bellevue. Holy shit, John, there's blood everywhere."

"I'm leaving right now; I'll meet you at the hospital. Okay?"

Without waiting for the answer, John broke the connection and looking at Melanie's questioning face said simply, "We have to go; I'll explain to you on the way."

The taxi ride to Bellevue seemed to take forever. Chambers cautiously gave Mel the information received from Gates, trying hard not to frighten or excite her. His concerns in that regard proved unfounded. She listened intently and when John finished, said simply, "Let's think positive thoughts and pray for Mo. I know how close the two of you are," she added, giving John's hand a slight squeeze. "It's going to be all right."

Looking across at Mel, John could hardly believe her calm attitude. Here she was in a strange city, hundreds of miles from home—and she was trying to comfort him.

***

Bellevue Hospital
Emergency Room

Chambers sipped cold coffee from a white Styrofoam cup. Nearly four hours had passed since his arrival at Bellevue's Trauma Center, and he was still trying to make sense out of the entire evening.

Mo hadn't been robbed. His wallet, credit cards and jewelry were all still on him when he was found. What could account for such a vicious attack—what was the motive?

He insisted Melanie return to the hotel and not accompany him to the hospital. Nerves still frayed with the uncertainty of the situation, he held the taxi at the door of the Cottonwood Plaza until the doorman escorted her inside.

Shortly after arriving at the hospital and being directed to a small waiting room in the emergency area, Michael Gates rushed to meet him.

"He must be really bad, John. They're calling in two specialists to work on him in emergency surgery. One young doc says it doesn't look good. What the hell does that mean? 'Doesn't look good.'"

"Easy, Michael. I'm sure they're doing everything possible, and it's probably too early to tell very much."

Chambers was surprised at how emotional Michael sounded. It was really out of character for him and undoubtedly had to do with his inability to control the situation.

"Why don't we sit down, discuss the sequence of events and see if we can come up with any reasons someone might want to hurt Mo. Want some coffee? There's a machine over there...."

Before Chambers could finish his sentence, several of New York's finest came through the swinging doors to the small waiting room. Two "suits" followed the uniformed cops; *probably detectives,* Chambers assumed. *This sure seems like a lot of firepower for a single stabbing assault. What the hell is going on?*

Before he could answer his own rhetorical question, the two detective types came over and began asking questions.

"Excuse me, Gentlemen. May we ask why you are here?"

The man asking the question was the smaller of the two. Chambers noticed he was wearing a well-cut suit with a broadcloth shirt and silk tie. The second man, larger and younger, was dressed in a similar style.

These are not New York City detectives. Wrong dress—and definitely—wrong attitude in asking questions.

Chambers waited for Gates to speak. When a moment of silence went by, Chambers decided to answer; "We're waiting for a colleague of ours to come out of surgery."

"And who might that be?" asked the taller of the two.

At that point, Gates' voice took on a familiar challenging tone as he said, "Excuse me...Gentlemen. Who are you and why are you asking?"

Gates' question and tone of voice seemed to throw the two momentarily off guard, and they took a quick glance at one another before the older of the two answered.

"We're here to be certain a colleague is protected from further injury...." He appeared to start to say something more, but reconsidered when the second man gave him a small slap on the arm. Turning abruptly, they walked over to a uniformed officer; and standing with backs turned, spoke to him in hushed tones.

Finishing the conversation, the two "suits" moved to nearby chairs, and the uniformed officer (a sergeant with three stripes on his sleeve) approached

Chambers and Gates. Judging by the three stripes on his sleeve, he was a sergeant.

"Good evening. We're on a protection assignment, and I need to see some identification if you plan to remain in this area," the sergeant stated in a controlled but firm voice.

"Look, Sergeant, we're with the *New York*...."

"Mister, you weren't asked who you're with; you were asked for ID and I want it now!"

Gates and Chambers had lived in New York too long not to understand the change in tone of voice. The streets of the city were a tough place, and uniformed cops didn't get far if they took any back talk—even if it was an attempt at explanation. It was better to comply with the request and explain later.

Glancing down at a laminated card with their photos identifying them as employees of the *New York World*, the cop looked at both of them carefully comparing the photos to the two men.

"Show me a driver's license."

"I...I don't have a driver's license," Gates said in a tone starting to show his frustration.

"Then show me some other form of identification," the cop said, not finding it at all suspicious a man living in the city didn't have a license to drive.

After being satisfied of their identities, the sergeant asked, "What's your business here in the hospital?"

"We're waiting on an injured colleague to get out of the operating room," Gates replied.

"His name is Mustafa; and if you check, you will find he was assaulted in our offices earlier this evening and brought here for treatment. What's all the cloak and dagger stuff about, Officer?"

The sergeant stood for a moment trying to decide how to answer and finally, deciding not to respond, returned to the plainclothes pair and began to whisper. The three men looked toward Gates and Chambers, then turned away and moved to chairs on both sides of the hallway leading to the operating room and sat down.

After an hour or so, Chambers persuaded Gates he would be needed at the paper to edit the inevitable story that would have to be written about the assault. It was finally agreed, John would stay and provide an hourly update on Mo's condition until—one way or the other—it was no longer necessary.

Chambers called Melanie and she wanted to come to the hospital to wait with him, but he convinced her that was not a good idea for the present.

Suddenly the three men sitting in the hallway rose from their chairs. A black woman came into the waiting room wearing the familiar green operating gown with a mask dangling from a string around her neck. The bloodstains on the front of her gown gave Chambers a chilling sense of foreboding.

The two "suits" showed some form of identification, and the doctor examined it carefully. Obviously satisfied they had a right to information, she spoke with them for several long minutes.

What is she telling the cops about Mo's condition? He felt an urge to rush over, but instinct told him it would be better to wait and speak with the doctor privately.

Something about this female doctor appeared familiar. The sanitary cap pulled down over half her forehead made features difficult to see clearly.

Now I remember—Dr. Charlotte Hammack.

After 911 he wrote a story on her heroic efforts to save lives. She literally risked her own life rushing into the danger zone to provide early emergency aid to the injured. Following Chambers' story in *Big Apple* magazine, Dr. Hammack received public acclamation—becoming somewhat of an overnight heroine. She had even been a guest on late night TV with David Letterman.

Hammack was an example of success coming from the very depths of poverty—both social and intellectual—having grown up under difficult circumstances in Harlem. A graduate of Princeton and Columbia Medical School, she had a growing reputation as an outstanding surgeon.

The conversation seemed to end, and Chambers walked quickly toward the doctor hoping to catch her before she could leave the waiting room.

"Excuse me, Dr. Hammack. Could I ask you a couple of questions, please?"

Weary from the hours of surgery and not anxious to attempt to answer questions for which she had no answers, the doctor's expression did little to hide her annoyance.

As Chambers came closer, the look changed to one of recognition, and a tired smile crossed her face.

"If I remember correctly, asking questions is what you do best. How are you, John Chambers?"

"I'm well, Doctor," he replied taking her extended hand.

"One of my associates—and closest friend—was brought in with stab and head wounds. Did you…did you by chance treat him?"

Chambers could see the two men coming toward them without any attempt to conceal the fact they wanted to hear the conversation.

"He's in critical condition and the next 24 hours will probably tell the story. Dr. Gerald Bair, one of the top brain trauma surgeons in the country is finishing up now. He feels the head wounds have been repaired successfully and barring complications should heal nicely. One of the stab wounds missed being fatal by millimeters, and the danger of infection will be present for the next couple of days."

The doctor turned the clipboard in her hands and began to write something across the paper.

The sudden change in behavior surprised Chambers, and he took it to mean the conversation was over. Fumbling for something to say, he finally spewed forth a seemingly obsequious—but sincere comment.

"I'm glad you performed the surgery, Dr. Hammack. Mo couldn't have been in better hands."

"Thank you, John" she replied, turning the clipboard toward him and holding it close to her chest in an effort to shield it from the policeman.

The letters jumped out at him—FBI-CIA.

Feeling the blood rushing to his head and realizing he was about to react to this unexpected news, Chambers took a deep breath to regain composure.

"Thank you for the information, Dr. Hammack," he heard himself saying in a surprisingly even voice.

It was all he could do to conceal his surprise.

What the hell are they doing here? An assault does not fall into the jurisdiction of the FBI and certainly not the CIA. What possible connection could they have to Mo, Chambers wondered.

"I'll let my boss know about his condition and be sure Mo's relatives have been notified."

As Dr. Hammack left, Chambers' mind began to race over this latest information.

What was the connection? Was Mo the subject of an investigation by the feds? Could he be a terrorist suspect? No way in hell. But what then, if not a suspect?

Walking toward a private area of the waiting room, Chambers suddenly froze in his tracks.

What was it the older of the two federal agents said? "We're here to be certain a colleague of ours is protected"...that was it. "A colleague of ours."

Mo wasn't being investigated; he was undoubtedly working for the FBI or CIA. It all fit—his background gave him the perfect cover needed to infiltrate potential radical Muslim groups. *The New York World* gave him access and credentials to move without suspicion into virtually any area of the country—and eventually back to the Middle East.

Did Gates know? It was hard to believe he would intentionally hire someone from FBI or CIA, allowing use of the paper as cover.

Anger mixed with indignation surged within Chambers as he considered what it all meant to their relationship. *What did this subterfuge by Mo mean with regard to their friendship? Was it, too, part of an elaborate cover?*

He pushed the speed dial for Gates, his mind still racing, uncertain what he would or should say about his suspicions.

The phone rang twice and an excited Michael Gates came on with, "Holy crap, John, I was about to call you. This place is swarming with federal agents. They come in here with a search warrant. Where the hell do you find a judge to issue a search warrant in the middle of the night? They are going over Mo's desk, your desk, everything in the office. What the hell is going on?"

"Michael, the good news is Mo's still alive. He came through the surgery and the doctors think if he survives the next 24 hours, he could make it."

"That's more than we could have hoped for," Michael replied in a somewhat less excited tone.

"John, you and Mo are close; probably know him better than anyone here at the paper. Could Mo be mixed up in some kind of terrorist activity, perhaps involving the sale of drugs? That might account for such a violent attack."

Damn, here it is; what am I going to say? After a long pause, John finally replied.

"No, Michael. No way Mo could be involved in anything of that nature."

"I needed to hear that from someone else, John—to be sure personal feelings weren't affecting my judgment. I have a good source in the FBI, and it's time to get him out of bed and find some answers. Keep me informed and get some rest when you can."

Chambers let out a deep breath and sat asking himself *why*? *Why did I deliberately withhold information from Gates?*

This is exactly the kind of misguided loyalty that gets reporters fired—and I don't even know why I'm doing it.

***

Exhaustion finally took its toll and Chambers slept. He was awakened by the noise of rubber-soled shoes padding through the intensive care waiting room. Rolling over on the small couch, he could see at least three medical personnel entering Mo's room.

Two NYPD uniform cops were on either side of the door—exactly where they stood before Chambers fell asleep—and that could only mean one thing.

It was obvious: whoever Mo was working for believed he could still be in danger. It could also mean he possessed information valuable to both sides.

Jumping to his feet, he almost fell down from the rush of blood to his head. Regaining balance, he rushed toward the glass door behind which laid his best friend—at least his former best friend.

Whatever is going down in that room can't be good. Screw this; I'm going to find out.

The burly officers held out their hands warning him to stay back.

"Listen, Officers, I've been here all night worrying about my friend and something is going on in there. Cut me a little slack, will you please. I only want to look through the glass."

The two men exchanged glances and the older of the two finally spoke. "Go ahead and step to the glass for a quick look. But that's all."

"Understood. Thank you."

What was happening? Two nurses and a doctor were standing around the bed without appearing to be conducting any kind of treatment or examination.

Aw no. Not, Mo. He must be dead, or they'd be doing something.

Seeing Chambers standing at the door, one of the nurses came toward him, opening the door and closing it quietly behind her.

"Let's talk over here," she suggested walking past the cops stopping just outside the waiting room.

"We've seen you waiting for the past several hours; are you a relative of Mr. Mustafa?"

"Not exactly. Mo is my co-worker…" and feeling his voice choke with emotion added, "and my best friend."

"We have some good news. He regained consciousness and the attending doctor feels he has a good chance of recovering. It was a close call; they nearly lost him twice on the operating table. He caught a big-time break when both Dr. Bair and Dr. Hammack happened to be on call; they are two of the finest emergency room trauma surgeons in the world."

"Awesome! That's such great news. I was so sure you were going to tell me…. Well, it doesn't matter now. Thank you very much. Any chance I could see him?"

"No, I'm afraid that isn't possible yet," the nurse replied. "You look like *you* could use some sleep; why not go home and come back later. Your friend is going to need all the rest he can get, but perhaps you'll be allowed to see him this afternoon."

Thanking the nurse for the information, Chambers located a seat in the waiting room and pulling a cell phone from his pocket hit the speed dial for Gates' home phone. It was late, actually early morning but he'd want to hear the great news.

The next few days were going to be unpredictable at best. There were a lot of questions to be answered and Gates would want to pursue the Bridger story now that his new position was public knowledge.

But what about Mo? How much would Gates be able to find out from his source in the FBI? How much should I tell him about what's gone down here?

Best to wait until later to call Melanie. No sense in waking her this early—and, what about Melanie?

The idea didn't appeal to him; but the facts were, it would be best for Melanie to return to Wyoming. *But how in hell am I going to suggest it without hurting her feelings,* he wondered.

***

FBI Resident Agency
Springfield, Missouri

In the Springfield RA ComRoom, Bridger looked over the latest communication to arrive from Seattle.

05-31-2007
VCF # 911-009342
OO: Washington
TO: SAC Kansas City/FIST Denver
FROM: SAC Seattle
RE: VCF Seattle dated 05-30-2007.

On 05-30-2007 SA Reginald Sanders conducted the following investigation at Hood's Body Shop, 2000 Aurora Avenue South, Seattle, Washington.

Forensic examination 2007 Pontiac Gran Prix, VIN 777D0984190 reveals the following:

Latent prints taken from vehicle identified as ARTHUR ALLEN SHIPMAN, DOB 11-22-69. (Reference earlier communication for further description and information.)

A second latent print identified as THOMAS EUGENE HOWARD, DOB 07-31-77. Army service records reveal HOWARD served US Army, serial # RA 174482768, honorably discharged 09-03-2003. Last assigned to Ranger unit with ordinance training. Records further indicate HOWARD's attempt to re-enlist denied upon recommendation commanding officer. (See attachment for complete copy of service records, listed relatives and psychological profile.)

Idaho DMV records list THOMAS E. HOWARD DOB 07-31-77, assigned license # 492-63-8703, with residence listed as P.O. Box 897, Rocky Creek, Idaho. Records further indicate 2001 Ford F-250 pick-up truck, VIN # 698T0048932, registered to HOWARD at above address.

On 05-30-2007, Richard T. Jackson, SeaTac Rental Car employee viewed random photos and selected HOWARD and SHIPMAN without reservation. Jackson indicated he was "positive" these were the two individuals who returned a damaged rental car to his workstation at SeaTac on 05-18-2007.

On 05-30-2007, SA Thomas Vortec submitted random photos to employees of Hidden Valley Golf Course, Spokane, Washington. Office Manager, Cynthia Ann Styles, identified photo of THOMAS E. HOWARD as friend of former employee at golf course. Styles further advised she had spoken with HOWARD on several occasions while he waited for one of employees to get off work.

Styles records indicated ANTHONY WATERS, employed 04-03-2007, as golf course worker associated with HOWARD. Records further reflected WATERS provided Washington DL 580-26-5903, DOB 10-25-88 address listed 1947 Cascade Ave. NW, Spokane, Washington. Styles stated WATERS employed golf course grounds crew and voluntarily self-terminated 05-04-2007.

On 05-30-2007, Jerry L. Worden, Superintendent, Hidden Valley Golf Course, viewed random photos and selected THOMAS E. HOWARD, as individual observed with ANTHONY WATERS on several occasions.

Worden further advised WATERS was employed on maintenance crew performing grass cutting and fertilizer duties during month of employment. Slothful work habits, combined with confrontations with two minority members of crew, resulted in fellow workers giving WATERS nickname "SLOW" WATERS. A verbal conflict with Worden culminated in WATERS resignation.

Worden stated WATERS' duties required full access to sheds containing fertilizer.

Worden advised he recalled seeing HOWARD driving a black Ford pick-up truck, bearing unknown Idaho license number.

Worden described WATERS as follows: WM, 6'3," 200, Blue eyes and shaved head. He further stated WATERS was known by younger members of crew to be member of local "Skin Heads" recognized for prejudice and violent actions against selected minorities.

Interviews conducted with Styles, Worden and other employees of Hidden Valley Golf Course failed to provide further information of possible individuals, addresses or vehicles, associated with HOWARD or WATERS.

LEADS:

Seattle will conduct the following investigation:

Spokane will conduct discreet inquiries to determine extent of relationship between SHIPMAN and WATERS.

Spokane will contact appropriate CI's in attempt to identify WATERS potential association with "Brotherhood of Aryan Warriors" known to have presence in Coeur d' Alene, Idaho area.

Spokane will determine identities of individuals living 1947 Cascade Avenue NW, Spokane, Washington. Appropriate tech EL-SUR (Electronic Surveillance) and related surveillances will be performed as directed.

Bridger realized this latest information served to all but culminate the investigation in Seattle. It was noon on Tuesday, and he had spent all day Monday in the communication room receiving and sending leads to consolidate possible locations and identities. There was a steady stream of communications flowing from the various leads, and each lead sent out generated its own source of further leads. The last several hours had been spent digesting and summarizing the vast amounts of information and transferring it to his Smart Board computer program. It was time for him to meet with the staff and provide parameters.

Bridger paused in front of the conference room door.

"May I have your attention. Please complete your immediate task and join me here for a briefing."

Ten minutes later, the last of the agents entered the conference room and settled weary bodies into the seats around the long table. Most had laptops and everyone was prepared to take notes and anxious to see how the investigation was coming together.

Blackwell stood near the light switch, "Karen, if you'll cut the lights, we can get started," Bridger said.

A few seconds later the large white board at the front of the room lit up with the first of the outlines of the investigation.

What a difference technology has made. When I was the age of these agents, this information would all be appearing on a chalkboard. These people were introduced to computers in elementary school and are far more adept than I at utilizing their tremendous potential in every facet of a complex investigation.

SYNOPIS SPRINGFIELD INVESTIGATION

Bird feather recovered from grill of perpetrators' Dodge truck traced to area of North-Central Arkansas.

FBI-Little Rock actively investigating Para-military group known to live and train on 220-acre farm located in area often referred to as Moark, Arkansas.

Group identified as Brotherhood of Aryan Warriors known to be actively training in the use of firearms and explosive devices.

Sale of .308 Nosler 180gr. Spitzer bullets, (factory marked C.T.) and Alipant 15 powder traced to Kelley's Shooting and Archery Supply, Little Rock, Arkansas.

Alipant 15 powder residue found in Chicago, on wall used by sniper, matches that traced to Little Rock store. Fatal bullet recovered from door of restaurant identified as .308 Nosler.

Photos of ROBERT HENRY JONES and MICHAEL WAYNE MATTHEWS identified by management and employees at Kelley's, as individuals having purchased shooting supplies on numerous occasions. Records indicate purchase of listed supplies on 04-15-2007 under the names

Jerome T. White and Alex G. Johnson. Photo identification indicated Little Rock addresses.

Addresses provided for suspects from store records found to be non-existent.

Stolen Dodge truck odometer readings compared with oil change records and owner driven mileage, reveal a total approximating 129 miles driven subsequent to theft.

Topographical map computer analysis by NRO (National Reconnaissance Office) agrees with probability the truck was driven from a North-Central Arkansas location to Springfield, Missouri.

Little Rock office advises CIs (Confidential Informants) currently working inside the Brotherhood of Aryan Warriors.

Informants to determine location of MATTHEWS and JONES and number of people currently at training site of Brotherhood of Aryan Warriors.

NSA providing appropriate intelligence from cell phone and cyber traffic.

Voice traffic analysis by NSA (National Security Agency) from Arkansas encampment positively identified suspect voice being that recorded on cell phone transmission from Chicago and Springfield subsequent to shootings.

Motive for assassinations linked with avowed violent hate crimes attributed to BAW (Brotherhood of Aryan Warriors) in the past and publicly stated violent agenda.

Chicago victim—Jewish and recently presided over trial of white supremist.

Seattle victim—African-American Congresswoman with platform of tolerance.

Portland victim—Talk show host with outspoken opinions against white supremacy and related hate groups.

Springfield victim—Prosecuting attorney with homosexual lifestyle publicly acknowledged in recent election.

Satellite surveillance is being initiated on the suspected area of encampment.

Evidence is being submitted to appropriate U.S. Attorneys, and the Justice Department is obtaining necessary search and arrest warrants.

Recommendations are being considered regarding strategies and tactics for raiding the Arkansas encampment.

Bridger expanded verbally on each of the numbered points trying to provide as much accumulated information as he felt was pertinent to enable the entire group of agents to see the big picture.

Finally, after over an hour, he stepped in front of the smart board and asked for the lights.

"Before we continue with a summary from Seattle, any comments on the Arkansas investigation? Are there leads or sources to tap we haven't utilized? Any comments or questions?"

The agents looked about waiting for someone to speak. There was only silence until finally—from her seat in the back of the room—Karen Blackwell spoke in a tone suggesting a degree of uncertainty.

"Our investigation thus far seems to pretty clearly identify the perpetrators involved in both the Chicago and Springfield assassinations—and their affiliation with Brotherhood of Aryan Warriors.

"I...I may be jumping the gun here, but communications from Seattle and Portland, strongly supports the probability the attacks there were planned and carried out by BAW from an Idaho encampment. This in turn suggests a strong likelihood there is a national coordination involved indicating a centralized leadership and source of financing. Can we, or should we make that determination prior to raiding a single training sight and possibly driving the leadership to deep cover?"

Damn, she hit the nail square on the head, Bridger conceded. *"Follow the money...It's always about the money." I've been wrestling with that question all morning, trying to decide how I'm going to respond when the Secretary or one of the Directors asks what I recommend.*

"Damn good question," Bridger replied.

"On the one hand, we are faced with the possibility of delaying and incurring another assassination, or seeing the leaders of a dangerous extremist movement go underground. This is a question best resolved in Washington. After all, they get big money for making all those great decisions."

There were polite chuckles from the agents, followed by a few whispers.

"Anything else come to mind?" Bridger asked and waited several seconds for a response.

"If we could get the lights again, we can look at the results of the west coast investigations."

Bridger spent the next hour outlining the results from Seattle and Portland also presenting compelling evidence for the identity of the perpetrators and their probable location. He concluded by again asking for comments or questions, and this time there were none.

"There is a lot to do strategically to bring a successful conclusion to the efforts the various agencies have made. I'll be leaving for Denver tomorrow. I expect to have some input into the final solution, but DHS and the President will make the decisions when, where and how.

"Domestic terrorism has the potential to be absolutely as devastating as any perpetrated by foreign entities. We only need remember Oklahoma City and the turmoil and anxiety created by that tragic event.

"Allow me to take this opportunity to thank each of you for an outstanding effort. It's been a rough few days, but I trust you'll agree the results have made it worthwhile. You can be justly proud of your effort and the expertise demonstrated in this complex investigation. Well done!"

Bridger began to gather his notes and was putting them into his briefcase when he heard Sterling's voice asking for attention.

"If I may have everyone's attention for a moment, I'd like to make a quick comment."

Pausing until it was quiet, Sterling continued.

"The idea of having a new unit compiled of individuals from the various federal agencies appears to many as one more example of bureaucratic bungling. The potential for such an endeavor to succeed is fraught with obstacles from the beginning, ranging from power struggles, to selection of personnel, to perhaps most of all, leadership."

As Sterling paused, Bridger's face flushed with anger.

I would never have believed this SOB had the balls to verbalize what he has undoubtedly been thinking since he met our flight the first day. I'm surprised and disappointed—he appeared to be getting with the program.

"The past few days have been the most intense experience of my 13 years with the Bureau. They have also been the most rewarding, both from the standpoint of what we accomplished and because it has refurbished my enthusiasm for the work we are doing."

Sterling again paused and Bridger let a small sigh escape—his worst concerns were not being realized after all.

"It's become clear to all of us in this room what cooperation among agencies can accomplish, even in such a pressure-filled investigation as this.

"It's obvious FIST has great potential for success, and it is equally obvious it has the ideal leader to make it happen. I'm really proud and happy Mr.

Bridger was—and is—one of us and especially pleased we were able to make a contribution to the success of his new team in its first official investigation.

"Director Bridger, thank you on behalf of myself and the entire office. It has been a pleasure to work with you and we wish you and FIST the very best!"

The small FBI office in Springfield, Missouri, filled with applause as the agents stood in recognition of Bridger's leadership.

It was no time for speeches. Everything had been said worth saying and Bridger again felt his face flushing as he made his way around the long conference table—shaking hands, one agent at a time.

***

CHAPTER 20

Swan Lake Apartments
Springfield, Missouri

Arriving home earlier than usual, Blackwell decided to take a short run to loosen stiff muscles and let the exercise rid her mind of tension. The short run turned into several miles, and feeling the comfortable fatigue, she arrived back at her apartment to a ringing telephone.

Cripes sakes, let them get someone else to run their errands. Screw it; I'm not going to answer, she grumbled, knowing full well she would.

To her surprise, it was Aaron. Even more surprising—the reason for the call. He wasn't asking to be picked up so they could return to the office for yet another round of interagency communications—but rather inviting her out to dinner.

Blackwell wiped the steam from her bathroom mirror. A hot shower never felt quite so invigorating. The previous days were frenzied, with no time to exercise or do anything but work, eat and sleep.

She turned on her powerful little BOSE radio; a favorite FM station came on blaring country rock. Friends in California would find it amusing to learn her taste in music slowly underwent a transition after moving to the Ozarks; and without realizing it, she had become a fan of various styles of country music.

As Gretchen Wilson sang an award-winning song, Karen reflected on Aaron's invitation.

He seemed shy on the telephone, or could it have been reluctance? Why would he be asking me out the night before leaving town? Is he looking for a "quickie" or only tired of spending time alone in a hotel room?

Their last encounter at *Jennie's Restaurant* had been anything but encouraging—on her part at least. She felt sorry for her sharp comments that morning and tried since to be especially careful how she spoke to Aaron—until tonight that is.

"What kind of date asks the woman to pick him up? You could rent a car or call a taxi," came her facetious reply on the phone.

There was a momentary pause followed by his puzzled reply, "Yes, I could...."

For a long moment, he said nothing further.

Realizing she may have gone too far, Karen said, "I'll pick you up at your hotel. About 7, okay?"

Why am I being such a sarcastic little shit with him, she wondered. Is it because he's leaving and I envy him his new job or because I'm going to miss having him around?

This was not her typical attitude toward male contemporaries. For the most part, she considered herself professionally aloof. Snide remarks and a mocking, insulting demeanor were not part of her personality.

She slid the closet door open and began to shuffle through her wardrobe looking for something to wear. Hangers slid along, with various outfits being eliminated, before she finally concluded. *Damn! Nothing to wear for even a casual date. What does that say about my social life these past few months? Howard Hughes went out more in the last year of his life than I have.*

Finally settling on a pair of khaki capris pants, with a sleeveless black turtleneck and matching black sandals, she went back into the bathroom to dry her hair.

Martina McBride came on the radio singing "California Girl" and Karen smiled at the irony. Looking into the mirror she considered eye shadow and a touch of make-up.

What the heck—she decided—might as well give the boy a thrill on his last night in the big city.

***

University Plaza Hotel
Springfield, Missouri

Aaron stepped out of the hotel elevator 15 minutes before Karen was to pick him up. Time enough to look around the hotel gift shop. He considered buying flowers or a bottle of wine, but the fact she was picking him up somehow made both seem awkward. Besides, he really didn't know if she liked wine, and she certainly didn't seem like the type woman you give flowers.

What kind of woman is she then, he wondered. *Her built-up defenses were obvious and were probably necessary to enable her to work in a male-dominated profession that could still exhibit chauvinism in all its forms. Nevertheless, something was attracting him; but he wasn't really sure what it might be or why. She was attractive—but not beautiful—and her attitude toward him was only slightly short of offensive. She must think I'm really a "glutton for punishment." Perhaps that was it; his ego was challenging him to win her affection.*

In the small gift shop he was greeted by a young female employee busy restocking magazines on a long rack.

"May I hep ya?" The young woman asked in a friendly tone with an Ozarkian accent.

Turning from the stack of news magazines, she gave Aaron a dimpled smile displaying slightly uneven white teeth. Dressed in slacks and blouse worn by all the hotel employees, her blond hair was worn long, parted in the middle.

As she approached, her bright green eyes held a questioning look, and she appeared to be genuinely interested in "hepping" him. *Probably a college student,* he decided, *and perhaps she can help me.*

"I'm looking for a 'happy gift'—something suitable to give on a first date to a young professional woman. Any ideas?"

The young woman's brow creased, and she appeared to be seriously contemplating the problem. "How about a small stuffed animal? It's something a woman can keep in her car, take to work and put on her desk, or simply leave it in her bedroom."

Glancing at the shelf full of animals ranging from giraffes and lions to every type of dog imaginable, he was about to walk away when a small bear caught his eye.

"May I see the bear, please," Aaron asked. "That one, the gold colored one."

Back in the lobby of the hotel, Aaron looked down at the small sack containing the bear. The young woman had apologized for not having materials to gift-wrap and searched under the shelf, finding a small piece of bright ribbon and carefully tying a small bow around the hotel sack. She then used a pair of scissors to cut around the top of the sack creating a wavy design.

"That looks terrific! Not many people would take the time or be so creative. Thank you very much."

"You're very welcome," she said with a toss of blond hair. "I hope she likes your gift," she said smiling and reaching to flick the hair back from her eyes.

Aaron sat down in a large overstuffed chair near the front entrance, where he would be able to see Karen arrive. Cohn felt his stomach turn over slightly and realized he hadn't eaten since morning. The day passed quickly and was far too busy to take time out for lunch.

Bridger was giving him more to do each day, and he took that to be a sign the Boss had confidence in his abilities; he was making an extra effort to be sure not to prove him wrong.

Looking down at his Polo slip-on casual shoes, he began reflecting on the time he spent preparing for this tryst with Karen. It brought a nervous chuckle, and he took an embarrassed look around to see if anyone was watching.

It took him a full hour to get ready for what he should be considering a casual first date. First off, getting out of the shower, he shaved so closely he cut himself in three places. After using half a box of tissues, the bleeding finally stopped from a combination of wet soap and toilet paper.

Next, he tried to settle on what to wear. Conversation with Karen ended before they discussed where they were going, and he was not sure whether to dress in suit and tie or casual.

Finally, electing to go casual and pulling on a pair of tan Docker slacks, he stuffed a dark blue golf shirt into a still comfortable waistband. The lack of workout time hadn't shown up yet, probably because he was missing as many meals as workouts.

Damn, he admitted, *I haven't been this nervous about going out with a woman since the high school prom.*

Movement outside caught his attention, and he recognized Karen's red Acura pulling into the parking lot.

He waited for the electric sliding doors to open and waived to Karen, pleased to see she was dressed casually, as she opened the car door to get out.

Good, at least we're starting out on the same page.

Aaron, got into the car, fastened his seat belt and without hesitation made his first faux pas of the evening, "Good evening, Karen. Thanks for picking me up; it saved me having to rent a car."

Realizing how that might be misinterpreted

"I…I didn't mean…."

Before he could say more, Karen interrupted.

"Aaron, I'm terribly sorry for my earlier comments to you on the phone. I can only claim fatigue as an excuse. Forgive me?"

"No problem; it's been quite a week for all of us. Let's enjoy the evening and try to relax for a few hours. How about a pact? No job talk, agreed?"

"Agreed," Karen replied.

Aaron looked at the sack with a ribbon wrapped around it and suddenly felt very awkward about giving it to her. It seemed like an OK idea in the shop, but now he wasn't so sure. *Too late—she's seen it and I have to go through with it.*

Feeling his face turn warm, Aaron handed the paper sack to Karen and mumbled, "It's a really small token as a reminder of the evening...and me sort of I guess."

Karen carefully untied the ribbon and reached into the sack pulling out the small bear.

A delighted smile came to her face as she recognized the gesture. It was a golden bear—the athletic mascot of the University of California.

"I'm sorry I wasn't able to get something to remind you of me. The drugstore was all out of Trojans."

They both broke into laughter, and then Karen did something which totally surprised both of them. She stared at him for several seconds with a puzzled expression—as though trying to make a difficult decision.

Then, quite unexpectedly, she leaned toward Aaron very slowly and kissed him ever so tenderly on the lips. Pausing for a moment to look into his eyes, Karen then abruptly changed the mood and asked, "How about Italian? Sound good? *Zio's* here we come."

The red Acura sped onto James River Parkway and accelerated quickly to merge smoothly with the evening traffic.

"One of my favorites," Karen shouted over the blaring radio. "It's Garth Brooks singing about an old girlfriend he had in high school and how fortunate he is not to have married her. Ever hear it?"

"I don't believe so," Aaron shouted in reply. "Are you a country western fan?"

Reaching down and turning the radio down slightly, Karen said, "You know, I don't think I've ever been asked that before. Simple answer is yes, by necessity at first and inclination at present. This area's radio stations are full of Bluegrass and Country, and I've learned to enjoy the music."

The conversation continued in a carefree manner, with Karen nimbly weaving the Acura through traffic. After several miles, she turned off the freeway onto National Avenue and a couple of blocks later pulled into a parking spot next to an ornate Italian style building. A sign near the roof read: *Zio's Italian Kitchen*.

As Karen came around the car, Aaron realized he was seeing her for the first time as a woman—rather than a professional colleague.

Form fitting capris pants and a sleeveless turtleneck revealed her slender figure to perfection. *She has a great body,* he decided. *Her breasts are small, but really well shaped, and what a great ass.*

"Nice," he heard himself say.

"I'm sorry, Aaron, what did you say?"

"I…I said nice restaurant. Very nice."

Karen gave him a puzzled look before moving around the car and putting her arm in his. "Shall we?" she asked.

As they approached the hostess desk, people to the left sat casually sipping a drink at a long bar. The kitchen on the right was open to scrutiny of the patrons and occupied one entire side of the restaurant.

Wooden tables were randomly spaced around large vine encircled columns reaching to the roof, and the Italian motif was completed by mock laundry hanging from a rope clotheslines stretching high from imitation balconies.

Patrons of every description were sitting at small tables, with young college-age servers moving swiftly between tables and kitchen. Great smells filled the air and suddenly Aaron felt famished.

"Good evening, Ms. Blackwell—your table is ready."

"Thank you, Manny."

Manny was a manager of Zio's and knew Blackwell from her frequent visits. He seated them at a table toward the back of the nearly full restaurant, handed them menus and signaled for a waiter. "Enjoy your meal," Manny said with a smile before leaving.

Picking up a piece of crayon, the waiter quickly wrote his name—*Eric*—upside down, so they could read it on the paper tablecloth.

Interesting touch, Aaron conceded; *also a good way to establish a more personal connection in the interest of a better gratuity.*

Looking over the menu, Aaron asked, "What's good, Karen? Anything you can recommend?"

"I love the seafood pasta combinations, but any type of Italian food is outstanding here."

Eric returned with water and lemon wedges, plus great-smelling fresh baked bread.

Setting the bread on the table, Eric poured some virgin olive oil into a dish and mixed in several spices to be used for dipping the bread.

Electing not to have hors d'oeuvres on Karen's advice—"The portions are huge and there is usually enough for another meal with what I take home in the doggie bag."—Aaron asked if she would like wine.

"Please. A glass of wine would be nice."

"Eric, please bring two glasses of house Chianti with the meal," Aaron requested.

Reaching for the fresh bread, Aaron deftly cut the small loaf into several pieces and placed the bread between them. Picking up a piece and dipping it into olive oil, he wasted little time in downing the delicious warm morsel.

Looking up, he caught Karen watching at him with an amused smile.

"I haven't eaten since breakfast, and the great smells in this place are getting to me. Better keep your fingers clear of the bread dish," he offered with a mock warning.

Eric delivered the main course as Aaron was swallowing the last of the bread. The lasagna covered the entire plate; and hungry as he was, it would be difficult to eat it all at one sitting. Karen's shrimp pasta looked equally appetizing.

"Will there be anything else," Eric asked.

"How about more bread and we're good to go," Aaron replied.

For several minutes they sat in silence enjoying their first meal since breakfast. The food proved to be as delicious as it looked. The conversation was casual with both electing to stay away from business topics. Taking a sip of Chianti, Aaron looked across at Karen, "Great choice of restaurants! First *Jennie's* and now *Zio's*; you're on a roll!"

After declining dessert and ordering "doggie boxes," the two sat finishing the Chianti. Offering his glass in salute, Aaron said, "L'Chayim!" (Too life)

"L'Chayim," Karen repeated.

Aaron suddenly felt the urge to offer a compliment.

How will she take it, he wondered. *Don't all women like to be complimented? Would it be considered sexual harassment? Come on, pal, you're on a date—remember?*

"Karen, you look *great* this evening," he blurted right out of the blue.

Karen's gaze lasted several seconds—her dark brown eyes questioning— before speaking.

"*You* look *great* too, Aaron," she said with a pleasant smile.

That was nice. My grandmother would be bursting with pride to learn I'm on a date with "a nice Jewish boy." "Finally," she would say," finally you will make me great grandchildren. I was beginning to think you would be older than Abraham's wife Sarah before making babies."

"Thank you for dinner. It's been good to relax and get the job off my mind for a time. However, speaking of the job, what do you think Mr. Bridger would say if I asked to join FIST?"

The question caught Aaron completely by surprise. It must have shone on his face, and Karen quickly began to apologize.

"I'm sorry I asked you that, Aaron. It…it's really putting you on the spot, and you don't have to answer. We weren't going to talk…."

"No. No that's okay. I'd like to answer, but first answer one question. Why would you want to join FIST?"

Karen hesitated, carefully considering the question.

"The past few days have been more what I joined the Bureau to do than all the rest of the 2½ years combined. I've been treated as a professional with an opportunity to perform and gain credit for results. That's all I've ever wanted or expected. I would like to be part of a new organization, setting new policy with new ideas on working together as a team and capturing the potential success and rewards it offers."

Aaron did not speak for a moment, carefully considering what he was about to say: "I obviously can't speak for Mr. Bridger, Karen, but he has been very complimentary of your work. Have you considered the implication moving to FIST could have on your career?"

"To be honest, Aaron, I'm not sure whether it will ultimately hurt or harm my career, but I'm certain of one thing. If I have to return to crappie assignments like before, I will be leaving the Bureau when my three years are completed."

What am I saying? You don't know this guy well enough to trust him with those kinds of comment; besides, it makes it sound like a desperate move to get away from your current circumstances.

She needs to be very careful about making such comments, Aaron realized. *The Bureau doesn't respond favorably to that attitude.*

"Karen, I'm certain that's not information you would want shared with many people, so let's be sure this conversation remains mutually private," he added before continuing.

"I'm confident FIST will have some assignments more rewarding than others, but the very reasons it exists suggests the potential is there for us to be on the cutting edge of high profile investigations.

"As you have seen first hand, the Boss expects a lot from people around him and isn't bashful about letting you know if you aren't carrying your end. If it's a working environment that appeals to you, I suggest you make your interest known before he leaves tomorrow."

"Did you say Mr. Bridger's leaving?…Won't you be leaving tomorrow too?"

"Not yet. The Boss has assigned me to act as liaison until the case is closed. Looks like you'll have to put up with me for a little while longer."

***

Standing in the hotel waiting for the elevator to arrive, Aaron impatiently pushed the already lighted button a couple more times. It was nearly midnight.

Was it only wishful thinking, or did Karen's expression take on a pleased look when she heard the news about my not leaving?

Tomorrow will be another busy day. The boss would be leaving around noon, and the conversation with Karen on transfer ended after Chambers recommended she make her desire known before Mr. Bridger left town.

After the meal, they had gone to *Manning's*, a local watering hole with dance floor and karaoke style music. They spent a couple of hours dancing, drinking draft beer and even going to the microphone and singing a duet. Fortunately, Karen had a nice singing voice and covered his weak effort at harmonizing. They actually received some scattered applause from the patrons who were mostly in their twenties, and Aaron seized the moment to take Karen's arm and get her off the stage. Seemed only fair to give someone else equal opportunity at embarrassment.

At 11 pm they mutually agreed to call it an evening, and Karen drove back to the hotel, parking at the main entrance.

Without hesitation, she leaned toward Aaron and kissed him—gently at first and then more pressing with soft wet lips followed by a small flick of her tongue.

"Thanks for a great evening, Aaron."

Aaron could only come up with a very hesitant "you're welcome" as he exited the car.

How lame was that, he bemoaned. *You're welcome…you're welcome?*

But holy cow, she was the first woman he ever dated who not once but twice initiated the first kisses.

Strangely enough, I think I liked it—heck, I know I liked it.

***

FBI Resident Agency
Springfield, Missouri

It was moving day for Bridger. He spent a little over two hours at the RA, wrapping up loose ends and speaking with Secretary Ramirez for an update on strategy.

"I'm leaving for a meeting with the Intel Directors," Ramirez had said. "The President will be sitting in and I'm certain he will be pressing for a speedy resolution. The media is eating us alive and the recent "Opinion Polls" show a decline in confidence relating to the handling of the situation."

A successful conclusion demanded a coordinated effort—if they were to avoid the blunders of the recent past—and would be an early test of the ability of FIST to contribute in that regard.

It will be asking a lot of FIST to respond to such complex circumstances while still in a neophyte stage of development. Would they be up to it, Bridger wondered. *Now is the time to rely on the experience of good people and give an ear to them in the planning stages.*

It was time to call Bill Johnson.

After bringing Johnson into the loop on discussions with Washington, Bridger decided to make him aware he would be recommended to command the unit going into Idaho. Johnson received the news without comment and neither man spoke for a moment.

Both were aware of the sensitivity the situation demands, along with the physical danger to personnel involved. The last time a Seattle SAC led a raid into Idaho (near Coeur d'Alene where the Bureau was unfairly blamed for returning fire and killing two of the perpetrators of earlier murders), he got his head chopped off. It's a law of physics that "water runs down hill"—and in politics so does crap; they don't refer to Congress being on "The Hill" for nothing. Someone was required to pay the price for perceived public embarrassment—as often is the case, it would be the individual least responsible.

"Bill, our preliminary intelligence indicates the camp is heavily fortified with anti-vehicle and projected charge bombs, along with small arms and possibly grenade launchers.

"NRO (National Reconnaissance Office) is conducting satellite surveillance as we speak. Get what you can from informants, but be careful—the last thing we can afford is a leak that could give any warning to the camp.

"I'm leaving for Denver this afternoon. You can reach me through the Kansas City field office or on my cell until I arrive. Talk to you soon."

He then contacted Harmison in Denver who was patiently attempting to work out of the new office space, along with several of the new FIST personnel from the various agencies.

Connie Long was trying valiantly to bring some degree of organization to the complex effort of setting up a new office. The situation was made even more complicated by the very fact it was a completely new endeavor. There were no blueprints outlining supplies, dictating the size of spaces for personnel and equipment. For now, Long would have to make these decisions, and Bridger could think of no one better qualified.

"Shawn...great job with the profiles. You impressed the hell out of some people in Washington. Ramirez really went out on a limb for the both of us, and I'm glad as hell we didn't let him fall off!"

"Thanks, Ted. Coming from you, it means a lot; and I haven't thanked you for going to bat for me when my career was dead in the water. I won't soon be forgetting."

"Cripes sake, Shawn—if you care to recall, it was I who helped put your career in the toilet in the first place. We're both fortunate to have a new opportunity in a situation with interesting potential—and best of all, we may have some control over our own destiny.

"I'm headed your way in about an hour. I'll be arriving on a DHS plane and plan to use the ranch's ground transportation until we get up to speed with some drivers and vehicles. See you soon."

As Bridger disconnected from the secure telephone in the ComRoom, the buzzer signaled someone asking to enter through the sound proof door. Pushing the button to engage the electric solenoid and opening the door, Karen Blackwell was standing in the doorway.

"I'm sorry if I'm interrupting you, Sir. I can come back later...."

"No, it's okay, I'm finished here. What's up, Karen?"

Closing the door behind her, she began to speak with an uncharacteristic abruptness, "Sir, I would like to speak with you about the possibility of my joining FIST. I know you're not familiar with my professional skills and I'm only in my second office, but I'm confident I can contribute to the new unit."

"Karen, you are correct in saying there has been limited opportunity to observe your investigative ability. You would be wrong to assume I haven't taken the time to look at your personnel file. Your experience level is a matter of concern for the work we will..."

"I'm a quick learner and I'll work...." Karen blurted before Bridger could finish.

"Karen, Quantico surely taught you never to interrupt during an interview; someone may be getting ready to reveal something unexpected to you," Bridger suggested, hesitating with a look of amusement before continuing. "I would be very pleased to have you consider joining us at FIST. Now, having said that, have you considered the ramifications for your career?"

Karen's look of uncertainty, quickly changed to one of understanding and her fervor was evident as she spoke, "Yes, Sir. Absolutely. How soon can I start?"

***

Blackwell slowed the BuCar as they crossed the tall speed bumps installed after 911 to aid in security at Springfield-Branson Airport. Following her request to transfer to FIST, Bridger placed a call to Assistant Director Terrance Rainwater asking for yet another expeditious personnel action. When he finished the conversation and informed Blackwell, her enthusiasm was obvious.

She will be a good addition for FIST, and it is readily apparent a transfer from her current assignment will be best for everyone concerned.

Blackwell stopped at the closed gate to the entrance for private aviation and displayed her FBI credential to the armed security guard. After taking a long moment to examine it—obviously not something he saw everyday—he returned the credentials to her, opened the gate and waved her through.

The guard activated his hand-held radio as they drove past. Ahead, a second uniformed guard moved quickly to the gate opening onto the tarmac where the planes were parked. Pushing a switch, the large reinforced steel gates moved slowly across a track imbedded in the ground.

Allowing passenger vehicles into this area couldn't be standard operating procedures. The first guard must be aware the Lear Jet waiting is from DHS, Bridger reasoned.

A sleek Lear 31A sat sparkling in the sun; FAA number designations provided the only markings. The six-passenger jet could cruise at a maximum speed of .80 mach and reach altitudes of 51,000 feet to get over weather when necessary. The "clamshell" door stood open with the cabin entry ladder down.

Blackwell drove directly to where a man and woman stood waiting. The two were dressed in simple white shirts—with epaulets on the shoulder but no insignias designating rank or affiliation—black pants and black shoes. As the car stopped and the trunk popped open, the two removed the two pieces of luggage and walked briskly up the ladder disappearing into the airplane. A third individual, dressed like the first two, appeared from under the wing of the aircraft where he had apparently been conducting a pre-flight inspection.

"Good morning, Sir. I'm Darryl Uthoff. I'll be your pilot in command today. We have a full galley if you care for something to eat, and we have a supply of Maker's Mark bourbon. The plane is ready to roll when you are, Sir—feel free to board at your leisure."

Bridger extended his hand to Blackwell (he still felt awkward offering his hand to a woman even though it had long been PC to do so) and said, "Thanks for the lift, Karen. As soon as we wrap things up here, you can plan to transfer to Denver. And Karen, try to keep an eye on Cohn for me will you."

Blackwell waited while Bridger moved easily up the ladder, hesitating at the top and turning for a final wave before disappearing into the jet. *Keep an eye on Cohn? What did that mean? He didn't appear upset. I haven't been around him long enough to be sure, but he appeared to have a look of mischief. How much does he know? Probably knows about the date; Aaron may have mentioned it to him. What else is there to know?*

Driving back toward the RA, she began to make some mental notes of the myriad of personal details she would need to take care of over the next few days.

The apartment will be the biggest problem. They are required to cut me some slack. (All individuals involved in government employment-related transfers are by law released from contractual housing lease agreements.) *Still, I hate to take advantage of the situation, and it would be best if I could locate someone looking for an apartment to take over my lease.*

Furnishings will not be a problem. I don't have much in the way of furniture—just some personal items—and Uncle Sam will cover all moving expenses.

A smile crossed her face as she contemplated leaving. *I'll be getting away from the crappie assignments dumped on me here—and not to be overlooked, I will be working in the same city, in the same building, on the same squad as one Aaron Cohn. And I have instructions to "keep an eye on him." Damn, I like my first assignment already!*

***

Streets of Manhattan
New York City, New York

Chambers stared out the window of the taxi without really seeing anything. Forcing himself to focus on an approaching street sign, he become aware they were turning onto First Avenue, meaning Bellevue Hospital was only a short distance away.

His earlier fears Melanie would be reluctant and disappointed to leave New York proved to be completely unfounded. In fact, she broached the subject before he had the opportunity to do so, suggesting it would be best for everyone for her to return to Wyoming allowing him time to do what was being mandated by the unsettling circumstances.

In the end, John came to the realization it was he who was reluctant for her to leave. He fought a battle with himself over asking her to stay, almost giving in to the overwhelming desire on several occasions. Ultimately, they both did what common sense dictated; and after having made certain her plane left on time at La Guardia, he was en route to visit Mustafa.

Mo's very fortunate to be alive; what had Dr. Hammack said about the stab wound—"missed being fatal by a few millimeters." Today's the first day I'll be allowed to see him for more than a few minutes, and it's time for him to answer some overdue questions.

Gates' FBI contact had taken some time to check on Mustafa and then basically stonewalled Michael by saying he appeared to be only what he represented himself as being. Although Gates seemed somewhat skeptical of that report, he did not seem to be pursuing the matter.

Getting out of the cab at the main entrance to Bellevue, Chambers paid the driver and went inside to a large bank of elevators, waited impatiently for several people talking on cell phones to get off, and finally stepping in, pushed the button for Trauma Intensive Care.

Even the name is intimidating; he cringed as the elevator jerked to a stop on the 7th floor. Getting off, he rounded the corner to where the single uniformed cop still stood guard at the Mo's door.

John held out his identification as he approached the policeman, "John Chambers. I'm on the visitation list."

While he waited for the cop to scan his clipboard for the list of names cleared to enter the room, Chambers wondered what would happen when Gates finally got around to visiting later today and was asked to jump through hoops to get in. It would surely set off new suspicions about Mo's real identity—unless, of course, he already knew the answer.

Mo was sitting up in bed and John was relieved to see there were fewer tubes and wires protruding from various parts of his body.

"Hey, Mo—how you feeling today?"

"Not bad, JC. Most of the pain in my chest has disappeared, and I'm not having headaches when I sit up. Have a seat. Something we need to talk about before we're interrupted."

For several moments Mo said nothing, as he appeared to be wrestling with a decision. Finally he began to speak in a weak whisper of a voice.

"Most of what you know about me, or think you know, is part of a cover story. It's been carefully developed to enable me to have the credibility necessary to successfully infiltrate certain radical elements of Islam in this country and eventually abroad. The original mandates and charters for many agencies have changed dramatically since 911, allowing more flexibility; CIA and FBI have adjusted their areas of operation accordingly.

"Before I go any further, let me tell you the friendship we have developed over the past few months is very real so far as I'm concerned. It was not my desire to keep you in the dark regarding my identity; but as you will hopefully understand, I had no choice."

John could not contain his rising anger any longer and lashed out at his friend, "You're obviously about to tell me you're working for CIA, or some equally bizarre agency, but what I want to know is how many people at the paper are aware. You almost got yourself killed. You selfish bastard—my neck is in a noose, pal!" He was close to shouting, "So spare me the friendship crap and tell me the truth, if you're capable of it!"

"Hey, man, don't blame you for being pissed. This business can get nasty around people you care for—but let me be clear on one thing. I'm not apologizing for the fact I've chosen to fight terrorism and I'm offering you as much explanation as circumstances will allow. Take it or leave it." Mo's face grew taut.

Chambers remained silent for a long moment. *This man in the bed has been a close friend.* "Okay, I'm listening…I'm not sure I'll believe anything you say, but go ahead try me."

"JC, I have to ask. Can I get your word that what I've already revealed and what I'm about to will be kept in strict confidence between the two of us?"

Chambers could not believe his ears. *This guy has more nerve than a burglar.*

"What the hell! I told you my ass is on the line…."

"If I tell you more, John, *my ass* is going to be on the line too and could include prosecution for revealing secure intelligence information. No farther without your word to keep it confidential, you decide."

Both men were quiet for several seconds, and it was Chambers who finally broke the silence.

"Okay…okay I agree with this exception. If I don't buy what I'm hearing I reserve the right to cut you off and from that point on—all bets are off. Understood?"

Mo said nothing, hoping JC would cool down and also allowing the meaning of his latest statement to sink in before finally agreeing. "Understood. The people I work for grew suspicious when they observed you exchanging information with Dr. Hammack the night of my injuries. The FBI was asked to look into it and discovered your relationship dated from the story you did following 911.

"Hammack admitted she made you aware of the presence of certain government agencies in the hospital waiting room. The question we now need answered is this: With how many people have you shared that information?"

Government agencies? Why the hell is it these spooks are so reluctant to call it like it is, John questioned. *The "company," the "bureau," always the subterfuge—why the big mystery?*

"Are you asking, or do you know the answer to that too?"

"I'm asking, JC, and it's important—*very* important."

"I haven't told anyone and I'm not even sure why. For some reason, when Gates got suspicious and asked me some questions, I came to your defense.

"Now it's your turn to answer a question. How many people at the paper are aware of whom you really work for?"

"We think maybe one person, JC—and we believe that one person is a deep plant attempting to use the paper's resources to implement some very ugly terrorist plans for this country.

"You can imagine what access to Press Credentials capable of getting through some of the countries' tightest security could do for terrorists bent on violence. Sources of information and 'leaks' from government agencies could be equally valuable."

"But who, Mo? Any idea who the mole may be?"

"In fact, we do—we believe it's Gates...."

"Gates? No way, man! *Gates*, you have to be kidding me. Hell, he's been at the paper how long—started as a beat writer—worked his way up through the ranks.

"You have to be wrong, Mo—not Gates—you could never convince me of that one."

"Listen to me, JC—listen and think. He has access, sources, gives the okay for credentials, *and* he is responsible for hiring Shaquille who we now believe was working as a double agent." Mustafa paused allowing time for what he was saying to soak in.

"Shaquille gave me information on the potential dirty bomb, if you recall, but didn't provide information as to where, when or who. It was virtually worthless—except to convince my people and me he could be of value.

"In fact, some of the information was accurate; when Gates became aware the plot was leaking out, he had to do everything possible to stall action until the 'cell leadership' could react.

"We have evidence Gates influenced the paper's policy board to reject publishing and/or notifying the authorities of the bomb information by convincing them Shaquille was a source without proven validity, and the paper might well be embarrassed by disseminating erroneous information.

"JC, it is imperative we uncover Gates before irreparable damage can be done and we need your help."

"*My* help? What can I do, I'm no spy. Damnit, I've already stuck my neck out by not telling Gates what I know. What more do you want from me?"

"I want you to do just that, JC—tell Gates you believe I'm probably working for CIA. Give him what you have and explain you have been trying to be sure before accusing someone falsely. He'll buy that—he has to. The last thing he wants right now is more attention from the administration at the paper. After a good dressing down, Gates will let it go—at least on the surface."

"But why? If he is the mole, why do you want him to know your identity?"

"JC, I've told you all I can. You're going to have to trust me on this one. It's very important you give this information to Gates—the sooner the better. Will you do it?"

"Trust you…shit I don't even know you. I have to think about this. I need some time to sort this out in my head."

"JC—I need you to do this!"

Suddenly Mo's expression changed and his face began to lose color.

Intensity of the conversation had obviously created strain. He let out a soft moan, and an alarm sounding loudly on one of the machines in the room.

Seconds later a plump middle-aged intensive care nurse rushed into the room, "What's going on in here, Mr. Mustafa? Your blood pressure's spiking wildly."

As Chambers moved to the side, the nurse lowered Mo's bed slightly. "Your body has taken a lot of punishment, and you need to take it easy before you undo everything the past few days have healed."

The nurse stood at one of the monitors looking intently at the blood pressure reading. After a few minutes, she went back to Mo's bed and placing her hands on wide hips she stood looking down at him; Chambers read the name on her identification badge: Head Nurse—B. GRABOWSKI. The messages that followed did not require interpretation.

"Now you listen up, Mr. Mustafa—you have been beaten over the head and stabbed in the chest narrowly missing your heart. You are **not** out of the woods yet, so you better start getting with the program—you understand me? A simple yes or just nodding your head up and down will do."

Turning toward John the nurse added, "You still here? You are going to have to leave the room—now!"

As head nurse Grabowski and Chambers left the room following Mo's assurances he would "get with the program," Mo relaxed for a time and then began to reflect on their conversation.

I've broken one of the cardinal rules of intelligence operatives: Don't let it get personal—and JC has become a good friend. He's been drawn into something he doesn't understand and now to add insult to injury, I'm using him.

The "Company" has concealed the fact Shaquille has been found tortured to death and beheaded, floating in the Hudson River. He was not a double agent—as I lied about to JC—but in fact was working to identify a deep sleeper cell and had provided names and locations that allowed the FBI to make arrests and recover the materials for the assembly of a radioactive dispersion device.

One of the people arrested is believed to be the highest-ranking terrorist leader in the U.S. and has been identified as a close subordinate of Osama Bin Laden. He apparently entered the country illegally from Canada. Kahdaffi el Shurache is being held in a safe house and questioned by a special interrogation unit. He can be held indefinitely under the current anti-terrorist laws we're hoping will ultimately provide a wealth of information vital to the war on terrorism.

It's possible, even likely, Shurache had access to some of the multitude of missing radioactive fission devices now making their way onto the world's black market. The former Soviet Union left huge numbers unaccounted for following its dissolution. In the hands of terrorists with even limited technical knowledge, their potential is too frightening to contemplate.

We leaked the information on a potential dirty bomb to smoke out the mole at the paper, and Gates bought it. Before we could pull Shaquille out of danger, the cell grabbed him.

Damn! Somehow I have to get JC to tell Gates about me for his own good. Right now, JC's life is in serious danger until the terrorists realize the undercover threat they believed he represented was in reality me.

Gates was instructed by his boss to assign Chambers to the Bridger interviews, and Gates construed that to mean Chambers was the government agent searching for the mole. It added up as far as it went; JC and Bridger would have time to discuss what he had learned and plan a course of action that might ultimately reveal Gates' treachery. In addition, Gates undoubtedly believed JC and my friendship was a move to develop a person of middle-east background and culture for information, at the same time diverting attention away from him.

Thank goodness, Chambers is under protective surveillance 24-7, but will not be safe until he tells Gates what I requested. It was a relief when Melanie stopped earlier in the day en route to the airport for her return to Wyoming. At least, I don't have to be concerned for her safety.

My assault by the terrorists attempting to get into Chambers' computer was accidental—occurring only because I was in the wrong place at the wrong time.

What were they looking for in his computer? Perhaps they assumed he would be keeping reports received from Shaquille. Or possibly in an attempt to stop the torture or extend his life, Shaq had provided false information to the vicious bastards. They could have been searching for leads on the location of Shurache when I surprised them.

Shaquille Abumotte was a brave young Kuwaiti citizen who remembered the atrocities he witnessed as a child when Iraq invaded his country. He wanted to make a difference in helping to stop the insanity of terrorism and volunteered his services to CIA. At 22, a time when he should have been enjoying college, parties, perhaps a youthful first love, he died an unimaginable grisly death at the hands of people who place no premium on life—that of others, or their own.

Shaq can't have died for nothing; there has to come a time of reckoning. Someone is out there who took pleasure in murdering this kind-hearted, courageous young man. I hope I have the opportunity to make those responsible pay—in spades!

***

CHAPTER 21

The White House
1600 Pennsylvania Avenue
Washington, DC

Secretary Miguel Ramirez moved with a resolute stride down the long hallway of the West Wing to the entrance to the Intelmet Room. A muscular young Marine sergeant, wearing a sidearm, examined Ramirez's credentials.

Undoubtedly, he recognized the Secretary of Homeland Security by now, having seen him numerous times, but he followed security protocol to the letter.

"Thank you, Mr. Secretary." he said and opened the door, waited for the Secretary to step through and closed it behind him.

The room was filled to capacity of those expected to attend—*everyone,* in fact, but the President.

Washington was a power-conscious city with protocol taking many forms. It hadn't taken him long to realize people tended to arrive for meetings in chronological order of rank. As a cabinet level appointment of the President, Ramirez should arrive at meetings only minutes before they were scheduled to begin. If he came too early, it could mean others would have to plan to arrive earlier at the next meeting, lest they risk offending him.

He found much of what was termed "Washington Protocol" to be comical at best and condescending at worst—a throwback to another time and place that was anything but democratic. Kings, Queens, Dukes and other leaders of the day created behavioral patterns designed to maintain their positions in a status conscious society. Some positive aspects of protocol came from Western European culture, responsible for much of our formal government procedures, including Roberts Rule of Order (better known as parliamentary procedure), which dictated the vastly important process of conducting legislative business.

Ramirez was baffled and amused to think an intelligent free society could continue to promulgate the fundamentals of maintaining power through such archaic ideas. *Why not keep the practical and discard the supercilious?*

A serving table held an array of drinks and fresh baked delicacies, and Ramirez looked over the tantalizing tidbits. *Damn, it's tough to turn down some of those sweet rolls with frosted icing and fruit centers crying out to be eaten.* Finally, exhaling a deep breath of resignation, he selected black coffee and a small glass of orange juice.

As the waiter in a white starched uniform approached, the Secretary waived him off, electing to carry the drinks to the table himself.

"Good morning," he offered in response to similar salutations from the gathered room.

A damn good morning it is. I have to admit; I'm look forward to this meeting. FIST initially created quite a stir within the intelligence power structure, accompanied by heat from every corner—including Congress.

No less than half a dozen members of powerful committees on the "Hill" contacted him in one manner or another suggesting he rethink the idea of a new investigative unit—particularly, some had added, with Bridger at the helm. The President remained firmly behind the idea, and the fact FIST is moving so quickly with its first investigation has certainly help.

Ramirez barely sat down and sipped from his orange juice before he heard the private door open and a voice announce, "Ladies and Gentlemen...The President."

Everyone sitting at the long conference table began pushing chairs back in an effort to rise.

"Keep your seats, please," President Anthony G. Roark announced in a pleasant voice.

Sitting down at the head of the table, the President looked across to Ramirez and said, "Miguel, I read the 'Synops Reports' on the assassinations; and I have to tell you, I'm very impressed. It appears *our* idea to form this new FIST team was right on...and, I might add, very timely.

"Bridger's suspicions from the get-go are evident now that essentials of the investigation are concluded. Even the motives for the various killings seem crystal clear and in retrospect appear obvious. This is not the time to rehash what we should have seen earlier on but to take what we have and deal with this domestic malignancy called—*Brotherhood of Aryan Warriors.*

"Please accept my congratulations, Director Barkley, Director Goode and General Winter, on having the foresight to see the potential for cooperation among agencies. Your attitudes and efforts in support of this new unit have not gone unnoticed by me…you can be certain of that fact."

Ramirez looked at Barkley and Goode shuffling in their seats and was pleased that the President's admonition had not been lost on them.

"Ladies and Gentlemen, if you will open the file reports in front of you," Roark continued, "I would like to start this meeting with recommendations for operational details on how we bring these bastards to justice."

On the table in front of each lay a thick folder. Emblazoned in large black letters across the red cover were the words, *TOP SECRET*. The folders were sealed with a tough nylon tape that could not be removed or torn away without evidence of tampering, and a razor-edged opener bearing the White House Seal lay conveniently along side.

One by one, people cut the tape and began opening files. Ramirez was reminded of something far removed from the present. It was a sudden flashback to Santa Fe, New Mexico, and Christmas morning in his small but comfortable boyhood home, surrounded by family. *Strange, how the mind often creates memories of past events sparked by a sight or smell, often in the most unusual and inopportune places.*

The idea of comparing this gathering to family made him smile, and he glanced around quickly to see if anyone noticed. Everyone was too busy opening "gifts," and he was thankful his change in demeanor had not been observed. It could easily be perceived as gloating—not a sentiment he wished to send to the already rebuffed directors whose cooperation he would require in the future.

The first section of the report was a synopsis of the investigations conducted at each of the crime scenes. It began: **"This report is a summary of immense investigative information stemming from a complex synergistic effort involving federal agencies under the direction of FIST."**

It contained references to more in-depth information to be found within the appropriate master file—located at DHS Headquarters. (Keeping the "master file" at DHS had been Ramirez's idea to send a signal to the intelligence community—contrary to Bridger's advice. Bridger felt strongly the FBI would be better equipped to disseminate.)

Reading the carefully abbreviated report for the umpteenth time, Ramirez could not help appreciating the skill required to pour over the vast amounts of minutia involved and summarize it in a form easily digested and understood by the layperson; and accept it or not, *layperson* was precisely what many in this room were—and that included the President and himself.

Aware the complex text was written by the seriously maligned Shawn Harmison, he thought about his own hesitation when Goode painted such a negative picture of Harmison's abilities. Bridger made his confidence clear, and Ramirez now realized his own reservations involved Bridger as well, questioning if he might be expressing loyalty rather than good judgment.

The content of this report could leave little doubt of Harmison's capabilities and raised the question of why his obvious talents had been put on the "back burner" of the "intelligence stove." *Could it be professional prejudice,* Ramirez wondered? *Guilt by association—stemming from Harmison's relationship with Bridger? Perhaps politics with a powerful enemy attempting to get at his uncle in the Senate—a relative with enough clout to save his job but not keep him out of professional banishment. Whatever it proves to be—this is no time for such pettiness. We are in a battle that will be tough enough utilizing all our assets.*

Reaching for a pad and pencil, Ramirez quickly scribbled himself a note: *Haugen—research details Harmison's problems. Expedite results to me personally.*

Haugen's a good man—a fair man—and can be counted on to deliver the facts in an honest and thorough fashion. A rare breed in Washington, Haugen understands politics better than most but refuses to let it corrupt him.

If Harmison got the raw deal Bridger suggested, something needs to be done to rectify the situation. This is a very bad time to have someone of his skills sitting on the bench; we need all our best players in the game.

President Roark left the meeting soon after the files were opened, and it was now the obligation of the professionals to implement a plan of action that would be both successful and politically tolerated. *Waco* and *Ruby Ridge* could never be far from the minds of those responsible for this type of logistical exercise.

The next several hours were filled with "parameter plans" for raids intended to search out and arrest those responsible for the latest domestic terrorism. Bridger submitted his recommendation for simultaneous coordinated raids to be carried out at the two confirmed encampments in Arkansas and Idaho.

Various assistant directors and supervisory personnel were asked for input before final detailed strategy was authorized. In the final analysis, they were the people who would determine the success or failure of the mission at hand and provide final impetus for carrying out the raids within the limitations approved by the politicians and amateurs in Washington.

The President would personally give the go ahead or, if necessary, send the plan back for further consideration. He made the urgency of the situation emphatically clear before leaving the meeting.

"The current state of affairs is unacceptable. We have a near panic situation with many of our citizens unnecessarily fearful and others ready to take inappropriate action against an imagined foe—in this case innocent Muslims. The media is having a field day and in no small way contributing to the confusion.

"Gentlemen...get final tactical plans to me promptly...and let me be clear on this point. You will not want to be that isolated individual found guilty of needlessly complicating this operation attempting to protect your turf."

Looking sternly around the table, emphasizing his last statement by making eye contact with each person, the President rose to his feet and left the room.

***

HRT Mobile Command
North-Central Arkansas

Aaron Cohn and Karen Blackwell listened intently through their tactical headphones to the growing stream of information being processed by the sound technicians and provided via satellite to a situation room in Washington, DC. They had been in position for over two hours. It was almost 9:30 am, and simultaneous raids were scheduled to begin at 10 am central standard time. Hypothetically at the scene because of their thorough knowledge of the subjects being sought, in reality, they were being rewarded for a job well done. Both were pleased and excited to be a part of the final solution.

They were sitting in an MTV (Mobile Tech Van), designed for use as a command center in situations calling for synchronization of personnel. The outside of the vehicle appeared very much like any other service van operating in the area. It might well be from one of the name brand appliance stores making delivery of a new refrigerator or repairing an old one. The exterior did not appear new (although it was in fact quite new) and had been carefully "aged" by specialists to produce a look designed to go unnoticed.

315

Inside the van, highly trained field technicians were operating complex electronic equipment, capable of sending and receiving audio and video signals from a vast array of sources, including satellites, miniature helmet cameras worn by HRT (Hostage Rescue Team) and highly sensitive audio devices. Screens and monitors covered the interior, and the technicians were kept busy monitoring and routing the streams of incoming and outgoing information.

The MTV was beside a small gasoline service station where Arkansas State Highway 16 and 27 intersect—a few miles from Ozark National Forest to the west and US Highway 65 to the east. (The owners and occupants of the station were evacuated for safety. Although the station was fully five miles from the encampment, it was far better to error on the side of the unlikely.) Because of the general remoteness of the area, it harbored white supremacy training camps in the past—and the latest investigation left no doubt it was obviously doing so again.

Special Agent Tim Laurie, an HRT supervisor assigned to this raid, was a veteran with multiple years' experience. Approaching 50 years of age, he maintained the same high level of conditioning demanded of his SWAT teams; and at 5'9" and 160 pounds, his wiry frame wasn't carrying any more excess weight than it had when he was a star running back at Virginia Military Institute. Wearing a dark blue cap with FBI across the front, short pepper-black hair showed around the edges, and his gray-blue eyes set in a chiseled darkly tanned face gave him a look of confident authority.

Prior to entering the Bureau at age 35, he served as an officer in Army Special Forces, participating in the "first" gulf war. His background included numerous scenarios, demanding instant decisions. This could well be another of those situations requiring tough on-the-scene calls—eventually to be replayed in slow motion and second-guessed for days after the fact.

The SWAT teams assigned were carefully chosen for their expertise in hilly and heavily wooded terrain—and the ability to generate controlled firepower should it become necessary. Deployed by SIOC (Strategic Information Operations Center) located on the fifth floor of the J. Edgar Hoover Building in Washington, DC, they were assigned to CIRG (Critical Incident Response Group) and are deployed to assist when local field offices do not have the resources to manage an operation alone.

The CIRG is home to several special FBI units developed to manage a vast number of potential domestic violent situations. Included in this group is HRT, an elite SWAT team trained to handle a myriad of incidents—including chemical and radioactive.

Assigned to their 91-member unit are hostage negotiators, clandestine surveillance experts, snipers and crisis managers. Subsequent to their initial establishment in 1994, they were used in numerous critical situations in the U.S. and abroad. Of the 91 total SWAT personnel in the unit, over half (51) were being used in the simultaneous raids in Arkansas and Idaho.

Each of the three teams in Arkansas was comprised of seven men. Supplied with the best weapons and technical equipment available, each man carried gear deemed necessary for the success of this particular mission.

The teams were wearing "woodland" camouflage suits, with Kevlar body armor and "fritz" style helmets, Nomex flame resistant gloves, black balaclavas and Bausch & Lomb ballistic eye cover.

An assortment of weapons included H&K MP-5 submachine guns in 10mm caliber with red-dot Holographic scopes and tactical lights. Rifles included Colt M-16A2 carbines in 5.56 caliber and Remington M-40A1 .308 sniper rifles with Unertl scopes. Each man carried an accurized Les Baer .45 SRP pistol built on a high capacity Para-Ordnance frame.

The close assault team was equipped with multi-shot 37mm gas launchers, M-79 40mm grenade launchers and "flashbang" diversionary devices.

Every man carried global positioning devices (accurate to within 3 feet) and tactical headsets for communication.

A single Bell-412 Huey helicopter and a smaller MD-530 "Little Bird" were available minutes from the scene—as was a specially equipped Medi-Vac helicopter.

Several vehicles used for transport were sitting off road and out of sight, including one LAV-Bison (Light Armored Vehicle) capable of withstanding 7.62 mm rifle fire.

A covert surveillance team, entering the encampment several hours earlier under the cover of darkness, reported the presence of 12 adult males inside the camp and an additional 6 males guarding vehicle and foot trail accesses. A variety of booby traps and IEDs (Improvised Explosive Devices) designed for use against personnel and vehicles were strategically placed along the route and in weapon storage areas.

A large quantity of small arms, including semi-automatic assault type weapons with large quantities of ammunition were observed in weapon storage as well as in sleeping quarters with the occupants.

A small cache of what appeared to be projected charges in the form of rocket propelled grenades were observed but could not be verified; closer inspection would have put the surveillance team in too much danger of being discovered.

Informants indicated the two subjects being sought for murder, Robert Henry Jones and Michael Wayne Matthews, were at the encampment as of 8 pm last evening—almost 12 hours ago. The CIs further stated both men were preparing to leave for destinations unknown—and packed gear in the living quarters indicated it could be soon. No individuals left the encampment overnight, and it could be assumed both subjects were still on site.

The tactical plan to conduct a simultaneous ASO (Arrest and Secure Operation) in Arkansas and Idaho was presented to the President and met with his approval. He gave the go-ahead to proceed as quickly as feasible.

***

"Point 1 to Command...we have activity at the main compound...stand by," reported a calm voice over the tactical headphones.

Everyone in the MTV stiffened, straining to hear what would come next. It was the point man on the tactical site survey team responsible for reconnoitering the encampment.

"Command...we have a green Ford Explorer with a single male driver stopping in front of the compound...two...no correction, three male individuals are exiting the building. The subjects are carrying duffel bags and...at least two assault rifles are visible. They are also wearing side arms...copy?"

"Copy Point 1...four individuals in green Ford Explorer...A&D (Armed and Dangerous)," came the reply from Laurie. "Maintain position and report movement, copy?"

"Point 1 Copy...maintaining position."

"Command to Bison...copy?"

"Bison...go ahead."

"We have a green Ford Explorer with four suspects, A&D...I repeat A&D approaching on Highway 16. Move into position to block the roadway short of the intersection with Highway 27. Repeat...block short of Highway 27. Hold out of sight until the vehicle approaches your position. I repeat...hold out of sight until the vehicle approaches your position. Affirm message now."

The LAV radio operator quickly and accurately repeated their orders.

"Command to Tact #2 what is your ETA to intersection?" Laurie asked.

"Tact #2 to Command. Current GPS positioning places us 1.25 miles west-northwest; we will be on sight in 7 plus minutes...copy?"

"Copy Tact #2."

"Damnit! At 60 mph the subjects will be on our position in approximately 5 minutes. Tact #2 won't arrive until after the suspect vehicle is stopped," Laurie said looking at Cohn and Blackwell.

"Point #1 to Command...four subjects are in the SUV and leaving the encampment...repeat...leaving the encampment, copy?"

"Copy, Point #1. Tact #1 and Tact #3 hold assault on compound until the vehicle leaving can be stopped and secured. Wait for my command before proceeding unless fired upon. Acknowledge now."

"Tact #1 copy, hold await command."

"Tact #3 copy, hold for command."

"The AV has a three-man crew, including driver; it's strictly intended for transportation and can take some small arms fire. The two techs and the driver are not armed. *We* have to give them some back-up," Laurie thought aloud.

Turning toward Blackwell and Cohn, he asked the question but already knew the answer, "You two up for it?"

Both were scrambling to put on the Kevlar armor vests, and Laurie held out a single MP-5 machine gun—one of only two extras in the van, the second of which he had already slung over his shoulder—and Blackwell grabbed it as she raced out the back.

Turning to the radio technician, Laurie issued a quick order, "Inform *HOT POTATO* (Code name Idaho operation) *COTTON PICKER* (Code name Arkansas operation) will be making aggressive contact in approximately five minutes. Update SOG on the latest development, and get this MTV to some cover away from this gas station. You're sitting on a potential bomb!"

Laurie nearly landed on Cohn as he jumped from the van; the three agents turned and sprinted toward the intersection where the LAV was slowly pulling into position.

***

Tactical Observation Room
The White House
1600 Pennsylvania Avenue
Washington, DC

"Whoa! That was a damn fast decision Laurie made. Get him on the horn and let's discuss alternatives before...." DCI Director Barkley began.

"Hold off on that," Secretary Ramirez said looking at the communication technician about to act.

"Ted, what do you think?" he asked

"Mr. Secretary, he has actionable intelligence in front of him…he's on the scene…we put him there. Let him do what he's been trained to do," Bridger stated firmly.

Looking around him Ramirez saw General Winter, Margaret Fleisher and Attorney General Clovis Stipp nodding in agreement—and to his surprise FBI Director Goode was doing likewise.

Stipp had been asked to join the assemblage to observe first hand what he could of the two operations being conducted simultaneously. It was a logical decision; at a later date, the Justice Department might be expected to defend in court the actions about to be taken.

Some of the proceedings would be viewable on the multiple video screens in front of them. Signals were provided by satellite coming from the personal miniature cameras worn on selected SWAT helmets. Ramirez observed the intense interest as everyone was glued to the monitors watching the action beginning to unfold in front of them. Representatives from each of the agencies working together in FIST were also present at Ramirez's request. Bridger had been brought in from Denver, somewhat against his will. He had expressed a desire to be at the scene in Arkansas after recommending Bill Johnson as the commander in Idaho.

I hated to nix the idea, Ramirez reflected. *But it was an opportunity for him to be here with me—solidifying FIST if things go well—picking up the pieces if they don't.*

This has great potential to let everyone see what cooperation can achieve and then be a part of the final resolution. This, Ladies and Gentlemen, is called teamwork.

It was up to the men and the woman on the frontlines now. *For cripes sakes people, for everyone's sake—let's get it right.*

***

There isn't much time to plan strategy, Laurie concluded, as the three of them stood across the road from the MTV. The LAV would block the roadway, and there wouldn't be room for a vehicle to pass on either side due to the large oak trees growing right next to the side of the narrow road.

The only course of escape was back where they came from in the SUV or getting out on foot and making a run for it. There was nothing that could be done for the latter, so cutting off the retreat had to be their first focus.

"Blackwell, if there is an exchange of fire, take out the tires on the vehicle. Set up over there in the trees with Cohn," he said pointing toward a heavily wooded area with good cover.

"I'll take the other side of the road and prevent their retreat on foot. Cohn, you do the same on your side. Remember, they have some assault rifles and no telling what else; keep your heads down. Help's on the way. Good luck!" And he was off to a wooded and brush-covered area across the road.

Running for their assigned post in the trees, Cohn heard Blackwell mumbling something under her breath. Stopping and settling in behind the tree cover, he turned toward Blackwell a few feet to his left and asked, "What...I can't hear what you're saying."

"I *said*, why didn't I grab those extra clips for this damn MP-5? They were in the gear right by the door.

Cohn didn't answer but pulled his 9mm Sig Sauer from the holster and checked to be sure he had a round in the chamber. Reaching around on his belt, he made certain two extra clips were still in their holders. He knew he was outgunned going against assault rifles, but at least he could take comfort in having 16 rounds in his semi-automatic pistol with two more 15-round clips in reserve.

Taking a couple of deep breaths to slow his heart, racing from adrenalin, he located Laurie, almost hidden by the heavy brush and trees. *What's that opening running through the trees in front of him?* It was some sort of trail; it ran several yards before disappearing into the woods.

Cohn looked across the road to the side he was on and saw the path continued, running a short distance into the trees before fading from view. *Probably a hiking trail or perhaps made by wild game,* he surmised before being interrupted by a sound in the distance.

A vehicle was moving down the road in their direction. And it was coming fast; only a few hundred yards and closing rapidly—it was the green Ford Explorer heading straight for them.

The driver of the approaching vehicle could not yet see the Bison still parked out of sight.

They're driving faster than anticipated, Cohn realized. *We're going to be on our own longer than expected before Tact #2 arrives. Shit, they're practically on top of us...what are those guys in the LAV waiting for!*

And then the camouflaged vehicle lumbered out of hiding and pulled across the narrow road completely blocking it.

The approaching SUV driver saw it about the same time, slammed on the brakes and skidded along the road before coming to a stop a hundred feet from the roadblock.

FBI! STEP OUT OF THE VEHICLE WITH YOUR HANDS IN THE AIR!

The sudden amplified announcement startled Cohn. Laurie had obviously used the LAV loudspeaker system for the announcement through his tactical headset. It was remarkable how cool he was reacting under pressure.

The occupants of the vehicle froze in place and appeared to be taken completely by surprise.

They may be ready to surrender, Cohn reasoned, taking his left hand off his weapon and wiping the sweat on his trousers.

Moments passed and Laurie made another announcement.

THIS IS THE FBI! You are under arrest! Step Out With Your Hands Raised!

Cohn strained his eyes seeing movement inside the vehicle as one of the subjects appeared to be scrambling over the backseat to the rear of the SUV.

Suddenly all hell broke loose. Three side doors sprang open, and the occupants spilled out—using the doors for cover—firing their assault weapons on full auto toward the LAV.

The fourth subject popped into view from the rear of the vehicle holding a round tube on his shoulder with a cone sticking out.

"No! Oh shit no!" Cohn yelled.

He heard a loud Whoooosh—the rocket-propelled grenade streaked past him headed straight at the LAV.

The explosion hit the small armored vehicle near the engine, rocking it up on two wheels—but failing to turn it over on its side. The thin armor plating combined with the heavy engine to prevent penetration. *They're probably okay, but everyone inside is going to have one hell of a headache,* Cohn thought right before the three occupants jumped from the rear door and sprinted for cover in the trees.

Judging from their speed getting across the road, they're not hurt; but they're unarmed.

Blackwell fired single rounds from the MP-5. Front and back tires on the SUV made loud hissing noises as the bullets struck the targets.

Cool. She's not wasting ammo and saving the automatic fire for suppression if needed.

Seeing the subject still at the rear of the SUV attempting to load another grenade, Cohn fired a couple of two-round bursts from his pistol and moved immediately to a new position.

"Fire and move...fire and move. Assume you will draw return fire," how many times had he heard that at Quantico?

From across the road came the sound of Laurie firing short automatic bursts, followed by the pinging of metal as the 10mm rounds hit the metal doors of the SUV.

So far so good, if we can only hold them a little while longer, Tact #2 will arrive and one way or the other—it'll be over.

At that moment, the situation changed abruptly.

The man at the rear of the vehicle had managed to reload and fire another grenade. In the confusion, the cornered subjects obviously believed the main threat was coming from the AV.

The whooshing sound was heard again—but this time it missed the target completely and continued on down the road.

First came a discharge from the grenade—followed moments later by a much louder explosion—and the first of three gasoline tanks went up. A fireball shot wildly into the sky followed by smoke and flying debris.

The service station...it must have hit the service station. Damn good thing Laurie had them move the MTV. Those tech guys would be toast.

The subject at the rear of the SUV was frantically trying to reload a grenade; and seeing only the smallest of targets, Cohn snapped two quick shots toward the grenade launcher and watched him tumble backwards onto the road. One or more of the rounds must have found their mark.

Quickly changing positions, he ran in a low crouch to another clump of trees. Hearing the clatter of an assault rifle on full automatic, he looked back in time to see bark flying from the trees where he'd been only seconds before.

Then, as if on signal, the three remaining subjects jumped from behind the open doors, sprinting for the trees—firing their assault weapons on full auto as they went. Clumps of dirt flew up a few feet in from of him, and Cohn instinctively ducked even lower.

The subjects were hoping for the explosions to create enough confusion to allow them to get to the cover of the thick woods. If they made it to the trees, they would be tough to find and might even succeed in escaping.

Laurie again fired short bursts, and one of the running figures went down, tried slowly to get up and then fell again—lying motionless in a growing puddle of blood.

Poor bastard, Cohn thought—*he chose the wrong direction to run.*

Then he saw movement to his right. One of them was running toward the path on his side of the road. He was carrying an assault rifle and firing wildly into trees in front of him as he ran.

Cohn fired a couple of two-round bursts from the Sig Sauer before the man disappeared in the trees.

"Shit!" Reaching down and triggering his mic (microphone), he spoke into his tact set, "Command, this is Cohn. I'm in pursuit east on the path in front of my position."

At least let someone know where to look for my body. This guy has an assault rifle and can stop anywhere he pleases to take me out. I've got no choice; can't just let him run.

There was still shots being fired behind, fading as he hit the trail on a dead run. The sound of automatic fire appeared to come from the area where he last saw Blackwell. The heavy dome of southern pines on both sides of the trail created a sudden dampening of sound and sent a chill down Cohn's back.

In a matter of seconds, the action had taken him from a scene of movement and thunderous sound, to a surreal atmosphere of silence, in which his heart beating loudly in his ears was all he could hear.

Moving to the edge of the dirt path and stopping behind a tree, Cohn peered carefully out and looked as far ahead as possible. No sign of movement anywhere.

He abandoned the cover of the trees and ran along the edge of the trail in a deep crouch. *How many rounds fired,* he wondered. *Eight...no ten. That leaves me six rounds.* He reached behind to his clip holder and his heart skipped...*Where the hell is it...I've lost the...no...no there it is. It slid on my belt.*

Grabbing a fresh clip, he hit the release on the Sig, caught the old clip and put it into his hip pocket. Sliding the new clip in and hearing it snap cleanly into place, he felt a small sense of relief knowing he now had 16 fresh rounds.

Looking ahead he could see nothing moving. He sprinted hard for 50 yards before diving behind a large fallen tree.

His breath came in short bursts, and the blood pounded in his ears so hard he couldn't hear clearly. Settling back on his heels—taking several deep breaths—he crouched there for a few seconds trying desperately to hear the sounds around him.

What was that—a noise from behind—I ran right past him! The realization came too late. Turning his head attempting frantically to swing the 9mm around—he never heard the single report from the .223 caliber assault rifle—before something smashed into his jaw.

The fast moving bullet hit with the force of a baseball bat—spinning him over backward and sprawling him out on the rocky trail.

Cohn felt the warm liquid oozing down his neck and tried to raise his head and shoulders. The burning pain and effort almost made him lose consciousness, and his head fell heavily back to the ground.

Then he heard the footsteps approaching on the run—perhaps it was Laurie or Tact #2 coming to his aid.

Blinking his eyes, he tried desperately to clear his vision...finally seeing through the growing fuzziness of semi-consciousness, first the barrel of the assault rifle pointing down at him—and then the face—*Michael Wayne Matthews. The killer of the Missouri Highway Patrolman—is about to kill me.*

It's amazing how calm I feel, Cohn thought—a second before the final darkness enclosed him.

***

CHAPTER 22

Kaniksu National Forest
Northwestern Idaho

Newly appointed Assistant Director of FIST, Bill Johnson, sat quietly in an MTV in the Idaho foothills of the Kaniksu National Forest. Located several miles north of beautiful Lake Coeur d'Alene, this was some of the most scenic terrain in the country as well as some of the most rugged.

As Bridger had indicated might happen, Johnson was the COS (Commander On Scene) of operation *HOT POTATO*. The irony of the code name had not been lost on either man, and Johnson followed Bridger's advice by contacting the former SAC who commanded the Ruby Ridge affair.

They would be dealing with a different extremist organization entirely, but there was always something to be learned from past situations—both positive and negative. The conversation with his predecessor proved candid and helpful in his tactical planning for this operation.

Surprise was the tactic of choice, meaning early strategy for Hot Potato revolved around inserting personnel and materials into position without alerting the subjects to their presence. The last piece of advice received from the COS of Ruby Ridge was "Don't let it become a stalemate." That advice had been playing over and over in Johnson's head all day.

Five teams composed of seven men each (four HRT and one Seattle Field Office SWAT) were assigned to infiltrate the heavily forested and mountainous terrain near Rocky Creek, Idaho, and carry out the mission. Once again, Johnson listened to the advice of the Ruby Ridge commander and opted for more than needed, rather than too little firepower. "And for shit sake, Bill, keep it all under your command. We had a bad combination at Waco and Ruby Ridge—too many people with too many Chiefs with too many ideas."

Johnson's assistant was HRT supervisor Jack Fox. The two had never worked together, but since he arrived on the scene, Johnson was impressed with Fox's professionalism and attention to detail. *Fox is a pro,* Johnson decided. *He understands our goal is to make arrests, conduct searches and seize whatever we find in the way of illegal firearms and explosives. Using the firepower available to us is a last resort—and one we damn well hope will not become necessary.*

Vehicles chosen for insertion of personnel were indistinguishable from the countless recreational vehicles coming into the area for the spring fishing and camping seasons. Several SUVs and pick-ups owned by agents in the Spokane and Coeur d'Alene FBI-RAs were utilized to move people into position without arousing suspicion.

A number of special pieces of equipment were brought in during early morning hours under cover of darkness. It would prevent speculation from curious onlookers who might wonder at some of the strange-looking vehicles. Medi-vac helicopters and a single MD-530 "Little Bird," were on standby minutes away at Rothschild Air Force Base in Washington.

Hot Potato caught a major break when CIs reported the women and children of the base camp were planning a daylong trip to Spokane for supplies and entertainment. The information proved accurate when the "point" man on Team #1 advised women (5) and children (9) were observed leaving the compound in the early morning hours before the scheduled incursion.

A combination of informant reports, covert surveillance and satellite overview all agreed: A small cadre of 9-12 men were well fortified and occupying the military style encampment.

Informants also reported the main body would be occupying the larger of the three buildings (designated Building #1) for the purpose of conducting a planning session for a new operation. Team #1 point confirmed movement of personnel from the smaller buildings into Building #1, shortly after women and children left the premises.

Three main buildings in the compound were built with reinforced walls capable of withstanding small arms fire. All windows contained heavy metal shutters, metal doors were set on re-enforced steel hinges and roofs were sheet metal sprayed with a fire retardant.

The buildings were in the middle of a circle, cleared of all trees and cover of any kind for a distance of over 100 yards to create a "killing field" reminiscent of those used by U.S. forces around the isolated "firebases" in Viet Nam.

The known occupants included trained former military personnel responsible for instructing BAW (Brotherhood of Aryan Warriors) members in the use of assorted small arms and explosives—all were considered A&D (Armed and Dangerous).

Weaponry was imposing and varied: Small arms, grenades, assorted explosives, bomb-making materials, assault weapons, sniper rifles—with at least one homemade armored vehicle carrying a .30 caliber machine gun.

The HRT surveillance team discovered several booby traps along paths and trails leading into the encampment and spotted two snipers in heavily camouflaged, elevated deer-hunter stands overlooking the camp on the north and south—the only two sides allowing access.

Informants confirmed two subjects indicted by a secret Federal Grand Jury for murder—Thomas Howard and Arthur Shipman—were at the compound as of late yesterday afternoon. Both men were now wanted for multiple murders in Seattle and Portland. It was probable the two were still on the scene since they would be principles in whatever operation the group might be planning.

Johnson glanced at his watch. *Almost time.* Fox was in the field with the lead element—Team #1. They approached the camp from the south along with Team #2; one member (Dolphin) was assigned to neutralize the sniper.

Team #3 approached from the north along with Team #4 also with one agent (Popeye) assigned to the sniper.

Each group included one highly trained marksman (radio code names "Pluto" and "Flintstone") equipped with a Remington Model 700 in 7.62x51mm NATO with m118 Ball Ammo. The 14.5-pound rifles carried Northrop-Grumman PVS-10 Sniper Night Sights that function day or night. The sights had a daylight viewing range of 800 meters.

Team #5 split into two groups slowly working their ways into positions on the east and west of the encampment. Their jobs were to block the path of escape. With stealth of movement critical to prevent alerting the camp, they began before dawn and were painstakingly inching their way into heavily wooded terrain, negotiable only on small game trails. (Satellite recon indicated these same small paths to be the most likely escape routes.)

All five teams had point men utilizing the latest high tech equipment developed for urban and jungle warfare to search for booby traps and anti-personnel mines. The roadway would be cleared of anti-vehicle explosives to allow two specially equipped Up-Armored M1114 HMMWVs (High Mobility Multipurpose Wheeled Vehicles) to be brought in. The HumVees contained two tactical weapons capable of keeping the situation from turning into a stalemate—something Washington had also decided they did not want to see occur.

Both operations had SOPs (Standard Operating Procedures) of "returning fire only if fired upon." The use of force necessary to make arrests and secure the encampment were the orders emanating from SOG, and every detail of what was about to occur would be carefully scrutinized by both government and public entities.

Be that as it may, Johnson decided. *I'll be damned if I'm going to see any of my men needlessly endangered by this bunch of murdering hate mongers. Let the powers in Washington have their pound of flesh if they want it, but I'll protect my men first and worry about oversight reaction later.*

"COTTON PICKER to HOT POTATO...copy?"

It was Arkansas command on satellite relay.

"Hot Potato, copy."

"Hot Potato, be advised Cotton Picker will engage in *5 minutes*...repeat *5 minutes* copy?"

"Copy...Cotton Picker will engage in 5 minutes," the com-specialist repeated.

"Oh shit!" Johnson blurted.

Something's gone bad in Arkansas, he realized. *We can't lose surprise here or we're going to have subjects scattered all over this mountain and beyond.*

"Steve, can we intercept and block any messages coming to the encampment here, from Arkansas?"

Steve Woolcock, a communication expert from NSA had been asked to join FIST by Bridger; he and Johnson worked together before, and Johnson had great confidence in his abilities, including knowledge of the highly technical capabilities of NSA.

"I'm on it, Boss. We'll scramble all signals coming to and from the encampment and record any incoming messages."

Johnson looked over at the myriad of technical equipment where Steve sat typing rapidly on a computer keyboard.

The question now is how much time will Fox require to get into final position.

"Com #1 to Com#2, copy?" (Com #1 is Johnson; Com #2 is Fox deployed with Team #1.)

"Com #2, go."

"Com #2, Cotton Picker's been forced off schedule and has engaged. Repeat, Cotton Picker has engaged. What is your TR (Tactical Readiness), copy?"

"Com #2 to Teams #2 through #5. Respond to TR in sequence...beginning...now!"

"Two...*ready*...three...*ready*...four *ready*...five *ready*."

"Com #1, we are in position...we are in position, copy?"

"Com #2, you are clear to commence operation Hot Potato at your discretion. Repeat, commence at your discretion."

"Copy...Com #1, Commence at my discretion."

"Com #2 to HumVees Adam and Boy...Move into tactical position.

"Com #2 to Little Bird #1...You are clear for fly over arrest announcement.

"Com #2 to Popeye and Dolphin...Stand by and prepare to secure sniper positions, copy."

Popeye and Dolphin responded in sequence with a single click—the sound made when the send button is depressed—used when close proximity to the enemy precludes using voice replies.

In the MTV Bill Johnson could only sit and wait. Leaders in far away Washington, DC—including the President—could only do the same.

***

Surprise was key to getting the main teams into position to make arrests with the least amount of confrontation possible. Taking out the snipers who were also acting as sentries was the first step.

On the small dirt track leading into the camp from the north, Jerry Carter (communication code name "Dolphin") depressed his send button one time causing a single *click* to be heard in the command headsets.

A former Navy Seal, Carter joined the FBI five years ago and had been assigned to HRT for the past two years. A veteran of the conflict in Serbia and Desert Storm, he was no stranger to covert action in the dessert, the jungle, or the water. A trained sniper, movement without detection—and remaining in a concealed position for long periods of time—was something to which he had grown accustomed.

Carter began his stalk hours before in the dark, slipping through the heavy brush and dense tree cover in his Ghillie suit (a burlap and cordura camouflage covering the entire body). A single snapping dead twig or rustling of a branch

330

indiscriminately pushed aside could give away his position, making every movement and footfall critical.

He also had to be aware of spooking a wild animal or bird into sudden flight and on this particular night came within a few feet of a mule deer and her young fawn without being detected.

Much of the last 100 yards were on hands and knees or stomach, literally moving forward inches at a time until ultimately making his way within a few feet of the target. Sitting to the rear of the tree stand where the sniper-sentry was smoking a cigarette, Carter had narrowly missed getting wet, when the man had relieved himself onto the camouflaged position where Carter had been crouching for almost an hour.

Carter carried a Beretta 9mm pistol equipped with an AAC sound suppressor and subsonic ammunition, along with a specially built air pistol for use up close.

The AEG (Automatic Electric Gun) powered by four 1.2 volt batteries could fire a BB—or in this case a small syringe filled with a drug causing instantaneous loss of consciousness—accurately to distances of 33 feet or more, depending on conditions.

A sudden movement by the sentry above was followed almost immediately by the distant sound of a vehicle approaching on the gravel road. The sniper shifted his position raising the rifle to his shoulder to look through the powerful scope at what was approaching.

"What the hell…oh f…!" Then he was on his radio. "We've got company on the north road…looks like a HumVee…could be the Feds!"

Next, came the sounds of the "Little Bird" swinging in low over the trees with loud speakers blasting: THIS IS THE FBI! YOU ARE UNDER ARREST! EXIT INTO THE OPEN WITH YOUR HANDS RAISED! I REPEAT….

Before the announcement could be repeated the sniper raised his rifle and began firing at the small helicopter. It was hovering in the air, like a duck about to land on water and presented an inviting target above the compound less than 200 yards away.

Carter carefully drew the air pistol from a shoulder holster made of nylon materials designed to prevent a static spark while allowing the lightweight polymer-metal gun to slip silently into ready position.

Slowly pointing the pistol through the brushy cover and waiting patiently for the sniper to expose his head and neck, Carter took careful aim and squeezed the trigger of the powerful air gun. The sound of the dart being fired was much like that of a muffled sneeze—not enough to alert anyone even if they had been near the target.

Carter's aim was perfect. The dart hit the man in the large vein of the neck. Reflexes caused a futile reach toward the wound before he crumpled unconscious to the floor of the tree stand. The sniper's rifle fell from his hands making a small rustling noise as it hit the heavy brush under the tree.

Standing up slowly allowing circulation to his blood-starved head and legs, Carter pulled a thin nylon string from his utility pocket, spread the arms on a small grappling hook and swung the device toward the end of the rope ladder used by the sniper to reach the tree stand.

The first toss barely missed catching the ladder rung; the second was successful snagging the heavy rope and pulling it down to the ground. Seconds later the powerfully built agent was on the small platform, slinging the unconscious sniper over his shoulder and carrying him down to the ground below.

Once on the ground, Carter secured the man's hands and feet with nylon restraints. He slipped the two-way radio off the sniper's neck and removed the power source before tossing it into the brush. He then placed a blindfold over the sniper's eyes and slipped a special nylon gag into his mouth, designed to allow him to breathe through the mouth if necessary but only emit small grunting sounds muffled by baffles.

The entire operation from start to finish could be measured in seconds rather than minutes. Keying his tact radio, Carter calmly mouthed, "Dolphin to Com #2, sniper position secure."

"Copy 'Dolphin', sniper position secure."

Moments later the message was repeated.

"'Popeye' to Com #2, sniper position secure."

"Copy 'Popeye', sniper position secure."

***

Jack Fox had moved to cover near the Team #1 point man and was assessing the situation in the armed camp. Sporadic small arms fire was coming from ports cut in the heavy steel shutters, and it was all too clear the worst possible scenario was underway—the inhabitants planned to fight it out.

The Little Bird made another pass hovering 200 feet over the compound, again issuing the command: FBI! YOU ARE UNDER ARREST! EXIT THE BUILDINGS....

Suddenly the message broke off as a smoke trail appeared from the roof of the main building. There was a bright flash followed by an explosion toward the tail of the hovering helicopter.

"Ah Crap!" Fox exclaimed, alarmed at the helicopter's struggle to maintain flight. He knew all too well—the pilot was now trying desperately to find a place for a "controlled crash."

"All teams…all teams…Little Bird is going down. Provide cover fire; do not approach the wreckage! Repeat…*do not* approach the wreckage."

The last thing we need is to move into the open and take a bunch of casualties trying to reach the chopper. We've got to determine whether anyone survives first—and pray there's no fire. Fox watched helplessly as the chopper pilot labored valiantly to control the crippled aircraft by auto-rotating the props while continuing to lose altitude.

The helicopter shuddered hard, then began to fall from a height of 100 feet, rolled slightly to the right and crashed with a bang in the cleared *killing ground* 80 yards from the main building. The appalling sound of metal crunching and tearing rose from the swirling dirt as the rotors dug into the ground before allowing the small craft to settle onto its side.

Immediately, another sound sent a chill up Fox's back. It was the unmistakable chatter of a machine gun firing on full automatic.

Dust kicked up from the earth close to the downed helicopter followed by the sound of bullets hitting metal. Fox saw the two men in the Little Bird moving; both were scrambling to the side of the wreckage away from the incoming machine gun fire. *They should be relatively safe for the moment unless…unless the bastards fire another RPG.*

"Little Bird to Com #2," came the breathless voice in Fox's ears. "My co-pilot has a leg injury; we're taking heavy incoming and fuel's leaking on the ground. It's only a matter of time before this thing goes up. We're going to make for cover east of our location. Request cover fire."

"Com #2 to Little Bird. Stay put as long as you can; we have help on the way."

The machine gun was firing from somewhere beyond the encampment buildings; but before an exact location was determined, it stopped.

"Com #2 to Com #1. We have Little Bird down inside the cleared area of the compound. Two survivors confirmed…one with a serious leg injury. They are taking cover in the wreckage and receiving machine gun fire from a concealed location. We are getting random small arms fire as well. Request

Permission to utilize LRAD (Long Range Acoustic Device) and MCFS (Mobile Counter Fire System)."

"Com #1 to Com #2. You are clear to use LRAD and MCFS. Repeat, you are clear to use LRAD and MCFS."

Damn, no hesitation at all—this guy Johnson has balls as big as his title, Fox realized with appreciation.

"Com #2 to HV-Adam, move into position and engage machine gun located north of Building #1. You are authorized to return fire; you are authorized to return fire.

"Com #2 to HV-Boy…move into position and prepare to lock on to Building #1.

"All teams go to PHP; go to PHP. (Passive Hearing Protection)."

The small arms fire was increasing from the main compound building, shooting blindly into the surrounding trees and continuing to direct fire at the downed helicopter.

There had been speculation from some corners in the planning stages, the entire encampment would surrender—but Fox knew from the history of paramilitary groups that wasn't likely to happen. It was an opportunity to use force against one of their perceived enemies—and they were highly motivated and prepared to do so.

Some of these people know they are going to face the death penalty— and they will most likely opt to take their chances on trying to fight their way out, Fox had told his surprised superiors.

Slipping on the Peltor-65 electronic earmuffs designed to protect hearing from intense high decibel reverberation, his attention was drawn to the sound of the .30 caliber machine gun firing again on full automatic. Fox peered out from behind the fallen logs he was using for cover. The bullets were punching holes through the metal of Little Bird's fuel tanks. Almost immediately, the small aircraft burst into flames; and before the heavy smoke blotted out his view, he watched the two crew members running, one behind the other, for the nearest cover.

They would have to run across 20 yards of open ground—the injured man was limping badly—the sound of the machine gun hammered loudly kicking up dirt behind him.

"You lousy bastards!" Fox shouted.

Shouldering his MP-5, he fired on full automatic into the cover beside the main building. It was an act of total frustration (serving only to reveal his position) since hitting the target with a 10mm bullet was virtually impossible at that range.

Just when it appeared the running pilots might make it to cover, the injured man went down heavily. The man in the lead had already reached the trees and stood staring back at his fallen comrade. He hesitated realizing going back would probably mean being shot—most likely killed.

No...don't do it...don't go back! "Com # 2 to Little Bird," Fox shouted into the radio already too late. Running in a crouching zigzag back to his fallen buddy, the pilot grabbed both arms frantically trying to drag the wounded man to safety. The injured man appeared to be unconscious and was "dead weight" making it even more difficult for the smaller of the two to move him.

The machine gun began to chatter again; dust flew first behind and then in front as the gunner methodically walked the fire into the target. There was no hurry; the target was slow moving and besides—it wasn't firing back.

Fox grimaced as the pilot jerked to his left and fell hard to the ground.

"Com #2 to Com #1...we have agents down...agents down. We need medi-vac to stand by. The area is hot! Repeat hot!"

He's still moving, but he can't last long in that open area. Where the hell is....

Fox's question was answered when he heard the sound of a heavy machine gun firing—not the .30 caliber being used by the Aryan killers, but a much heavier weapon...it was the M2 HB .50 caliber on HV-Adam

(The Mobile Counter Fire System was developed for the U.S. Marines. Using an assortment of acoustic sensing devices to pick up sound and direction of hostile fire, it locks the heavy .50 caliber weapon onto the target and allows the operator full control of returning fire.)

The loud "thumping" sound of the powerful weapon firing could be heard even through the earmuffs, and Fox watched as the brushy area beside Building #1 was literally chopped into pieces, until shiny metal began to appear.

Training his field glasses on the area 200 yards away, he could barely make out what appeared to be a steel shield with a gun protruding from a hole cut in the center.

It must be the half-track intelligence reported, Fox assumed.

The HV-Adam gunner fired off a short burst and the steel jacketed .50 caliber bullets struck the metal causing it to shudder violently with the impact. Moments later, Fox saw two men running toward the woods to their left.

"Com #2 to Team # 5, you have two 'Rabbits' moving *east* from behind Building # 1."

There was an audible "click" on the tact radio—message received.

"Com #2 to HV-Boy...direct 105 dB to Building #1...increase to 151 dB in controlled increments."

"HV-Boy to Com #2; copy, 105 dB to 151 dB."

The LRAD (Long Range Acoustic Device), originally designed for use in crowd control and as a sonic weapon to deter the approach of a combatant, would force the occupants out of the buildings and prevent a potentially devastating long-term standoff.

Seconds later, a 30-degree beam began to emit a high frequency (approximately the high pitch of a smoke detector), beginning at a warning level and escalating gradually to an intensity that could permanently damage the hearing of anyone not wearing ear protection.

The LRAD is effective to a range of 300 yards and at the closer range should produce rapid results. As the decibels increased, the comfort level inside Building #1 was going to degenerate very rapidly into an acoustic hell. Without high quality hearing protection, it would be next to impossible for anyone to remain inside for more than a few minutes.

The firing slowed from Building #1 and then grew totally silent. Even with the electronic hearing protectors, Fox could hear the high pitch of the LRAD bouncing back off the building.

Suddenly the door at the front swung open, and a man was silhouetted in the opening. He stood frozen holding his hands in the air, waving to signify he was surrendering and then clapped them over his ears bending forward at the waist attempting to shut out the earsplitting pain. Moving to the outside of the building, he was followed closely by two men, and then came two more in quick succession.

"Lie flat on the ground with your hands behind your head," came the order from HV-Boy's speakers. At the same time the LRAD was reduced to a low shrill, still uncomfortable to the ear—but no longer dangerous.

As the subjects began to comply, Fox waited for more to exit the building. There had been two snipers, two on the machine gun...and now five out of the building.

That could be all of them, Fox reasoned. *Intelligence estimated 9-12...but something doesn't feel right. Could they be setting some type of ambush...if so where and how?*

"Com #2 to all teams; remain in place. Remain in place. Team #5 what is the status of our two rabbits?"

"Team #5 to Com #2, we have two rabbits bagged and ready for transport…copy."

"Copy Team #5, two rabbits secure."

Damn, what's missing here? Something still doesn't feel right; they've thrown in the towel too easily after showing they intended to fight it out. What the hell is it I'm not seeing? Fox deliberated uneasily.

***

Carter secured his prisoner and then moved to a new position of concealment, giving him a clear view of the road while still allowing him to observe the unconscious sentry.

The sound of battle acted like a magnet, and Carter could feel himself being drawn to the action. Only discipline from the intense Seal and HRT training kept him from moving toward the conflict.

Listening intently, he could tell the LRAD had been reduced and the gunfire had completely stopped. He then heard the announcement for the subjects to lie down on the ground. *They must have decided to cut their losses,* he assumed.

Continuing to scan the heavy cover around him, the young agent moved his head very slowly, while allowing his eyes to dart quickly over every patch of brush and potential area of concealment.

A human eye can best pick up an object or detect motion if the eye is kept moving rather than stationary. Ironically, he had been skeptical of this bit of training information until he experimented with it to aid in finding his wayward golf ball hit into the jungle of various golf courses and was amazed how well it worked. With practice, it had since become second nature.

Fox said remain in place. He's uptight about something—I need to stay alert.

Carter could feel the slight movement of air on his face, and his sense of smell intensified picking up the sweet odor of flowers and pungent smell of rotting pine needles. Muscles of his body tensed with the sudden pump of adrenalin; unnecessary organs began to shut down to prevent taking oxygenated blood from the areas where it was in demand.

Carter recognized the feeling and knew his body was preparing for action. His eye caught a hint of movement coming from a patch of low brush sprinkled with the violet colors of wild flowers. The flowers were definitely out of place on this scrap of otherwise brown grass.

Damn, why didn't I notice that before. The flowers have been planted to cover something. He was almost on top of it—only twenty feet or so to his right.

At first the purple flowers barely moved in the calm air. Then they moved slightly more, raising barely an inch or so off the ground.

Shit, that's some kind of lid being raised off a hole; looks like the training tapes we were shown from Viet Nam.

Turning his body very slowly to allow him to look directly at the object, he began to examine it more closely.

The brownish brush blended with the area around it with only a sprinkling of color intended to match the distant mountain flowers. The section was away from the large trees, suggesting it could well conceal a tunnel that would have to be dug away from the roots of this heavily forested area. Someone had been very careful in selecting the terrain but made a serious gaffe with the flowers.

Could this be an escape tunnel dug from the main compound? It would only be a couple of hundred yards or so, and the Viet Cong dug tunnels far longer, in similar terrain, without the benefit of modern equipment.

Carter slowly laid the air pistol on the ground and carefully removed the 9mm Beretta 92 from his shoulder holster.

The camouflaged lid began to move again very slowly at first—and then suddenly flung open.

A man's head appeared, looking quickly around; and then he was out onto the ground clutching an automatic weapon. He squatted beside the opening in a covering position; immediately a second man came out of the hole staying low to the ground carefully searching the area.

This is not good; should call for backup...but they're going to scatter in the next few seconds.

"FBI! Freeze...."

The man squatting turned toward the sound of the voice and began firing. Carter had already moved and now fired two quick rounds from the silenced weapon. The subsonic ammo combined with the ACC silencer made only a slight "coughing sound" with one round finding the mark—catching the shooter low in the throat.

The second man ran hard for the cover of the trees, firing on full automatic wildly into the brush. It was impossible for the assailant to tell from where the silenced weapon was firing; but now that he had reached cover, Carter knew he would watch for movement and spray the area at first sign of a target.

"'Dolphin' to Com #2."

"Com #2, go ahead 'Dolphin.'"

"Com #2, I'm solo with two subjects exiting a tunnel…one subject is down, the second has taken cover. The perp has an automatic weapon and is approximately 40 yards south from my present location…copy?"

"Copy 'Dolphin'…hang tight, the cavalry's on the way."

Time is really my ally now. There'll be backup here in a matter of minutes, and the perp has to know that.

Suddenly the brush around him erupted as the automatic fire began splintering and breaking limbs.

He had taken a gamble in calling for backup. It was standard protocol—but *protocol* may have just gotten him killed.

The nearest cover was a couple of steps to the left—and it was going to be the longest two steps of his life.

Bursting out of the brush and pushing hard off his right leg, he felt the soft earth give way under his boot causing him to slip ever so slightly—just enough to allow the terrorist time to aim his weapon.

The .223 Remington round caught the running agent in the right hip and knocked him to the open ground. The 9mm fell from his hands and landed several feet to his right.

Damn—he's no amateur—he aimed low to miss my body armor and now he'll finish the job.

As Carter lay powerless on the ground, the terrorist left his cover and ran toward the young agent. Carter knew he was all that stood in the way of the fugitive's escape. Fighting through the racking pain in his body, he crawled toward the fallen weapon. Dirt kicked up from the ground in front of his head—and he knew that he would never reach his weapon in time.

It all happened so fast—one bad decision and now it's all over but the shouting.

"Com #2 to 'Dolphin'…copy?" came the worried voice of Fox.

Reaching to trigger his tact radio one last time, Carter suddenly realized his assailant had stopped running. Blood was streaming from what was left of the man's face. Everything was happening in slow motion. The M-16 flew into the air, and the man's arms swung away from his body trying to maintain balance. Then the knees buckled and Carter watched in astonishment as the cold-blooded assassin crumpled backward to the ground. It was only then he heard the distant sound of a high caliber sniper rifle.

*Pluto…that had to be Pluto. I got backup after all…*and then he felt himself relaxing as the first wave of unconsciousness engrossed him, bringing welcome relief from the intense searing pain in his hip. He never felt his warm urine soaking his pants.

***

CHAPTER 23

Mayflower Hotel
1127 Connecticut Avenue NW
Washington, DC

The President actually made that statement—in front of the all those 'Monday morning quarterbacks'? Damn, Ted, I would've given a lot to be there."

"Hell, Bill, you're too valuable to be back here sucking up to the establishment. You've proved your merit once again; and I'm here to tell you, it went a long way in getting FIST off to a great start. I'm in your debt for joining the team. You've already set a high standard for command in the field.

"Apprehending the two homicide fugitives coming out of the tunnel was a real coup—and we've delivered a severe blow to the Aryan Warrior leadership by catching Colonel T.S. Knight with his 'hand in the cookie jar.' He appears to be the man in charge of planning operations and may lead us to the money behind the movement.

"We got lucky in Arkansas, Bill. Laurie did a great job of thinking on his feet. Everyone at SOG watched a good deal of it on the big screen, and it was impressive to say the least. Both assassins tried to shoot their way out and got waxed—not really disappointing anyone.

"Cohn was the sad part of *that* situation. I'm on my way to Missouri to meet with his parents," Bridger said, his voice trailing to a whisper.

"What's the word on Carter and the two helicopter pilots?"

"Both pilots are going to recover. Parker caught a lot of shrapnel in the legs and is probably going to pension out on a medical.

"Thompson is going to be fine and Fox recommended him for an in-grade promotion plus a gold star for his mother's scrapbook. According to Fox, who witnessed the entire saga, Thompson is a bona-fide hero who deserves anything we give him.

"Carter is going to take some time to recover, but the doctors are optimistic he can return to duty. He's driving everyone in rehab nuts trying to push the envelope. I've been looking at his personnel file. He's seen a lot action and proven himself in tough situations calling for quick decisions. We need to bring him into our little club if he's interested. We can use another cowboy or two—no insult intended."

"None taken. You really think we need people with his qualifications in our organization?"

"Damn straight, Ted. In 10 or 15 more years, we're both going to be too fricking old to fight the bulldog. We need a few young 'phenoms' who still think they can't be bitten."

Ted chuckled. "I'll leave that up to you. How soon will you be back in Denver?"

"I'm nearly finished here and plan to leave Seattle sometime tomorrow."

"I'm looking forward to buying you a frosted one. Again my friend, well done."

***

Springfield-Branson Airport
Springfield, Missouri

Captain Darryl Uthoff maneuvered the DHS Lear Jet into a gentle left turn and began his approach to Springfield-Branson Airport.

"Mr. Bridger...we're on final, seat belt fastened please and secure any loose items. We will be on the ground in seven minutes. The Springfield RA has been notified of our arrival and are standing by."

This is not a trip I've been looking forward to, Bridger lamented. *It's amazing how quickly I grew to like Cohn. His attitude from day one was special and complemented an exceptional intelligence and work ethic. What might his future.... I've got to get off that or I'm not going to be able to deal with this. This is dangerous work and Aaron knew that going in—people can and do get shot.*

Bridger barely felt the slight bump as Uthoff landed the Lear, reversed the engines and began braking before making a right turn onto a taxiway leading to the small private aviation passenger building.

The plane came to a stop within a few feet of the chain-link fence surrounding the building; a black unmarked Bureau car immediately pulled up beside.

Uthoff appeared at the exit, released the door and extended the ladder to the ground.

"We'll have your luggage right out. I trust you had a good flight."

"Darryl, the flight was exceptional. Great landing, I'd give that one a 10."

"Thank you very much, Sir." Uthoff beamed. "That means something coming from another pilot. Aircraft will be refueled ready to fly on your notification."

Descending the stairs, Bridger was surprised to see Henry Sterling extending his hand and saying, "Welcome back to Springfield. We're all sorry it couldn't be under more pleasant circumstances."

"Thank you, Henry. I appreciate your taking the time to meet me."

"My pleasure. Do you wish to go straight to where Cohn is, or would you like to check into your hotel."

"I can check into the hotel later. Have Aaron's parents arrived?"

"Yes, Sir; and as you might expect, his mother is taking it pretty rough. His father has a better grasp on the situation."

***

Sterling had gone in ahead at his own suggestion and was now headed back down the long hallway toward an obviously distraught Bridger.

"If you will follow me, you can see him now."

Bridger could hear the echo of his own footsteps as he walked down the long cold corridor and instinctively found himself pacing more on his toes. The antiseptic smells of the tile floors and walls sent a wave of dread through him as his subconscious brought back memories of tragic past events.

Sterling paused in front of a door waiting for Bridger to catch up and then pushed it open for him to enter.

Stepping into the room, Bridger was greeted by a smartly dressed man who extended his hand.

"Good afternoon, Mr. Bridger. I'm Herman Cohn, Aaron's father, and this is his mother Ruth. It is very good of you to come. Aaron has told us so much about you."

Taking the extended hand, Bridger felt emotion welling up inside him and fought to keep it down. *They don't seem as upset with me as I somehow*

343

imagined they would be, he sensed as Ruth Cohn crossed the room and extended her hand.

"Good afternoon…it's very nice to meet you," she said with a tired smile.

"I certainly wish we were meeting under more pleasant circumstances, but we are all grateful it isn't worse," Bridger said.

"Good afternoon, Karen; and let me tell you in person, you did a great job in this investigation from beginning to end. I want to hear the details later, but for now—how's the *patient*?"

"Thank you, Sir. The patient's making progress, but I'm afraid he's 'gold bricking' a bit. It seems some of the nurses on this floor are giving him a lot of special attention."

Aaron Cohn was sitting partially propped up in the hospital bed with a bandage covering his lower face from the eyes down. Several tubes and wires ran to various monitors with bags of fluid still dripping into his system to prevent infection and blood clots.

Aaron's eyes reflected a mock look of disgust as he furiously typed on his laptop and then turned the screen so everyone could see what he had written.

"SIR, I'M NOT GOLD BRICKING. THEY ARE FEEDING ME THROUGH A STRAW AND IF THEY DON'T GET MY JAW LOOSE FROM THIS WIRE SOON, I'M GOING TO BE ABLE TO RIDE IN THE KENTUCKY DERBY."

Everyone in the room laughed.

Aaron was referring to the fact his jaw was wired shut allowing the wounds to heal. Doctors indicated the bullet entered under the lower jaw, destroying several teeth, and then deflected cleanly through the middle of the fleshy opposite cheek with minimal damage to jaw structure.

A dental surgeon had repaired the teeth, and his jaw required immobilizing until the body could assimilate foreign materials integrating them into a natural healing process.

Earlier conversations Bridger had by phone with Dr. Bob Guyette indicated, "Mr. Cohn will show few physical signs of his injuries after nature does its *thing*—and the plastic surgeons do *theirs*." Bridger had brought in Dr. Guyette from Scottsdale, Arizona, because of his reputation as the leading dental reconstruction surgeon in the country.

"Aaron, everything I said to Karen goes for you as well; outstanding job of investigating—right up to the time you chased the bad guy down the road and went up against an automatic weapon with a 9mm handgun. We're going to have to take another trip down to Quantico for some remedial training."

Once again Aaron began to type furiously on the laptop. Finally, looking up at Bridger with concern, he turned the screen.

"I REALIZE I VIOLATED PROTOCOL, SIR...BUT I COULDN'T ALLOW THE PERP TO RUN OFF INTO THE WOODS AND ESCAPE. IT WAS A SPUR-OF-THE-MOMENT DECISION—WAS IT WRONG?"

Bridger paused for several seconds regaining his composure before attempting to answer the question of the young, seriously wounded agent lying before him.

Finally raising his voice and showing a sense of humor he really didn't feel Bridger said, "No, Aaron, you made a good decision—despite violating protocol—and kept a dangerous fugitive from being on the loose to kill again. The really smart part of the decision was keeping that 'Trojan' handy."

Sterling and Cohn's parents were startled by the sudden laughter from Blackwell and Bridger.

Cohn's eyes mirrored amusement at the private joke Bridger had made referring to Blackwell's alma mater. It was good to see someone displaying a sense of normalcy. Everyone had been acting as if he were dead, and even the nurses and visiting agents were somber as if they were looking at a ghost. He had wanted to shout, *"Hey! Lighten up, will you—I'm alive and kicking."*

***

Karen Blackwell laughed—but gave a small shudder as she relived the horror of seeing Aaron on the ground 75 yards away, with a killer standing over him pointing a weapon at his head. She remembered all too well the jumbled scenario racing through her mind.

I have to make a kill shot...no, capture the shooter's attention and get that gun off Aaron!

Shouldering the MP-5 sub-machine gun, she fired two quick rounds toward the surprised assailant who quickly spun toward her. Before he could move to the side, she held slightly high on a sight picture intended to hit him in the center of the body and squeezed the trigger three times.

The autopsy later revealed two of the three shots hit vital areas: one in the chest piercing lungs and heart and one lower catching the liver before passing into the spinal column.

Sprinting to the two men lying motionless on the ground, her mind was racing and she expected the worst. *Please God, don't let him be dead! I care a great deal about this man.*

First, she checked to be certain the subject was down for good and kicked his weapon away; then she turned to the unconscious Cohn. Finding a pulse, she wasted no time in calling for medi-vac and giving temporary aid for shock while waiting for help to arrive.

The wait seemed endless as she ripped pieces of her shirt into strips and attempted to slow the bleeding from the gaping hole in one side of Aaron's face. When the paramedics came running up the trail, they discovered her sitting with his head cradled in her blood soaked lap. At first, the medics began to examine *her* for wounds before she assured them she was not injured.

At the helicopter, there was a short argument—quickly won by Blackwell—when she insisted on riding with him to the hospital in Springfield where she had scarcely left his side since.

Bridger called every day to check on progress and made it clear, he wanted Blackwell to act as his "on-the-scene representative" in being sure Cohn received the best treatment available. It had become clear—Bridger felt more than an obligatory sense of responsibility for the young agent injured under his command. There was something more. Some kind of bond had been established between the two in the very short time they had been together. She sensed it in the urgency of Bridger's voice and the immediate concern Aaron displayed when he first became lucid over whether "the Boss would be upset" with the way he handled himself.

A lot has happened in the past couple of weeks! Karen silently exclaimed. *My life looks entirely different from a professional point of view—and for the first time in a very long time, there is a man in my life. A very good man!*

***

CHAPTER 24

Bellevue Hospital
New York City, New York

E xiting Bellevue Hospital, Chambers was relieved to see a taxi unloading passengers and moved quickly to flag the cab. After giving the address of his apartment, he attempted to get comfortable on sagging well-worn vinyl seats still sticky from the last occupants and began considering his conversation with Mustafa.

Somehow it didn't make sense Gates would be supporting a terrorist organization. Gates still got misty eyed when the subject of 911 came up, and some things are difficult to fake. No...no. Gates couldn't be the mole the Feds are looking for—and that raised an interesting question: if not Gates, then who?

What do I do with Mo's request to tell Gates that he works for the CIA? He was emphatic in asking me to do so, but how much of what he said can I really trust? Some of this will have to make sense before I go any further in this subterfuge.

This has been quite a day—shortening Melanie's visit and taking her to the plane and then a mind-boggling conversation with my best friend. I need to take a shower and have a drink—give frayed nerves time to settle down and then decide.

***

Chambers' Apartment Building
Manhattan
New York City, New York

Dressed in the familiar orange coveralls of Empire State Cable and carrying a small toolbox, two men stood at the front door of the four-story apartment building and pushed the button marked TOM BEHRING—MANAGER.

After three long rings, a husky voice, showing obvious irritation, came over the intercom, "Yes, what is it?"

"Eem pire Cable. A Mr. Chambers een 412 call and say hees cabull no work."

"You'll have to come back," the husky voice replied. "He's not here right now." *Damn bunch of foreigners, don't even speak English good*, Behring grumbled.

"Chambers say come right now. We very busy and if leave, will be several days before come back."

There was a slight pause while the manager mulled over what to do. *Chambers probably came in while I was in the basement. If he's having cable problems and misses the Yankee game, he's really going to be pissed I didn't let them in.*

The door made a loud buzzing sound, signaling it was open for entry.

As the two entered the hallway, a baldhead poked through a half open door. It was policy to examine ID before admitting service personnel, but it'd been a long day. Empire Cable was in the neighborhood frequently, and he recognized those ugly orange uniforms. After a long look in their direction, satisfied by their dress, the head disappeared followed by a slamming door.

The two men stepped into an elevator and punched the button for the fourth floor. One of the men held the door for an elderly woman carrying a bag of groceries, and she thanked them as she entered the elevator and again as she exited on the third floor.

They exchanged glances but neither spoke. It was a short distance down the recently painted hallway to Apartment 412. One man removed a small case from his pocket and took out a slender metal instrument with a hook on the end and a second with small jagged teeth.

Inserting the lock picks into the deadbolt, he maneuvered them for a few seconds before turning the tools like a key and the lock opened. The second lock was a simple latch variety common on the handle of most doors. Sliding a thin credit card size tool between the door jam and latch took only seconds before the door opened.

The younger of the two men walked to the kitchen area, stopping at the two-burner gas stove containing a small oven.

"Gas line geev plentee gas in room," he commented in an excited voice to the older man.

"Good. Allah es weeth us," the older leader commented.

On the wall right of the front door, the leader found a light switch and flipping it was pleased to see it turned on two lamps in the middle of the room.

Excellent, much better than light on ceiling.

He stooped to open his toolbox carefully withdrawing a bottle containing a mixture of high-octane gas. Removing the cover from a specially-altered hypodermic needle and inserting it into the gas, he pulled back on the handle until the syringe was full.

Moving to the nearest lamp he inserted the super-sharp point through the bulb high enough to leave space for the gas being injected from the syringe. All that would be required from the bulb was a small spark.

The entire operation required only minutes, and they were ready to leave; just a couple more details—disconnect the gas line and lock the door behind.

***

Chambers alerted the driver in the middle of the block as they approached his apartment building and when the cab stopped at the curb, handed fare plus tip over the seat. Closing the door, he went up the steps of the sandstone apartment building.

Half a block away, a plain unmarked car slid unnoticed into a parking spot and stopped. The two occupants—FBI Agents assigned to follow and if necessary protect Chambers—both let out sighs of resignation. It was boring work and they had two hours before their relief arrived.

Chambers inserted the recently installed plastic key card for the entry door, waited for the green light and entered. Moving to the elevator and pushing the up button, he felt a sense of relief when the door swung immediately open. More often than not, he took the steps rather than wait for the apartment building's single elevator to arrive.

Melanie would be getting home around six, which meant several hours before he could speak with her. I miss her already. What we can do when things settle down is a question begging for an answer; but for the time being, it's best for her to be home in Wyoming.

He removed the keys from his jacket pocket and opened the heavy bolt lock first and then the smaller door lock.

How different from life in Wyoming, he thought. *Here I have a double lock on my door and I'm probably still not safe. Out there, most people leave their cars and houses unlocked. Maybe that's the answer—I'll move to Cheyenne and get a job near Mel.*

As the door swung open, a familiar pungent smell permeated the air. *Dead mouse...on top of everything else, I've got a dead mouse to find,* Chambers complained as he reached for the light switch.

***

CHAPTER 25

Chambers' Apartment
Manhattan

Scuse me, Mr. Chambers. Heard you come in. The cable crew must've missed ya, and I just wanted to let ya know they was here."

Turning around, Chambers saw it was Behring, the building manager.

"I'm not sure what you're talking about, Mr. Behring. I'm not having any problems with my cable. However, since you're here, any ideas about how to get rid of some mice. Smells like I've got another dead one somewhere in the apartment."

Behring walked to the door of the apartment and made a loud sniffing sound.

"Damn! Smells like gas to me. If ya don't mind, I'd better check."

Chambers reached again for the light switch.

"No…No! Don't turn on any lights. If it's gas, a spark from the switch could be enough to blow us to hell and back."

Entering the small dimly lighted apartment, Behring coughed once before moving quickly to the double windows. He tugged hard to break them free of years of dried paint. Grabbing a towel from the sink he covered his mouth and looked behind the stove.

The gas line was making a hissing sound. Even in the dim light, he could see the conduit lying loose from the stove connection!

Chambers heard two more loud coughs.

"Mr. Behring, you okay in there? You'd better come out and we can get some help."

Behring pushed a shoulder into the small stove shoving it out of the way to get room to reach the line. Grasping the line he stuck it back onto the fitting and gave it a couple of hard twists.

Not enough to completely stop the leak, he realized. *But I'd better get out of here before something sets this fricking thing off.*

Sprinting through the door and slamming it behind him, Behring coughed hard several times.

Approaching the bent-over apartment manager, Chambers asked, "Are you okay? What the hell is going on in there anyway?"

Behring didn't answer but went to the closed door as he removed the towel from over his mouth and quickly tucked it along the bottom of the door.

"It's gas all right," he said pausing to cough, "Damn line was completely loose."

"You got your cell phone, Mr. Chambers?"

"Right here," he said reaching into his pocket and holding it out.

"Better call 911 and get the fire department up here. It won't take much to set this off. I need to start warning people in the building."

***

"What the hell!"

Jack Daily and Art Burgason, two FBI Agents assigned to keep an eye on Chambers were startled when the NYFD truck, sirens blaring, came speeding past them and stopped in front of Chambers' apartment building.

They jumped from their car and rushed to the firemen already sprinting up the steps. Holding out credentials, the two quickly identified themselves.

"Special Agent Daily and Burgason. What's going down here, Lieutenant?"

"We got a call for a gas leak in one of the apartments. We're here to check it out and try to prevent a fire or *worse*."

"Which apartment?" Daily asked.

"Apartment 412," the fireman replied as he hurried up the stairs.

The two agents stood staring at one another.

"Nuts! Jack, we've got a fricking problem here," Burgason said looking at his partner. "We're supposed to be keeping a low profile watching this guy, but screw it man, this is too much. We're using the guy for bait and we could get him killed. It's time to let him know what's going on."

Flipping the cover on his cell phone, he pushed the speed dial for his supervisor. After two rings, Special Agent Ed Newman picked up the phone. Newman was supervisor on a desk for terrorism investigations in New York City, and he was a loyal protégé of the man he referred to as the best—Ted Bridger.

***

352

"I really can't be sure; they was down the hallway and I really didn't get that good a look."

Tom Behring stood talking with FBI Agents Burgason and Daily. They had asked him to view photos on their cell phone. The photos were of several known members of a terrorist group believed responsible for the killing of Shaquille Abumotte and a knife assault on CIA Agent, Mozarab Mustafa.

"Thanks for your help, Mr. Behring. If you recall anything you feel may help us, please call me at the number on the card," Burgason said handing him a business card.

Behring walked away leaving the two agents standing alone. "Not much to go on here. It looks like we're going to have to count on getting something out of Kahdaffi el Shurache," Daily suggested.

"Newman said our interrogation people are making progress—whatever that means—and I hope he's right. These people are totally ruthless and I get a *bad feeling* they have a *nasty surprise* coming our way."

***

ACRONYMNS/DEFINITIONS

1099-JR— J-4 designation—following the 1099 felony fugitive radio call—indicates Armed and Dangerous
A&D—Armed and Dangerous
AEG—Automatic Electric Gun
AI—Actionable Intelligence
AMFO—Ammonium Nitrate and Fuel Oil (Bomb)
APBs—All Points Bulletin
ASO—Arrest and Secure Operation
ASRA—Assistant Senior Resident Agent
AV—Armored Vehicle
BAW—Brotherhood of Aryan Warriors
BuCar—Bureau Car (FBI)
CIA—Central Intelligence Agency
CIRG—Critical Incident Response Group
CIs—Confidential Informants
ComRoom—Communications Room
ConSum—Communication Summary
COS—Commander on Scene
CTS-1—Confidential Top Secret (Priority Highest)
DCI—Director of Central Intelligence
DEAF—Definitive Expected Accuracy Factor relating to potential accuracy of a situational assessment.
DHS—Department of Homeland Security
DIA—Defense Intelligence Agency
DNI—Director of National Intelligence
DTSC—Domestic Terrorist Screening Center
EADI—Executive Assistant Director of Intelligence
EC—Electronically Communicated
EFP—Explosive Formed Penetrators
EL-SUR—Electronic Surveillance
ERP—En-route Rally points
ETA—Estimated Time of Arrival
FAMs—FBI Automated Message System
FBI—Federal Bureau of Investigation
FIDS—FBI Intranet Dissemination Source

FISA—Foreign Intelligence Surveillance Act
FIST—Federal Investigative Strategic Team
GPR—Gun Powder Residue
GPS—Global Positioning System
GS grade—Government Service grade—Ranking and pay levels for federal government employees
HAZMAT—Hazardous material
Hezbollah—Iranian and Syrian sponsored terrorist vowing destruction of Israel
HMMWVs—High Mobility Multi Purpose Wheeled Vehicle (Hum-vee or Hummer for slang)—M1114 Up-armored built in 1996 after use in Kosovo revealed their vulnerability to small arms and RPG fire.
HRT—Hostage Rescue Team
HV—Adam - Hum-vee #1
HV-Boy—Hum-vee #2
I-3AP—Immediate Attention Appropriate Administrative Personnel
IAIP—Information Analysis and Infrastructure Protection
IDF—Israeli Defense Forces
IED—Improvised Explosive Device
Intelmet Room—Intelligence Meeting Room
LAV—Bison—Light Armored Vehicle
LRAD—Long Range Acoustic Device (Built by American Technology Corp. of San Diego, California.)
ManPads—Man Portable Air Defense System—missiles for bringing down planes.
MCFS—Mobile Counter Fire System
MTV—Mobile Tech Van
NCIC—National Crime Information Center
NIBI—National Integrated Ballistics Information Network
NRO—National Reconnaissance Office
NSA—National Security Agency
OCS—Officer Candidate School
Operation Cotton Picker—Arkansas operation
Operation Hot Potato—Idaho operation
PHP—Passive Hearing Protection
PIA—Presidential Intelligence Assessment
QAL—Quantico Audio Laboratory
RA—Resident Agency
RPG—Rocket Propelled Grenades

RURs—Rossum's Universal Robots from Karel Capek's play
SAC—Special Agent In Charge
SCI—Sensitive Compartmentalized Information
SCION—Top secret Sensitive Compartmentalized Information Operational Network
Signet—Signal Intelligence Network
SIOC—Strategic Information Operations Center—Located on fourth floor of J. Edgar Hoover Building, in times of crisis serves as intelligence collection and dissemination site.
SOG—Seat of Government
SOP—Standard Operating Procedures
SSRA—Senior Supervisory Resident Agent
SWAT—Strategic Weapons Assault Team
TDY—Temporary Duty
TEDAC—Terrorist Explosive Device Analytical Center
TR—Tactical Readiness
Tsunami Priority—Top/Highest Priority
Unsubs—Unknown Subjects
USSS—United States Secret Service
VCF—Virtual Case Files
WM—White Male
WMD—Weapons of Mass Destruction

Printed in the United States
97446LV00003B/42/A

9 781424 178988